I0789481

Jacob

Walk of the Messengers

EAMON BLAKE

ISBN: 978-1-7385182-6-5

Acknowledgements

Book 2

This book, **Jacob - Walk of the Messengers**, is the second in the Jacob sage. This one tells a story about the amazing journey of four groups of teenagers who were tasked with putting together the greatest army ever created. For me, writing the books was a labour of love that began in 2016, and who would have thought it would grow to be told in a series of five books.

> Book 1 - Jacob - Journey of a God
>
> Book 2 - Jacob - Walk of the Messengers
>
> Book 3 - Jacob - War of the End Times
>
> Book 4 - Jacob - Children of the Gods
>
> Book 5 - Jacob - Battle for Olympus

These books would never have been written if it wasn't for the support and encouragement of my amazing family and friends who listened to my relentless telling of the stories and the ideas I had. A special 'Thank You' to you all, you know who you are.

I would like to take this opportunity to thank those who took the time to read and proof-read this book in a genre that, in a lot of cases, is alien to them. They were the ones who particularly encouraged and cajoled me into taking this epic story to its conclusion. Thank you, a million times, to Teresa

Carroll, Rita Foley, Sean Blake, Tom Lillis, Vincent Reynolds, Eamonn Maguire, Raymond King, Vanessa Keogh and Thérése McGarry.

To my friend Damien Carroll: What can I say. Your regular emails and phone calls were a great help in getting some of my Dublin 'isms' out of the story making it a far better read. I am filled with gratitude.

I am eternally grateful to two groups of very special people, the Poets and Authors in the 'All About Writing Group' and the 'Dublin Writers Forum' for assisting me in getting my book to print ready; this would not have been possible without their valuable critique and editorial assistance, especially with grammar, layouts and storylines.

To my amazing niece, Niamh Blake, thank you so much for your wonderful cover designs.

I would also like to acknowledge PerpetuityPublications.com for their assistance in formatting my books and getting them ready for release. Thanks again Perpetuity Publications.

And finally, for my wife, Connie - forever in our hearts , R.I.P.

𝕬𝖚𝖙𝖍𝖔𝖗'𝖘 𝕻𝖗𝖔𝖋𝖎𝖑𝖊

Eamon Blake is from Crumlin, a Southside suburb of Dublin, Ireland, a place he still has a great love for. It was there, between 1970 and 1975, where he attended the local secondary school, Meanscoil Naomh Colm. During fifth and sixth year, he had the pleasure of being taught English by the late Michael Condon, an inspirational teacher who had an amazing teaching technique commanding the greatest of respect from his pupils. Eamon believes that as a result of that teacher's style and perseverance he developed an interest in writing. It was in that same school where he developed his passion for real and classical history. *The history and mythology learned during that time lingered in Eamon's mind and those early influences only resurfaced in recent years, inspiring him to pen a series of five fantasy novels recounting the tale of a Dublin schoolboy discovering his extraordinary powers, and who he actually was.*

A widower with one son, Eamon, over the years, has successfully navigated various employment roles involving procurement, sales and marketing. His professional journey included delivering marketing presentations to major wholesale and retail chains, as well as participating in monthly sales and planning meetings. He believes the wealth of experience garnered during those years helped him develop his own writing style, ultimately leading to the Jacob series.

Eamon's first foray into writing began with him researching and publishing a book detailing the history and genealogy of his own family in central Dublin, dating back to the 1780s. Motivated by a desire to share this heritage, he produced and published enough copies exclusively for his extended family.

The idea for the Jacob series came to Eamon in the late summer of 2016 after he witnessed a charming yet humorous incident in Temple Bar, Dublin. This event led to the realisation that a fantastical story could be crafted by intertwining major historical events from Africa, America, Europe, the Far East as well as the Near East, linking them, and drawing inspiration from worldwide mythological realms featuring Centaurs, Dragons, Elves, The Gods, The Little People, Mer-Peoples, The Yeti and Wizards.

Contact author:

Email: thejacobsaga@gmail.com

Table of Contents

Prologue

Jacob's journey began in an enchanted cave on the island of Crete; the very same cave where Zeus, the king of the gods, was born. After his birth, he was taken by his mother two thousand years through time, to a small village in the north of England where she felt they'd be safe from prying eyes.

On reaching his twelfth birthday his godly powers were showing prompting his mother to move him again, this time to Dublin where she enrolled him into one of south Dublin's renowned rugby schools. Almost immediately he was seen by his classmates as being different, he excelled academically but it was on the sports field where they noticed he really stood out. He was well liked and was known for possessing a formidable strength of character with morals to match. He constantly challenged issues he felt were wrong and never flinched in his efforts to set them right.

Very quickly he became an awe-inspiring rugby player and it was his prowess on the pitch that encouraged his school to build their team around him. One player in particular, Shane, was to become his closest friend. It was Shane who listened on a daily basis to Jacob's very disturbing nightmares and it was he who encouraged him to share his night terrors with his mother, Maria, who immediately took action.

Maria began by telling him his story, and the very personal story of her own amazing life. She used her magic to show him how powerful she was and then encouraged him to explore his own powers. During those conversations he discovered his mother was in hiding from the wrath of her father who happened to be Zeus, the King of the Gods.

After listening to her story his anger grew, causing something deep within him to awaken. This encouraged him to seek a confrontation and his opportunity arose when his mother offered to take him back to the time of Olympus.

On arrival in Olympus he was captivated by its grandeur and immediately knew he belonged. He was in awe when he saw the amount of columns that ran the full length of the Great Hall and was amazed by the statues that nestled between each one of them. Viewing each statue his power of prophecy enhanced, allowing him to see how each god was destined to play an important part in his future.

He loved his time in the temple, especially the day when he saw four naked girls swimming in a nearby lagoon and decided to join them. One girl, Ealasaid, was destined to be the love of his life and the mother of his children. He then met eight boys and soon all thirteen were to become inseparable friends.

That same day, he met Poseidon, the God of the Sea, who was one of the senior gods and this meeting was quickly followed by the arrival of his grandparents and the opportunity for his confrontation. After an initial hostility he began to gain an understanding of his grandfather and soon learned to love and respect him. He discovered he had brothers and also discovered his father was the most powerful Thunder God.

In the realm of the gods it was long ago foretold that the arrival of a boy into Olympus was to be a precursor to many dramatic changes and it was obvious that Jacob was that boy, especially when his first action was to use his new found powers to convince Zeus to allow his twelve mortal friends into Olympus. He used those same powers to show the gods how his friends were going to be instrumental in carrying an important message to all corners of the world. His power of prophecy showed how his brothers were to become his most staunch allies and be responsible for keeping him grounded. He became very close to Odi, his twin, and their meeting led to many exciting adventures together. Throughout all this, his friend in Dublin, Shane, was never too far from his mind.

During this time he sensed the power of the Light but he also felt the deceit of The Darkness. His visions showed him how the Archangel Lucifer had escaped his imprisonment and how he was preparing to conquer the Underworld. The visions showed how Lucifer was going to use the Underworld as a stepping stone to attack Earth, destroy the gods and seek revenge on the Ancient One. They also showed how the plans became easier when the dismembered body parts of the Titan Cronus were found and brought back together. Jacob knew Cronus was the one Titan most feared by the gods and saw how it was this fear that emboldened Lucifer.

With the assistance of the War Gods, Jacob trained his friends to become his messengers before sending them on a journey that would take them to all corners of the world. He gave them the powers and skills to survive the journey as well as everything required for them to lead the forces of the Light during the battle of the End Times. What they didn't know was that, just like Jacob, their destiny was also set at the beginning of time and, in their own right, they too were fated to become very powerful gods. Those that received the message were to become known as the Carriers and the backbone of a worldwide army that, one day, would answer the call to defend the realm of man.

Soon after the messengers left Olympus the gods entered their two thousand year sleep but for some it wasn't to be a restful one. Jacob slept lightly and was always ready to assist when the need arose. His eldest brother, Magni of Asgard, with a heavily armed force by his side, almost immediately began patrolling the Northern skies. The Wizards never slept, they kept a constant vigil while the Centaur, Dragon, Elf and Mer-armies spent the two thousand years preparing for the call.

Meanwhile Lucifer sent his minions to search for those who had received the message, and those they found were slaughtered, and their captured souls taken to the deepest recesses of Hell. Their search included seeking out the messengers especially Ealasaid who was pregnant with Jacobs children.

- And so the story of the Messengers of the Gods begins

Panya's Journey North

Chapter 1

Jacob stood at the entrance of the portal watching Panya, Baldor and Thanases preparing to make their way to join him. While waiting, he satisfied himself, and was confident the boys were well trained and strong enough to be worthy guardians of Panya whom he foresaw as destined to one day be Queen of Asgard. He knew by looking at them that they were the correct choice to ensure the message was delivered during the dangerous journey towards the northern Ice lands.

Panya appeared as a regal and beautiful messenger of the Light, her sparkling blue eyes and luscious red lips were framed by flowing fair and wavy hair, accentuating her beauty. When she walked her gown and fur-lined cape rested perfectly on her hour-glass figure ensuring those watching were unable to divert their eyes. Her jewellery and headband contained so many diamonds, the refracted light, when split, enhanced the spectrum of rainbow colours surrounding her. She was known for compassion and empathy, always ready to assist those in need. Her only weakness was her love for Jacob's brother Odi, and Odi was never far from her thoughts.

Those first steps were difficult, her mind being flooded with thoughts of happier times. She thought of her night of passion and how Odi made her feel. She thought of how he described her warm alluring smile drawing him in and how her body touching his, electrified him. She longed for his embrace but brushed those thoughts aside and concentrated on the journey ahead. She walked a few more steps and remembered Jacob saying, "You will be crowned with the laurels of victory and the north will kneel before you. I see you as a Queen..."

Before meeting Odi, a journey like this was something Panya could only dream of. She had always wondered about the lands of her ancestors, aware she was a descendant of merchants who had set up the trade routes between the Persian Empire and the Nordic lands. There was no turning back; it was this knowledge that drove her desire to see the frozen mountains, the fjords and the dark, vast forests that continuously appeared in her dreams.

Jacob looked at Baldor and Thanases, and was taken by how striking they were, tall majestic youths with blond, shoulder-length hair and piercing blue eyes. Their robes and armour enhanced that appearance. Resting under their right arms were their helmets and on their left they held their shield. They weren't aware of their heritage but the Asgard gods were, and to them Baldor's and Thanases' Nordic ancestry was clear.

Baldor was the quiet one and a bit standoffish, keeping to himself for fear of betraying his loneliness. He remembered every word Jacob said to him when they first met, especially, "...you, my friend, will be the quiet one yet you will be the god who carries a beacon of light in the dark lands of the frozen north. You will be the torch bearer Asgard will follow". Although good looking he didn't exude the same confidence as Thanases but he certainly held his head high. He was equally as athletic and agile but not as muscularly powerful.

Thanases on the other hand was a more rugged good looking youth who liked to always take the lead. He had a reputation for being vengeful when not getting his way. He was also known for his loyalty and how he would sacrifice everything for those he loved. Fear was an emotion he held at bay especially when he remembered Jacob's comments, "... a warriors son. You will change the ways of the North and have the power to grant immortality, use it wisely, stories of your life will stand the test of time. Many will fall under your protection and you will be tested..."

Jacob embraced all three, holding the longest grip for Panya. He said very little, afraid anything he said would deter them or shatter their confidence. He opened the portal for the first time and as they stepped through he bowed and wished them well.

Chapter 2

On exiting the temple grounds they turned right and moved towards the crossroads, walked through, and made their way towards the ice lands of the north. Baldor walked a short distance ahead, ensuring no danger awaited them. Although there was no danger, he suddenly stopped, closed his eyes and received a vision where he saw himself carrying a torch. Moments later another vision showed him leading an exodus into the Ice lands. He was annoyed with himself for not challenging Jacob after being referred to as 'the god who carries a beacon of light'. He didn't feel like a god, he felt lonely and troubled.

Thanases walked several paces behind Panya, continuously glancing back and always alert to any movement in the surrounding fields. He welcomed his task, and Jacobs's words emboldened him to be ever vigilant, to constantly train, especially for the arrival of the Light, and to maintain his weapons like a seasoned warrior.

They eventually reached a small village where they decided to rest. As immortals, 'Time' meant nothing and when resting they found that days, weeks, even years may have passed. This made 'Time' difficult to get used to.

While in the village, Baldor and Thanases removed their armour, materialised and made themselves known to the villagers. Panya, on the other hand, remained invisible and chose to begin her task - passing on the message.

She moved among the people, and to one after another, whispered the same thing; "Go now, tell your children to tell their children's children for all time, that one day, they will be called upon by the gods and they must answer." Within moments, and as if by magic, those who received the message developed tactical and combat skills, with the ability for those skills to be passed on to their descendants. Using this message Panya began assembling the ancestors of Jacob's army. After a few days it was time to move on. They gathered their belongings and made their way to the great city of Jerusalem.

On reaching the outskirts, they followed a road that took them to the summit of a small hill. From there they watched thousands of people enter the city and those people were on their way to witness an execution. Panya, in particular, was horrified to see so many people walking in darkness and baying for blood.

In the distance, a bright light was shining and it surrounded a lone traveller. He was a pilgrim and was journeying to pray at the Temple on the Mount. Panya ran to join him and on reaching him whispered, "My visions tell me you are Simon. They ask you to show your compassion and carry the burden. You must climb the hill of the skulls and assist an innocent man. Your reward will be a reverence that will last throughout all time."

Simon, seeing nobody, was startled, "Who, who, who's there?" he asked, A...a...answer me." No matter which way he turned he couldn't see the source of the voice.

He continued his journey and soon reached the centre of the city where he witnessed the crowd, still shouting and chanting. He watched the death march of three cross carrying men who were each being brutally treated, the cracking sound of the whips and the screams of pain will forever be etched in his memory. He saw one man fall and immediately stepped forward to help, only to be grabbed by a Roman soldier and told to bear the burden. He lowered his head, nodded and smiled; somehow knowing this to be his fate, and it was an ordeal he willingly accepted. When his eyes met a brief glance from the beaten man he felt humbled. Here was a man carrying the weight of the world upon his shoulders. Tears clouded his eyes as he listened to the cruel taunts of the crowds. But fearing the soldiers and trying not to show any sign of weakness he reached out to support the suffering man. He wiped his face with his sleeve, and bore the weight of the cross without complaint. At times the soldiers laughed and pushed Simon away, forcing the suffering and heavily bleeding man to continue his walk unaided.

As the procession passed through one of the long and narrow streets, Simon raised his eyes from the road. He saw three figures standing upon an arch looking down at him. He looked around and was surprised no one else seemed to notice them, but he was wrong. The suffering man also saw them. It was Panya, Baldor and Thanases and the look of horror and disgust on their faces showed how appalled they were. "I'd forgotten how cruel and savage man can be," Panya said, trying not to weep, "our journey has hardly begun, and already we're witnessing barbarity and viciousness."

Her tears trickled down her cheeks before falling upon those walking below. Some of those teardrops reached the man's face and then gently flowed across his shoulders, giving him a warm feeling and bringing on a serene calmness. Like the man, Simon also received that same calmness strengthening his resolve.

Panya left the arch and walked slightly ahead of Baldor and Thanases. They followed the procession 'till reaching a hill, and watched in horror and disbelief as the three men were nailed to their crosses. They were shocked and sickened at the scene, they fought the urge to help, knowing the gods would fail to approve if they intervened. They remained in silence as the hours passed.

Dark clouds gathered and the atmosphere became sinister. The last time Baldor felt something similar was when he and Jacob travelled through time to visit Jacob's school. It was when he used the power of the Light to expel the demon from Jake.

Baldor and Thanases had had enough. It was time to raise their staffs to call on the Light and when it arrived they had difficulty keeping control. "We should have practiced more." remarked Thanases.

"Fear not," replied Baldor, "trust the gods."

Thanases wasn't convinced, "How to use the Light is something not taught in the temple. What if we fail?"

Baldor raised his staff again, "We're good learners and will soon master its power. Trust the gods, I do," he released his light, "too late, we can't worry about our light skills now."

Thanases walked ahead and climbed a little higher, "See how your light travels across the hill," he pointed in several directions, "see how it reveals the whereabouts of disguised Dark Angels."

Baldor joined him, "I hear them, do you? They are encouraging the people to call for a terrible death. They chant the name of the innocent man." he again looked around, "Remember what Jacob said?" He reached for his sword and rubbed his fingers along its edge, "'Use the Light to identify any threat, eliminate the threat before it can develop to endanger your task.'" They both knew what they had to do.

The dark clouds thickened bringing on an eerie shadowy light and behind the clouds the moon had moved to block the sun, blending day and night into one. From among those same clouds, one bolt of lightning flashed, and struck the centre cross taking the spirit of the man.

At that very moment the people changed, they quietened as though suddenly awakening from an evil induced trance. At the same time the earth beneath them trembled, causing many to stumble and fall in terror. The crowd remembered well known stories from Greece, about the return of the Titan Cronus. They imagined him walking through deep caverns beneath their feet, and this terrified them.

Baldor and Thanases decided it was time to make their move. They were unsure if their invisibility would protect them but knew, as guardians it was now or never. They attacked, and proceeded to eliminate the Dark Angels until none were left, but unknown to them they had an audience. It was Lucifer, he could clearly see them, he had earlier opened a portal to view the crucifixion not knowing he would also witness the first offensive move made by the guardians of a messenger. As his angels fell his temper rose.

Up on the Mount, Panya watched the fall of the Dark Angels, she also observed a figure staring out through a portal and assumed it had to be Lucifer. She watched the expression of rage cross his face. She memorised every muscle twitch, every hair bristle and most frightening of all, she saw the evil orange fires of Hell light up his eyes. She now feared for her guardians and when she looked to their future she saw attacks and they were relentless. Her visions were interrupted, "I see you," she briskly turned to see one of the women who wept at the base of the cross standing before her, "fear not for your guardians, they will also have many happy times."

The woman returned to the base of the cross and waited for the body of the Man to be taken down before being carried away. Panya followed the women and watched them clean and prepare the body then take it to its final resting place.

She called Baldor and Thanases to join her and together they waited for what her vision showed would be something special, something that was destined to change the world. They waited patiently and on the third day they watched a burst of light arrive, and from within it an angel appeared. He was tall, with brilliant white wings and the strength to push the boulder from the entrance of the tomb. The Man stepped out, paused for a moment and acknowledged the angel. An expression of happiness crossed his face with the arrival of one of the women who wept three days earlier. He reached in, kissed her and put his arms around her. He waved across at Panya and slightly bowed, before he and the woman walked away.

Back in the Underworld Lucifer's anger sent shockwaves throughout his domain causing many of his generals to hide. One brave general cautiously approached him and said, "Need I remind you of how easy it was for you to enter the Temple of Zeus and possess Jacob? Can I remind you of how during that possession you forced Jacob to say? 'You fools! You think you can defy me? I have seen and heard your plans. I will be waiting at every crossroad, every bridge, every valley, on every mountain. You cannot hide from me...' My Lord, seek your revenge on the guardians by unleashing the legions of Hell on the villages, towns and cities visited by those same guardians. Target the ones where the message has already been delivered."

Another general arrived and presented an alternative plan, "My Lord, let us not be hasty, let us not unleash Hell's legions at this time. Instead, we should instruct the serpents who have already reached Rome to infect any boy they find alone. Let them nurture him to grow in power and stature. Let them assist him in becoming a most powerful general who under our instruction will then use the resources of Rome to destroy Jerusalem.

Lucifer liked this plan and soon calmed down. This suggestion suited because he knew Hell was ill-prepared for a full scale attack at this time. More generals arrived and together they put in place their plans for an attack on Jerusalem and they chose the year 70CE.

恢恥

It was now the year 49CE and on one particular warm and clammy evening in a small yard, hidden from view and near the colosseum, a young Roman boy was playing alongside some friends. His name was Titus Flavius. He was the ten year old son of General Vespasian and a member of the powerful Flavian dynasty. He was popular among his friends and even at such a young age, he was already showing signs of leadership.

As twilight approached Flavius was summoned home. On the way he found himself passing a number of dark alleys, one of which unsettled him. He panicked and began to run but didn't get very far. A piercing pain raced through his body causing him to collapse, writhing in agony. He fell unconscious but within minutes recovered and was a little confused. Oddly he was unfazed by his experience so continued his journey home.

He grew to be a strong and forceful young man and was tutored by the best teachers. He joined the Imperial Army and during his training it became apparent that he was the kind of young man who excelled at everything he touched. As a result he quickly rose through the ranks to become a decorated general. His father, on the death of the Emperor Nero, was elevated to become Emperor of the Roman Empire, thus ensuring that Titus, as next in line, would become commander of the eastern legions.

In a wide cavern, deep in the Underworld set among the lapping flames Lucifer sat. The incessant cries of terror and shrieks of pain were like music to his ears. The stench of searing flesh wafting from every nook and cranny brought on a contentment from which he took great pleasure. He sunk back into the comfort of his blackened stone carved throne and stared out into the vastness of his domain. Those watching witnessed a devious smile cross his chiselled good looking face. His plan was now coming to fruition especially when he was informed that Titus had aligned himself with Tiberius Julius Alexander, an older and more ruthless general.

Chapter 3

Panya, Thanases and Baldor remained near Jerusalem, and for forty years continued to train themselves in controlling the arrival of the Light. They were also developing their prophetic power, a power they were very aware was random and only available to them on occasion. Using this new skill they foresaw a great calamity was imminent, and as time passed their visions became more vivid.

Between 66CE and 70CE the continuous uprisings of the Jewish people reached a point where the patience of Rome grew thin. In response they sent General Titus who, with the assistance of his friend Tiberius, led four experienced legions from the eastern armies to lay siege to, and then ruthlessly take this historic city.

On the 14th of April 70CE Panya observed the Roman legions arrive. She watched them commence their siege which went on for five months. During this time the Jewish citizens enjoyed some victories, most notably when they tunnelled under the city and set bitumen fires causing the tunnels to collapse, destroying many of the breaching towers but this only delayed the inevitable. At the end of August everything changed, the legions broke through and so began what was to become the total annihilation of an ancient way of life. At this point Baldor had had enough, he raised his staff and prepared to call on the Light to assist but was prevented when Panya lowered his arm,

"I've seen the future and it tells me this is a battle in which we can't get involved." Baldor wasn't happy but knew if Panya spoke he must comply.

The murderous actions of the legions not only targeted the resident men, women and children but also visitors and pilgrims not associated with any rebellion. Rome's intention was to leave no one alive and no dwelling intact. Brick by brick, buildings were demolished. For the soldiers their greatest pleasure was when they reached the Temple, which was the second to be built on the Mount. They immediately destroyed its archives, successfully erasing over five hundred years of Jewish history. The western wall of the temple is all that remains of what was once a sacred Semitic site.

The death toll throughout the city was so high the stench of decay permeated throughout the land for weeks after the army had left in pursuit of the few residents who had escaped. Although this slaughter was foretold, Panya, Baldor and Thanases felt ill-prepared for the savagery they witnessed. After a few moments of reverence they sought out those survivors hiding in the surrounding countryside and assisted them as best they could. When no more could be done, Thanases sent out his light, "Even the Light grieves," he said. "See how it dims," He went to his knees and cupped a mound of sand in his hands, "see how the grains fall through my fingers, I fear each one represents a soul so brutally taken in this god-forsaken city." When he stood, Panya and Baldor saw tears had gathering but hadn't flowed. They watched him raise his arms and utter a prophecy. "Let the year 70CE be forever etched in the memories of those who survived this brutal attack. Their descendants will not forget and as the centuries pass, they will return to help rebuild. From among them will be the swords bearers of Jacob's army, warriors destined to answer the call of the gods."

They gathered their belongings and travelled east. Their walk took them high into the mountains and led them to the entrance of a well camouflaged cave, from which was glowing an inviting and bright light. On reaching the light they were surprised to find an elderly woman sitting alone, staring into the flames of an orange-glowing fire. She was a broken woman who seemed to be deep in grief. Panya recognised her as one of the women who, thirty seven years earlier, had wept at the base of the cross. She was the same woman who greeted the man outside the tomb.

The women blankly stared into the flames and didn't seem to care on realising she was no longer alone. It was obvious on looking up she could see who stood before her. "I know who you are," said Panya. "You are Mary, they call you the Magdalene; you were there when he died and when he left the tomb." She knelt and gently touched Mary's arm, "From you his message will be spread for all to hear."

Mary lowered her head, "I have seen the future; they say I am fallen, they question my love and loyalty to him, they do not want a woman to carry his message but what they don't know is that it was I and I alone who was the closest, I...KNOW... EVERYTHING."

For many hours her stories were listened to, and when finished Panya prophesied, "The lies they create will sadly travel through time. For two thousand years those lies will spread but there will be those who know the truth and to you I say, be assured for the truth will always prevail. The enlightened ones will name schools after you. They will build houses of worship in your name. Kings in the future will be anointed in Cathedrals built in your honour. Then, near the end times, your gospel will be found and all will be revealed." Mary managed a smile, "I have seen many things but that future is blind to me. What is it I'm expected to do?"

Panya continued, "You must go to the port of Jaffa where you will meet James, he waits with a small fishing boat. He will take you, and your family, to a new life in the far west. James will forever rest in a place that one day will be known as the city of Santiago de Compostela and you will rest in the land of the Gaul's. Before that time comes, you will both keep his message alive," she continued while reaching in to part the embers, "I see you everywhere, in the future you will be known as the Apostle to the Apostles."

"Ah, James," said Mary. "He was a favourite." She stood, bent forward to place her hand on Panya's cheek. She whispered out of earshot of Baldor and Thanases, "I see their light, they are goddesses; your babies will be safe and out of his gaze. From this day there will be War Gods and they will close by. They will always be watching."

Panya was taken aback, "I'm not pregnant." Mary tightly embraced her, "Yes, my dear, you are."

This news was troubling. Forty years had passed since leaving the temple and never once did she have feelings of being pregnant. "The gods work in mysterious ways," said Mary, "you must now put this news from your mind. Your task was set by the Ancient One and must be completed."

Panya was startled, "You know of our task?" to which Mary replied, "As I said, I know everything."

Mary went to the cave entrance where she waited for the sun to rise. When its rays reached her face all the lines of time faded before disappearing. She glanced back and bowed and left to meet up with her family.

On reaching a small farmhouse she was greeted by one of her sons, "Mother, you're back, last night many of us dreamt of a voyage. What does this mean?"

"My son!" she said kissing his cheek, "it wasn't a dream. It was a vision. Last night I spoke with a messenger of the gods and she foretold of a journey, she said we must leave immediately and sail west. James is waiting." When she met with the rest of her family, they listened and didn't need much persuasion. They packed and made their way to meet up with James.

৵৹৵

Way out in the cosmos the temple of Zeus was floating through time and space. A light covering of dust had gathered on the statues of the gods. When Mary spoke of Panya's babies, dust began to fall from the statue of Odi and be begun to awaken. At the same time, in Asgard, dust also fell from the statue of Magni. He was first to waken and immediately used his powers to reach Odi, "Go back into sleep little brother. Remember how Jacob tried to leave the temple on discovering Eala was pregnant; remember how he was prevented? By the power of the gods, you too will be prevented. For you, walking towards the northern Ice Lands is not part of the plan. Trust me, I and a legion of elite Asgard warriors will patrol the skies above where Panya and her guardians walk. Rest assured she will be well protected. Brother, for your daughters I will give my life."

Odi absolutely trusted Magni and knew Panya and his daughters would now be safe. He relaxed and fell back into his deep sleep but not before a very faint message was heard. It was Jacob, "Congratulations brother, you've got your wish."

৵৹৵

Panya and her guardians remained in the cave for many more years. They particularly enjoyed those nights when Roman soldiers arrived to investigate the fires that seemed to just ignite even though no one was present. The look of confusion was always priceless especially when armed guards near the cave entrance confirmed the cave was vacant. Baldor and Thanases loved teasing those searching the cave. Their teasing could be something as forward as throwing a rock against the wall or something as mild as blowing in their victim's ears.

The supernatural reputation of the cave spread far and wide, especially among the younger inexperienced soldiers who, when drunk, would enter the cave acting very brave. It always ended the same way. They'd race out in terror, resolving never to enter again. This all ended when, one cold winter's night, General Tiberius decided to investigate and because of his ruthless reputation he was known not to easily scare. He arrived with an armed escort determined to solve the mystery of the self lighting fires.

When he entered the cave Panya noticed two puncture marks on his ankle and became alarmed. She gestured for Thanases to remain still and for Baldor to call on the Light. When it arrived it was undetected by Tiberius, or his escorts, but it quickly confirmed that the general had in fact been bitten and was now a disguised Dark Angel.

Tiberius moved deeper into the cave. He occasionally paused, looked around and sneered, indicating he sensed something. The slightest sound of the smallest pebbles being disturbed didn't escape him causing him to strain his neck trying to identify where those sounds came from. His sneer changed to a permanent smile when he surmised he had potentially stumbled upon a hiding place of a messenger. His arrogance showed when he instructed his escorts to leave and ordered them not to allow anyone near the cave. "Messengers of the Gods," he said in a rasping and sinister voice. "I know you're here. There is no escape; you have failed in your task. My legions will soon arrive and your souls will be fed to Lucifer before this day is out."

Thanases was nearest and silently gestured for Baldor and Panya to follow his lead, knowing they would do exactly as he did. When he lifted his left leg they followed, and as they each swapped their steps they eventually ended up in single file, with Thanases almost eyeball to eyeball with the general.

Thanases had his sword drawn, ready to strike when the general raised his nose and sniffed the air, "Ah, the smell of fear; Lucifer and his serpents are hungry this night. You will not pass me."

Thanases became alarmed causing his hand to shake and he began to doubt himself, He felt a presence, it was Jacob, "Fear not the threats, they are hollow. You were a pupil of the War Gods, do what you were trained to do."

Thanases materialised and without a moment's hesitation, lunged forward and plunged his sword into the general's armour to slice through his heart. The general sniggered before laughing loudly and slowly moving his head closer to Thanases, "Fool. Do you not know? We have no hearts." Baldor managed to get behind Tiberius, materialise and with the swiftest of swordsmanship he decapitated him.

Everything went quiet for just a few moments. Tiberius' eyes widened and his mouth opened allowing a brief intake of breath. His throat gurgled before his head fell forward and tumbled to the ground. On impact a black mist rose to whisk his spirit back into the bowels of Hell.

Watching the mist disappear Panya knew they were now in mortal danger. They quickly packed and when ready, they moved to the mouth of the cave. Baldor sent out his Light and it highlighted several hundred Dark Angels mingling among the thousands of soldiers billeted in the encampment below. Many were young and innocent conscripts who had just arrived and these were soldiers who didn't have blood on their hands. Panya was troubled watching sporadic white mists rise towards the heavens, she knew it meant there were other soldiers worth saving and this, for her, was a dilemma. She wanted to intervene but her instincts were telling her to leave. Her decision was made easier when Thanases confirmed there were hundreds of serpents slithering towards the valley and they were coming from all directions.

When briskly making their way out of the valley they came across a young centurion who was preparing to leave. Panya approached him and placed her hand on his shoulder. The centurion felt something, stood still for a moment before raising his hand to rub his neck and shoulder; he then shrugged and continued with what he was doing. On whispering Jacob's message in his ear the seed of greatness had just been planted. Panya was also aware he was destined to meet a messenger again. The centurion's name was Trajan and he had been reassigned to the far west as general of the western legions.

Chapter 4

Their journey took them north into many small villages and towns before they arrived at the hills overlooking the ancient city of Palmyra, where they stood and marvelled at its vastness. This was home to over two hundred thousand citizens who were very proud of all they had achieved, they were especially proud of how its architecture attracted students from all over the known world. It was a city of diverse tribes, all speaking the same Semitic language. The Palm trees, that gave their name to the city, grew out as far as the eye could see, confirming this place to be the largest oasis in all of Mesopotamia. The green pastures and tilled fields provided all the food the city needed. It was now part of the Roman Empire and all the main trade caravans travelling the Silk Road stopped there just for its refreshing water and as a result it became extremely wealthy and a target for envious neighbours.

The Temple was the predominant structure and attracted the most attention. For Panya it was the resident god who interested her. She used her powers to look back through time, to the year 32CE, when the temple was built and dedicated to the god, Bel Marduk. She watched Bel Marduk arrive and take up residence without him being seen by the masses.

She chose not to make contact because something wasn't quite right so she decided to remain in a cave overlooking the city. As the days turned into weeks and then months before turning into years it was noted how a bleak sadness and fear appeared on the faces of the people. It was a fear brought on by a sinister evil that took control of Palmyra and it would seem Bel Marduk himself had turned malevolent. The people learned to hate him and as a result, they avoided making offerings at the temple.

Baldor and Thanases never let their guard down, they remained outside the cave and once a day would release their Light until one day, the presence of serpents was detected and to their horror they found the city had been overrun.

Around that time they observed a young boy entering a scrub-hidden smaller cave that was close by. It was so well hidden they hadn't detected it when they were securing the area. They called for Panya and together they went to investigate.

On entering the cave they were awe-struck viewing the most amazing wall and ceiling paintings. Panya materialised near the boy and attempted to reassure him, she encouraged him to sit and tell his story. Although frightened, he struggled not to cry. He managed to ask, "Who are you? Are you going to hurt me?"

Panya again attempted to calm him, "No, why would I hurt you? I worry that such a little boy is alone in this remote place. Tell me, what is your name? Why are you hiding?"

"M-M-Michael is my name." He looked more frightened and said while backing away, "The serpents bit my mama and dada and they tried to get me so I ran; my dada used to bring me here to watch him paint and I knew it would be a safe place to hide," his tears began to flow, "I miss them, my tummy feels very sore. I'm, I'm hungry."

Panya offered him food. She could see he was beginning to really grieve so she took him into her arms and held him as he wept. It broke her heart to hear him say, "I saw the white mist rise as they fell." When he finally slept she again looked around at the paintings then whispered in his ear,

"You will carry forward the art of your father, your descendants will also be artists and one of them will become the greatest of them all." She had planted in him the seed of art.

In the meantime Baldor and Thanases stood guard at the entrance of the cave from where they saw strange streaks of light moving slowly across the heavens. Suddenly the streaks stopped moving, all except for one that kept travelling before turning and descending to land on a dirt-track a short distance away.

It was an Asgard chariot carrying a fully armed warrior who walked towards them with his head lowered. Baldor wasn't fooled; he immediately recognised the warrior and ran to greet him. Thanases wasn't fooled either, he too ran close behind. It was Magni and they both showed how happy they were to see him after so many years.

He willingly returned their embrace, sensing they were still traumatised by the terrible events they had witnessed in Jerusalem. He also felt they needed reassurance and pointed to the heavens, "See the streaks of light? You are watching a legion of Asgards best charioteers and they will be escorting you from now on. I'll be with them and will be watching at all times. We will not interfere in the task set for you. Everything has changed now that Panya is carrying the daughters of Odi."

Baldor was shocked and first to speak, "Panya's pregnant? When? Where? Why didn't she tell us? And, do you not trust us?"

"Of course I trust you," smiled Magni. "You are the most trained of all the immortals, Jacob saw to that, but as I said, everything is changed now," he paused for a moment, giving them time to absorb the news, and then said, "We can't risk Lucifer discovering Odi is going to be a father, especially as we believe he knows Jacob's children are already born. His serpents are searching throughout the western lands. Trust me, they are wasting their time, they won't succeed."

Thanases struggled to find the words but he managed to say, "Eala, Ealasaid had babies? Jacob's a father? Are they boys or girls? How did this happen?"

Magni asked, "Did your parents not tell you of the birds and the bees?" Baldor sniggered. Magni continued, "Eala gave birth to two boys and a girl, they're safe and hidden, even from the gods."

He left them shocked and walked into the cave where he saw Panya sitting with a young boy sleeping in her arms and could see she already had the heart of a mother. He placed his hand on her shoulder and her excitement on seeing him was obvious. He sat beside her and whispered in her ear, "The gods are aware you are pregnant and so is Odi. He wanted to come for you and it took all my powers to stop him from fully wakening, I encouraged him to return to sleep. His part in this story will come to pass in the not too distant future. My task is to provide for your protection, I promised Odi his children would be safe in the hands of Asgard and for that I have deployed a legion of warriors."

She wasn't interested in her own safety. She only wanted to know about Odi, and asked, "When he woke did he think of me?"

"It was his concern for you that woke him," said Magni. He left her and went back to the other cave to sit and listen to the stories Baldor and Thanases had to tell. After several hours, he asked, "Tell me about your plans for tomorrow."

Baldor was glad he asked. "Tomorrow," he said, "we will face battalions of serpents and possibly Dark Angels but what worries us the most is, we will also have to face a turned Sun God who has now been walking on the path of evil for almost sixty years. His name is Bel Marduk. We know nothing of him."

"Panya needs to enter the city," said Thanases, "she senses a struggling force for good and needs to get the message to them so we plan to enter unseen until the last second."

Neither saw how pale Magni got but they did note how he went very quiet. When he composed himself, he said, "It hurts me to hear this news. Marduk is a dear and special friend; I cannot believe he's been turned." He continued after standing to leave, "This news changes my plans. Tomorrow I will join you and deal with him myself. He's not only a Sun God, he is a War God and much too strong for you." He then left and made his way to brief his warriors on the plan for the following day.

The next morning Michael woke and seemed much happier. He said as he hugged Panya, "I was dreaming; there was an angel who looked just like you. She showed me Rome and then another city. I think she said 'Florence', what does it mean?"

Panya took him into her arms and moved to leave the cave, "I too saw your dream, you will go to Rome and then the city of Florence, your future lies there. You will have many descendants and I ask you to ensure they always pass on the love of art because, it is your art that will help keep mankind in the Light."

Michael cuddled into her and after a short time asked, "Do you think the angel would mind if I took her name, I would like to be called Michael Angel." Panya nodded, "I think she would be honoured if you took her name."

They left the cave and moved down towards the road where they met up with a young couple who were walking towards the west. Panya approached them and established they were travelling to Greece in the hope of starting a new life there. She used her powers to encourage them to take Michael as one of their own which they did and soon they were on their way. Panya blew a kiss to Michael and with a tear in her eye watched as he continuously turned to wave her his last goodbyes. When he was out of sight she sobbed softly. Magni after watching from the cave went to join her and listened as she wept, "I wanted to keep him by my side and protect him, but I knew it was not to be. Look at him, my little hero."

"For me," said Magni, "you are showing that you will be a warm and loving mother to my nieces. One is destined to be an Asgard War Goddess and the other a powerful Goddess of the Sun."

She linked Magni's arm and said snuggling closer to him, "Linking on to you helps me feel close to Odi, I really miss him. He is so considerate, so loving and attentive to me. You must be so proud of him."

Magni stopped and slowly turned to face her, "Are you sure we're talking about the same Odi? The one I know is cheeky and insubordinate; he is insolent and doesn't respect authority." They both laughed and she said,

"No matter what, the one I remember is the one I really miss. I love him so much." Magni said no more.

The time soon came for them to make their way into the city and it wasn't long before they reached the five hundred meter great colonnade that stretched out before them. They noted how each column held the images of the great and the powerful elite who once ruled Palmyra. They passed the renowned valley of the dead and the western wall of the Necropolis where they stopped to gaze at the tower style funerary tombs.

Baldor kept his staff high for the full journey allowing the Light to shine in all directions highlighting the whereabouts of all serpents enabling them to avoid contact for as long as possible. They continued their walk and soon arrived at the steps leading up to the Temple of Bel.

Magni pushed open the doors and when he did, the sickly stench of death almost overpowered them. Magni called out, "Bel Marduk, old friend. How is it, the warmth is gone from your halls? And where is the light of a most powerful Sun God? Can your dear friend enter in safety?"

A reply was slow in coming but when it did, it answered in a sinister and ominous voice sending shivers across the Cosmos, "Enter my halls at your peril, War God. There are no friends here. Look upon the fallen priests, the results of my wrath? Be aware of how the Light offends me."

Magni cautiously stepped forward and asked, "How is it a Sun God can be offended by the Light? Show yourself, my friend."

Thanases was slightly to the left when he noticed a rapidly moving spear heading towards Magni. It was travelling at such a speed that all he could do was push Magni to the ground. The spear continued its journey outside the temple where it turned to ash as it met the rays of the sun.

Magni struggled to focus for a moment; the sunlight behind him didn't quiet reach the back of the temple so he waited for his eyes to adjust. Then he saw him, the Dark Angel, and he was standing at the back of the temple in his colossus form. "I challenge you, my friend," said Magni, "reach out to me. I know you are within him. Expel the evil that binds you."

He was met with a menacing sneer and decided he had no choice but to take his colossus form. Magni was always impressive as a man but when he grew to full size he put the fear of Odin into all who stood against him. He raised his shield and positioned his sword before stealthily moving forward for the clash of two colossi to begin.

Baldor in the meantime discretely walked behind one of Magni's legs allowing him to get half way through the temple before jumping to hide behind a column near where Marduk was standing.

Thanases by now had rejoined Panya and was horrified when he realised he and Baldor had left her unprotected long enough for her to be surrounded by serpents and Dark Angels. He placed her behind him and took up an attack position and raised his staff to call on the Light. His staff vibrated violently and when the Light came its radiant beams held the Dark Angels at bay.

Meanwhile in the temple, hidden behind a column, Baldor watched the battle unfold and waited for the opportunity to call on the Light. He worried when he saw Magni was having trouble getting the better of Marduk and could see how every move Magni made was being undone by what was obviously a very well trained Dark Lord. They were both using every move and skill they had acquired since they first became warriors and as a result the fight seemed destined to go on for an age; that was until Magni finally lost his patience.

He lunged forward with such force he was unable to stop himself when the Dark Angel leapt aside and this was the opportunity the Dark Angel was waiting for. He spun around and used his sword to pierce Magni's shoulder, tearing into his muscle and shattering his bone. Magni dropped his weapon and collapsed to the floor.

As he fell he managed to turn and land on his back, this allowed him to use his foot and flip his sword across to his uninjured hand giving him a chance to strike back, which he did, forcing the Dark Angel to his knees. Magni, with great difficulty, stood knowing he had to finish this battle there and then. He hesitated when he thought of the time he spent with Marduk, and it was breaking his heart to be the one to kill his dear friend.

This moment of hesitation was his undoing, it allowed the Dark Angel to rise to his feet and spread his massive black wings out across the span of the temple. Magni could see that all semblance of what was once a Sun God was gone confirming Marduk was now totally possessed. What he was looking at was a being, much taller than the Dark Angel who led the attack in Dublin, suggesting he was a senior general from Hells armies.

The Dark Angel used an ancient magic that was strong enough to propel Magni backwards and out through the door of the temple. As he fell and hit the ground he turned his head and saw the standoff between Thanases, the serpents and the Dark Angels, he was pleased to see the Asgard army was descending from the sky above.

The Dark Angel wasn't finished; he was determined to destroy an Asgard god. He raced forward with his spear raised but was stopped when Baldor leapt out from behind the column and challenged him. Baldor yelled, "You will now suffer the power of the Light, Dark Lord."

The Dark Angel retorted with a hideous sneer. "A messenger of the Light, or are you just a guardian? You will be my dinner this coming night." He lunged forward but failed to capture Baldor who was faster and better trained.

Baldor leapt from pillar to pillar and made his way to the rear of the temple and calling on the full force of the ancient source Light for assistance. When it came, it came with such brilliance, that it sent the Dark Angel plummeting to the floor, squirming and thrashing about in pain. Baldor increased its intensity and watched the Light do its work, he was again reminded of the first time he used its power to expel a Dark Angel from Jake just after the battle of Dublin. He was ruthless and was determined not to make the same mistake as before.

When he was sure the evil was expelled, he backed away so as to open the blinds that covered the windows on the south facing side of the temple. This allowed the sun to shine through to make its way towards a peaceful looking Marduk. Within minutes Marduk sat up but his recovery was sluggish, that was until a powerful beam of pure sunlight arrived. When he stood, he waited for his powers to be completely restored before walking to the centre of the temple where he closed his eyes and raised his hands towards the heavens.

Baldor watched him transform back into a most powerful Sun God, he watched the golden halo form and a crown of flawless white light rest on his head before it glowed brighter. He watched body armour miraculously form around him and then his pure white cape drape from his shoulders. He had no weapons; there was no need because all he required was the power of the sun.

Marduk made his way out of temple, stepped over Magni, and immediately raised his hands to summon balls of molten lava which he used to incinerate the serpents and Dark Angels who were attempting to capture Thanases and Panya. He was now in a rage and determined no soldier of Hell would survive his vengeance.

The Asgard charioteers had arrived and their blade laden axles were a weapon the forces of Hell were unprepared for, they were so precise they decapitated the remaining Dark Angels who were in the surrounding lanes and alleyways as well as the forecourt.

Baldor joined Thanases and together they climbed upon the portico where they raised their staffs to send the Light across the hills. They quickly identified serpents scurrying towards the mountains, allowing the Asgard charioteers who were in pursuit to quickly locate and vanquish every last one.

Marduk then sat on the steps and looked devastated, he was horrified at how easily he fell to the power of Hell. He gazed across at his friend and wondered how he could ever again look him in the eye.

Panya rushed to Magni's aid and began nursing his shattered shoulder only to discover his wounds were more serious than seemed at first. He was poisoned and was beginning to lose consciousness. Marduk watched her efforts and saw she was struggling; he joined her and offered to help. He whispered in Magni's ear, "My friend, it seems the poison has taken you. I may be a Sun God but I am also a Healing God, let my power assist. I know you probably hate me right now but let me help. Please remember the love we once shared."

He asked Panya to step aside before raising his hands to call on the power of the sun and when it arrived his body glowed. Soon beams of light flowed from his fingers to reach across and enter Magni's forehead. From there they made their way towards his neck and shoulders allowing its heat to begin melding the sliced veins, smooth the torn bones, and generate enough extra blood to give him the strength to begin his recovery.

It was twelve hours before Magni came around; his first question was an enquiry as to the safety of Panya. His fears were assuaged when she walked in and sat with him. She could see he was subdued and offered him comfort, "When you fell I felt real fear until I looked at the stoicism of Thanases. I saw his power and his valour and this helped me feel safe again. I saw the flashes of light as Baldor did what he was trained to do and knew then I was safe in their hands," she paused and assisted him to sit up, "Magni, when I look at the night sky and see your army I know I am close to my Odi, I long for him to hold me one more time. Today I held myself and sensed their presence. How is it I don't feel pregnant? I don't understand. How did I travel for so long with nothing showing?"

He leaned forward and placed his hand on the cheek, "You are carrying the life force of two goddesses. Only they will decide when it's time." He then managed to stand before making his way into the main hall where he found Baldor, Thanases and Marduk sitting in a very sombre mood. Baldor and Thanases immediately jumped to their feet and bowed. They extracted, then offered their swords, because they felt they had let the gods down and were ashamed at how they had left Panya so vulnerable.

Magni looked at them quizzingly, backed away and then turned to Marduk who still couldn't look him in the eye. He gripped Marduk's arm, "Please look me in the eye. We are brother gods who were the closest any could be," he raised Marduk's head, "Why do you look so ashamed when it was your use of the sun that won out this day. Think back and remember how it was you who always came to my aid when I was in trouble."

He turned back to Baldor and Thanases refusing to accept their swords, "Need I remind you of how one of you took on a supreme general of Lucifer's army, vanquished him and send him back to Hell? The other stood alone before a legion of serpents, protecting Panya. It is I who should be ashamed; I was the only one who fell." He asked Baldor and Thanases to leave and prepare for the rest of their journey.

When they left he and Marduk hugged each other. Magni whispered, "Strange how my feelings are the same after all these years? Why did you leave me?"

Marduk tightened his grip, "I never wanted to leave. You were the reckless one and always looked over your shoulder to see if anyone was watching. I was a mere Sun God and you were the most powerful of the War Gods, it would never have worked. We would never have been accepted. You know that."

"I would have given up everything for you," said Magni.

"And that was the problem," was Marduk's reply. "How long would it have been before you resented me?" he hesitated for a moment, "How long would it have been before you learned to hate me?" he hesitated again,

"Your whole life was built around being a War God and a general of Asgard. You would have blamed me if anything went wrong and I would never have been able to live with that."

Marduk moved away and said as he sat on a step near the exit, "This temple is so polluted by the Dark Lords I want nothing more to do with it so I have decided to leave. I fear I will be remembered as an evil god with my name being forever associated with the demon, Beelzebub."

Magni wasn't happy, "I've just found you after all these millennia and you are already talking of leaving. How do you think that makes me feel? I'm prepared to give up everything for you. Apart from my feelings, think of your people, need I remind you of how you are not only their Sun God! You are also a most powerful Storm God. What will your devotees do? You bring the rains when they pray and bring the sun when they call on you yet again. Before the attack from Hell you never failed them. They will remember this before the visit of the End Times."

After a few moments of silence Marduk said, "I hope you never thought I forgot you, I didn't. I'd look at the northern skies and hope that one day we'd meet again. Little did I know it would be under such terrible circumstances?"

He then lifted his tunic to reveal two puncture marks just above his left knee. He rubbed his hand across them, "The Dark Angel may be gone but his poison still races through my veins. I fear this evil of Hell."

Magni placed his hand on the wound for a few moments before fetching a large carafe of the finest Palmyrian wine and a basin of cold water from a nearby shelf, "Apollo identified wine as a foe of the poison. Trust me, you will fully recover but tomorrow morning, the pounding of a stonemason will be nothing compared to the pain you will suffer." They drank every last drop of wine and after some time fell into the deepest of sleep.

They woke early the next morning and were really suffering. Their heads were pounding and their groans could be heard out in the courtyard, much to the amusement of the Asgard warriors. Magni stretched his hand across to the basin and called on Poseidon to come to his aid but was surprised when instead of Poseidon, the voice he heard was that of Jacob, "I'll help you brother, but you must give your blessing for Marduk to leave. Your place is at the head of the armies of Asgard and there can be no distractions. Your time for happiness will come but it's not this day. Place your hand on Marduk's forehead and wait for the pain to leave."

Magni wasn't happy, he felt something special being rekindled and didn't want the magic to end but he knew his place. He closed his eyes and placed his hand in the water. He felt it slowly trickle up his arm and move across his chest. He then placed his right hand on Marduk's forehead and they both began to recover.

Marduk turned to embrace Magni, "Last night you gave me amazing memories. You gave me your body, your heart, your soul and I'll be eternally grateful. My friend, you must understand, my decision is final," he stood to walk towards the door, "I'll be leaving to find a sun somewhere out in the cosmos, where one day I hope to finally find the happiness that has evaded me for so long."

Magni was upset but accepted Marduk's decision. He also knew Jacob's advice was sound and trusted his prophecy would come to pass. Seeing Marduk after so long helped him understand the loneliness he was feeling, especially when he saw the love his younger brothers had found. It was then that he imparted a most profound prophecy and asked Marduk to share it with his people.

Out in the courtyard Baldor observed a delegation of citizens moving through the colonnades prompting him to call Magni and Marduk to join him. The gods watched the people reach the temple and ensured the only immortal visible was Marduk.

When the delegation reached the steps they went to their knees and bowed to their god. They spoke of how many citizens had witnessed the battle and had seen the charioteers attack the Dark Angels; they said they had seen everything. They told Marduk of how they loved him and hoped he would stay to protect them because they felt more vulnerable now that they know how the forces of Hell could attack so easily and without warning. They asked about their future without the guidance of their priests and oracles.

Marduk looked out past the courtyard and watched thousands more survivors approach the temple. He could see they were straining to set their eyes on the face of a god, their God. He could also see the grief and despair in the faces of those who lost loved ones, and was beginning to feel guilty about his decision to leave.

He stepped out to walk among them, "It's time for me to leave but before I go, I will impart a most profound prophecy that will help you prepare for what's coming." They all listened carefully, "This city will thrive for another two hundred years before falling yet again to the Roman armies. Another three hundred years will pass when it will fall again, this time to a new religion and will never know peace again. Nine hundred years will then pass when it will suffer two earthquakes causing your descendants to finally leave. Just before the End Times, what is left will be attacked, one last time. This attack will be by a most evil force and then this magnificent temple will be lost forever. When this happens, people all across the world, will know of Bel Marduk. They will know I am a true God of the Light and not the demon whom some will try to say I am. I promise you, my friends, I will be by the side of the gods at the battle of the End Times. I will stand with your descendants and together we will assist to finally defeat The Darkness. Go now and rebuild your lives. The time has come for me to leave."

He then did something unusual, something that was unknown among the gods, he bowed to his people and they reciprocated. He closed his eyes as he accepted one last hug from an invisible Magni.

Soon after, a beam of light arrived and formed a bridge to the now high sun. Its golden rays assisted by lifting him towards the heavens.

Magni was crestfallen while watching the golden rays fade causing Baldor to ask, "Magni, are you OK? Is there anything I can do?"

Magni appreciated his concern, "I'm fine, I just. I just." he went quiet for a moment then turned to face Panya, "I'm so proud of what you achieved today, go now and spread the message of hope. Remember, if you need me, look to the stars." He mounted his chariot and left to join his warriors.

The journey north was set to continue, any fears Baldor and Thanases had were now gone, Magni had given his seal of approval which gave back to them their confidence. They walked through the crowds, all the time identifying those worthy of receiving the message. Baldor and Thanases assisted Panya by whispering in the ears of the chosen ones, they whispered the same words used back in the villages outside Jerusalem, "Go now, tell your children to tell their children's children for all time that one day, they will be called upon by the gods and they must answer."

Each carrier chosen felt a calming hand causing them to stop what they were doing while a new purpose for their lives showed itself. In time they grew to become happier people, full of ideas. Some destined to be compassionate healers and helpers. Over time they would migrate out throughout all lands spreading the message of hope.

Chapter 5

Gathering their belongings and making their way towards the city limits, they stopped and looked out towards the north east, across a vast desert that would eventually take them to the Kingdom of Ararat in ancient Armenia. Walking for several months they eventually stopped by Lake Van where they decided to stay. They often sat in the hills above the lake which gave them a view of a circle of fire, volcanoes that were continuously erupting and their glow, especially at night, conjured up images of primordial times. The one that really caught their attention was the violently erupting Nemrut Dagi volcano. They watched it spew its molten rocks high into the night sky before it send a rain of fire out across the land. It was the highest and stood proudly over the western end of the lake dominating a vista of peaks, standing majestically as though the guardian of these most foreboding highlands. When the snowflakes settled, it never allowed them rest for too long before sending its heat to create the melt-waters keeping the lowlands irrigated and fertile.

For many decades they remained in the caves above the lake where they were happy and always felt safe, from there Panya watched out for people to whom she could pass on the message.

In the year 264CE, while out on one of her long walks, Panya met seven year old Gregory. Intrigued that he could see her and looking forward to speaking with him she was surprised he was so articulate for one so young.

She sat with him and talked for many hours. When it was time to leave she said, "This country has a future mired in difficult times and will suffer much pain, I see your future and it tells me you will be the founder of a great religion."

"Are you an angel?" asked Gregory.

She smiled, "No, I'm just a messenger." She returned to the cave where, alongside her guardians, she spent many more years.

It was now the year 301CE and Gregory was an established preacher who had succeeded in converting the Armenian monarchy as well as the sceptical nobility to Christianity. He was responsible for the Armenian people becoming the first peoples to declare Christianity to be their state religion.

Many more years passed bringing a steady increase in pilgrims to the capital city. Panya felt this should be investigated and on reaching the city soon found out why. They were just in time to witness the opening of the great cathedral of Echmiadzin, and remained to watch it being dedicated to St Gregory the illuminator. After the dedication Panya foretold, "For Armenia, this is one of the golden ages but it won't last. Gregory will forever be known as St Gregory, patron saint of Armenia and this cathedral will remain a pilgrimage site destined to always be the beating heart of the Armenian nation."

When leaving, she heard her name being called and on looking back she saw it was Gregory running to greet her. He was wearing his priestly robes and was being accompanied by his wife and two sons. He said when he excitedly reached her, "Panya, my angel, you've come back." He couldn't see her guardians.

Everyone present, including Gregory's family, were shocked and concerned, watching him speak into thin air. His wife, Miriam, became very alarmed and attempted to drag him away but there was no moving him. She stopped when he began writing. Gregory knelt, his writing becoming more feverish. The people who gathered could see no one near him, and when they saw the fear in his face they began to believe he was receiving messages from God. Little did they know that what he received was a prophecy showing sad happenings destined to befall Armenia over the next seventeen hundred years?

When he finished writing he read aloud the prophecy, "I will be the first patriarch of Armenia and like my successors I will preside over a nation steeped in the blood of its people. Over the next two thousand years, time and time again, our country will be attacked. From the east there will be the Agars, from the north it will be the Kingdom of Rus, from the south the Persians and from the far west the remnants of the Roman Empire. From the near west, it will be the Ottomans. By the sword there will be forced conversions to a new religion. The worst will come near the End Times, when genocide will happen and millions of Armenians will fall. Some of these attacks will be led by men bitten by the serpents of Hell, but all is not lost, for there is hope. Through all this mayhem the spirit of our people will persevere and before the End Times battle a bright light will shine and for our people a new nation of Armenia will be born."

Visibly shaken Gregory closed his eyes in prayer. On opening them he was disappointed to find Panya was gone.

Heading back to the cave Thanases said, "You really scared Gregory and you didn't hold back, I think I saw him visibly age as you spoke."

"I don't believe what I said to him will be the worst prophecy given by me before our journey ends," said a forlorn Panya.

For the remaining twenty eight years of his life Gregory travelled throughout Armenia preaching in the hope of strengthening his people's faith in preparation for what was to come.

Their time in Armenia was over and it was time for them to make their way to the north east where they would cross the mountains of Georgia into the Mid Lands. It was then when they realised they had been travelling for almost three hundred years. On looking up each clear and starry night, they were comforted to see the patrolling Asgard chariots. They often played games identifying shapes created by the erratic formations and always felt it was safe to assume Magni's chariot was the one forever out in front.

Chapter 6

They set up camp in a secluded forest close to the Black Sea and made it their base for the next few years. Once settled they made plans to visit local villages and, after visiting the first one, Baldor got very excited. He felt something special and believed this was the place where his hero fought the fire-breathing dragon. He sensed the battle and the spirit presence of Jason and the Argonauts. He was convinced it was the location from where Jason took the Golden Fleece back to Greece. Thanases got great pleasure in teasing him and after much mirth reminded him of how it was at least fifteen hundred years since Jason had lived.

Baldor wasn't swayed, he really believed the spirit of Jason was about and it caused his senses to go into overdrive. Although he sensed Jason, his skills were telling him a more sinister menace was rising and this prompted him to reach for his satchel to retrieve his armour and weapons. On raising his staff he sent out the Light but nothing showed and this confused him, he was certain something was wrong.

Panya and Thanases sensed nothing untoward so they fell asleep leaving Baldor to watch over them.

There was no fire lit that night, there was no need. It was so warm and balmy it soon brought a creeping restlessness to Thanases and Panya, causing both of them to twist and turn in their sleep. Baldor remained alert and as the night progressed he got more agitated; he felt the evil presence getting stronger.

In the stillness of that night's darkest hour he heard what sounded like subdued chanting as well as muffled cries coming from over a nearby hill and decided to investigate. He reached the crest of the hill and to his horror, he saw a party of serpents, assisted by a coven of warlocks, burning the bodies of Georgian youths. He concluded the young men and women wouldn't succumb to the call of Lucifer. There were other youths who were gagged and bound to the surrounding trees and assumed they too were being prepared for torture and death. He raised his staff and again called on the Light which quickly came and using this light he established that those before him were the only forces of evil in the vicinity.

He withdrew and made his way back to waken Thanases, telling him to prepare for battle. They woke Panya and when ready all three moved up the hill where they remained invisible, allowing them get close enough to the tree line to plan a rescue. From there Panya observed the warlocks mix a concoction of herbs and powders before adding the bones of some unfortunate creature. She watched them pour water into the mix and then listened to them chant the words of an old magic spell that called on the powers of Hell. She was startled when from among the flames a Dark Angel appeared.

This Dark Angel was different to any other she had known; he had the power to see through her invisibility putting her in great danger. The only advantage she had was the fact he couldn't see her guardians or the Asgard warriors patrolling the sky above. She knew she was caught so she folded her arms in contempt and showed no fear. She called on the Dark Angel to leave or face the wrath of the gods but her threats didn't faze him; he just sneered and then laughed menacingly before moving towards her.

In the meantime Thanases worked his way through the ranks of the serpents, decapitating each one as he passed. This action allowed the Dark Angel to work out there were at least two immortals before him. He didn't detect Baldor who never left Panya's side.

The warlocks saw the slaughter of the serpents and were feverishly conjuring up all kinds of ancient dark magic in the hope of illuminating the sword bearer; they found one that made Baldor and Thanases visible, robbing them of their advantage. The Dark Angel now knew there was two immortals not one, and he immediately released a powerful blast of fire that was so strong its intensity took them by surprise. It penetrated Thanases' armour and instantly he succumbed to its power and fell. Panya and Baldor went into shock watching Thanases' life drain away and when they saw his white mist rise they began to grieve. They thought immortality meant death could never come their way and this confused them; especially when they saw the now three hundred and fifty year old body of Thanases wrinkle and wilt. In the sky above Magni and the warriors of Asgard hadn't time to react.

Baldor soon snapped out of his shock and went on a frenzied onslaught against the warlocks, his attack was so swift and ruthless he dispatched them in a matter of seconds. The first four fell immediately and the second four fell when he leapt over the pyre to decapitate them while still in the air, the remaining four were taken out as he pirouetted his way back to protect Panya.

He challenged the Dark Angel and then began to use all the skills taught to him by the War Gods but found he was out of his depth and no matter how hard he tried he couldn't bring the angel down, he soon realised he was just being played with. It seemed the Dark Angels had developed their skills over the years and were now able to deal with most of what the guardians threw at them.

Baldor never gave up, he harried and harassed until the Dark Angel finally had enough and retaliated by raising his arm in a left to right motion. This action sent Baldor hurtling towards an old tree which had long, sharp branches protruding from its trunk. He was slammed against it with such force he was impaled on those same branches to let out a heart wrenching cry

Meanwhile the spirit of Thanases drifted through the clouds and floated across the sea; it crossed the nearby mountains and made its way towards a light shining from the far west. He soon arrived on a pristine sandy beach. He took a few moments to get his bearings then walked towards what looked like an ancient temple. He walked up the steps to be greeted by the Archangel Raphael who gestured for him to turn back, "It's not your time," he said, "there is no place for you here; you must return and assist Panya in spreading the message."

Thanases felt a great calmness. He didn't want to leave but he had no choice. The world around him was fading rapidly, and soon he found himself hovering just above the site of his demise. He saw the devastation the serpents and Dark Angel had caused and was pleased to see that the warlocks had been destroyed. Drifting down towards his almost totally wilted corpse he saw Baldor impaled on the tree and became angry. He entered his corpse and waited a few seconds for the Light to arrive and begin his recovery.

While all this was going on several archers from the Asgard army had their arrows primed and ready for release. Many more charioteers were on their way to rescue Panya. Their assent was stopped by the arrival of Raphael who appeared alongside Magni and requested he let Thanases do what he was trained to do. This confused Magni because all he could see was a dead Thanases, an unprotected Panya and a seriously wounded Baldor. He was struggling with the request but trusted the Archangel so he ordered his warriors to take a holding position with their arrows drawn and ready for release.

The Dark Angel had turned his attention back towards Panya and began taunting her, "Lucifer will have great pleasure in using you as his plaything; we know you are a favourite of the Boy King and will use your anguish to draw him out. Ah, I see the light dim in your face." He paused as he looked down her body and then with great delight continued, "My, my. Two goddesses grow within you, their life forces shine brightly. He will cherish you until they are born and then force you to watch as he grows them to be his consorts. When he is finished he will tear you apart before delighting in devouring your soul."

Panya still showed no fear, she could see the Asgard army were close by and in her peripheral vision, to her right, she saw the bound youths free themselves and work towards assisting Baldor down from his impalement. She moved slightly to the left hoping to hold the gaze of the Dark Angel. At the same time the youths stuffed a cloth in Baldor's mouth to prevent him from screaming as they lifted him from the tree. He began to heal almost immediately but he had lost so much blood he was too weak to be of any assistance.

To Panya's left Thanases was fully restored and floating into an upright position. She moved towards the right still holding the gaze of the Dark Angel and preventing him from noticing the resurrection of Thanases. Baldor also saw what was happening and stood with difficulty so as to create a further distraction.

Thanases continued floating and soon reached a boulder where he drew his dagger from the scabbard below his knee. At the same time he held his sword ready to attack. He soon floated into a position just behind the Dark Angel and hovered while Baldor continued to distract.

Magni and Raphael watched in awe as Thanases raised his dagger above the head of the Dark Angel then plunged it into his thick skull. This action gave him a solid grip allowing him to swing his sword so as to decapitate him in one swift move. For a moment, The Dark Angel stood motionless, wide eyed with shock before his head, then his body; fell to the ground. They watched the black mist rise before falling into the nearest crevice to make its way back into the bowels of Hell.

Raphael bowed to Panya and her guardians then disappeared. Magni ordered his warriors to return to the higher holding position before travelling down to meet with Panya.

When he landed he saw Baldor and Thanases were still in shock staring blankly into space. He could see they were having trouble taking in all that had happened and how precarious their position was.

When Thanases came around and saw Magni approach he exploded into a fit of rage and ran at him. He was so angry he didn't care that he was attacking one of the most powerful War Gods.

Baldor was struggling and the way he approached showed he too was determined to attack. Magni noted his fist was clenched and braced himself for an impact he chose to allow but he didn't expect it to cause him to hit the ground. Baldor's punch was a lot stronger than he expected and it touched a nerve. Magni stood and composed himself while suffering a now verbal onslaught. Baldor was the most vocal and didn't care that he had assaulted a prince of Asgard.

The Asgard warriors, watching from above, were astonished at how Magni had allowed the boys assault him so violently and knew he would reach a point where he would put them back in their place. They were right, his patience finally ran thin and he grabbed both boys by the scruff of the neck and pulled them closer, "Enough!" he said. It took some time for them to calm down and then Thanases screamed, "I was dead. I travelled across the seas and over the mountains before I reached the sands at the ancient temple. I...Was...Dead."

Baldor yelled, "Did you not see I was impaled? Did you not see Panya's life was in danger? All this is not supposed to happen: We failed again."

Magni was exasperated, "Let me yet again make myself clear, you are not failures! You have fought a coven of warlocks; a scouting party of serpents and you defeated a new type of Dark Angel who seems to have more powers than those we met before. Your skills, need I remind you, were given to you by the War Gods and that training assisted you in winning out this day. Most importantly we have learned how Lucifer's angels are evolving into a greater threat than we ever imagined."

Baldor was inconsolable, "All I thought about was Panya's safety; she was in real danger and there was nothing I could do."

"Yes," said an exasperated Magni, "she was in danger but I had a thousand arrows trained on the Dark Angel, he would never have laid a hand on her, trust me."

Magni saw both boys were exhausted and arranged for them to rest near the beach. He then joined Panya who was comforting the still trembling and severely traumatised youths. She introduced him to each of them but emphasised one in particular, "This is Mia, she saw us when no one else could; I believe her to be an oracle and in her I see a Goddess of the Light."

Magni received a vision, "Mia, a beautiful name, I too see your future, there is a dragon Lord and I see you by his side."

Magni backed away and joined a boy who was rubbing his hand off the handgrips of the chariot. The boy said, "I only ever heard of golden chariots in the stories and legends spoken of in my father's court."

Magni was intrigued, "You are of this realm? Who are you?" he asked.

"I am known as Prince Georg. I've fallen in love with Eliza; she makes me feel like the luckiest man in the world. She lives nearby and by this very lake we meet in secret. It's a secret that can never be spoken of; my family will not accept her because she's not of royal blood." Georg pointed across to her, "See how calm she is, she will help us recover."

Magni proffered "I too am of royal blood as are my twin brothers, both of whom met girls who are not. Asgard and Olympus have taken these girls into their hearts. If the gods can accept this, why can't man. Do you wish me to speak with your father?"

"No! My Lord," said Georg, "I will deal with this myself."

Panya heard what Prince Georg said and brought him and Eliza together, she held both their hands, "Let it be known that you will never rule but your descendants will. Six hundred years from now the golden age of Georgia will begin and those descendants will still be on the throne. One will be known as Queen Tamar and of all the Queens of Georgia, she will be forever revered."

Panya re-joined the remaining youths and proceeded to give each of them a prophecy. When finished she said, "Each of you have now been touched by the gods and will go on to be ancestors to many renowned Georgian teachers, artists, authors, composers, leaders and scientists. I have also given you a message where you must tell your children and their children's children that one day they will be called upon by the gods and they must answer." She then took away the trauma they suffered and sent them home. Magni left and rejoined his army.

The following morning there was a lot of tension. Thanases was still numb, a little listless and said he needed time alone. He went to the water's edge and then proceeded to walk off. He couldn't get the images of his death from his mind and it was tearing him apart. When he finally sat he was in turmoil and unsure if he wanted to continue; giving up his immortality was something he was now considering.

Baldor and Panya caught up and sat each side of him but all three had difficulty thinking of something to say until Thanases mumbled, "I saw the tombs of the heroes." He went quiet again then rested his head on Panya's shoulder, "I saw the warm light and it made me feel so happy and contented, then I got a vision. It showed me with a woman, and then two children appeared from behind her- a boy and a girl." Panya reached in and kissed his cheek and when he looked at her he saw a smile prompting him to say, "You saw the vision, didn't you?" She didn't answer, just continued smiling.

"That was some punch you landed on Magni, Baldor," said Thanases, "he'll bide his time then make you suffer."

Panya sniggered, "Trust me; Baldor is the last one he would ever hurt. In Magni's eyes Baldor can do no wrong."

"What do you mean by that?" asked Baldor

"Nothing," said Panya

Thanases relaxed as the banter between them increased and he remembered the support and encouragement he got from Jacob as well as the wonderful time he spent walking among the gods back in the temple. He thought of what Jacob said in the lagoon when they first met, 'You will change the ways of the North and have the power to grant immortality, use it wisely; stories of your life will stand the test of time.'

His strength had returned and with a new purpose he suggested they move on. They gathered their belongings and made their way towards what was to become known as the Empire of Rus.

Just as they were about to leave the beach, Baldor paused and said, "I still have the feeling Jason is about."

On the crest of a nearby hill about twenty spirits has gathered, "Ah, there they are," said Panya. "Look up, Baldor! See the spirits of Jason and the Argonauts. They were waiting to come to your aid but saw you didn't need them."

"How do you know?" asked Baldor.

"I've always known they were about," she replied, "and I sensed they were here for you."

Baldor was delighted to see them especially when they waved. He waved back and knew he had just met his heroes.

Chapter 7

After leaving Georgia, they made their way to the southern flank of what was to become part of the Kingdom of Rus, and there they spent almost two hundred years. They travelled through numerous villages and towns passing on the message, still hoping that one day their descendants would answer the call of the gods. They walked among indigenous tribes, talked with their oracles, and imparted prophesies knowing they too would help with the turbulent times ahead.

The trauma and pain suffered during their time in Georgia faded into a distant memory, allowing them to enjoy this peaceful land. They felt safe knowing they were under the protection of the Asgard army who were patrolling high above, yet all three knew danger was close.

One particular day while strolling along the banks of the Sea of Azov, they met a fisherman who offered to take them across to the Middle Lands, a place now known as Ukraine. The fisherman was a seer and had been expecting their arrival. His visions showed a beautiful woman escorted by two guardians, and he knew his task was to see all three safely across the lake. He had a wealth of knowledge and told them of the advance of the Goths, then the Huns. He warned them of the Horse Lords who were now rulers of this land, and alerted them to a new threat, the expansion of the Slavs.

On the western shores they set up camp and they were there when the land was overrun by the Bulgars, a formidable tribe who ruled the steppes with an iron fist and maintained their power by integrating their languages, customs and skills with the remnants of the Goths and the Huns. They witnessed the arrival of the Khazar Kingdom that reigned from the Caspian Sea to the Caucasus Mountains.

Travelling towards the north-west brought them to an area known as the flat lands where, in the centre, was a low hilly area. It was here, many years earlier, where a small village had sprung up, and this village became a town, then a city. It was founded by Viking travellers from the north who brought with them government skills and a desire to expand the influence of their Norse Lords. This city became known as Kyiv, and was a hub for trading routes between the north and the south as well as the east and the west. It prospered for many years; until the year 882CE when the city was destroyed. It was invaded by a tribe called the Varangians, led by a ruthless leader known as Prince Oleg.

Soon after that assault, Baldor located a protected site, forested and pockmarked with sinkholes and many hidden caves. The site overlooked the city and it was from here he spotted a small papal caravan leaving the city, it was a caravan of five carriages, flying Yellow and White flags and bearing the markings of the Vatican. It was escorted by a company of Papal guards.

Panya decided to intercept and used her powers to enter the main carriage before materialising alongside the papal legate. The legate's name was Giovanni Da Pian del Carpine. On seeing Panya, Giovanni's eyes widened and shock was written across his face. He thought an angel was sitting alongside him. "Be not afraid," said Panya, "Tell me what befell the citizens of Kyiv."

Giovanni was afraid, and continued to visibly shake. When he calmed he produced a letter he had written to Pope Steven V, it read -

'They destroyed cities and castles and killed men and Kyiv, which is the greatest city they besieged; and when they had besieged it a long while they took it and killed the people of the city. So when we went through that country we found countless human skulls and bones from the dead scattered over the field. Indeed it had been a very great and populous city and now is reduced almost to nothing. In fact there are hardly two hundred houses there now and the people are held in the strictest servitude'

Panya fell back after reading the letter, visibly upset. Her complexion paled, her lips quivered and tears gathered. "After the savagery we witnessed in Jerusalem I thought man would learn, but no," she looked out the window to see wolves feasting on recently killed bodies. "Their hearts are filled with darkness and its power knows no bounds. It gets harder to see the Light." She left to rejoin Baldor and Thanases and told them of the pain and the slaughter. Thanases reacted by pounding his staff against a nearby tree. He was furious until he felt a presence in his head. It was Jacob, "Thanases, my friend, calm down. Remember your training; remember what I said 'You will change the ways of the North'. Now is your time, begin to make those changes."

"Jacob has spoken to me," said Thanases while walking away. "I need to go. Wait for my return."

"But where are you going?" Panya enquired, and he replied, "It seems it's time for me to change the ways of the north."

Thanases made his way into the city, and moved unseen through the streets. Watching Varangian soldiers ill-treating those citizens still alive caused his anger to grow. He grew sickened by the constant beatings and resolved to relieve the citizens from their pain.

Thanases climbed upon what remained of the archway above the main gate, and materialised in full golden armour. He raised his staff high calling on the Light, and when it arrived, he released its power out over the city and got the result he desired. The abuse of the citizens ceased, and the soldiers moved cautiously towards the archway. They were curious but at the same time they were preparing to take down this strange warrior.

Thanases waited until he was sure all soldiers were present then released another blast of light. This time the light rose high into the sky, before falling back to form a cocoon imprisoning those it surrounded.

"I am immortal, and of your lands - the ice lands of the north," announced Thanases. "You are my prisoners and before this day ends you will have changed your ways. You will help the citizens of this city to rebuild their lives, and then you will leave and return to your homeland."

Soldiers giggled, a nervous laughter, they were dealing with something new and were unsure of how to proceed. One commander aimed his bow and shot at Thanases. The arrow only travelled ten feet before being obliterated by the strike of a golden arrow sent from above. Thanases' gamble was paying off. He knew Magni would act, providing he took the lead.

Thanases said as he pointed north, "You are of the ice lands, as are the remaining citizens of this city. They are your kin." A second soldier shot an arrow towards him and again it only travelled ten feet before being destroyed, this time a third golden arrow was fired, impaling the foot of the soldier. A few moments later, at least a hundred arrows arrived and landed between the feet of those soldiers closest to the arch. There was silence, then the majority of soldiers, realising they were trapped, dropped their weapons.

The senior officers continued to challenge Thanases, threatening him with the imminent arrival of reinforcements. Thanases assured them no reinforcements were coming. He reminded them of how he was an immortal and prepared to remain where he stood forever. The commander became more alarmed when he looked around and saw his remaining soldiers disarm themselves. He grew fearful when he saw the citizens gathering around the shield. The pain and terror he and his army visited on them was easing and their injuries were being healed. Hope had arrived; Panya and Baldor were whispering in the people's ears, "The Light has come to your aid." Each survivor heard the same thing, "Go now, tell your children to tell their children's children for all time, that one day, they will be called upon by the gods and they must answer."

It took some time for all citizens to recover and during this time the soldiers wilted under the burning heat of the midday sun. They removed their armour and outer garments before falling to their knees for the want of water. They couldn't understand why Thanases was able to stand there, wearing heavy robes and armour, unflinching, and unaffected by the relentless heat of the sun.

Thanases lifted the shield, but only when sure the soldiers were seriously dehydrated and incapable of violence. And then a wonderful thing happened. The citizens drew water and helped the suffering soldiers to drink. Thanases' faith in mankind was restored. Before the soldiers were fully recovered, Panya materialised and spoke with each in turn. She placed her hand on the shoulders of those she felt worthy and gave them her message. A soldier asked, "Are you an angel?" and as always, she gave the same reply, "No, I'm Panya."

The will of the soldiers had changed. They began to undo the damage they had caused. It took several years, but between the soldiers and the remaining citizens much of the city was rebuilt.

Four years had passed when the time came for the soldiers to leave, but before they left they stood in awe as a gilded chariot descended from high above. They bowed to the Asgard warrior they recognised immediately as Magni, their War God. Magni said nothing, walked among them and gestured for them to begin their journey home.

Magni joined Panya and told her how proud the gods were of the way they rescued what remained of Kyiv. "Brilliant, magnificent," he said, "you are a true warrior and have fulfilled a part of Jacob's prophecy. Watch those soldiers walk away, be happy for them to bring the Light to the north." And then, he left.

On returning to their camp, Panya, Baldor and Thanases remained there until the end of the ninth century, long enough to watch the arrival of the Kingdom of Kyivan Rus. A kingdom that protected Kyiv, by helping it to flourish, until the middle of the twelfth century.

At the dawning of the thirteenth century there was awareness throughout Kyivan Rus and beyond of evil times approaching. There were skirmishes on the borders, and rumours of villages and towns being destroyed. A new menace was showing itself. Panya's visions showed the advance of a vast army. They showed the demise of the Kingdom of Rus and the time of destruction was near. Baldor and Thanases being alert to the danger sent out their Light, but no serpents or Dark Angels appeared. As each year passed the sense of foreboding increased, so Baldor rode to the southern mountains where he found a high protruding rock giving him a clear view out towards the Far East.

Chapter 8

It was now the year 1223CE and a formidable army of twenty thousand horsemen appeared on the horizon. They were riding west led by Jebe; a general in the imperial army of Genghis Khan. Baldor, from his vantage point saw how vast the army was and how they were fulfilling Panya's vision. His powerful sight showed him the systematic annihilation of any village, town or city that refused to submit. He later found out that those that did submit, survived, but were subject to the most severe taxes.

Rumours of this advancing army soon reached the Kings of Kyivan Rus, forcing them to gather together an army from across all of Russia. They rode out only to find they were no match for this new threat, they were slaughtered at the battle of the Kalka River, fulfilling a prophecy given by Panya. After their victory, the Mongols returned to their homelands, a decision that was found to be very confusing.

The sense of foreboding didn't abate as fourteen years later a far larger army, this time led by Batu Khan, general of the Golden Horde and grandson of Genghis, invaded under orders of his uncle Ogedei Khan. Their intention was the annihilation of the remnants of Kyivan Rus. This army didn't stop with the taking of Rus; they attacked the Kingdoms of Poland, Bulgaria and Croatia.

The armies of Austria and Hungry repulsed the invaders but only after the death of millions of Europe's citizens.

Batu Khan's attack strategy was simple. He split his army in three, ordering one to follow the course of the Danube, the second to cross the Carpathian Mountains and the third to attack Poland. After the devastation caused in those three areas, they regrouped resulting in another attack on Hungry and this time the Hungarian army was crushed, causing the death of half its population. It also caused the loss of the Great Plains, Transylvania and the Carpathian Mountain region.

Thanases again recalled Jacob's prophesy 'You will change the ways of the North' and decided to take action. He raised his staff and sent his light across the heavens. He called on Zeus to bring the thunder, lightning and the rains. He called on Chione, the secretive Goddess of the Snows to bring on her blizzards. They both answered his call and soon the thunder came, then the rains followed by the snows, turning the flatlands from dry grasslands to marshy and swampy terrain. This action by Thanases deprived the war horses of food causing great difficulty for the army and prompting Batu Khan to reconsider his battle plan. His decision to retreat was made easier when he received word his uncle had died. His duty was to return to Mongolia for the council to elect a new Khan. The rest of Europe was saved by Thanases' action and in part by the death of Ogedei Khan.

It would be another eighteen years before the Mongols returned for the first of two more attacks, one in 1259CE, and the second in 1287CE. During this time Thanases took the opportunity to continue changing the north. He called on Pegasus to send him his strongest stallion and when it arrived he used its speed to travel to all realms. He called on the wisdom of his teacher, Chiron, to help him convince the various kingdoms to follow his advice.

His first call was to the Kingdom of Poland where he met with the fragmented Princes of the realm. He hoped to get them working together and encouraged them to form an alliance with the Kingdom of Hungary. When he left Poland he used the speed of the black stallion to call to the Kingdoms of Serbia, Lithuania, Georgia and Armenia.

Being invisible, his arrival at the various palaces always caused consternation. Palace guards could hear the sound of horse's hooves approaching followed by the palace gates magically opening then closing. On reaching the halls he always materialised and greeted those present in the same way, "I am Thanases, guardian of Olympus. Do not to be afraid." Time and time again palace guards released their arrows but those arrows never reached their target. He never retaliated. He continued to allay their fears and when he felt they had sufficiently calmed, he'd warn them of what was coming and advise them to change their ways, unite with their neighbours and form alliances with old enemies.

His trip to Georgia was emotional when he met King Georg V, known as 'The Brilliant'. Thanases was startled and just stared, prompting King Georg to comment, "It seems I remind you of someone?" He took Thanases by the arm and pointed him towards a painting hanging near the rear of the great hall, "Many centuries ago an ancestor of mine claimed to have met an angel and her two guardians, his name was Prince Georg. See in the painting, your image. The story of how you saved my ancestor has been passed through the generations. You fought off evil forces, an action that helped Prince Georg to convince his family to accept his choice for his bride. Her name was Eliza. They never ruled but many of their descendants did, one of them is my direct ancestor."

Thanases remembered Prince Georg well, but the memory also dragged him back to a dark place, and this unsettled him. "I remember him well. He and Eliza were destined to be together. The way he looked at her, the way he held her hand, the way he always made sure she was safe. Their love is a love written in the stars and built from all that is good."

He made his excuses and left to call on the Saxons and the Vlachs, urging them to rise up and assist in the expulsion of the Mongols from their territories. He chose not to visit Hungary aware they had learned many lessons since the initial attack. They had built walled cities with vast formidable castles. These castles were built throughout their remaining territory which was the most important lesson.

When Thanases felt no more could be done he returned to meet up with Baldor and Panya and together they watched the Mongols continue their destruction of eastern and northern European cultures.

Then it happened, in 1285CE the Saxons and Vlachs attacked. That same year as ten thousand Mongol soldiers began to cross the Carpathian Mountains; Chione, yet again at the behest of Thanases, came to the assistance of the Hungarians and unleashed her wrath. She launched the blizzards, smothering all the passes from the late summer through to the following spring, bringing about the destruction of that army. They had no protection against the extreme cold and the continuous barrage of arrows from the remnants of the Hungarian army based high in the mountains. Two years later as a Mongol force of thirty thousand horsemen headed towards Poland and Lithuania, the alliance with Hungary was activated and together they successfully repelled the invaders.

For the next sixty years there were many skirmishes until finally, in 1350CE, and as a result of a further intervention by Thanases, all of Europe united and drove the Mongols back to their homeland. Baldor assisted King Casimir 111 in uniting Poland leading to a period of prosperity. Thanases assisted the Kingdom of Lithuania to reclaim their lost territories. He returned to Georgia and helped King Georg V reclaim all that was his. The lands of Kyivan Rus never recovered, but from the ashes arose three new countries, one became Russia, the second Belarus and the third became the Kingdom of Ukraine.

It was now time to move on, and for two hundred and fifty years Panya and her guardian's criss-crossed Eastern Europe ensuring the message was everywhere. From Ukraine they travelled into Belarus before walking into the eastern lands of the Poles. After Poland they walked through the Baltic countries before making their way into Russia. They reached Moscow where they remained for several years before moving to the foothills of the Urals Mountains where they found a safe and secluded cave near the Hot Springs in the ancient district of Turinsk.

Chapter 9

At the beginning of his journey Baldor was the lonely one, and over the centuries he grew from being a shy youth to becoming a powerful and confident young man. He had grown taller and broader, and now looked even more formidable. He was always on alert, especially now, he feared a long overdue attack and used his time to continuously send out his Light. He was always happy to report no sightings of serpents.

Thanases on the other hand seemed to have lost his confidence. On leaving the temple, all those years ago, he was the self-assured one, the vengeful one, especially when not getting his way. Although equally as broad and formidable as Baldor, he no longer took the lead choosing to spend a lot more time alone. He was continuously suffering flashbacks even though it was over twelve hundred years since the Dark Angel took his life. He had difficulty suppressing the memories of the attack, or his soul's journey to the tombs of Elysium. He particularly hated the way the Archangel refused him entry.

It was now the year 1600CE, and resting beside the hot springs near Turinsk in central Russia was what all three needed, especially Panya who easily tired. Her babies were beginning to grow.

Where they set up home was generally inaccessible, hidden deep in a dense forest and the nearest village was a good distance away. Occasionally, teenagers made their way through the undergrowth just to enjoy the freedom of swimming in the warm waters, particularly when the weather was at its coldest.

Thanases spent much of his time swimming and floating in the warm and soothing waters. There he suppressed the bad memories and allowed himself to think of the times when he was at his happiest. His mind drifted back to his home village where he loved being with his family, it also reminded him of walking among the gods in Olympus.

Day after day he swam in the same spot until one day he heard a soft and gentle humming. His curiosity got the better of him and he quietly paddled over to the far side of the pool. This was one of the coldest days causing thicker steam clouds to rise, obscuring his view of the snow covered bank. He left the water but could barely see six feet ahead. He noticed footprints, sunk deep into the accumulated snowfall, and decided to investigate.

After a few paces and through the rising steam he saw the outline of a most beautiful girl who, to his delight, proceeded to undress and dive into the appealing water. He gently lowered himself back in, and being invisible, he was able to slowly and silently paddle over to where she was swimming without causing any ripples. He was fascinated, and moved closer until they were almost nose to nose. His mind drifted back to the vision he received in Georgia, where he was in the company of a woman and two children. Suddenly, from deep within, he felt something stir and wondered if she was the woman in his vision. He put those thoughts aside when he saw her looking around, seemingly uneasy. He feared she sensed him and was being scared off, so he backed away.

The continuously rising mist obscured his view forcing him to edge closer to the bank where he became besotted by what he saw. During his time swimming in the Olympus lagoon there were many naked women but never one as perfect as the one that was now no more than three arm lengths from him. His eyes took in everything, and he had no intention of diverting them. It wasn't only her nakedness that attracted him, it was her face. It was a face that framed the bluest eyes showing him the gateway to her soul. She quickly dried herself, humming and singing a soft lullaby while dressing. He watched her lips release her words to echo around the spring. When she moved away he leapt from the water and followed her. On reaching her village he watched her run to greet her parents, and then enter a small house.

He returned to the spring and quickly dressed then ran to join Panya and Baldor. For a short time he said nothing, which wasn't unusual, but it was obvious something had changed. He continuously smiled to himself prompting Panya to comment, "If I didn't know better I would think Thanases got his first kiss." He just continued smiling and said nothing.

The following day he returned to the spring hoping to see the girl again. She wasn't there, and to say he was disappointed would be an understatement. Another three days passed before he heard a soft singing voice drifting from deep within the forest. He knew it was her, and his heart began to burst. When she arrived she glanced about, and then proceeded to undress. For Thanases this was too much. He was fixated on every contour of her body and when she entered the water all he wanted was to dive in and join her.

He watched her swim about and became concerned when she dived to spend an abnormal length of time beneath the surface. He was relieved when she reappeared to shake her long and dripping hair, causing water droplets to fan out in all directions. The winter sun shone through the droplets and brought on all the colours of the rainbow and this, in Thanases' mind, made her perfect.

Thanases undressed and entered the water; he decided to move closer and reveal himself but was concerned his sudden appearance would terrify her. He plucked up the courage and said, "Hello." She was startled and raised her hands to cover her breasts while looking around to see where the voice came from. He spoke again, this time he said, in a low and calming voice, "Please don't be afraid."

She was afraid. "Who's there, show yourself," she yelled.

He again tried to reassure her, "My name is Thanases, please, please, don't be afraid."

She continuously spun around and her widened eyes showed how terrified she was. "You're frightening me, show yourself."

He feared she was about to run away then suggested, "Look at the tree line and tell me what you see." She turned and saw nothing unusual. This distraction gave him enough time to materialise without her seeing it happen. When she turned back, she didn't run; she was mesmerised. She stood there, frozen to the spot and had difficulty taking in what she thought was a vision of an Asgard god.

She had the sun behind her and it was shining directly on to Thanases giving her a sunlit view of the most handsome man she had ever seen. She noted the water dripping from his neck length, fair hair and found it difficult to prevent her eyes from looking down on his rippling muscles to gaze at his toned torso. When she saw his muscular arms she felt a desire to have them wrapped around her.

He interrupted her gaze, "My name is Thanases, and yours?"

"I'm Irina," she nervously replied.

There was an awkward silence, interrupted only by chirping birds and the sounds of cracking branches from deep within the forest. He was enchanted by everything about her, especially her amazing pale blue eyes and the way they were drawing him in. The sallowness of her perfect skin served to enhance her beauty and increase his desire to step forward and touch her face, but he too was frozen to the spot and for the first time ever he didn't know what to do. She had the same feelings.

Their trance like state was interrupted by the arrival of Baldor who was on his daily check for serpents. He called to Thanases and was surprised when, from behind him, stepped a naked and beautiful girl. Irina was equally startled and she panicked. She left the spring, grabbed her clothes and ran into the forest. Thanases had no time to arrange for them to meet again. He wasn't happy, he turned back to give Baldor a furious look, suggesting it would be best to stay out of his way.

Baldor backed away and ran to the cave; he couldn't wait to tell Panya how he had caught a naked Thanases in the hot spring with a beautiful girl. Panya didn't seem surprised, "I wondered when this was going to happen. A thousand years ago Thanases and I had a similar dream. We both saw his future and it showed him to be with a beautiful woman and two children. One is a boy, destined to be very powerful, and an ally of the Asgard gods."

Thanases arrived back to a waiting Panya. Baldor had decided to hide; he knew it was best to stay out of Thanases' way for the moment. "I suppose he told you?" Thanases said, looking around to see where Baldor was.

"He did," replied Panya. "And need I remind you that you are an immortal; if she is not the one, it will end badly for both of you."

"Why can't you be happy for me," he retorted. "These are feelings I've never experienced before and I like them. Since I met her she's all I think of. She has stolen my heart and ......"

"I am happy for you," interrupted Panya, "I just want to remind you that you cannot allow your feelings prevent you from completing our task."

"I was about to say before you interrupted me," responded Thanases, "nothing will interfere with the task; I'm well aware of my duty."

Baldor appeared. "Is it safe for me to be here?" he asked.

Thanases gave him a threatening look, "Your timing is terrible and a real passion killer. I could kill you."

"At least you are getting a chance at some passion," Baldor sarcastically responded, "I've no hope."

Panya pulled Baldor closer. "Baldor, Baldor, Baldor, you poor thing," she said, "trust me, your time for passion is not too far away and you might be surprised as to who it is."

"I suppose you're not going to enlighten me?" said a confused looking Baldor.

They all laughed and then the questions began to flow.

The following morning Thanases left the cave earlier than normal and when he reached the springs he was delighted Irina was already there. All he saw above the water was a bobbing head with beautiful eyes. His heart raced as he stripped, and he hoped hers too was racing. He dived in and when he reached her, he stretched across for their first kiss. It wasn't one of those first awkward kisses, it was soft and sensual, and it quickly ignited a deep seated primal desire to get closer.

Thanases looked around at the snow covered banks seeking somewhere he and Irina could go. He pleaded for help from The Ancient One, and within seconds his right hand involuntarily moved away from Irina's back. It began a continuous left to right motion causing a clearing to form, revealing a grass verge. His thumb and forefinger came together and when they clicked an inviting fire appeared. "It seems the Ancient One is looking upon us this day," he said with a beaming smile, "look what has been gifted to us." Irina was impressed.

Thanases fetched his cape and laid it on the grass. He gestured for her to join him and together they sat and enjoyed the warmth of the now blazing fire. They both knew everything in their lives was about to change, and knew they were going to share their bodies but didn't really know where to begin.

Eventually Thanases plucked up the courage to stretch his hand across and gently slide it along Irina's arm. His touch caused goose bumps and tremors to cascade through her body encouraging her to move closer and give him another gentle kiss. Her breath on his neck caused his hairs to rise. When she nibbled his ear lobe, his eyes automatically closed. When she moved her soft and sensuous lips along his jaw line to reach his waiting lips, he felt a throbbing sensation, one like he'd never experienced before. He was now breathless. He responded by moving even closer, all the time using his hands to stroke her back and then find their way to explore her soft, warm breasts. He didn't expect them to be so responsive to his touch but they were, and what followed were kisses that were more probing, deeper and sensual. He gently moved her to her back without parting their lips, and within moments their bodies fitted together in a rhythm that was meant to be. Their love-making was so intense the biting cold wind, every sound, every smell, everything, seemed to just fade into the background. For them the heat of the fire was no longer required. Their passion was so hot no other heat was needed. They were madly, deeply in love.

Soon the winter sun began to set and it was time for Irina to return home. They dressed but even then, they couldn't keep their hands from each other.

Thanases escorted Irina through the forest and before he let her go he insisted they meet again the following day. She didn't hesitate and for the next seven days they met and made love until it became obvious to Magni that he would have to intervene.

The following morning Magni arrived at the cave entrance and was just in time. Thanases was leaving, and although delighted to see Magni, he had no intentions of missing his time with Irina. He acknowledged him with an embrace, "Good to see you but your timing is terrible, I need to leave but will be back in a few hours; will you still be here when I return?"

"I don't intend to remain any longer than is necessary," said an unimpressed Magni, "the reason I'm here is to instruct you to end your relationship with the village girl; she will distract you from the task."

"How did you find out?" said Thanases turning to look sternly at Baldor who showed his indignation, "Don't you look at me like that. I said nothing."

Magni scolded Thanases. "I'm surprised you think Baldor would betray you," said Magni. "He's your best friend. I think you forget that I and the Asgard army travel above and see all that goes on below."

Thanases stumbled backwards, closed his eyes and felt quite sick. He went bright red and gulped, "You, you...you saw everything?"

Magni bit his lip, trying to contain himself, "Don't worry, we turned our heads when the passion got too much, we also learned that the winter sun is as potent as that of the summer, it burns everywhere. I'm surprised you can sit down."

Thanases got more flustered. "You don't mean to tell me your whole army was watching?" he said.

Magni was now having real difficulty holding a straight face and did his best to prevent a smile. Thanases was mortified, he thought of Irina and how embarrassed she will be when she finds out they had an audience.

"I love this girl, Irina is her name," said Thanases, trying to regain his composure. "She has stolen my heart, and I can't, and won't end my time with her. Meet her and judge for yourself." Magni agreed and they both made their way to the spring.

On arrival they found Irina sitting on a rock and she was obviously in distress. Thanases ran to her and when she stood, his eyes widened and panic set in. "I don't believe this?" he gasped. He was in shock but knew he had to quickly snap from it.

Irina collapsed into his arms, "The bump appeared last night just as I went to bed. When I woke this morning it was so big my father and brothers accused me of bringing shame on the family and threw me from my home. I don't understand?"

"I'll always be there for you, I promise," said Thanases, although still in shock.

Magni placed his hands to his head before yelling at Thanases, "You idiot, you have created an immortal child, that's why your baby is growing so fast. You should have known better, this will change everything and means I can't rely on you to protect Panya."

"I don't need you to tell me I have created an immortal child, I can see that," responded Thanases angrily. "Trust me, we will find a way to raise our baby. Another thing, don't ever question my dedication to the protection of Panya."

"Fine, if you say so," responded Magni, "there's not much time, your baby will soon be born, tell me what you propose to do?"

Thanases paced back and forth, thinking and mulling over his options, but the one obvious one didn't come to him until he felt a presence, it was Jacob, "Thanases, my friend, remember my prophecy. 'You will change the ways of the North and have the power to grant immortality, use it wisely, stories of your life will stand the test of time.' Thanases, remember."

He turned back to Magni, "Jacob gave me a power and asked me to use it wisely. My plan begins with me granting Irina immortality. Will you assist me?"

Panya and Baldor joined them and heard most of what transpired. "Magni, we've seen the changes in Thanases," said Panya. "Since he met

Irina, he has never been so happy. We trust him with our lives and if he chooses to grant Irina immortality, we will support him. We too ask you to assist."

Magni took time alone to process this new situation before turning to Irina, "Do you know who I am?" he asked.

"Thanases addressed you as Magni. The War God of the Asgard realm is called Magni," she replied then asked, "Is that you?"

"I am that same Magni and I'm providing extra protection to Panya," he placed his hand on her bump. "Your baby is strong and rapidly growing, he will soon be born. He is an immortal and is entitled to the protection of the gods."

Irina gently moved her hand across her bump and said, "My baby is a boy?"

"Yes, your baby is a boy and he will be very powerful," replied Magni, "I see him with a queen of Asgard. I see the Ancient One and he blesses him."

He took her by the arm and walked along the banks, "Thanases intends to grant you immortality. I'm not so sure. Do you understand that if you become an immortal you will watch those whom you love die of old age, leaving you feeling very alone?"

Irina slowed down and took a sharp intake of breath, "Of course I'll miss my family, but at this moment in time, all but my mother has rejected me," she stopped and turned to stare Magni in the eye, "we love each other and spending eternity with him just seems right."

Magni sensed her sincerity and the love she had for Thanases. He kissed her forehead, and gave his blessing before joining Thanases and preparing to recite the most ancient prayer of immortality.

Thanases joined Magni and together they raised their staffs. They called on the Light and when it came it was stronger than the light of the midday sun. It hovered above Irina before making its way to enter her body. She glowed as a light-filled aura formed around her. Magni and Thanases placed their hands on her forehead, closed their eyes and began reciting the prayer.

"From the depths of the heavens I call on the Light. Come, life giver and show your might. Let the minutes pass and the hours be gone so the weeks and months are merged as one. Father time come and see, a goddess of beauty let her be. Make her life be never-ceasing, make it endless, long and pleasing."

She opened her eyes to be met by a beaming Thanases and knew then her immortality was complete. Magni, before leaving, whispered to Thanases, "You are so lucky to have found love and to soon be a father. I wish I had what you now have." He then left to continue his patrolling of the sky above.

Panya said after embracing both Irina and Thanases, "I'm sure you have much to talk about, go and enjoy the crispness of the freshly fallen snow. Walk and talk, make your plans and see where the path takes you."

Their walk took them deep into the forest and then to the outskirts of the village. They were so engaged in conversation they didn't realise they had travelled so far. Thanases was surprised and immediately went into invisibility hoping no one had seen him. He reached into his satchel and extracted his robes and armour and prepared for any conflict that might arise. "We're close to your home and maybe we should meet with your parents," he cautiously looked around, "it would be nice to make your peace before we leave, remember I'll be by your side at all times."

Irina was apprehensive walking through the village, especially as her bump was now very pronounced. She got reassurance when she heard Thanases say, "Hold your head high, be proud, you have been blessed by a god and remember I'm with you." They tried not to get upset listening to the crass and cruel comments of the gossiping villagers.

On reaching her parents house she faltered but then felt her strength return when Thanases gently kissed her on the cheek. When the door opened she was greeted by her mother but not her father, or brothers, who went to strike her causing her mother to intervene. They made a second attempt to attack but were stopped when they felt the blade of a sharp sword, and the tip of a dagger resting against their throats. Thanases materialised giving them all a severe shock, and when things calmed he announced, "I'm Thanases, guardian to a messenger of the gods and father of this baby. I love Irina and have called on the Light to give her immortality. This has been granted," and when no reaction came he continued, "Our baby will soon be born so you have a chance to make your peace. Soon after, we will be leaving for the northern ice lands." Irina's father and brothers, to the disappointment of Thanases, didn't relent. They made her so unwelcome she was left with no choice but to leave.

On leaving the house Irina was met by a gathering of hostile villagers who were preparing to stone her. They had no idea an invisible guardian was walking alongside her.

"Now would be a good time to use your new powers and join me in invisibility," suggested Thanases.

"This is all new to me," she said trying not to panic, "I don't know how or what to do."

"Just think about it and wait for it to happen," he suggested.

Suddenly Irina received a violent kick from her unborn baby causing her to fall to her knees and scream out in pain. Like all cowards, the villagers took the opportunity to start stoning her knowing she was at her most vulnerable, but their stones never reached her. Thanases was so swift he used his sword to send the stones back at those who threw them. Many were injured and had difficulty understanding what had happened. Thanases then repeated, "There are too many. Call on invisibility, do it now."

Irina stood; she placed her hand on her abdomen and could still feel her baby kicking. She closed her eyes and thought of the Light and it came, bringing a glow that surrounded her. As it grew brighter it illuminated Thanases causing the villagers to back away in fear. When the light faded neither Thanases nor Irina could be seen.

"Today you have experienced many strange things," said Thanases as he leaned in to kiss her again, "trust me; there will be even stranger things to come. Always remember we have each other."

Over the next few days Thanases, Baldor and Panya made every effort to assist Irina, making her as comfortable as possible. On the fourth day Irina went into labour and within two hours a handsome baby boy was born. For Irina there was no real pain and the actual birth was very quick. When the baby arrived he was strong, alert and already attempting to sit up.

Thanases was mesmerised, and very quickly became besotted. He cradled his son and asked if he alone could name him, Irina agreed. He left the cave and raised his son towards the heavens, "Let the gods of Asgard know that my son is of them, and destined to be a free spirit. No laws shall bind him and restrictions will be his enemy. I name him Viktor."

Viktor was indeed special, he grew rapidly, in fact, no more than seven nights had passed when he went to sleep as a baby and woke the next morning as a toddler.

It was now time to move on and preparations were being made to start the journey to their next destination, St Petersburg. Thanases was first ready and he waited outside the cave. From there he saw two elderly people exiting the forest and recognised them to be Irina's mother and father. He re-entered the cave and said as he placed his hands over Irina's eyes, "I've a surprise, come outside."

He carefully walked her to the entrance and then removed his hands. Irina covered her mouth, struggling to prevent her tears from flowing. She ran to meet her parents only to get a shock when she saw how they had aged. She also sensed they were near death.

Her mother embraced her. "My beautiful daughter," she said as she kissed Irina's cheek, "how I've missed you. For years I've heard stories of ladies in the woods, guarded by two warriors. In my dreams I too saw the ladies and over the last few nights, I saw one of them was you. I know my time is near and to set my eyes on you one last time is all I ever wanted."

Raised his arms, her father said, "Please forgive me."

"Father," she said as she moved to hug him, "there's nothing to forgive. You, coming here today, means everything to me," she continued hugging him then asked, "my brothers, where are they?"

"They seek forgiveness," said her mother. "They are too ashamed to meet you. They are fathers themselves and now understand the love a child can bring."

Irina was about to speak again when Viktor stepped from behind her. Tears flowed as his grandmother moved to lift him into her arms. She longed to meet him but was very confused. It was thirty years since Irina left the village and the baby she was carrying should by now be a man.

"I see your confusion," said Irina as she tried to explain, "We are immortals, time moves much slower for us. Sometimes when we sleep a day might pass, other times a year."

They were introduced to Panya and Baldor who made them very welcome. Panya saw they were both in pain and offered to help. She saw how the ravages of time had taken a toll and said after placing her hands on each of their shoulders, "My visions tell me your time is close and soon you will pass. There will be no suffering; this is my gift to you."

It was agreed that the journey would be delayed for a few hours giving Irina as much time as possible for her to say her goodbyes, but the call of the Ice Lands kept getting louder. It was now so loud Irina could also hear it, she said on reaching in for one last embrace, "The time has come for us to go, even I can hear the call from the north and it's very loud," she reached in to kiss her father, "a great weight has been lifted from me this day. I can now travel in peace."

Irina, Thanases and Viktor walked her parents towards the tree line and to their surprise her brothers were waiting. They spoke of how they were beaten through the forest by their wives and told to make their peace. They had difficulty looking Irina in the eye but lit up when she approached them. They had a brief conversation and soon all was good.

Viktor approached his uncles who each in turn hugged him. When in their arms he whispered a warning, "Terrible danger, coming, you must leave. Go far west, find a new home. He frightens me. They slither, they bite. There's poison, pain, suffering."

Thanases saw Viktor getting upset and said when taking him into his arms, "He might frighten you, my boy. Trust me; it will be over my dead body that he'll get his hands on you." Thanases was troubled. He was concerned his son was developing his powers while still so young.

Irina took Viktor into her arms, held on to Thanases and watched her family move down the hill. She remained until they went out of sight before letting her tears flow, she then ran into the forest to be alone. She found a secluded spot and sat on an upturned tree stump. There she thought about her family and the happy times they once shared. This sent her deeper into grief, until she felt a small hand move up and down her back, it was Viktor. When she saw his little face her heart melted and she was reminded of what she now had. She wiped away her tears and took him into her arms. She rejoined Thanases, Baldor and Panya and began what they were hoping would be the last leg of their journey.

Chapter 10

This part of the journey began uneventfully, allowing Thanases and Irina to get on everybody's nerves with their constant kissing, cuddling and general 'lovey doveyness'. Panya on the other hand was beginning to feel different; she sensed changes in her body. She confided in Irina but asked her to say nothing for the moment; she didn't want to cause alarm.

In the meantime Baldor and Viktor became great friends. Viktor treated Baldor as the mad, carefree uncle all children deserved to have. Baldor on the other hand treated Viktor like the son he dreamt of having, and brought him everywhere, especially on his Light patrols. They played games, pranked Thanases, teased the girls, and most of all just had fun.

The next destination was St Petersburg which was just over five hundred miles away. They had travelled over a thousand miles from Turinsk without any threatening incidences.

Viktor became very quiet, unsettled and scared. Still too young to properly express himself, he did what any frightened child would do. He wrapped his arms around Baldor's leg and held on tightly, he then raised his arms demanding to be carried. Baldor took Viktor into his arms and was taken aback by how he was trembling. He sensed nothing untoward but remembering his training, he placed Viktor back on the ground, opened his satchel and extracted his armour, weapons and his staff, before taking Viktor back into his arms.

Thanases, Panya and Irina were walking some distance ahead and at times were out of view but this time was not one of them. Baldor increased his pace and was relieved when he passed a protruding rock and saw a fully armed Thanases walking back towards him. He too sensed danger. When Viktor saw his dad dressed as a warrior he got more upset and ran to his mother who tried to reassure him. He was very agitated especially while trying to express the smell he detected.

To make matters worse a loud rumbling was heard and this terrified Viktor even more. The rumbling was the sound of chariots from the Asgard army. They were returning from one of their patrols. They had earlier seen both Baldor and Thanases arm themselves and decided to check the road ahead, where they observed villages being attacked by small groups of serpents led by at least one Dark Angel.

The Asgard commander informed Thanases that Magni had instructed them to take Irina and Viktor up to the holding position for their own safety, a decision he had to except especially when he recalled being warned that his family responsibilities were never to interfere with the protection of Panya. Thanases was crestfallen and didn't hide it; he felt it was his place to not only protect Panya but to also protect his family. He saw that Irina and Viktor were upset and moved to reassure them. When they calmed he assisted them onto the lead chariot where he covered them with warm furs for their journey, and kissed them goodbye.

Soon after the chariots left, Panya insisted they continue their Journey. They reached the first village to be met by scenes of wanton destruction. Houses were burnt and still smouldering, animals slaughtered. Villager's bodies lay everywhere and many were ripped apart. Survivors wandered aimlessly. There was blood spatter on the ground, the walls, the rocks and the trees. There was black blood mingled with foul flesh, torn from the serpents of Hell, showing the villagers had fought valiantly.

Panya sent out her Light then said, "The white mist will rise soon, many of these people fought off the power of Hell and protected their souls." She went to her knees and leant forward to close the eyes of a young girl. "It seems ripping bodies apart is a tactic the serpents use when not getting their way."

As happened in the past the serpents left a few survivors, but they were so traumatised they couldn't speak of their experiences, and as a result, the terror Hell wanted to spread never did.

On arrival into each village Panya moved to heal the injured and traumatised. She used her powers, breaking through the trauma to find out what the serpents were after, "They know of our last location and have attacked Turinsk," she said while turning to Baldor. "The spirits of the dead tell me of rage and anger, all because the serpents missed their chance to capture us when we were at the spring. The good news is, many villagers left and travelled to the west, heeding the warning given by Viktor." She turned to Thanases, "He knows Viktor is an immortal child, he fears him and the powers he will one day wield." Thanases replied, "I have to trust Asgard, they promised to keep him safe."

The litany of carnage continued, and as they entered village after village they were met with similar scenes; bodies and traumatised survivors. They dealt with each devastated village in the same compassionate way. What was becoming clear was the serpents still hadn't learned how to detect Panya or her guardians, unless they were close by. It was also obvious the serpents had worked out that their destination was the northern ice lands.

After spending many years assisting traumatised villages and passing on the message, they finally reached St Petersburg. Strangely enough, it wasn't attacked.

It was now the year 1703CE, and in the distance a Royal caravan carrying Tsar Peter the Great was sighted. He and his army were on their way to turn St Petersburg from being a small northern port into one of the greatest cities in the Russian empire. Peter realised his dream of founding a majestic city based on Venice. He personally oversaw the creation of canals and grand bridges to connect his palaces and the great houses, ensuring the city would become one of the most important commercial and cultural hubs in Russia.

This period was during 'The Great Northern War' and Peter had led the Russians to victory, taking many of the lands and provinces belonging to the Kingdom of Sweden. He used the captured soldiers as slave labour and also brought in a law requiring every ninth households in his realm to provide one worker to contribute towards the city's completion. This decree amounted to forty thousand serfs being taken and shackled together for the journey towards St Petersburg. The shackles were used to avoid desertions.

The city was built in difficult terrain and during continuously dreadful weather, causing the deaths of thousands of workers. The engineers came from Germany and Holland. Stonemasons came from Italy and local stonemasons were prevented from building anywhere else in Russia until the city was completed. When completed Peter insisted the city become the capital of Russia, a title it was to hold until 1918CE.

Panya decided to remain in St Petersburg for a number of years. She walked the streets hoping to pass on the message but found it difficult to find many whom she deemed worthy. It bothered her to see so many citizens, especially those in the military, who were carrying the mark of the serpent. Her uneasiness prompted Thanases and Baldor to maintain their alertness.

During one search for serpents, Baldor's Light illuminated what seemed to be a village deep in the forest. It was several miles north of St Petersburg and well hidden by a thick tree growth. He decided to investigate and soon discovered it to be a shanty town that was home to slaves, the very slaves who had been used to build St. Petersburg. He observed, over several days, how those who secured work were allowed to enter the city but had to leave by night fall.

He followed one column of workers at the end of another hard day only to be horrified when he discovered the squalor in which they were forced to live. He became aware that many were surviving prisoners taken from the Swedish army. The rest of the inhabitants were women and children captured during raids on Swedish villages and towns during the war.

The more he looked upon the young men, the more he realised they bore a resemblance to him and Thanases; he felt an affinity and believed they were all of the same ancestry. He decided there and then to develop a plan for their rescue; he visited every street, all the time sending out the Light just to be satisfied there were no serpents in the vicinity.

It broke his heart to look upon the youths and young men who seemed fit and strong, yet they came across as lost and broken. It hurt him to see the desperate women and their waiflike children. He tapped into the despair and absorbed their pain as he inhaled the ungodly stench. When he reached the last street his heart sank watching the old men warming themselves around small fires. He listened to them recall the stories of their ancestors hoping those stories were passed on to the young, he noted the young were listening; then he heard them express their feelings of no hope. His anger had risen and was about to explode when he heard a voice travelling on the cold winds blowing from the North West. It was the soft and calming voice of Jacob, "Baldor! Now is your time, be the God of Asgard you have grown to be. Remember my words, given to you when we first met, 'You will be the beacon of light in the dark lands of the frozen north. You will be the torch bearer the Gods of Asgard will follow. It's time to be that torch bearer, release the Norse Lords now."

Baldor returned to St. Petersburg and told Panya and Thanases of the squalor he had found. He told them that many of the elderly were once of royal blood from within the Swedish realm and many of the young are unaware of their heritage. He took control, becoming assertive, and insisted a plan be prepared to rescue the people. He began formulating that plan.

Panya and Thanases were troubled, they were in sight of their final destination and didn't want any distractions but as before they always worked as a team and trusted each other's judgement. Panya called on Magni, and he duly arrived. Baldor told him of the shanty town and suggested they visit it together. Magni, without hesitation, agreed and immediately left to see for himself all Baldor spoke of.

On arrival Magni opted to walk alone through the streets. He was shocked looking into the drawn faces of the beaten soldiers. Etched in the faces of the old he saw their ancestors calling out to him, they were warriors of Asgard and loyal to Odin. His tears gathered as he continued his walk, and everywhere he went there were those he thought he recognised, some were the descendants of those he once knew.

He said when he rejoined Baldor, "This can't continue. Some of these people are descendants of my friends. You have my armies at your disposal."

"How is it Asgard allowed this happen?" asked Baldor.

"Asgard has been asleep, now it's time to waken," responded Magni.

"No!" insisted Baldor, "Asgard must stay asleep and stick to Jacob's plan. I'll deal with this under your protection."

Magni was intrigued, so he decided to stay and watch Baldor put together his plan. They both returned to the city and met up with Thanases and Panya.

Baldor said, "You all know what Jacob said to me when we first met. So let it now be known that I am the beacon of light in the dark lands of the frozen north. I will be the torch bearer the Gods of Asgard will follow. Today my Light will lead these sad souls away from their misery and toil. They will know the gods have come to their rescue."

Thanases backed away and looked towards the sky. He raised his hands to call on an old friend, "My lady Chione, Goddess of the Snows. Hear me: Once more I call upon your power. Follow the beacon and protect the exodus. Watch us walk, before bringing the frosts, then unleash the blizzards." Within seconds a biting cold wind developed, and her reply was heard, "Yes, my friend. I hear your plea and will wait and watch. The wrath of the gods will soon be unleashed."

All four left St. Petersburg and travelled the short distance to the shanty town. Magni again chose to walk alone into the town as the Asgard War God. He was visible to all, and his appearance caused house after house to empty. The people were in awe and followed him through the streets. A sense of hope had arrived and everyone felt it.

The young had no idea who he was but were captivated. The old knew exactly who he was and many lunged forward before kneeling and paying homage. When Magni was sure all old soldiers were present he looked to the heavens and commanded the now very thick snow-clouds to part, allowing the people see the Asgard army in a holding position in the sky above. Magni then asked for silence, "I am Magni, God of Asgard and grandson of Odin. We knew nothing of your suffering and now that we do, it's time for it to end. You will be taken from this place and returned to your ancestral homes. Follow the beacon into the ice lands of the north." Baldor then materialised with the most dazzling light surrounding him, his golden armour shone so brightly some had to shade their eyes. He announced,

"I'm your beacon of light," he announced raising his staff, "I will lead you to your northern homelands, you must pack immediately and we leave before dawn."

Baldor's plan was clear, but unknown to him there were a number of Russian spies permanently placed in the town and these spies managed to leave and alert the Russian authorities. A five thousand strong army was assembled and sent to prevent the departure of the Swedish prisoners because they, along with their descendants, were considered in Russia, to be the spoils of war.

Word of the advancing army reached Baldor who immediately changed his plan. He began the departure of those already prepared. He worried about the speed of their departure until Asgard again came to his assistance; they sent enough chariots to take the very young, their mothers and the elderly into the sky, leaving only the strong to face the harsh walk. The rumbling sound of the approaching horse-drawn artillery caused panic until two more immortals appeared. Panya and Thanases were now visible and were standing facing St. Petersburg ready to release their Light in the hope of temporarily blinding the horses.

Baldor took his position at the head of the exodus, ready to lead the way. His cape fluttered in the now wild wind, his armour continued to glisten and reflected the torch lights as the walk began. He raised his staff and called on the Light and when it came, it lit up a path they were to follow. Over twenty thousand people walked in anticipation of freedom and were full of hope. Thanases and Panya waited until the last person left before changing the direction of their Light to ensure there were no serpents in the surrounding forest.

When they joined the exodus Panya took the opportunity to pass on the message; and to everyone she touched she said the same thing, "Remember this day. Go now, tell your children to tell their children's children for all time, that one day, they will be called upon by the gods and they must answer." Each one she touched received a new strength and many of the old soldiers magically changed into the strong warriors they once were.

In the sky above Magni remarked to his commanders, "It's been three thousand years since last I watched a great exodus. At that time I watched one man lead his people back to their homeland, Moses was his name. He was touched by the gods and placed in the land of the Pharaohs. I watched his mother place him on the river and I saw the princess find him. I watched him grow to be a powerful prince of Egypt; secretly I became his friend and mentor. I watched him slay the slave master and become a fugitive. I helped him to realise he was not of Egypt but of Israel. I worked with him, and encouraged him to meet the Pharaoh and demand the freedom of his people. When this was refused I gave him the plagues that ravished Egypt. Soon after, I gifted him the power to part the waters in the sea of reeds, allowing him to lead his people through the deserts to reach their promised land."

He paused for a moment then said while looking down with pride upon Baldor. "Today, I am watching Baldor, son of a baker, become the great leader he was always destined to be. He brings the Light to the north; he is a Warrior King, an immortal. He is now a God of Asgard."

It wasn't long before the Russian army reached the shanty town where they cautiously entered to be met by an eerie silence. Occasionally they saw into the far distance and observed a dim light, leading them to believe the people were not that far ahead. They followed the exodus and it was then when they began to feel the full wrath of the Goddess of the Snows. The hard frost she sent had taken the land and the light dusting of snow quickly became a blanket. She then unleashed the blizzards, causing their march to be slow and sluggish. Soon their horses succumbed. The trees on each side of the valley provided no protection because the northern ice nymphs arrived and parted the branches allowing the biting wind through.

The Russian army was well used to bitter weather but this onslaught of nature was too much causing many soldiers to fall. By the time they reached the open lands over a thousand men had succumbed. What was left were the best trained and the strongest. They were determined to continue their pursuit but it was to no avail, many more were to succumb to the incessant and freezing wind.

Several days later the exodus reached the small village of Vassa in Finland. It was on the coast and in an area beside the Gulf of Bothnia which was where Baldor decided the ice was deep enough for them to safely cross.

Their crossing was uneventful, and on viewing the sight of their homeland all began to feel a long missed and ancient stirring awaken. The march quickened and on reaching a stone beach they quickly turned to walk along the coast towards the town of Nordmaling which wasn't too far away. Their arrival caused the town's people to leave their homes just to watch the spectacle of this great throng walk through their streets, but what they were most in awe of was the warrior holding his staff high to emit the brightest light they had ever seen.

Baldor was still on alert when he reached the centre of the town. He climbed a nearby roof allowing him to look out across the frozen sea. From his vantage point he saw that the now seriously diminished Russian army had begun to cross. He wasn't concerned, he was joined by Thanases and together they focused their light to melt the ice between the rear flanks of the exodus and the forward ranks of the Russian army, forcing a retreat.

Chapter 11

On the hills above Nordmaling was stationed a company of border guards who, on seeing the throng crossing from Finland, immediately sent a message to the Swedish palace requesting assistance. Their king was Adolf Frederick, a cautious ruler. He immediately gathered his armies, and rode north to investigate. When he arrived, he was shocked by how many people had arrived. His cautious nature came from the many tough lessons learned after the sad experiences of the Swedish armies over the centuries. As a result he fanned his army out across the hills as a precaution. He was unsure as to whether what was before him was friend or foe. His fears were allayed when a golden chariot arrived carrying one whom he recognised as Magni, the Asgard God of War.

Magni was not one to stand on ceremony, he said as he approached the king, "Standing before you are your people and they are returning to the lands of their fathers. Asgard expects you to feed, house and protect them. They are carriers of a message, and in the not too distant future their descendants will be called upon to answer the call of the gods."

Magni then ordered his charioteers to descend, allowing the mothers, babies and small children to be reunited with their men folk. The last chariot to arrive was the one carrying Irina and Viktor, causing Thanases to throw all caution to the wind. He ran so fast, and was so focused on his family he barely managed a bow while passing Magni and the king. His heart was bursting with excitement, and everyone watching saw the great love he had for his family.

In the meantime the king said after turning back to Magni, "In my family we speak of our dismay at how the gods never came to the aid of Sweden during our times of need,"

"I understand your dismay, replied Magni, "But be assured, it was necessary as the gods have been dealing with a far more sinister threat. It's a menace we believe, if unchecked, will bring on the End Times for all."

The king knew it wasn't his place to question the gods and said no more. He promised all survivors would be provided for, and said he will ensure no harm would befall them.

The following morning the survivors left, escorted by the king's army. Some travelled south and others over the mountains to the west. Magni also departed to continue his patrols of the sky above.

Panya was struggling and her pregnancy was now showing. She indicated she wanted to leave and without further discussion she just walked away. It was a walk that took her higher into the mountains, through well hidden valleys and around many of the beautiful Swedish lakes.

After eight days they reached the small village of Vindeln where they spent ten years before moving on to Rengard to spend another ten years. They left Rengard and settled for twenty years in Vidsel, then Luvos before reaching the Tarfala valley. From there they travelled to the land known for its midnight sun, to settle near a small lakeside village called Abisko. It was there, at the base of Mount Nuolja, when they realised they had reached their journeys end. During they travels through Sweden Panya continued to spread the message. Baldor and Thanases remained vigilant.

It was the year 1800CE and the time for their long sleep was rapidly approaching. Panya looked out over the lake and felt the ice caps calling, prompting her to begin her final walk along the Kings Trail. She was moving so quickly Baldor and Thanases were getting concerned. Irina calmed them, and after handing Viktor to Thanases she ran to catch up with Panya.

"Remember how fast Viktor grew in my womb?" she said as she gripped Panya's arm, "your babies are now growing equally as fast." She looked down at Panya's growing bump, "You need to rest."

"We've been walking for almost eighteen hundred years," said Panya while taking a breather, "I'm tired and I know where we're going my babies will be safe. I do need to rest, but not just yet." She continued her walk but this time she had no choice but to link on to Irina.

Night was falling when they reached the glaciers of Mount Nuolja. It wasn't total darkness, it never got that dark; it was a kind of twilight. On reaching a high ice platform, they were greeted by a most enchanting sight. It was a gothic style Cathedral sculptured from ice and when they touched its walls it didn't feel cold. The buttress's held the carved images of Asgard heroes of old. The ice walls reflected the ever changing bands of the Northern Lights, colours that were so vivid they mesmerised all who saw them travel across the sky. It was as though they were dancing to bewitching music that could only be composed by the gods. Viktor pointed to the starlit sky, "Look, army gone." Magni and his army had returned to Asgard.

They climbed the steps and soon reached massive ice doors that just magically opened, and when they entered the great hall, there before them stood four exquisitely carved ice thrones. The burning torches gave off a light that shimmered off the walls, and the massive fireplace held a most inviting fire bringing warmth into all their hearts.

They were greeted by a steward whom Baldor recognised as one of the Asgard servants who attended Odin in Olympus all those years ago. The steward had a banquet prepared and encouraged them to eat, "Odin left this magical place as your sanctuary," he said as he took his seat. "Be assured you will be safe and protected until you are awoken near the battle of the End Times."

Panya was no longer uncomfortable; her babies had fallen asleep and had stopped growing. She smiled while gently rubbing her hands across her bump and felt an intense warmth flow through her. She thought of Odi and how he made her feel that night they conceived. She thought of her babies and longed for their birth.

"It's good to see you smile again," said Baldor putting his arm across Panya's shoulders. "Bet you're thinking of Odi?"

"I was," smiled Panya, "then I thought of that first time we all met." She moved her hands to hold both Baldor's and Thanases', "remember that time when eight, sixteen year old boys, watched four naked sixteen year old girls, swim in the lagoon. Remember how we objected to you seeing us naked, then challenged you to reveal all you had, it was you Thanases who was first to strip, revealing all your glory. You Baldor; you stood behind him, all shy and bashful, before sliding into the water." Thanases furrowed his brow and said as he leaned forward to stare at Baldor, "Were you looking at my ass?"

"I was," said Baldor. "I was wishing you would get it out of my face."

"Don't worry Baldor," said Panya trying not to snigger "His ass is big enough to be shared." Thanases continued to furrow his blow, Baldor wondered what she meant and Panya changed the subject.

"When I think about it, we must have given the message to millions," said Panya, "considering how many descendants there must be by now."

"We certainly did," said Baldor.

Thanases wondered aloud, "Remember the time we slept for what seemed to be a hundred years? We woke to find putrid bodies everywhere. It was the Black Death, Remember?" Panya and Baldor nodded.

Thanases continued, "All those we gave the message to, prior to that event. Did they die? Did we waste our time?"

"Your time wasn't wasted," assured the steward, "the survivors went on to repopulate. Your message is safe. The gods know that because of you, millions will answer the call." he moved closer to the thrones, "You have assembled one-fourth of Jacob's army, and when fully assembled, it will be formidable."

Thanases yawned and was having difficulty staying awake. Viktor also yawned and became agitated; he was only comforted when Baldor took him aside and played with him just like he did on the walk from Turinsk. The playtime didn't last for too long; it was now time to sleep. They prepared themselves and happily walked towards the thrones.

Panya was about to sit when the steward requested she wait. He removed a crown from a velvet covered receptacle before asking her to kneel. When she knelt he said, "Odin has decreed that you should go into sleep as a queen. He wants all of Asgard to know that when you waken, you and Odi will become the rulers of our realm. This crown is but a token, the real crown will be yours when you stand alongside Odi." After she was crowned, she moved to take her seat and very quickly, she was frozen in time. Her beauty radiated through the ice and because she was now heavily pregnant so did the light emanating from the goddess's she was carrying.

The steward stepped back and bowed, he then stared for a few moments, before closing his eyes. When he closed his eyes he used his mind to send the image of a sleeping Queen Panya to all in Asgard including Odin.

In Olympus, the statue of Odi slightly moved and a tear trickled down his face.

Next to sit was Thanases who took his place on the throne to Panya's left, he waited for Irina to join him and before she took her seat she leaned in for one last kiss. Baldor placed Viktor on her lap and together all three began to freeze. To Baldor and the steward, they looked like a loving family who were touched by the gods, given a love destined to last forever. Above Viktor's head, a light shimmered then took the form of an archangel before disappearing. Baldor briefly became alarmed but was reassured when the steward said, "Don't ask."

The steward invited Baldor to take his seat, which he willingly did. He looked around one last time, and was tempted to send out his Light just to be sure, but he trusted Odin, smiled at the steward and allowed the ice to take him.

- The walk north was over -

Oba's Journey South

Chapter 1

Jacob turned back to face the temple, waiting on Oba, Jomo and Jahiri to walk towards him and when they did, they too oozed power. Oba wore a yellowy white gown designed to deflect away the constant glare of the southern sun. Her lightly embroidered cream coloured cape gently fluttered in the light breeze as she walked. Her hair was hidden beneath a brightly coloured Geles head wrap, common among the Yoruba peoples. Jacob remembered their first meeting and how he was besotted by her beauty. It was her deep brown eyes, set in an oval face and highlighted by a radiant smile he remembered the most, then he remembered her semi afro hair, and the cascading beads adorning her black braids. He then remembered her hour-glass figure and had to banish those thoughts. Her jewellery was understated for fear the sun would threaten to reveal her using the jewellery as a conduit. As she approached she too presented as a powerful Goddess of the Light.

Jahiri and Jomo stood each side of her, looking majestic, each wearing the robes and armour of Olympus warriors. Jahiri looked like a true African god, sculpted to perfection. He had the height and striking good looks of the Maasai. His dark, semi braided hair framed a chiselled and youthful good looking face that lit up each time he revealed his smile. He was the son of a blacksmith, a trade not common among descendants of the Maasai. He had their height and stamina but not the distinctive red hair of the Rift Valley tribes. His face drew in all whom he met, it was his wide brilliant white smile and youthful good looks, all framed by his darkest black, semi braided hair. He was known to be vivacious, full of life and always looking for fun.

Jomo was equally as tall but not as striking, he was quieter and very shy. His hair was much tighter and his face rounder. He too had a smile that would brighten any day. His eyes were spellbinding, the kind that was able to reach deep into anyone's soul. He was stronger and broader than Jahiri and each time he flexed, even under his armour, he revealed his muscular and titan-like shoulders, confirming him as one who was to become the Brute of Africa because of his unnatural strength. He was the son of a crafts-man who specialised in working with stone, another trade uncommon among descendants of the African tribes.

Chapter 2

Oba glanced back seeking reassurance from Jacob. He continued to wave her off, hoping to encourage her. He knew she was frightened, even terrified, and it worried him that she was the most nervous of them all. He also knew that when she breaks through her fears, she will become a most powerful Goddess of the Light. He reached into her mind in the hope of allaying her fears, instead he saw her problem. It was the sad memories of her ancestors having to travel under the searing heat of the desert sun while escaping the violent tribes of the south, and those memories were flooding her mind. He saw how her visions were showing the relentless attacks on her ancestral village and how they were etched into her very being. He now knew why she was so filled with dread but it didn't concern him because she was chosen by the Ancient One.

Oba continued looking back, and even when Olympus had gone out of view, she sensed Jacob's presence; he continued to use his power to raise her confidence and reassure her. He reminded her of how powerful she was and how her powers will be used to protect the natural world. Each memory, each vision, everything he shared, helped strengthen her resolve.

Even thought she felt reassured her emotions were not easily hidden and her pain was very evident. It was her dark eyes and creased brow that was betraying her mixed-up feelings, that was until Jomo turned and offered her one of his disarming smiles. She felt him look deep into her eyes and knew he would soon reach her soul to reveal all the beauty of the cosmos. She sensed his burning passion and knew then she was safe with both him and Jahiri as her guardians.

Walking along the narrow dusty road gave her time to pull herself together, before their journey took them deeper into the desert. The incessant heat took its toll, prompting Jomo to suggest removing their armour. Jahiri needed no persuasion; he was quickly followed by Jomo. They removed their armour and robes so fast they stood there with no more than a calf-skin wrap to protect their modesty.

"I have this nervousness in the pit of my stomach," said Jahiri, "and it's getting the better of me! Can we rest here for a short time? There's something troubling me and I don't know what it is."

At this point, Oba hadn't removed her robes. She was still wearing the yellowy white gown she wore on leaving Olympus. She was fidgeting with her Gele head wrap and finding it uncomfortable. Jahiri enquired, "Are you not dressing down?"

"I will, in a moment," she sniggered, "I'm just enjoying the view."

Jomo looked out over the desert and wondered what view she was talking about. That was until Jahiri slapped him across the neck, "Idiot, she's talking about our bodies." Jomo was embarrassed and moved to sit on a nearby boulder.

Oba removed her head wrap, revealing a hairstyle that contained a semi afro, and a cascade of bead adorned black braids that fell to rest just above her shoulder blades. She looked amazing, and when she removed her gown she stood there as though carved in the image of the goddesses of Olympus. Her hourglass shaped figure caused Jomo's mouth to drop in awe. Her radiant deep set brown eyes and her dazzling smile electrified him. These were feelings he knew he would have to suppress.

Oba extracted a thigh-length linen chiton from her satchel and proceeded to dress. Jahiri assisted by securing the pleats along her shoulders with a series of fasteners. She was still having slight pangs of nervous tension until she raised her arms to look at her completely flawless ebony skin and noted how it was glowing, Jacob was in her head again, encouraging her, and helping her relax.

When she again relaxed she looked across at her two semi-naked guardians and smiled each time a light breeze blew, causing the calf-skin wraps to flap and then raise. On a serious note she recognised them to be two powerful immortal warriors who seemed to be totally unflinching in their alertness. Little did she know that terror and fear was racing through their minds and they were dreading the journey. She watched them slowly move into invisibility and wondered how long it would take before she too would disappear. She didn't have to wonder for too long, her invisibility came almost immediately.

While invisible Jomo proposed using their time learning how to use their powers. He faced the west, and raised his staff to call on the Light, and when it arrived it was very faint, prompting him to try again. This time it came with such force it sent him wildly tumbling over twenty feet out into the desert. When Jahiri and Oba reached him they had great difficulty containing themselves. His legs and bare back side was all they saw sticking out from the dunes, is calf-skin nowhere to be found.

Oba composed herself and suggested they try calling the light when standing together, a suggestion agreed to. Jahiri was first to raise his staff, followed by a reluctant Jomo. This time the Light arrived a lot more sedately, but they still had difficulty controlling its power. They resolved to continue practicing until confident they, as a team, had gained complete control.

The time came for them to individually try, Jomo reluctantly agreed to go first. He raised his staff and just like before he was sent tumbling to the ground. On each failed attempt his frustration grew but his determination was stronger, he refused to stop until he felt some semblance of control. Jahiri was encouraged by his determination and followed his lead, after many attempts he too was showing signs of becoming a master of the Light.

That evening the conversation flowed and they really enjoyed each other's company. They wondered about their friends and how they were managing, they particularly wondered if they had the same difficulty with the Light. Oba closed her eyes and searched, "Yes, some of our friends are having trouble; Girish and Garuda have been seriously injured but are recovering. You are not alone." She then suggested, "Maybe we should remain here until you're sure you have fully mastered your light skills." The boys nodded in agreement and for the next few days, practiced until happy they had total control and able to call on the Light at will.

As each day passed and their confidence grew, they not only mastered the arrival of the Light; they also acquired other powers. They gained the ability to see as far as the horizon with such clarity, it gave them a major advantage over any future adversary. They also enhanced their power of prophecy, it was a random power only showing itself when least expected. They were disappointed to find the prophecies only showed fleeting glimpses of their own future.

They continued to hone their warrior skills and particularly enjoyed their spear throwing competitions. Jomo excelled at this. Each time he threw his spear he thought of what Jacob said, 'You will be the carrier of the flaming spear; armies of the south will fall before you'. In time, his spear travelled further into the desert, eventually it would travel out of sight before turning back and landing by his side.

108

Jahiri and Jomo continued their training, and as time passed their calf skin wraps seemed to be getting smaller revealing more of their sun kissed dark skin and rippling muscles. The skirts weren't getting smaller; it was their muscles that were growing. Oba found it more difficult to avert her eyes, especially from Jomo. Having said all that, she felt more secure knowing her guardians were much stronger and more confident.

Chapter 3

The time came to move further south. Jomo and Jahiri were well prepared and full of confidence but Oba wasn't ready, she decided to take a slight detour, which took them towards the western edge of the magnificent city of Petra.

On reaching the city they listening to the guides speak with pride of how much Petra had achieved, especially since it became a hub for the caravans carrying exotic spices from India and China to the Roman Empire. Oba was in awe of the city because, apart from Olympus, she never thought she would visit a place as beautiful or as ancient. Jomo and Jahiri were intrigued by how well hidden among the rose coloured sandstone cliffs it was.

They continued listening as the guides spoke lovingly about how within those cliffs were the most amazing buildings, monuments and carvings that made the city so famous. They spoke of how it was considered to be a city built way before its time because of its channels, cisterns and dams, all designed to provide an endless supply of water for citizens and visitors alike.

The city was situated in the valley of Moses, the very place where Moses used his god-given power to strike a rock to create a flow of water that still runs today. For centuries the city fought off many attackers. The Edomite's lived in, and ran it for hundreds of years. Then the Nabatean Arabs successfully made it the most important trading post between the east and the west; that was until the year 106BCE when, for the second time, it fell to the Romans, who ran it as an important staging post for many more centuries.

When Oba and her guardians arrived, it was bustling with over thirty thousand people and was considered by the scribes to be 'half as old as time'. The aromas rising from the wide variety of herbs and spices pervading the air were breath-taking, reminding Oba of home.

Jomo located a cave high in the cliffs giving him a wide view of the city and from there he saw how peaceful it was. He was pleased to see the gatekeepers disarm visitors without exception. From the safety of the cave he and Jahiri used the power of the Light to seek out the forces of Hell, and for them, it was always a relief never to find any. They were also pleased to see Oba's confidence grow, allowing her to walk alone among the citizens, seeking out those whom she felt were worthy of receiving the message. She did this for many years until she reached a point where she felt there was no more to be done, indicating it was time to move on.

Just as they were about to depart, Jahiri said, "Look at the gate, see how many pass through. Traders, tribesmen and farmers, my powers tell me many are soldiers who have as yet, not tasted war."

Oba insisted on making her way back to the market where many of the new arrivals had gathered. Those she chose for to carry the message had the same striking characteristics and colouring as her, Jahiri and Jomo. To each she said, "Go now, tell your children to tell their children's children for all time, that one day, they will be called upon by the gods and they must answer." Each one she touched showed a slight reaction by rubbing their shoulders before taking a trance-like state. Within moments they began walking south along well worn roads that took them home to their farms and villages that just happened to be located in Kush. The very place Jacob and Magni spoke of as the source of allies to fight by the side of the gods during the battle of the End Times. Oba remembered what Magni said, 'Modi will lead the armies of the south and call upon the Kingdom of Kush.'

Several hours later, the delayed journey resumed. On reaching the southern gate Oba was surprised to meet an elderly man who clearly saw through her invisibility. There was no threat so no defensive action was taken. "Greetings!" said the elderly man while bowing, "I'm Mygon, the third of the three ancient wizards. I'm a great friend of Merlin and Apollonius." He waited for a reply, and when none came he continued, "I've been looking forward to this day. It's a pleasure to meet a messenger of the gods, especially one so beautiful and wise."

"I'm sure you have already gathered that our meeting is no coincidence," he said as he gestured for them to look into a portal he opened. "What you see is the year 551CE. Now listen for a violent rumble and feel its wrath. A great earthquake it is. It will close all passes. See how it destroys the water courses and damages many of the dwellings causing the surviving citizens to leave. Look upon the wind storms and see how the sands will gather to conceal and preserve many of the monuments especially the Treasury and the Monastery, two of the most handsome buildings ever carved into a cliff face."

"Petra is beautiful and peaceful," said Jomo. "It treats its people as equals. Why are the gods allowing this to happen?" There was no reply.

Mygon again pointed towards the portal, "Observe the passage of time. See how the sands continue to build until not a stone is visible. Petra's story still waits to be told and in the year 1812CE an excavation will begin. Petra will be reborn. Its remains are destined to become a future wonder of the world."

Mygon quietened, he received a vision and looked pained, "Beware the guardians on the mountain," he warned. "They are not what they seem. I fear they wait and mean you harm." He took Oba by the arm and moved her out of earshot of the boys. "Be happy Jomo is the bearer of the flaming spear; it will be your saviour. I see the White Mountain. There you must look to the forests and wait for his greeting. Trust him for he is Emperor of the Tuskers." Oba closed her eyes for a moment and took in a deep breath; she had many questions she never got a chance to ask. Mygon just disappeared.

৵৵

A gentle breeze developed, and from within, a soft whispering invited Oba to make her way towards the land of Sinai, an invitation she accepted. On looking out across an endless, featureless landscape of sand, Jahiri suggested they walk along its western edge and hope for inspiration. This suggestion gave Oba the opportunity to pass on the message to all the Bedouin tribes and settled villages they encountered.

After spending many months on the western fringes a slow rhythmic drum beat was heard and it seemed to be calling them deeper into the desert.

It was drawing them to an area dotted with many low lying hills, beyond which stood the mythical Mount Sinai.

Jomo began having visions showing him the first exodus and the closer he got to the Mount the more vivid his visions became. When he closed his eyes his other senses took over, and he felt he was there among the throng. There were times when he reached out only to feel the terror, especially from those who kept glancing back out of fear the remnants of the Egyptian army might regroup and catch up. He quickly learned he was among a migration taken the Jewish nation to their promised land. He was also aware there was a presence of a far greater power.

Jahiri felt nothing like what Jomo was experiencing and just continued walking ahead, that was until he crossed the hills. Suddenly there was an overwhelming feeling of dread encouraging him to extract from his satchel, his robes, armour and weapons. Jomo watched him prepare and he too got ready, it was one of the most sacred rules given by Jacob - 'if only one feels a threat, both should prepare'.

Extracting so much from such a small and unassuming satchel fascinated them. How so much was magically carried, with no feeling of weight, never failed to amaze them. For Jomo, his fascination quickly turned to fear because he too was now feeling a sinister menace. Within minutes they were both fully prepared, wondering if they were about to enter their first battle.

While Jomo and Jahiri were preparing, Oba continued walking away. She was making her way towards a passageway leading to the summit of Mount Sinai. From what they could see she was being drawn, in a trance-like state, by some invisible force. She soon went out of view.

Chapter 4

Although Oba was in a trance, she was aware of everything around her. Up ahead, she saw a strange charred black tree stump that to her, seemed to be frozen in time. Her senses told her it was special. It was the remnants of a large bush she felt were once touched by the gods. Drawing closer, she saw four guardians; four stone Pleurants in hooded cloaks. Oba wondered were these the ones Mygon warned her about.

She cautiously passed, and kept walking until she reached a smooth cliff face, where the smashed remains of stone tablets engraved with Aramaic writings lay scattered on the ground. She sensed they were the first true tablets, the ones given to Moses all those years ago. Something troubled her; she feared the broken fragments were laced with an evil magic, making them powerful weapons, created to harm the carriers of the Light.

She placed her hand on one and received a shock so violent, it slammed her against the cliff face, knocking her unconscious and making her visible.

Jomo and Jahiri were a good distance behind, rushing to catch up. They sensed danger, panicking that their carelessness had left Oba vulnerable. While running they called on the Light for assistance, and when it came it travelled out into the desert, across the hills and over the mountains highlighting hundreds of serpents slithering across the sands. They were moving briskly and making their way towards Mount Sinai. "Jomo," said Jahiri, "you're the fastest. Follow her; leave me deal with the serpents."

Jomo ran up the hill and soon reached the burnt tree stump. Up ahead he saw four cloaked, hooded beings moving towards an unconscious and visible Oba, lying on the ground. They walked in single file, their swords raised about to slay her, but no matter how fast Jomo ran he knew he had no chance of reaching her in time. He prayed for assistance and suddenly felt a presence, "Jomo, my friend." It was Jacob. "Relax, you are powerful, remember what I said in the lagoon, 'You will be the carrier of the flaming Spear.' Now is your time, use it and watch them fall."

Jomo, confused and worried, trusting in Jacob, reached into his satchel and withdrew his spear. He rubbed it between his hands then scraped it off the rocks but couldn't figure out what Jacob meant or how to ignite it.

Watching the first figure preparing to slay Oba, Jomo panicked, threw his spear and watched it gathering speed. A bolt of lightning shot from the burnt tree stump and suddenly there was a flame. The spear ignited and continued its journey. It hit the nearest hooded figure, travelling through him and into the other three, impaling all four against the cliff face.

He ran to be with Oba and on reaching her was horrified to see her so helpless. His temper rose and he turned to behead three of the hooded figures, keeping the fourth alive. When the hooded figure looked its face was that of a Dark Angel, a demon from Hell, just like the ones Jacob and Odi fought in the battle of Dublin.

Jomo placed the tip of his sword against the remaining demons throat and waited for Jahiri to join him and when Jahiri arrived, together they used their powers to enter the demon's head. What surprised them was how devoid of empathy and compassion the demon was, it was as though it was bred just for one thing and that thing was 'Terror'. Nevertheless, they were able to force him to disclose the reason why demons were in this most sacred of places.

Oba, in the meantime, had regained consciousness and listened to Jomo apply more pressure in the hope of extracting as much information as possible. It was then when the demon finally spoke, "There's no hiding. The power of Hell is everywhere, in all sacred places, awaiting the arrival of Jacob's messengers," he sniggered then continued, "We know Jacob is building an army of the Light and our plan is to destroy it before it has a chance to grow." He continued to threaten, prompting Jahiri to lose his patience and with one swift swoosh of his sword he sent him back into the fires of Hell.

Jahiri rested against the cliff-face and when he composed himself he bent forward to pick up one of the remnants. "Stop!" screamed Oba, "I fear the remnants have been taken by the forces of Hell, laced with an ancient magic." Jahiri backed away.

"Why did you enter such a trance-like state," Jomo asked, "putting yourself in so much danger?" Oba linked his arm,

"I've been thinking about it," she said snuggling closer, "I believe what happened had something to do with the tablets. My instincts tell me they were the true ones given at the time of Moses. Why did Mygon warn about the guardians? The more I think about it, the more I feel it was his plan to bring us to this most sacred of places."

She then laid her head on his shoulder with her hand resting on his hip, betraying her feelings, "I can't relax. This evil! It's insidious; it's seeping into my very being."

She turned to Jahiri, "Call on your light, rid this place of Hell."

He did what was asked and it quickly came. It lit up the cliff-face and then cleansed all around. It also shot across the desert showing how close the company of serpents were getting. It highlighted the serpents being led by two Dark Angels.

Jomo moved towards the cliff ledge to monitor the progress of the serpents. He was joined by Jahiri and they decided to make their way to the tree stump where they chose to make their stand. While waiting they heard footsteps and assumed it was Oba joining them. It wasn't, it was Mygon, "You did what was expected, you brought the Light back to this most holy of places. Merlin and Apollonius have great faith and said I should watch out for you. They said you will be the instruments of the gods sent to reclaim what belongs to the Ancient One." Looking down at the advancing serpents, he said, "Fear not my friends, together we defeat this evil."

The pangs of anxiety grew as the serpents got closer especially when some of them transformed into winged demons. They then watched the demons take to the sky and fly as escorts above the remaining serpents. They were a terrifying sight and again they reminded Jomo of the description of the Dark Angels in the battle of Dublin; they too had the faces of demons. He tried to find inspiration from the success Jacob and Odi had, but his nerves were causing him to struggle; that was until he looked across at Jahiri who was standing tall and looked formidable. His fears abated and his strength grew; he now found the confidence and determination needed to assist in winning out this day.

Mygon suggested they retreat to a more secure vantage point which they did, and on their way Jomo closed his eyes and thought of the flaming spear. This time it just ignited and he planned was to use it against the winged demons.

The flying demons moved closer revealing how they were armed with crossbows and primed to attack. The initial volley they launched was unsuccessful. The shields, created by the Asgard shield makers, did what was expected. The second volley had more success when some of the arrows pierced the defences and hit Jahiri's shin bone and foot, leaving him in severe pain. He fell to his knees and went into shock, but even with such a disadvantage, he summoned his skills as a swordsman and staved off an attack by the forward ranks of serpents.

Jomo waited and watched the winged demons regroup. He waited for an opportunity to present itself, and it did when they flew out over the cliffs and formed a straight line, at a right angle to him. He threw his spear and just like earlier, it gathered speed and because of the angle the demons were at, it was able to take out all but the furthest two who managed to evade its path. Jomo recalled the spear and when it returned he threw it again and this time it penetrated one of the remaining two flying demons.

Mygon saw Jahiri was struggling, getting no relief from the relentless onslaught, and the intense pain. He pointed his staff towards Jahiri and called on the Light. It answered and immediately began the healing process giving Jahiri some solace. This action by Mygon was his own undoing; the remaining winged demon was close by and used this distraction to release his arrows and take Mygon down.

Jomo moved to assist Jahiri and succeeded in driving back the serpents allowing Jahiri to use his staff as a crutch. As Jahiri composed himself Jomo again threw his spear and this time took out the last winged demon.

Jahiri and Jomo summoned all their strength to attack with a new purpose. They used the swift swoops of their swords to decapitate any serpent that came close but their efforts weren't enough. The serpents identified Jahiri as the weakest and concentrated their attack on him; it was so focused they quickly broke through his defences. The first serpent to reach him sunk its fangs deep into his thigh, causing him to collapse from the effects of the poison of fire that was now racing through his veins. It was the very same poison that almost killed Jacob and Odi back in the village outside Olympus.

Jomo was now fighting alone and was seriously outnumbered. He had over twenty serpents and two Dark Angels before him causing him to fear for his chances. He then felt a new presence. It was Ares, the God of War, "Jomo, my friend. You stand alone and need the power of the gods, let me in."

Jomo discarded his spear and momentarily closed his eyes; then everything changed. He felt the power of Ares enter him to take control. A new light shone causing him to raise his sword and reach for his dagger. He ran forward and unleashed the power of the Olympus gods. His actions were swift, ruthless and showed no mercy, he quickly eliminated all but one of the Dark Angels. This Angel stood in defiance. Ares then left.

Jomo paused for a moment, composed himself, then stepped forward with his sword ready to strike. "We stand alone, spawn of Hell," he said allowing a sneer to cross his face. "My training tells me to use my advantage and interrogate you. You've hurt the ones I love so I've reconsidered. I'm going to send you, as painfully as I can, back to where you came from." He hadn't even finishing his sentence when he plunged his sword and disembowelled the Dark Angel. After retracting his sword, he swung it high and this time, removed the Dark Angels head.

When he looked around he was horrified by the black blood spatter covering the rock face and was shocked at how much there was. He saw Mygon was in trouble but felt, as a wizard, he would survive. He looked up at Oba and saw she was traumatised and looked lost. He turned back and glanced across at Jahiri, the white mist was gathering.

Jomo's heart broke to see his best friend in real trouble; he was losing his battle with the poison of fire.

Oba pulled herself together and ran to Jahiri's aid hoping to help. She knew the only antidote was wine, a lesson she learned back in the temple.

She said this to Jomo, who lit up, "Before we left the temple," he said, "Jahiri pleaded with the kitchen staff to supply him with two small casks of wine. We were hiding it from you until we had a reason to celebrate. I have a cask."

He opened his satchel and quickly produced his cask. He raised Jahiri's head and gently poured the wine into him, then held him close until the first signs of recovery began. It took two days for Jahiri to wake, and a further two weeks before the marks of the serpent disappeared from his thigh. In the meantime Mygon had fully recovered.

Another two weeks passed when Oba sensed it was time to make their way further south, and when she looked across the desert she saw her next destination. Mygon, Jomo and Jahiri joined her, "I too hear the call but it's not for me," said Mygon, "my place is to guard the remnants of the tablets." Together they put in place their plans to assist in building a defence against any further attacks.

Later that night all four sat around a warm and inviting fire. They used this time to share their fears; Jahiri spoke about how troubled he was by how easily he fell during their first attack. Oba was upset by how helpless and vulnerable she was, even after getting a warning. "Why are you so fearful and full of doubt?" said a surprised Jomo, "Jacob gave us all we needed to survive an attack; even Ares came to our aid. We survived and are all here in one piece. We've even enjoyed our supply of wine that we thought would be used for partying, but the gods must have known we'd need it for something else. He paused for a moment, "the only thing that really surprises me is the attack happened so soon after we left Olympus."

"Jomo, you fought alone," said Oba taking his hand. "Ares wasn't with you. I was there and saw you fight like a warrior possessed."

Jahiri disagreed, "He was possessed; I heard Ares say 'Let me in'."

Mygon reminded them, "Surely you never doubted that the senior gods would come to your aid when there was a danger of all being lost; Ares saw that danger and acted." He turned to Jomo, "You didn't leave Olympus in the last few months. It's nearly fifty years since your journey began."

Oba didn't seem surprised but it bothered Jahiri, "This news means our parents are long gone, is it time to grieve? I have this strange feeling."

Oba closed her eyes and thought of her home village, she saw how it had changed. She moved from house to house and noted their parents were nowhere to be found. She saw their brothers and sisters as well as many children. She saw they were all happy. "Our parents are gone," she said, "time has moved on. What remains of our families are still there and they're happy. Our brothers and sisters have many children between them."

Mygon reached over to comfort the boys, "Tonight, you both grieve; tomorrow we prepare the sanctuary for the protection of the tablets."

Jomo had a restless night; he was grieving and missed his family. He wondered how his brothers were managing in their father's workshop, he also wondered about the stone sculpture he was working on during his training to be a stonemason and hoped someone had finished it. He then fell asleep.

Oba also had a restless night; the sound of running water was disturbing her. She remembered the prophecy Jacob gave 'you will be my River Goddess'. She rose to walk over to the smooth cliff face and placed her ear close to the wall. She stood back and just like what Moses did over a thousand years earlier, she tapped, and a small crack appeared. Water trickled through and as the crack expanded, the water flowed as though it was the birth of a new river. The flow continued, bringing its life force to all the seeds lying dormant and buried in the dry sands. The river soon found its level and provided a small yet continuous flow of water destined to nourish and quench the thirst of the grasses, flowers and shrubs that began to sprout and then bloom.

When Mygon, Jahiri and Jomo woke they were amazed at the changes that occurred over night. The hole in the cliff face continued to expand and soon it became the mouth of a large cave. When the cave was fully formed they entered and were in awe at how vast it was.

Mygon was happy for this to be his resting place. He magically moved a large boulder to the centre of the cave and asked Jomo to use his skills to create a throne seat. Jomo, as usual, was prepared for all eventualities; he had his tools in his satchel and within twelve hours created an ornately carved stone seat, fit for a wizard. He then walked to the entrance of the cave and began creating two large columns, one on each side.

Jahiri was the gatherer. He brought together all the rubble he found and used it to form an airtight seal around the entrance. Jomo then created two large and aged looking stone slabs before placing them on each side of the entrance so as to camouflage the rubble. The next problem was to create stone doors, strong and heavy enough to withstand the test of time, and it was concluded that this was a job for a wizard.

Mygon agreed and conjured up two magical doors, using large slabs that were eight inches thick. He used his magic to raise them into place before securing them against the two columns. They remained ajar until all other tasks were completed.

While Jomo and Mygon were working on the columns and doors, Jahiri and Oba gathered together the remnants of the tablets. They laid them out before reassembling them, and they worked on this task until they were satisfied every last piece was in place. Jahiri then made a paste, using water and a mixture of lime, sand and a special soil he had located, to secure the tablets to one of the walls. When they placed them on the wall all cracks and signs of damage disappeared allowing each commandment to be clearly read. It was a job well done. They had just put the tablets, carrying the words of the Ten Commandments, back together.

Seven days had passed before the sanctuary was complete, in fact, in real time it was well over two years. Mygon was really impressed especially with the ornate etchings carved on his throne depicting the symbols of the earth, wind, fire and water as well as all the signs of the Zodiac. After thanking Jomo, he said, "It's time for you to continue your journey. The call to move on is now becoming overpowering and I can see you all getting restless. Today I will use my magic to protect this most holy of sanctums, then I'll sleep. Before this happens I will enhance your gift of prophecy, a gift which will come to your aid when you need it the most. Need I remind you, prophecies can be random and will never be your own?" He placed his hand on both Jomo and Jahiri's foreheads and said the prayer of prophecy.

Goddess of Time, guardian of the age

Help them to see and become a sage.

Give them the power to know what is to come.

Keep them with you and be as one.

He then called Oba aside. "You no longer need my help; you are a Goddess of the Light and have become most powerful but I caution you, bury your feelings as they will become a danger to the task. You should not act on them before reaching the land of the Tuskers."

He placed his hand on her forehead and showed her a future that has been hidden. She saw a future where she and Jomo shared a loving embrace.

She wept with joy when she saw in that future, happy children playing and enjoying a free and a peaceful life. She promised not to succumb to her feelings until they left the land of the Tuskers.

He then spoke of a kingdom coming to its end and said she should be there to send its remnants on their way; he reminded her that Modi will need their descendants at the End Times.

It was now time. They stood back and watched Mygon enter the cave to sit on his throne and continued watching as he raised his staff to call on the Light. They bowed when the Light arrived, and then listened to him conjure up his spell to begin sealing the entrance. They got upset watching him turn to stone. The doors closed and the hollow thud of the clash of rock coming together will forever be imprinted in their minds. Jomo then carved above the doors -

Here rests the guardian of

The Ten Commandments

- Mygon, Wizard of the Light -

Jomo and Jahiri produced their staffs and rotated them at such speed that the winds came and lifted the sands so as to conceal the doors, providing extra protection. It was a magical protection that was to last for eighteen hundred years.

Chapter 5

It was late morning when the descent of the mount began. Before leaving, Oba placed her hand in the river commanding its waters to cease flowing. Immediately the nearby grasses struggled, wilting under the incessant heat of the sun. At the base of the mount, a sea of grasses spread across the desert as far as the eye could see. The grassland had become home to herds of Dorcas Gazelle, Nubian Ibex, Lizards, Camels, mice and Egyptian Hares. There were also predators - Jackals, Leopards and Sand Foxes.

Oba froze and covered her mouth, "Did I make a mistake? The grasses, they were nurtured by the life-giving waters I commanded to cease flowing."

"Your water certainly nurtured the grasses," said Jomo, "but now you have a dilemma. Either you restart the waters and endanger the sanctuary, or you leave the waters locked away and endanger the lives of all who have made these grasslands their home." Oba was very concerned.

"Jacob referred to you as his Goddess of the Rivers, said Jahiri, "Be that goddess. You can't allow the water to flow but there is something you can do. Walk to where the grass meets the sand, seek an outcrop of rock. Use your magic and tap the rock, your water will flow and the buried seeds will soon sprout and bring forth more grasses. I promise the animals will follow. Move on a few more leagues and again bring forth the water. Do this time and time again, until you reach the western edge of the desert; the animals will follow to start their new life elsewhere."

Oba took his advice and walked many miles out into the grasslands, she worried the waters wouldn't flow but she tried anyway, and to her surprise the springs came and formed small lakes allowing the water to spread and bring forth life. The animals did follow and within two months they were grazing on the shores of the Gulf of Suez.

On reaching the gulf Oba entered a small fishing village near modern day Abu Durbah and from there she arranged their crossing to Egypt. Jahiri and Jomo remained on alert during the four hour crossing, fearing another attack. On reaching the bustling village of Ra's Gharib they located a small house close to the port where they remained for a few days. From there Oba used her time to pass the message to many of the villagers. At night, sleep was difficult; the call of the ancients was pounding loudly in their ears and drawing them north. When they finally left, they walked west to the banks of the river Nile and from there they followed its course north towards Giza, before moving north-east towards Heliopolis, the City of the Sun.

On reaching the outskirts they were surprised to be greeted by a Sun God. It was Ra-Atum. He was in his partial human form, wearing his falcon head surrounded by the sacred cobra and crowned by a sun disk. "I've been expecting you and have been asked to make you welcome," he said folding his arms. "But be aware, I'm an angry god. Not being invited to Olympus for the gathering of the gods is a great insult."

Oba acknowledged his displeasure and assured him no insult was intended. She then gracefully accepted his invitation to join him in his temple. On their way they passed the Al-Masalla obelisk. Oba remarked, "When the great battle ends this monument will still stand tall. I have seen it."

They soon arrived in the temple and were ushered through to the library where its vastness overwhelmed them. Between each column were floor to ceiling alcoves containing countless scripts, codices and books, all containing the history of nations going back to the fall of paradise. There were tables set in order, running from the entrance to the rear of the hall. At each table sat three novices and one tutor, an expert in hieroglyphics. Ra's priests were the guardians of documents dating back to the beginning of time.

They were greeted by the chief priest, considered to be the most knowledgeable when it came to the history of all the Africa's. "Through that passageway is stored the history of the ancient ones," he said pointing towards an archway near the rear of the hall, "it's there where the royal records are kept, records that speak about the rise of the Pharaohs. Among those records is a prophecy that today has come to pass. Your arrival has fulfilled that prophecy." Walking through the hall Oba observed the priests copying the codices. She also noted Ra's pride by the way he constantly looked over the priest's shoulders checking the progress of what was being copied. When he rejoined her he said, "I've had the pleasure of visits from Homer, Plato, Orpheus and Solon, among others, each of whom lectured within these hallowed walls."

Jahiri sniggered. "We met Homer,"

Jomo quipped, "He was one funny little man; he never stopped talking."

Ra-Atum smiled then spoke of meeting Alexander the Great. "He halted his long march just to visit my city. I was deceived and it saddens me when I think of how he used my temple as a template for building Alexandria to become far more important."

Ra continued walking until reaching the alcove containing the history of Rome, "I was furious with Julius Caesar," he said lowering his head, "in 48BCE, during his attack on Alexandria, he refused to take responsibility for the great library being burned to the ground, I swore vengeance on him;

how could his armies show such disregard for the ancient documents carrying the history of so many people's? It was then when I decided nothing will ever again leave this temple without being copied." He calmed for a moment then his anger showed again; he repeated his annoyance at not being invited to the gathering of the gods

"When Zeus called the council," said Oba, "the heralds of Africa beat the drums and that sound travelled to the furthest reaches of these ancient lands, how is it you didn't hear them? Shango, Isis and three other powerful deities attended; they represented all of Africa."

"I'm the most powerful of the African Sun Gods and should have been there," responded Ra-Atum, "every effort should have been made to wake me. Why did I not wake? Is it because I'm no longer revered and the more my peoples reverence falls away, the deeper I fall into sleep?" He lowered his head in sadness, "Isis, on her last visit, spoke of the gathering and assured me Africa was well represented. When she told me of your journeys, I longed for the day the messengers from Olympus would visit for I have a message of my own to impart, listen carefully to what I have to say and see all I have to show."

He opened a portal and said showing them the end of Heliopolis, "This is the ancient 'City of the Sun', my city. See its future, it will be torn down brick by brick to provide building material for the northern quarter of a city, the descendants will one day call Cairo." He moved the portal, "See also the fall of Alexandria, and the future burnings of its great library. Look forward to 270CE and watch how most of its rare manuscripts are destroyed by the Aurelian invasion. Look again and watch how in 391CE, the Coptic Pope Theophilus, will order the destruction of what he calls pagan documents. And then finally, watch how in 642CE, a new religion, will result in a conquest leading to the complete loss of this most renowned library."

For many hours Ra imparted more and more prophesies and they were getting more horrifying. He spoke of the relentless march of the deserts and the destruction of the rain forests. He showed them the extinction of iconic wild life and the poisoning of the lands, then told them of famine and pestilence, destined to forever stalk his realm. He brought up images of slavery and genocide, so terrible Oba and Jahiri went into shock. His constant prophesies of doom suggested there was no hope. Jomo mused, "All you show us makes me wonder are we wasting our time spreading the message."

Oba reacted, "What you have shown us suggests there's no hope. I don't agree. In Olympus we were taught that the future is not set in stone. There are many paths, and depending which one we chose, some of what you showed may not happen. We have faith in mankind and will assist them whenever we can."

Ra Atum shook his head, showing his loss of faith, "I wish you well and will give you a blessing. It's my gift of continuous sunshine." He linked Oba and said as he escorted her to the courtyard, "My time is coming to its end and it saddens me. Maybe you're right? Maybe one of those paths will take these lands to a different future? I pray the future treats you well and sits safely in your hands but beware, there are many dangerous times ahead and if you fail, the light in these lands will be extinguished forever. The Darkness and its ally will always be close by, waiting for your mistakes." He then suggested, "Walk to the coast until you reach the passes of the mystical Atlas Mountains, then cross the great desert to the oasis of Timbuktu. Find the grasslands and wait for the first migration of the Yoruba peoples. Use your power and help them, they have been loyal to me. When with them you will need the assistance of an old friend, one whom you know, Lord Shango. Continue your journey until you reach the Kingdom of Kush, just in time to see its end. There you will find the ancestors of your army."

He turned to Jomo, "You worry too much about the flame. Worry not; it will come, especially when you need it the most."

"It won't ignite," replied Jomo. "Everything I try fails."

Ra Atum opened another portal, "Have faith," he said, "look upon your spear and see how it ignites time and time again. See how its flame travels across the sky and returns each time to rest in your hand."

Before saying his final goodbye he turned and was moved by how handsome Jahiri was. He reached across and imparted another prophecy, "Jacob chose you well. He saw the essence of eternal youth but didn't look any further. I see everything else. I see the mischief and fun but your prowess and valour will bring out the true leader that you are. I also see your great love and she will forever be by your side. Your statuesque and striking appearance will, when you materialise before the tribes, take their breath away and you will stand before them as a god, they will swear their loyalty and rise up to follow you."

Jahiri was excited to be recognised by a most powerful god as statuesque and striking, but wondered what relevance his appearance was to what was ahead. He never thought of himself in this way until he caught his reflection in a shield resting against the wall. His image forced him to his knees and drew him in. He then realised the strength of the power he had. He was also intrigued to be told there was a girl in his future.

Oba and Jomo placed their heads in their hands, they knew they would have to listen to Jahiri speak of his good looks and watch him preen and groom himself for the next thousand years. They also knew no girl would be safe until he finds the one Ra-Atum spoke of.

Chapter 6

The walk towards the Atlas Mountains was unremarkable. On their way Oba, Jomo and Jahiri visited many villages where Oba chose children whom she felt were worthy to receive the message. Those children found they could see her and many asked, "Are you an angel?" She always gave the same reply, "No, I am Oba."

While walking through the ancient city of Carthage they felt the sadness of the enslaved descendants of this once great city. Oba wanted to help but knew her task was just to spread the message. In Carthage it was difficult to find anyone worthy of receiving the message, their spirit was broken and Oba felt there was no hope for them. She discussed her concerns with Jomo and Jahiri, after which they agreed they should continue their walk. This took them to the foothills of an arc of mountains that spread for two thousand miles across the north and into the far west.

The foothills weren't steep and the climb was easy. There were many villages along the way and Oba used every opportunity to spread her message. Jomo and Jahiri remained alert, they were aware of a powerful presence they couldn't identify. They climbed higher and soon reached a narrow plateau that on one side gave them a view towards the sea and on the other, gave them a view of a semi-arid landscape that stretched towards the horizon. Jomo pointed, "That presence I felt earlier is stronger, and it draws me towards that mound." Jahiri agreed.

Just as they reached the mound, three gods materialised, two male and one female. They stood roughly two meters apart. Oba whispered, "I've seen images of them before, they are three ancient gods of the Berber Pantheon. We must show them respect."

Jomo and Jahiri bowed, Oba slightly lowered her head. The god on the left was first to speak, "Welcome, travellers of Olympus. I am Ammon, the Life God of Africa. Lord of all Creation."

Ammon stood almost seven feet tall. Above his head was a colourful double plumb taken from a long extinct bird of paradise. He wore a well trimmed beard that was bound below his chin by golden threads. His hair was soft curled and flowing. He was of mixed race, neither black nor white. His ankle length wrap was held in place by a gem encrusted belt. On his arms were golden bracelets, spreading from his wrist to his shoulder.

The female Goddess then spoke, "I too welcome you. I am Afri, Goddess of Fortune and Fertility."

She too was almost seven feet tall. Her high cheekbone, sculpted face was framed by bead tipped braided hair. Above her head was a sun disc that captured sunrays before beaming them in all directions. She wore the horns of a water buffalo, draped with dense strands of hair taken from the manes of long gone male lions. At the tips the hair was white, before changing to cream, then tan, then brown followed by the blackest of black. She was naked but for a mesh style fabric that left nothing to the imagination.

The third god needed no introduction. He stood at just over six foot tall, and occasionally, when a globe appeared on his shoulder, his muscles would strain until the globe disappeared. "In case you don't know, I am the Mountain God. I am Atlas."

Oba was in awe, she had seen the life-size statues of a naked Apollo, Eros and Ares and they were impressive. Even the statue of Odi didn't compare to the naked god who now stood before her. At first she forced herself to keep eye contact. She found herself admiring his tightly cropped hair, his handsome face and his coal black flawless skin. She could no longer avert her eyes from his rippling muscles. They were so big; everything was so big she became breathless.

Jomo and Jahiri also had difficulty; finding it hard to avert their eyes. Atlas noticed how uncomfortable they were and teased, "Do I make you feel inadequate?"

"What do you think?" replied Jomo.

"Definitely not," said Jahiri puffing out his chest. Atlas's attitude changed,

"Tell me, guardians of Olympus. Tell me of Heracles, the thief. Has he choked on my stolen apples? They were my golden apples!"

"We know nothing of golden apples," replied Jahiri, "Heracles has been nothing but kind and generous. He has assisted Jacob in preparing us for our journey."

Afri intervened, "Now, now, Lord Atlas. Enough of this teasing, let us make our guests welcome."

Atlas apologised, and ushered everyone into a nearby mountain cave. He conjured up food and wine. And after dining, many stories were shared. Although the stories varied, some fantastical, some troubling, it was the news from Olympus the gods were really interested in. Afri enquired after her long missed friends, Isis and Aphrodite. Ammon was intrigued by Maria and Jacob wanting to know how Zeus reacted to their arrival and Atlas still only wanted to talk about his nemeses, Heracles.

The following morning Oba rose early and went to sit by a nearby lake. She was joined by a distressed Afri, who had a vision to impart.

"In the future my people will be forced to follow a new religion leaving me alone with no one to love me," she gently wept. Oba hugged her, attempting to comfort her. Afri continued, "This realm is destined to know no peace and the time is not too far away when an invasion by the Vandals will come to pass and many will die," she went quiet for a moment and got more distressed. "Less than a hundred years later an invasion by the Byzantine Empire will bring great pain. The loss of my realm will be complete when armies from the east bring a new religion. Their conversion of my people will be brutal and many will die. There is nothing I can do, but I plan to remain close by. With the assistance of the gods, one day my return will be sought."

While continuing to hug Afri, Oba got a fit of the giggles, "Forgive me, My Lady. I have just watched Jahiri and Atlas leave the cave, they walk higher into the mountains." Afri looked up, Oba continued, "Jahiri always wears the skimpiest of calfskins, leaving not much to the imagination. Not since that time in the lagoon have I seen him naked. Today, now he's naked, he looks good." Afri agreed, "Two unrelated and powerful gods, same height, same build. The Ancient One forgot to throw away the mould."

Afri raised her finger to her ears and strained, she was listening to what Atlas had to say. "Atlas is telling Jahiri of sad times due to befall these lands." She assisted Oba to listen,

"Look around friend, at these beautiful lands; listen to the sounds and breathe in what nature has to offer. This is not to last," said Atlas while moving to sit on a nearby rock. He gestured for Jahiri to join him, "There are times I hate mankind, their greed and ruthlessness repulses me. Since their expulsion from the Garden of Eden I have carried the weight of the world upon my shoulders, you have seen it appear and disappear. I am tired of using my powers to keep these lands in balance and wonder how long I can continue," he stood and pointed back at the grasslands. "See the great herds, I assisted them to grow. Now, in my dreams, I see empty spaces. My favourite, the Atlas Bear has no future - they will hunt him to extinction. Listen to the trumpeting of the Northern Elephants; a subspecies destined for a tragic end, it is a sound soon to fade forever. Why does man hate the elephant? Look up at the majesty of these Algerian Oaks; they are the last of their kind and soon to perish. Does man not recognise their beauty?"

Atlas stepped back and placed his two hands on Jahiri's shoulders, "I was there at the creation. It was written back then that from among the Maasai a warrior will come, one who is destined to be a God. That Maasai warrior is you Jahiri, my friend," he bowed then continued, "all I ask is that you bring succour to the herds and assist them, especially when the End Times approaches. Bring the tribes together and teach them to respect all of nature. Make them understand how even the lowliest animal has a place in the balance of life. Guard those you can, and help them to safety." Jahiri said nothing, he was in shock.

While Jahiri and Atlas climbed higher up the mountain Jomo and Ammon, who had left the cave earlier that morning, crossed the central plains. Everywhere they walked some form of life came and took root in Ammon's footsteps. When they approached any tree, Jomo shook his head in disbelief; the tree would bow before its god.

On reaching the first of many rivers Ammon kneeled to stare at his reflection. He beckoned Jomo to join him, "Kneel beside me, look into the river and tell me what you see."

Jomo gasped, "You and I? Is it possible we are the same, am I of you? Or am I a descendant of the Orisha? Is this why Jacob chose me as a guardian?"

"I see the power of the Orisha in you. The Gods of Africa are your ancestors. Jacob must have recognised you to be a descendant waiting to shine. So today, I give you the strength of a god. Your flaming spear gives you great power and as its bearer you will be followed into battle but with this new strength you will be unbeatable." He stood and looked back at the mountain, "By now Jahiri will have learned a terrible truth. He will be aware of a great calamity due to befall the natural world. I sense his devastation but he is strong, his plans to assist will prevail for he too is a God of Africa. He is a God of War and will unite the tribes. They will listen for the beat of the Djembe drums and will answer that pounding call. When they see the flaming spear, they will gather and follow you both into battle."

Ammon struggled for a moment, "Beware! I see pain, a great pain. From the mountains of fire, the servants of evil and the serpents of Hell will begin their onslaught on the tribes. They will bite, and from those bitten will come the tyrants and dictators of the future. They will lay the ground for the End Times and will assist 'Him' in bringing on The Darkness."

For Jahiri and Jomo the prophecies weighed heavily, and they felt they had been given a greater responsibility than what was intended. When they returned to the cave they discussed their fears with Oba and were reassured when she used her powers to calm them.

The next morning Oba, Jahiri and Jomo said their goodbyes and continued their journey through villages occupied by the Amazigh peoples, later known as the Berbers. They were an ancient tribe, noble and wise. Many were nomads who over time migrated across the mountains, through the plains and into the vast deserts of the south. They were a people who valued their freedom, and their way of life was fiercely guarded by a council of elders.

Over the next hundred years Oba used her time visiting as many villages as possible knowing the nomadic nature of the Berbers would ensure her message will spread far and wide.

When the time came to move on they travelled deeper into the Atlas lands. They had many adventures, none more so than their confrontation with a giant who had the ability to see through their invisibility. He was angry and hated the gods of Olympus. He knew messengers had left Olympus and expected them to pass his way. He intended to make the journey difficult by refusing to allow them pass. Jomo attempted to negotiate until he realised the giant was not for moving.

Who are you?" asked Oba.

"I am Antaeus, guardian of these passes."

"Why challenge us?" asked Jahiri.

"My grandfather was killed by a god of Greece, the one they call Heracles. Not only a thief, he's a murderer. I swore revenge on Olympus."

"We know nothing of this and shouldn't be held responsible, let us pass," pleaded Jomo.

Antaeus thought for a moment then said, "My grandfather was the wrestling giant who guarded these passes, I too can wrestle. If one of you can defeat me I'll allow you through."

Oba said, "We shouldn't pay for the sins of Heracles."

"You are blessed by Olympus and I will get my revenge," said Antaeus with a sneer.

Jomo stepped forward insisting Antaeus step aside and when he got no response he removed his armour and readied himself for battle. Oba and Jahiri tried to intervene but Jomo had lost his patience and was determined to end the impasse. He recalled Ammon saying 'I give you the strength of a god'. He felt that strength take control of his body. His blood raced and his muscles ached before expanding for him to become a colossus. "Now will you allow us through?" asked Jomo.

"Defeat me and I'll allow you pass," replied a defiant Antaeus.

The bout began and Jomo outmanoeuvred Antaeus in every way. His training and prowess meant it wasn't long before he had Antaeus on the ground. He held him down, hoping for a submission, not knowing that the only way to defeat a giant was to raise him from the ground long enough for his ribs to crack and damage his heart. They parted and took a breath.

Antaeus paused for a moment before lunging forward; this time forcing Jomo to the ground where he held him so tightly the air no longer entered his lungs causing him to become semi-conscious. Antaeus believed he had won. He loosened his grip which was a major mistake. Jomo quickly recovered and raised his arm to pull Antaeus over his head, upending him. Jomo leapt upon Antaeus, again hoping for a submission but there was none, so Jomo held him even tighter, and this went on for many more hours. Neither submitted so Jahiri suggested they part and prepare for another bout. They agreed and it was decided the loser would be the first one to hit the ground.

This time it was Jomo who lunged forward allowing him to grip Antaeus just above his waist. He manoeuvred him into an upright position; he tightened his grip and totally incapacitated him. He then called on the strength of Heracles and in a moment that led to victory he raised Antaeus high above the ground in a plan that involved throwing him out over the grass lands.

Although Jomo had great strength, he was also compassionate. When he felt Antaeus's life drain away this troubled him. His compassion grew and he asked if they could end the battle and live in peace. Antaeus agreed and when he was lowered to the ground he went to his knees and bowed.

"There's no need to bow before us," said Oba, "you fought well but you need to let go your anger. My visions tell me you are the last of the Giants. Your strength will be needed when Pegasus calls together all those of myth and legend. Will you answer his call?"

Antaeus agreed. "When the lord of all horse's calls," he said, "tell him the last of the giants will answer." Antaeus stood aside, he allowed them pass and they soon reached the forested part of the mountains.

Walking through the forest, Jahiri received more visions and was getting more upset, especially when he realised how close the End Times battle was. He recalled the tragic prophesies shared by Atlas making his distress more acute. He requested time alone and left to walk deeper into the mountains where he met up with a family of Barbary Lions. He sat alongside the dark-mane male and rubbed his back only to receive another vision, this was another species destined to become extinct. He moved on and met with a herd of Barbary Deer led by a powerful stag, they too faced extinction. He continued and met the last of the Atlas Bears only to see their final days were close by. He sensed the presence of the mythical Barbary Leopard but never saw her. He marvelled at the black shiny feathers on the northern Bald Ibis as well as the call of the elusive Dipper. He sat and played with the cubs of the Mountain Badger and grieved, for they too would soon be gone.

The enhanced power of prophecy given to him by Mygon was now so strong he saw into the distant future and was devastated. He saw the extinction of many species and the destruction of numerous intricate habitats. He saw the ruthless slaughter of the great herds, especially the elephants and rhinos. He even saw across to the New World where he witnessed the mass destruction of the bison herds on the Great Plains. He was enraged by the burning of the scrublands and the destruction of the lush forests, all falling to the relentless greed and continuous land grab of mankind. He even tasted the polluted air brought on by man continuing to destroy all environments. Near the End Times he saw the glaciers slide into the sea causing the lowlands to disappear and this was the final straw. He wondered why Jacob wanted to save this third age of man.

He continued his walk through the mountains and reached a forest of Black Pines and then a stand of Atlas Cedars. His walk took him into a semi-secluded valley where some more Algerian Oaks still existed but they were under severe house building pressure. There he was surprised to be greeted by a small gathering of Atlas Elves who were packed, and beginning their journey to seek the protection of their northern friends, they had lost hope and felt everything was soon to change. They spoke of their inability to protect the trees into the future.

Jahiri calmed, he felt Jacob's presence, "My Friend, I know how despondent you are but I need you on my side. Find the strength and ask the elves to reconsider. Use your powers and show them that there is hope. Tell them of enlightened people who, in the future, will become protectors of the natural world, including the great Algerian Oaks. Have faith my friend." Although not completely convinced, Jahiri negotiated with the Elves for many hours and in the end they agreed to continue their nurturing of the forests.

Several days later he returned and met with Oba and Jomo, "I've had many sad experiences over the last few days. The visions I'm receiving are really upsetting, and I'm having severe doubts about saving this age of man. Jacob came to me and tried to encourage me but I'm still not convinced. In fact, I'm really annoyed with him."

Just then he heard what sounded like an egg cracking, he looked around and in a small bank of rocks there was a great deal of activity. He decided to investigate. He was taken aback to see a small desert lark standing over a nest of five eggs and they were beginning to hatch. He watched the first chick continuously chip away at the shell, struggling to be born. He was besotted. As egg after egg hatched, he realised their struggle showed they had a right to life. He was inspired and it became clear to him that he should increase his efforts to prevent The Darkness. He rejoined Oba and Jomo and said, "I think Jacob is still watching over me, I bet he arranged for the eggs to hatch within my earshot. The hatching chicks made me see the light so forget all I said earlier. I'm ready to move on. We should continue our journey."

Chapter 7

As immortals, the journey into the Sahara Desert wasn't daunting. Although at times they struggled, they were immune to the incessant heat of the sun and thirst was never an issue. They also used this time to have some fun by using the numerous dunes as giant slides. They particularly looked forward to the highest ones by using their shields as sledges. They descended at such speeds it became addictive. More often than not, Oba sat behind Jomo, gripping him so tightly she was again betraying her feelings. She cherished these moments although fleeting, and looked forward to the next time.

It soon became obvious to Jahiri that something was stirring and he was curious. He waited for the right moment, and when the chance came he questioned Oba about what he had observed. Oba confirmed her feelings for Jomo and said she was having difficulty controlling them. She reminded Jahiri about Mygon's warning telling her to bury those feelings until reaching the land of the Tuskers. She whispered, "I shouldn't be surprised you noticed but I wonder why Jomo didn't."

"I love Jomo, he's my best friend," quipped Jahiri, "but when it comes to matters of the heart he's a bit slow. It could be two or three hundred years before a 'eureka' moment hits him, so I think you're in for a long wait."

She was about to respond when Jomo returned from a brief Light patrol, the conversation was dropped. He announced, "I've located an oasis, the nomads call it Timbuktu. It shelters a number of small family groups and

I feel we should travel there." Oba agreed, and on reaching the Oasis she passed the message to many of the inhabitants before moving on.

That night, resting deeper in the desert, Oba received a vivid vision encouraging her to travel south-east into the grasslands. She recalled Ra-Atum asking her to watch out for the migration of the Yoruba peoples and knew the visions had something to do with that.

It took several weeks to reach the northern edge of a vast plain. It was the grasslands, vast and open, with only the odd tree or bank of rocks to break the view. The grass itself had grown tall, and swayed in steady waves as far as the eye could see. The stalks were yellow and brittle, heavy with seed and waiting on the long overdue rains. Everything seemed natural and wild. Ants and termites studiously foraged and prepared their defences, expecting a deluge but something was wrong. The grasslands were devoid of animals. The herds were gone - no grazers, no predators, nothing. Jahiri crouched and placed the palms of his hands on the ground. "Ah, there they are. They move deeper south and further west. I feel the rumble and sense their fear, even the predators are terrified." Getting to his feet, he said, "They know of Hell, they fear the serpents. Jomo, find us a safe place."

Jomo quickly identified several outcrops of rock, all ideal sites to set up camp. He chose the highest and went to investigate. Evidence of recent kills and the stench of lion was everywhere but no lions were sighted. Oba and Jahiri joined him. Together they climbed to the highest point and faced the northeast.

In the distance they heard a slow drumbeat. It was the first sign of the Yoruba migration. When it came into view it was many miles long, and moving at a steady pace. Jahiri send out his Light and the response was unclear. As the migration got closer he sent a second burst and this time it showed the presence of a small number of well hidden serpents.

Passing the outcrop Jahiri again sent out his Light guiding Jomo to discreetly make his way among the people to locate the serpents. His invisibility allowed him to get close enough to destroy them. Many serpents masqueraded as young teenagers making it difficult for him to carry out his task. His compassion encouraged him to attempt bringing the teenagers back into the light but it was never to be, he ruthlessly eliminated every last one.

Jomo noticed a lone warrior moving behind a dense growth of bushes and decided to intercept. He materialised causing the warrior to collapse in fear. Jomo smiled and reached out, "No need to fear, warrior of Yoruba, I'm Jomo, a friend. Tell me your name."

The warrior struggled to his feet, "Ojore" he replied, "They say I'm a man of war."

"I walked through your people and feel sickened," said Jomo. "Your elderly, many of your women and all of your children are gaunt, starving and thirsty. Why? When all warriors seem well fed."

Ojore lowered his head as though in shame, "Please don't judge us, we made many decisions to be ashamed of, but there was no choice. Everything was against us."

Jomo sat near him, "Tell me your story," he requested.

Ojore began, "There was no uprising, no whisperings of discontent, no violence. We all realised, almost at the same time that we were not of Egypt. In our dreams we saw our homeland and it was calling for us to return. Many of us are traders, craftsmen, seamstresses, farmers, stall-holders. Many were wealthy but they too weren't happy. Our dreams got more vivid and then they appeared. It was the Gods of the Orisha and they were calling us home," Ojore moved to sit on a nearby rock. "None of us were warriors. None of us were trained. Every territory we entered involved murderous attacks by savage tribes who seemed terrified by our presence. We didn't understand. We still don't, but we quickly learned how to defend ourselves. We captured their weapons, replicating them and taught ourselves to fight. We also decided to divert as much of our food and water as possible to the warriors, that's why so many look gaunt and are suffering. Of all the difficulties we faced the worst was the debilitating effects of the continuous and relentless sun. More of our people died from thirst than the ongoing tribal attacks."

Ojore stood and pointed back towards the distant hills, "Back there the determination and valour of our warriors helped stave off many tribal attacks. The constant assaults have weakened us, each skirmish wore us down. Beyond those hills the pursuing Egyptian army prepares, and I fear we have no defences against them. We need to rest and will camp here overnight, but tomorrow...."

"All might seem lost," said Jomo trying to reassure him. "Today you have the power of Olympus by your side. Go back to your position and say nothing of our meeting. We will put together a plan."

Jomo said after rejoining Oba and Jahiri, "They're a brave people. How they survived the relentless attacks amazes me." He turned to Oba, "It's the thirst that's killing them; you need to work your magic."

Without hesitation Oba fetched her staff and tapped it against a smooth faced rock, and like in Sinai, a crack developed allowing a trickle of water to flow. She tapped again and the water volume increased, creating a new river. Within an hour the river reached the encampment bringing great relief.

Oba waited a few hours before making her way to walk among the people. She passed the message to the first few she met. Those people lost their gauntness and began to recover. Oba noted her likeness in their faces and felt that in a past life, she was of them. While walking among the people she remembered the request of Ra-Atum, 'Use your powers and help them, for they have been loyal to me. You will know when you need assistance; seek then the power of my friend, Lord Shango.'

After a number of hours Oba returned to the outcrop where she, Jomo and Jahiri spent time looking out across the vast encampment. "I fear tomorrow," said Jahiri taking in a deep audible breath.

"Do you sense it?" asked Oba.

Jomo stood and rested against his staff, "The warrior I met, Ojore is his name. He spoke about all they suffered and feared tomorrow. Now I understand what he means. Their drums are silent, the tension is everywhere."

The following morning the sun had difficulty rising, stubborn clouds prevented the brilliant orange-red glow from shining. When it finally broke through its light highlighted a shocking and alarming sight. Across the eastern hills were thousands of Egyptian chariots, each containing a driver, a shield bearer and an archer? On the hills to the west many of the smaller indigenous tribes had come together to form a formidable force so vast it blocked the only escape routes to the Yoruba homelands. Deeper in the southern grasslands a far bigger army had gathered, they were more numerous than the combined forces of the other two armies. To the north lay the unforgiving desert. All seemed lost.

Oba placed her fingers to her forehead seeking out the reason the Yoruba were so hated and soon found out. "It seems the Oracles told the tribes of a frightful evil due to travel through their lands. An evil so demonic that if not stopped it would bring about the end of all life, they believe the Yoruba are harbouring that evil."

"How do we convince them not to attack?" wondered Jahiri, "There are so many."

"The Egyptians?" continued Oba, "They're furious so many Yoruba left causing the collapse of their economy. Their army has instructions to annihilate the Yoruba men-folk and enslave the women and children."

"Maybe we shouldn't try to convince them," said Jomo, "maybe we should show them our power?" No one answered, everything changed. The light winds ceased blowing, and all across the grasslands not a sound was heard. It was an eerie silence that became unnerving. Each army watched and waited for the other to make the first move.

"What's your plan?" asked Jahiri as Jomo stepped on to the highest rock. Jomo raised two fingers to his lips and whistled loudly in short sharp bursts. Two Arabian stallions, corralled near the edge of the Yoruba camp, broke free and galloped towards the outcrop. Jomo mounted one and gestured for Jahiri to mount the other. Jahiri rode off to a high ridge near where the western tribes had gathered and Jomo rode towards a higher ridge in the south east, next to where the eastern flank of the forest warriors were camped.

Oba, in the meantime, surveyed the battle field from her position high on the rocky outcrop. Her concern grew when she saw how completely outnumbered the Yoruba were, and knew that without divine help they had little chance of surviving the imminent attack. Her compassion and concern prompted her to call for the assistance of the gods even though she knew they were well into their long sleep, she wondered would Lord Shango answer.

Jahiri from his vantage point also surveyed the battle field. The forest warriors were preparing to attack and he hoped Jomo was ready to deal with them. He then walked among the western tribes listening to their stories and their fear of the evil they believed was being brought through their lands.

Sensing they were itching for a fight, he waited for the first warrior to move then materialised.

His appearance was so sudden he startled all those before him. It was an explosion of a most prismatic light, with colours emitting in all directions and its intensity sent them tumbling to the ground, many were temporarily blinded. Those who quickly recovered were met by the amazing image of a now visible Jahiri standing before them as a god. His golden armour glistening under the midday sun, and his cape fluttered wildly in the returned wind. He was armed, helmeted and shielded, ready for any attack.

From among the tribesmen a spear was fired but it never reached Jahiri. A bright light appeared, forming a magical shield diverting the spear away. This terrified the tribesmen who had never seen, or experienced, a vision such as what was now before them. They were unsure of what to do.

Jahiri didn't move. He waited until all warriors recovered before saying, "The evil you fear has been eliminated. I am Jahiri and of these lands. Look on me and see how we share the same ancestors. I am guardian to a Messenger of the Gods, and now I demand you rise up and follow my lead."

The tribesmen looked confused, they didn't understand how he was like them; all they saw was golden armour. Jahiri saw their confusion; he removed his helmet and immediately got a reaction. All knelt before him, they were in awe of his statuesque and striking appearance and acknowledged he was not that unlike them. They sensed his power especially when shards of brilliant coloured light shot out in all directions. They swore allegiance and vowed to follow his lead, just as prophesied by Jacob.

On the south side of the grasslands the forest tribes took the first tentative steps of their advance, and this was the cue for Jomo to take action. He raised his spear and sent it on its way. It travelled at first slowly then gathered speed. As its speed increased the flame came and ignited the shaft. It descended towards the warriors and travelled just above their heads causing them to fall before it. After reaching the furthest ranks it climbed higher before returning to Jomo, who yelled, "Warriors of the forest; look to me. I am Jomo, guardian to a Messenger of the Gods."

Like with Jahiri, shards of colourful light shot out from around him, not only from his armour but also from the tip of his spear. He held his spear high for all to witness his power. The tribes were in awe; they were forest dwellers and knew of ancient magic but never before saw it in action. Jomo rode down from the ridge and stood before them holding the spear high. He removed his helmet showing the tribes that he was just like them. "When this spear shows its flame and travels across the sky," he raised his spear higher. "You have a choice, follow, or fall before it. Make your choice." To the warriors this was a magic so powerful they knew they had to follow. Jahiri and Jomo now had control of the African tribes.

In the meantime Oba watched the approaching Egyptian army, and to her they looked ruthless and formidable. The sound of the chariots was so intimidating she feared the Yoruba's spirit would break. She watched the charioteers follow a typical attack strategy by driving the chariots at great speed into the forward ranks of the defenders using weapons that were the most lethal and advanced for the time.

She feared the Yoruba had no chance even with the assistance of the southern and western tribes. She felt being led by two well trained Olympus warriors was no guarantee of success; such was the reputation of the Egyptian army. She concluded there was no alternative but to again call on the gods for assistance.

The attack by the charioteers was indeed ruthless and without compassion. It penetrated the young defenders by employing their well rehearsed swarming tactics. The defenders were cut down without mercy and many were lost, but the survivors held their spirit and prepared for a second attack. When the second attack came the charioteers rode circles around the main defenders, showering them with arrows and then feigned a retreat. This gave the Yoruba breathing space to prepare many traps and plan ambushes. The older Yoruba used their experience to assist with reinforcing the defences by using any commandeered chariots as barricades, forcing the Egyptians to attack from the south side.

When that attack began the forest warriors led by Jomo were waiting, but they were at a disadvantage because behind the charioteers were legions of well trained foot soldiers, and it didn't take long for them to get the upper hand. The shields of the forest warriors were no match for the weaponry of Egypt.

Jomo surpassed himself in his efforts to assist but he was leading a now weakened force and this concerned him. He changed his strategy and targeted one of the Egyptian generals by sending the flaming spear and was shocked to see him just step aside and survive. He couldn't understand how this happened until he saw Jahiri sending out his Light which showed the general was, in fact, a disguised demon.

Jahiri moved the western tribes to the north of the Yoruba's and climbed the ridge above them. It was then when he saw a second army, comprising thousands more foot soldiers. He sent out his Light only to be bewildered by the amount of serpents and demons mingling among them. He gestured across to Jomo indicating they were in trouble, but they need not have feared. Oba succeeded in her efforts to contact the gods and Lord Shango dually answered. He announced his imminent arrival by sending a low almost inaudible rumble across the heavens. It was the kind of rumble normally ignored, but not this time. The rains were overdue and the tribes prayed for relief.

Shango sent a second rumble and this time the forest warriors sensed something unusual, the western tribes also felt the change in the air. For several moments all went quiet, then four bolts of lightning struck the ground igniting the grasslands and from among those bolts stepped a colossal figure who appeared to be a warrior god of immense stature.

Jomo was first to react and he rode at speed. Jahiri followed and when they reached the new arrival, they both dismounted, and to the surprise of the tribes, they bowed. Shango took his human form and moved to embrace them, which sent a message to all, showing these two warriors to be blessed by the gods.

The Yoruba people by now were traumatised. They had borne the brunt of the initial attacks and were finding it difficult to brace themselves for the next attack but couldn't take their eyes from the new arrival. With one eye they watched the advance of the Egyptians and with the other they watched what looked to them to be three immortals.

The people were intrigued when three elders and an oracle exited the protected area and walked towards the new arrival. On reaching him the oracle instinctively went to her knees bowed and said, "My Lord, Shango." The elders immediately went to their knees followed by the whole nation of the Yoruba. For them hope had arrived when they heard Shango say, "The gods listened and heard your prayers. I'm here to show you the way." The western and forest tribes also heard what was said.

Shango, Jomo and Jahiri made their way to the crest of a low lying hill and from there they assessed the strength of the Egyptian army. "I'm not happy." said Shango, "All we see is the charioteers, where are the foot soldiers? The Egyptians never show their full strength."

Jahiri replied pointing towards the northern ridge, "There's a second army, hiding behind that far ridge. I intend to return there and eliminate any serpent and Dark Angel I find."

Jomo left to join Oba. Shango retook his colossus form while Jahiri, as planned, went on an onslaught so vicious that by the time he finished, he left the Egyptian army almost leaderless. The few generals still standing assumed command and ordered their foot soldiers to attack Shango. At the same time they ordered the charioteers to recommence their attack on the Yoruba.

When Jahiri was satisfied he dispatched all agents of Hell he summoned his mount and made his way to retake control of the western tribes. Oba insisted Jomo rejoin the forest tribes while she remained safe on the outcrop to observe the battle unfold. Shango stood alone. He crossed his arms defiantly and watched the charioteers approach. He then observed them split to form two columns, one making its way to attack the Yoruba from the east and the other from the northwest. From behind the charioteers thousands of foot soldiers formed into battalions, each comprising two hundred well trained men.

From Oba's vantage point she counted fifty battalions and they were splitting. Ten battalions took up positions along the nearest ridge and when signalled, began moving towards Shango. The remaining forty battalions split and in groups of twenty followed the charioteers into battle.

Shango telepathically reached Jomo and Jahiri instructing them to do nothing until he signals, not realising Jomo and Jahiri were ahead of him. They had moved their elite fighters into an advance position. These were the warriors with the strength and stamina to sprint while carrying the heaviest shields in one hand, and a forward facing spear in the other. They planned using these warriors to assist the Yoruba fighters against the chariot onslaught, and the remaining warriors to attack the side and rear flanks of the foot soldiers. They waited for Shango's signal.

The arrogance of the remaining Egyptian commanders knew no bounds; it blinded them to what they were dealing with. They had no idea a god, let alone the African God of Thunder, was before them.

Shango waited. He stood there as a twenty foot high giant. His waist to foot, brilliant red skirt flapped in the gathering wind. His iron war-crown glistened under the sun. He held his axe at the ready while continuously monitoring the movements of the charioteers. When they got too close he unleashed continuous bolts of lightning before bringing on rumbles of extremely loud thunder. This was followed by torrential rain, instantly turning the grasslands into a quagmire preventing the charioteers from getting any closer to the Yoruba. This was his signal for Jomo and Jahiri to make their move. Jomo raised his spear allowing the flames to leap high, a signal for the forest tribes to advance. In the west, Jahiris army was already on the move.

The Egyptians were undaunted by the numerical superiority of the tribes. The dismounted charioteers joined the foot soldiers and together they quickly formed unbroken lines around the Yoruba defenders, and a second defence line facing the advancing tribesmen. The order was given and the pounding of shields began, so did the attack. The Egyptian outer lines moved towards the tribes and the inner line targeted the barricades.

"Only in the great stories did I know of shield pounding," said Jomo, talking with a warrior chief. "The noise of war is so deafening, it feels like a great weight resting on my chest, crushing my heart. Right now it scrapes my bones and is wrenching every organ in my body, even my head. It feels like a parasite gnawing its way beneath my skin."

Jomo moved into position ahead of the forest tribes. He spread them in an arc from the northeast to the south and had his elite warriors within striking distance of the advancing Egyptians. Jahiri was at the head of the western tribes. His elites were already engaged with the northern ranks of the enemy.

The Egyptians drew first blood. They were better trained in the use of swords and bows. Their shields provided almost full body protection and were made from toughened ox-hide, stretched on wooden frames making them very light, yet strong enough to repel travelling arrows and spears. They were adept at slaughtering any adversary. They attacked on all fronts and took no prisoners. They systematically sliced their way through the ranks of the tribes leaving an untold amount of decapitated bodies behind. There was no compassion, no mercy. It was a ruthless frenzy of violence with no escape. All semblance of humanity was gone, each soldier fought like a beast with only one focus - to kill. Death was everywhere; it was in the soil, in the wind, but most of all it was in their eyes. They knew they were winning but what they didn't know was - the more warriors they killed the more that arrived to fight alongside Jomo and Jahiri.

The tribes fought valiantly and their bravery was boundless. Every warrior strove desperately to break through the attacking Egyptians. When those in the front ranks fell, their bodies helped raise higher those who came from behind and when they fell, and the pile of bodies grew even higher, the mound was used as a vantage-point for firing spears targeting their enemy's commanders.

In the ensuing melee the Egyptian lines weakened then broke allowing the tribes through to rescue the Yoruba defenders, who were now involved in hand-to-hand combat. The tide had turned and the tribes now had the advantage. They used their numerically superior power to put the Egyptians on the run. The Egyptians were now in trouble and they knew it. They were completely surrounded with nowhere to hide. Many tried to flee and were ruthlessly struck down. Those still fighting soon realised all was lost, they threw away their bows and quivers, discarded their swords, hatchets, spears and other weapons.

When the fighting fully ceased, thousands of dead and wounded covered the battlefield. In some places, tribesmen were forced to walk ankle-deep through puddles of blood slowly congealing in the quagmire. All around the grasslands of slaughter was the distressing sight of the dead. And the sound of the dying, wailing in pain and suffering shattered arms, legs and thighs. This grated on the survivor's nerves.

In the meantime the ten battalions of foot soldiers got closer to Shango and, in large volleys, they released their arrows. Shango wasn't fazed. He used a continuous flow of lightning, building an impregnable wall of light to protect himself. It was a shield so bright; blindness became a friend of the soldiers near the front. Those soldiers had no chance, Shango's temper rose. He extracted a lightning rod from beneath his skirt, and used its power to slice through those who had been blinded, and any soldier that came too close.

From the rear ranks more volleys were launched and as each arrow hit the shield they were shattered, unable to do any damage. Shango's temper had reached boiling point and he decided to unleash the power of an angry god. He lowered his axe and raised both hands. He parted his fingers and from each finger he sent shards of light targeting knees, groins, arms and anywhere else that caused maximum pain. He showed no mercy, every soldier who fell was left writhing in agony before being finally put out of their misery when a final bolt of forked lightning appeared, and penetrated each of their hearts. Of the ten thousand soldiers who attacked that day, no more than three thousand were still standing, forcing them to surrender.

Oba's face showed her disgust at the ruthlessness of Shango. The rising white mists showed there were many soldiers worth passing the message too. She believed they could have been saved. Shango sensed her unhappiness and called her to join him, "I know you are hurting but I had no choice, look at what they did to the warriors. They never would have stopped. You were wise to call me, fighting an army led by Hells demons is unwinnable without the power of the gods. Today you have fulfilled the prophecy Ra-Atum."

"Did you not see the white mist?" cried an unconvinced Oba, "I saw it, there were many. Apart from that," she continued, "my visions show the End Times battle, and what happens there is much worse. That's what worries me."

Oba left Shango and walked among the surviving Egyptian soldiers. She passed the message to many and was pleased to see them change.

Out in the grasslands the bodies of the fallen were gathered and treated according to their tribal traditions. Later that night Shango, Oba, Jomo and Jahiri met and talked about all that had happened since they left Olympus. The tribes, when the funeral ceremonies ended, came together for a celebration of music and dance that lasted throughout the night.

The following morning a delegation of elders and oracles arrived requesting a meeting, which was granted. During the meeting they sought advice about what to do with the captured Egyptian soldiers who were now their prisoners. One elder suggested taking the soldiers as slaves to assist in the rebuilding of their homeland; another suggested executing them in retribution for the losses suffered and the third suggested freeing them, allowing them to take their chances in the desert.

Shango said nothing but Jomo did, "Slavery is wrong. Killing them is wrong. Sending them to die in the desert is wrong. How can you think like that after all you've been through?"

Oba materialised and was furious with what she heard, she raged, "Yesterday I walked among your people and gave many of them a message, a very important message. Trust me; the gods will not be happy with any of those options." She raised her hand when one of the oracles attempted to interrupt, "I must insist you release the prisoners and assist them home by providing enough food and water. Make sure there is transport for the sick and injured. Only then should you prepare to continue towards your homeland." There was no further discussion and the following morning arrangements were made to send the Egyptians home. They were assisted by the western tribes who promised to provide protection. In the meantime the forest tribes returned south.

Shango agreed to assist the Yoruba peoples during the final part of their journey but before he left he called Oba aside, "Don't judge me too harshly, war can be ruthless. Think instead of what you achieved over the last three hundred years. Look at my people. Your message has brought them the Light. Did you not see the Egyptians or the western tribes? Did you not see how your Light is now carried safely among them? Today I give you a prophecy of my own, 'Your message will travel among the forest tribes for the next twenty years before you reach the Mountains of the Moon. Near there you will bear witness to the last days of the fourteen hundred year rule of the Kingdom of Kush.' Be safe, Oba. Jacob chose you well."

Chapter 8

After spending twenty years passing the message to the forest tribes, and others encountered along the way, Oba, Jomo and Jahiri finally reached the great White Nile, and with the help of local fishermen they managed to safely cross. They reached the holy mountain of Gebel Barkal and there they met with three senior gods of the African pantheon, one was the goddess Isis whom they last met in Olympus.

Oba was a short distance ahead and was first to greet Isis. Jahiri, out of earshot, nudged Jomo while staring at the other two gods, "Who is she?" he asked.

"I've no idea, but she is more beautiful than Aphrodite," replied Jomo.

Isis introduced the two gods, starting with the goddess to her right, "Meet the lady Hathor, she's of these lands and is the Goddess of Love and fertility."

Jahiri couldn't help himself; he lowered his head, whispered to Jomo, "I bet she is." Oba wasn't impressed.

Hathor stood before them as a most beautiful goddess, wearing a straight, full length gown held in place by the thinnest of shoulder straps. The gown was black with green and blue wide threads woven into the pleats draping from her hips. On her head she wore her iconic headdress - a golden sun disk framed by cow horns, decorated with stunning enamel and exquisite gold inlays.

Taking Oba's hand she said, "Welcome, travellers from Olympus, welcome to our domain."

Next to greet them was Apedemak; the lion headed God of Africa. To Jomo and Jahiri he looked impressive. He was tall and muscular, wearing the traditional white linen wraparound kilt of an east African God. Unusually he was winged, not that unlike the Arch Angels who appeared in Olympus. In his hand he held a gem encrusted sceptre. Upon his head he wore a Hemhem crown set on top of two spiral rams horns. Each side bore the images of Egyptian cobras. In the centre were reeds camouflaged by black and white ostrich feathers and attached to the reeds were three golden sun disks. By his side sat a young lioness.

From the holy mountain they viewed the ancient city of Napata and its many temples, built in honour of the various gods who were present. The largest by far was the Temple of Amon-Ra where, without fail, the priests conducted daily religious ceremonies in his honour.

When the ceremonies ended, the priests left giving the gods the opportunity to visit the temple. Isis used her powers to open the main doors and just as they were about to pass through, they turned and looked towards the Nile, which was a good distance away. Apedemak remarked, "It never fails to amaze me when I look down on this vast colonnade of stone rams, so meticulously painted in such vivid colours, it is a wonder."

Oba was more amazed at what met her when she entered the temple. It wasn't as vast as that of Zeus, but like Olympus it had statues depicting not only the eight ancient African gods; it also had images of powerful gods from all across Africa. Unlike Olympus the images of the gods of Africa were highly decorated and full of colour. On the floors were the skins of many iconic animals, and seeing this caused great distress for Jahiri who refused to countenance walking over them: Isis noted his distress, "These skins were gifted to the temple by devotees, and I'm assured there was no suffering; they were taken from those whose deaths were natural." Jahiri still refused to walk upon them.

All enjoyed the hospitality and used the time to share many stories. Oba told Isis of her meeting with the goddess Afri and how she spoke so highly of her. She also spoke of Afri's grief and sadness when foretelling the end of the African pantheon especially with the arrival of a new religion that was less than three hundred years away.

Jahiri expressed his concerns for the natural world; he spoke of visions showing how man will use many species as his playthings, "It was bad enough during the games in Rome," he said, inching further away from a nearby lion rug. "It'll get much worse, and many species will become extinct. All because of greed and something man likes to call sport. The worst thing is; they do it because they just can."

Apedemak responded, "My visions are similar except they show extinction events especially near the battle of the End Times. What saddens me the most is many of these animals are my guardians and my friends."

Hathor showed she too was upset, "It brings on a great sadness when I see I'm no longer revered in these lands. I too can see the end of the African pantheon." A tear was seen to fall.

"We all know why we're here," Hathor said after composing herself. "We're about to witness the end of a most amazing era, the end of the great Kingdom of Kush. Its name will be removed from all memory but in the distant future people will begin to wonder and ask questions, codices will be found and Kush will again be remembered."

She turned to Oba, "Speak fondly of the story I'm about to tell."

Jahiri interrupted, "I too will remember."

Hathor began, "Time is a strange thing; it's when the mists rise when all is forgotten. Many thousands of years have passed since, in these very lands, there was once the Garden of Eden. From there came the oldest race of people on earth, here we stand in the Kingdom of Kush," she pointed towards the city, "for centuries all were happy because the two great rivers flowed slowly before gathering together in force to flood the plains down river. This allowed the Kushite's to provide harvested food, enabling their empire to grow. They established their first capital near here before moving it to the royal city of Meroe. It was in this city where the cult of Amon-Ra, our King of Kings was at its strongest, allowing it to become the custodians of Egyptian culture and religion. Trade routes were opened to the far west, to the red sea, north to the Mediterranean and east towards Indus."

Apedemak then continued with the story, "Kush became extremely wealthy, they mastered the art of iron works and weaponry, they supplied gold, silver and ivory, all prized in Greece and Rome. Because of this they found themselves targeted by the surrounding tribes who dwelled on the mountains, in the deserts and to their south. Time and time again the tribes formed alliances and attacked, but they were always repelled as Kush had the strongest armies. The Kushite's bred a horse, and over time this horse became a large and resilient War Horse. Their archers became known as the 'Bowmen of Nubia'. They developed the Sudanic quilted armour enabling them to withstand any onslaught of poisoned arrows. Kushite kings always wore Egyptian style armour and used Egyptian weapons bringing terror to any adversary. At times they succumbed, but their political skills allowed them assimilate their attackers. This ensured they grew into a powerful expanded Kushite state. In truth history will recognise them to be the only true African empire and civilization ever to have existed."

Isis then spoke, "It pains me to say that tomorrow we will travel to Meroe to wait for the fall of Kush." She turned to Oba, "Remember Magni's words, 'Modi will call on the Kingdom of Kush'."

Just after dawn all six travelled together to take up residence in a large temple which was north of Meroe. From there they had a panoramic view of the city and all its approaches. Oba left to walk alone through its streets and alleyways where she targeted the very young. Touching their shoulders she always said the same thing, "Go now, tell your children to tell their children's children for all time, that one day, they will be called upon by the gods and they must answer." The children always ceased what they were doing and rubbed their shoulders. She was pleased to see many of them encourage their families to leave and migrate north. For over eighteen years she walked through the city only stopping when she realised there was no more to be done.

The city was now in political and economic decline, unrest manifesting itself everywhere. Residents suffered from food shortages caused by the over use of the once very fertile lands, and as the years passed the desert began to make itself felt, leading to the desertification of the Meroe area. This was the final straw for the city and its decline was now complete, allowing for a successful invasion by the Kingdom of Aksum.

Oba returned to a hillock, close to the main gate into the city. From there she watched the invading army approach. It was led by, Azana of Axum, their King of Kings. He was a descendant of Menelik 1, son of the legendary King Solomon and the Queen of Sheba. He became known as Azana the Conqueror, one of the most powerful warrior kings of all time. He was the first African leader to declare for Christianity, bringing his whole Kingdom with him. In his short reign he achieved many things, none more so than improving the fortunes of Meroe by reopening the trade routes to Egypt, Greece and Rome.

Oba watched the army enter the city and was pleased not to be watching a slaughter or an enslavement of the citizens. When Azana passed she was taken aback at how majestic he looked. His brilliant white robes where offset by his golden gem-encrusted crown and he was protected by an equally ornate shield.

Oba resolved to meet with Azana and when she reached his encampment, she entered his tent and materialised before him. His initial reaction was one of fear and when he calmed, he asked, "Are you an angel?" to which she replied, "No, I am Oba and I have come here to give you a prophecy."

She sat opposite him, "Your time, King Azana, will soon come to an end. You will be succeeded by your brother, your twin, Se-Azana and it is his descendants who will be the kings of this great realm. They will be the guardians of the treasures of Christendom. The Ark of the Covenant and what will become known as the lost Gospels will be under their protection. In an age, not too far from now, his descendants will provide shelter in a time of need to one who will become known as the Prophet Mohammad, and because of this kindness the Kingdom of Aksum will survive until 1974CE. It is then when the last Emperor, Haile Selassie, will pass into history."

Azana asked why she came to him and she replied, "You will always be remembered as a just king, your legacy is secure. Tell your brother of me; ensure he passes my message to his descendants. One day they will be called upon to assist a powerful god." She then returned to invisibility and rejoined Jomo and Jahiri.

Chapter 9

The journey towards the Land of Punt was uneventful. Many areas were peaceful, with friendly tribes who, after witnessing the flaming spear, swore their allegiance to Jomo. Other tribes, when seeing the striking appearance of Jahiri, knelt before him and also swore allegiance.

On reaching Punt, Oba not only used her time to pass on the message. She used her powers as the River Goddess to assist by opening wells, and staving off the thirst among those same tribes.

In Punt Jahiri changed, he became restless and didn't understand what was troubling him. His visions were no longer negative. There were nightly dreams showing him an oasis surrounded by jaw-dropping sunsets, sometimes beautiful sunrises. Each dream had the same ending, feet, legs, his hand moving up that leg, then nothing. Every morning, he woke breathless and feeling uncomfortable.

Being first awake he always volunteered to emit the Light only to report no sightings of serpents. As the weeks, then months passed he travelled deeper into the bush, taking longer and longer to complete his tasks. When day trips turned to overnights Jomo became concerned and decided to investigate, only to be taken aback when he stumbled upon Jahiri in a very passionate embrace with a beautiful Samalle woman. He discretely withdrew and returned to their encampment never to mention to Oba what he had seen, even though he knew she too was aware of how Jahiri had changed.

After several years the time to move on arrived and just before departure Jomo noticed how distressed Jahiri became and suggested, "Go to the oasis and send out your light one last time. Make sure the tribes understand and are safe." Jahiri wondered, 'Does he know?' but didn't ask. Three hours later he returned and seemed more relaxed. Oba said as she greeted him, "The trumpeting of elephants is louder, they're calling us to 'Gods resting place.' We need to leave now."

The journey took them into the Great Rift Valley where they spent many years crisscrossing from north to south and east to west. They passed numerous fresh water lakes, walked across grassy plains, struggled through treacherous swamps and experienced hot springs with violent geysers. Their journey brought them in contact with many tribes especially the Maasai, the very tribe Jahiri wanted to meet. His family lore told him his ancestors were of this tribe.

On reaching the foothills of an extinct volcano, Oba said, "Ah, Finally. Kirimara or, as our friends the Maasai call it, 'Gods resting place'."

On climbing higher they walked through the scrublands into the woodlands before reaching the tropical forests circling the mountain. Climbing up they observed elephant herds arriving from all directions, gathering near the tree line.

"Listen, not a sound," said Jomo. "They are so big, yet not a sound!"

"Something momentous is happening," said Oba. "We should show respect. Materialise." They materialised.

"Listen," whispered Jahiri. "A faint rustling in the undergrowth, do you hear it?"

Two enormous bull elephants emerged, each carrying tusks, so large they were within touching distance of the forest floor. They were two of the four elderly tuskers tasked with the protection of the old one. They parted and allowed Oba, Jomo and Jahiri to continue to a clearing where they were met with a most astounding sight. Before them was the elephant known as the old one. He was almost sixty years old and his tusks were so long, they reached the ground forming two shallow grooves as he walked. He was magnificent and was known throughout the animal Kingdom as 'Emperor of the Tuskers'.

Oba approached and when she bowed he placed his trunk on her shoulder saying, "Welcome to the realm of the Tuskers, emissaries of Olympus."

Oba responded, "My lord, The Darkness travels the universe and has many allies. The gods of Olympus are assembling an army, they need the wisdom, your wisdom, gathered since the beginning of time to be passed to your descendants so they will know what to do when the time comes."

The emperor acknowledged her request then said, "Strange how you come to us this day, my last day. Join me on a walk."

As they left the clearing and entered the forest, they were surprised how such a large beast walked without making a sound. When they reached the grasslands, they were escorted by thousands more elephants.

They finally reached a narrow pass leading into a well camouflaged valley where all around them rested the sun-bleached skeletal remains of tuskers dating back to the creation. They were resting in the mythical elephant necropolis.

"I have seen the future of my species and it's not good," said the emperor. "There will be a slaughter. I see our heads as trophies and our tusks as ornaments. Why is Olympus so interested in saving the third age of man? How can a herd as vast as the one now gathered be so threatened in the future?"

"Jacob is my friend and I trust him," said Oba, "he lived among man and knows many are worth saving. Our journey will find those who will become guardians of the natural world but it'll be a difficult road for them. I know they will prevail."

The Emperor continued his walk to the far side of the valley where he found a comfortable spot and lay down to prepare for his long sleep. With his last few breaths he said, "Rest among my guardians for as long as you need, befriend four and when ready, they will be your escorts into the deepest south. Oh, my descendants know what to do; they will answer the call of the gods."

His breathing was now shallow but he was resisting passing, he was worried. Oba whispered in his ear, "Rest peacefully. The future I showed is but one path and sadly it is the most likely, but it also shows there is hope. Near the battle of the End Times there will still be twenty five known tuskers, eighteen bulls and seven cows. The guardians I spoke about will come to their rescue and will succeed. As a result of their efforts the four hundred young tuskers who still exist will have teachers among the remaining old ones. The ways of the tuskers will be saved." The Emperor smiled and then passed away. For the rest of that day the vast herds raised their trunks and sent out the most mournful call, a call heard all across the heavens.

For many years Oba, Jomo and Jahiri remained among the tuskers. It was a happy time and never once did they feel threatened. All this was to change when Oba received visions of a dormant three-coned volcano. Jahiri also received a vision, his showed a battle, and it was vicious. It was time to move on.

With four Tusker escorts they travelled towards the Serengeti grasslands and from there they had a clear view of the three coned volcano as seen in Oba's vision. The highest cone, known as Kibo, stood majestically above the other two, its snow-capped summit glistened like a beacon and it was guiding them. They reached its foothills and with the help of their four escorts they made their way through the dense undergrowth of the rain forest. On exiting the forest they reached an area covered in scrub and lichen, with sparse tree growth

Oba froze, she sensed an evil presence. The four tuskers became irritated; they also felt a presence and it manifested itself as a low rumbling tremor. Oba turned in panic, "This Mountain no longer sleeps; we should return to the forest." It was too late; Jomo and Jahiri were now on alert and had reached for their armour.

Jahiri raised his staff to call on the Light but found no signs of serpents yet the sense of evil was all around them. Jomo tried and he too failed. They both feared Hell had yet again evolved and releasing serpents invisible to the Light.

Jahiri suggested, "Let's not panic. Thank the gods it's a clear day." He turned to the nearest tusker and asked to be raised above the tree line. The tusker obliged by raising himself on his hind legs and using the strength of his trunk he hoisted Jahiri high above the canopy. From this new vantage point Jahiri saw up the mountain towards the highest cone. There he saw an orange glow emitting from a crack near the summit, and this troubled him.

The forest quietened, not a sound, the mountain became sinister causing the tuskers to get more alarmed and they began trumpeting their fear. On the foothills and across the plains, herds of elephants began racing to their aid. They too felt the tremors and got more agitated as time passed. They formed protective groups around the mountain.

The orange glow grew brighter and pulsated, causing part of the ridge on the south western face of the cone to break away revealing a large semicircular cave. From that cave, dark figures emerged and were seen to be ushering serpents out into the now twilight, and there were so many, they just kept coming.

The four tuskers rushed to protect Oba but they had no defence against the serpent onslaught that followed. Suddenly one fell; it seemed the serpents knew how to target giants of the forest and relished the destruction of such powerful beasts. The remaining three tuskers found themselves in a battle for their lives and soon all three fell. As the serpents attacked, Jomo and Jahiri did their best to eliminate as many as possible.

So many serpents fell, the remaining serpents worked out that there were invisible guardians about prompting some to retreat back to the cave and report their suspicions.

Four Dark Angels responded and arrived at the battle site, it was obvious they were different; they had the power to see through Jomo and Jahiri's invisibility but not Oba's. This was an unexpected situation. Jomo and Jahiri knew Hell would evolve over time, and trusted their training prepared them for all eventualities so showed no fear.

All around them many more serpents had arrived, some were searching behind every rock, crack and crevice, obviously looking for Oba. The others were ready to join in the attack.

"What a pleasure," said one of the Dark Angels. "To think our search for the messengers started nine hundred years ago, and now we find you as a gift before a gate to Hell, this day cannot get better!"

Jahiri's heart actually missed a beat and no matter how hard he tried he was obviously in shock; he thought a mere few months had passed since the Land of Punt. He had trouble composing himself, but he did. The Dark Angel continued, "We cannot see the messenger but we know she's here. Trust us, we'll find her and feed her to the Hounds of Hell."

Just then a large herd of elephants arrived; they were answering the dying calls of the tuskers. They achieved a silent and brisk climb taking the remaining serpents by surprise. On reaching where the serpents had gathered

174

they trampled many before continuing their onslaught until every last one was destroyed. When sure their work was done they surrounded the Dark Angels allowing Jomo and Jahiri to commence their attack.

The attack began and Jomo took the lead. He secured one of the Dark Angels in a headlock using him as a lever to jump, and by manoeuvring both his legs; he grabbed the second Dark Angel. This allowed Jahiri to step in and decapitate both.

The two remaining Angels immediately retreated, they used their powers and managed to escape back to the cave with Jahiri and Jomo in hot pursuit, but the cave was sealed as soon as the angels passed through. There was no more to be done so Jomo and Jahiri returned to rejoin Oba.

Descending the mountain Jahiri wondered aloud, "That Dark Angel. He said something that's bothering me; he said they were searching for us for nine hundred years! Jomo, I feel sick, how can this be?"

Jomo shrugged his shoulders, "I gave up questioning the magic of Time years ago. What's on your mind?"

"It's bothering me because......." Jahiri said no more. After a few moments Jomo asked,

"Do you not think it's time you told me?"

Jahiri reacted, "What do you mean? What are you talking about?"

Jomo thought for a moment, "Obviously you are not ready to talk." Jahiri just stared and wondered.

The following morning thousands of elephants, both young and old, silently walked up the mountain. As they passed, each one touched and caressed the fallen Tuskers; then departed. Many months later they returned to lift the sun-bleached bones and carry them back to rest among their ancestors.

Chapter 10

After the herds left, Oba insisted they begin the final part of their journey and seek out the ancestors of the Zulu nation. For almost a hundred years they crisscrossed the southern regions of the Rift Valley. When with the elephants they learned how to communicate with many from within the animal kingdom and this ability was their greatest asset as they travelled through the land of the thousand hills especially when they met with the Mountain Gorillas.

During their journey they crossed arid savannahs, wetlands and marches. They penetrated dense tropical rain forests only to be besotted when they saw the beauty of the lands called, The Pearl of Africa. They zigzagged north to south, east to west, all the time passing the message to the many tribes they met. The only time they felt threatened was when backtracking towards the Mountains of the Moon, the sight of volcanic cones alerted them to the possibility of encountering serpents.

They rested for a further hundred years on the shores of Lake Nyanza, the world's largest tropical lake. It was near there while passing the message to many of the Bantu tribes when they realised these tribes were in fact, the ancestors of the Zulu nation. A further one hundred years passed and those years were also uneventful.

One morning while swimming they were interrupted by the appearance of a young boy, no more than ten years old. This boy had the ability to see them and the sight of three ghost-like figures terrified him. His eyes opened wide and shone like pebbles washed by the lakes waves. His brow creased betraying his tense face. Occasionally his eyes glanced at a nearby bank of rocks looking for somewhere dark to hide, somewhere that felt safe. He backed away but his knees betrayed him, he wobbled to and fro, before impacting the ground. He couldn't speak, for him there were no words in Bantu to describe such a vision.

Oba rushed to reassure him. She placed her hand on his shoulder and encouraged him to relax. When he relaxed he asked, "What are you? Why are you here?"

"We are Messengers of the Gods," said Oba. "We are here to find the Zulu. I need look no further, when I touched your shoulder I realized we have found them."

"What do you mean?" pleaded the boy.

"I know who you are," said Oba. "You are Shakaone, you are the first. From you will come the greatest warriors, one will be Shaka, he will be the most powerful and he will become the greatest King of the Zulu," she opened a portal and invited Shakaone to view the future of his descendants. "Look across the hills, thousands of warriors, all in battle dress. Their plumes stand high, their spears sharpened and their battle shields at the ready. See the one who stands alone, look upon the face of Shaka, a descendant of yours. See him grow to be a great warrior who will earn the support of many chieftains. He will quickly rise to lead the Zulus to victory in many campaigns, creating the greatest nation in the southern lands. He will become King of all the Zulu and will bring a wealth unheard of, but his reign will not last because madness is his destiny. He will be supplanted by his brother who will try to erase his memory but he will fail. From among his great nation will be born the carriers, and they are the ones who will be called upon by the gods: Shaka will forever be remembered as the creator of that nation." She stood back and watched the Light arrive to surround the boy before passing the message to him.

Shakaone returned to his village escorted by Oba and Jomo and when there, Oba used her time to pass the message to the villagers. When done she felt a sudden tiredness. She felt it was time to find their place of rest but had no idea where that place was, her instinct told her it lay somewhere to the north.

On rejoining Jahiri, she said, "It's been well over twelve hundred years since we left Olympus and the journey was taking a toll. I'm so tired. We have more to do - we must find our resting place."

✿

Resting by the lake Oba noticed something strange flying high in the northern sky. Jahiri and Jomo also noticed. There was no threat but they prepared for one anyway. The strange sight was a giant bird and it was flying towards them. When it landed it stood over seven feet tall. It was Garuda and he was quite emotional. He said running to embrace Oba, "You look amazing for someone who is nine hundred years old. You haven't aged a bit."

She was confused, "Garuda, twelve hundred years have passed."

They both felt a presence; it was Jacob, "My friends, you are immortals and Time should mean nothing to you, it has moved slower for some and faster for others. It will realign near the End Times."

Oba continued to hold Garuda much to the ire of Jomo; that was until Garuda turned towards them and they saw who he was. They ran at him with such speed they sent him tumbling to the ground and when their excitement waned, Garuda said, "I too am excited and can feel the tears well up but this is a fleeting visit. There is a new magic and Mulan is in danger." He paused then asked, "On your travels, have you ever heard mention of 'The Phoenix'?"

"Yes, we did," said Jomo. "In Heliopolis, the city of the sun, there were images engraved on the temple walls showing the rising of an immortal bird called The Phoenix. Go there and meet with Ra-Atum, he is a Sun God and will help."

Jahiri warned, "Be aware, he was near leaving and that was over a thousand years ago, it's possible he may have left."

"Fear not," said Oba. "The temple may be gone and the library burned but he will know how much he is needed and will have waited. Go now and seek The Phoenix." She went silent as though in a trance then whispered, "I see them and you are right, Mulan and Girish are in great danger, many monks have fallen. I see the Wraiths and they are near; you must hurry."

Garuda quickly took to the sky and circled several times before swooping one last time. He yelled, "Be safe!"

Chapter 11

For some time all Oba, Jomo and Jahiri spoke about was meeting Garuda after so long. They were happy to hear that he; Mulan and Girish were still travelling and hadn't succumbed to either the forces of Hell or to The Darkness. When all memories of his fleeting visit were exhausted they decided to begin their journey north to the Land of Punt, to an area close to the elephant graveyard and soon they were on their way.

It was a carefree journey with little or no interaction between them and the villagers they met along the way. Oba was now free to show her feelings and used every opportunity to attract Jomo's attention, not realising that he too, centuries earlier, had developed feelings for her but hadn't an idea how to show them. Although now a powerful African god, Jomo was still as shy as he was when he left Olympus all those years ago. When it came to affairs of the heart he had great difficulty expressing his feelings. Even trying to broach the subject with Jahiri didn't help, so he chose to say nothing.

Oba was determined to get his attention but didn't want to seem too interested. She followed him on his trips in search of serpents. She watched his every move especially when stripping to swim in any lake or river he came across. She knew he was now a powerful god with all the powers required for his protection but still she should have known better. His powers ensured he was always aware of being followed, and anytime he sensed her presence his confidence grew. He teased her by deliberately choosing the same flat surfaced rock near his favourite river to strip naked, sunbathe while gently massaging his legs and chest. He kept teasing until she began to suspect he was leading her on. She finally lost patience and changed tactics.

One particular day she followed him until he entered a nearby forest. She made herself known, and then walked in a different direction. Jomo's curiosity grew and he decided to follow her just in case anything untoward was to happen. When he reached where she was, he hid behind a fallen tree and watched her stand on the bank of a clear and slow flowing river. She knew he was watching and called him to join her, he didn't. She called him again and when there was no response she moved her plan to the next level. She seductively disrobed before sauntering slowly into the water.

She hummed softly and gently rubbed the clear water over her body. His mouth dropped and those stirrings he always felt when thinking of her became potent, he gasped for breath, his shyness and inexperience no longer an issue. The stirrings were taking control and encouraging him to join her. When he reached the bank of the river she coyly looked up. "Well," she whispered, "What are you waiting for?" Finally, he seemed to know what to do.

He briskly removed his calfskin skirt to reveal the body of a god, all chiselled, toned and ripped. He moved cautiously towards her, slowly placing one foot ahead of the other for fear of stepping on any sharp pebble. He never took his eyes from her stunning and perfect body, "Hey, big boy," she said with one of her disarming smiles, "my eyes are up here."

He giggled, "I've seen your eyes everyday for a thousand years and they always drew me in. Today, it's time I saw everything else."

His guard was down while staring into her eyes and he wasn't watching where he was walking. He tripped on a moss covered rock, fell forward, plunging both of them under the water with him lying upon her. When they came to the surface again, he said, "I didn't think I was in this much of a hurry."

"Ha! This much of a hurry?" She laughed and placed her finger across his lips, "I've waited a thousand years; I'd hate to be in a real hurry."

He smiled, "Can't believe I fed you that line."

Moving their heads closer they softly kissed for the first time. Their tongues explored each other's mouth causing a series of cascading sensations to race through their bodies. A thousand years of pent-up passion was about to be released and when he held her closer he found he was in total control as they became one. At that very moment, touching each other electrified their bodies and gave them something words couldn't describe. It wasn't just lust, it was pure love. Their bodies already had become one and now their minds were melding, taking them to places they never dreamt existed.

They left the water and lay facing each other, touching and caressing until the need to start all over again arrived, and when it did, Oba said, "I think it's my turn to take control," she gently placed him on his back and said while straddling him, "be a good boy and move your arms above your head." He nervously obliged then closed his eyes. She bent forward and kissed his chest, then his neck, followed by his ear and then his lips. "I'm going to drive you crazy," she whispered as she slowly slid along his legs. "I'll tempt you by pausing and leaving you wondering, tease you until you reach a point where you will beg me to take your breath away. I mightn't stop, I might keep going until your mind and body can take no more."

"Trust me lady," he said, "I can take anything you throw at me. Do you worst, I've been thinking about this for a thousand years."

Her slow yet deliberate gyrating along his legs moved higher until she reached his special place. Nothing he thought of for the longest time prepared him for what happened next. She rose and fell, occasionally leaning forward to kiss his now parted lips. Each time she tensed, his muscles tightened and his back arched, he wanted every ounce of pleasure she could give and he was certainly getting it. Once again they were in bliss before falling into a loving embrace, then starting all over again.

Day after day they went to the same spot near the river and never tired of each other. They were now so madly in love, they were totally inseparable. At night they lay together not considering that Jahiri was always alone.

Some weeks later Oba began to change. She felt strange and didn't go to the river as often. Although feeling sick her concern about Jahiri grew when his light patrols took longer, sometimes taking all day. She decided to follow him and was shocked to find him sitting on a high cliff overlooking a bend in the river. His head was resting on his knees and he looked distressed. Oba approached and placed her arms around him but said nothing, knowing that if he wanted to talk it would be on his terms. Eventually he said, "It's not what you think."

She responded "What do I think?"

After a few moments he said, "You think I'm jealous of the love between you and Jomo. I'm not, I'm really happy for you."

She pulled him closer, "Jahiri, I never thought you were jealous but we were wrong to show our affection when you were present. This still doesn't explain what's upsetting you."

Neither noticed Jomo had arrived and heard some of what was said. "It's time you knew something," he said after sitting alongside Jahiri, "I saw you with a beautiful girl when we passed through the Land of Punt, it must be over a thousand years since that day. I saw how you and she had gotten so close you became one. Why didn't you talk about her? Tell us, is she what's troubling you?" Jahiri just nodded then struggled again. Jomo held him a little closer hoping the sadness would pass.

184

"Her, her name...," he mumbled. "Her name was Jamilah, it means 'beautiful' and she was beautiful. I knew my duty was to protect Oba but my heart was trying to get me to do something else. I always planned to go back for her but Time deceived me. When the Dark Angel said 'nine hundred years' I realised she would be long gone and now I'm broken."

He turned to Oba, "I loved her more than life itself. She made me feel complete. She made me smile and made me the happiest man alive. Oba, why have the gods done this to me?"

There was nothing anybody could say so they remained quiet. They sat for some time until Oba needed to move. She stood; then retched, before running behind a boulder, "How can this be your fourth day of illness?" yelled Jomo, "You're an immortal! You're not supposed to get ill."

Jahiri slapped him across the back of the head. "What the ....," yelped Jomo. "What was that for?"

"You're so slow, a thick idiot! Haven't you noticed?" snapped Jahiri.

Jomo rubbed his head, "Eh, no!" He was annoyed at the smirk on Jahiri's face. It took a few more moments before he began to understand. He jumped to his feet and ran behind the boulder. When he reached Oba he gently turned her to face him and for the first time he saw the slight bump. He was ecstatic, so much so, he lifted her and swung her around in the only way he could express his absolute happiness. He put her down and ran back to Jahiri, lifted him so high, forgetting his strength and nearly crushing him.

"I'm happy for you," gasped Jahiri. "Do you think you can put me down, you're squeezing my life from me?"

That night it was Jahiri's turn to go on a Light patrol and he soon confirmed there were no serpents about so they retired early but didn't sleep peacefully.

It was a restless night. Jomo was dreaming of a future playing with his children. Oba was dreaming of Jahiri when he was in the Kingdom of Punt. Jahiri couldn't sleep.

Oba's dreams showed how Jahiri and Jamilah were both very much in love. She also saw how they were meant to be together and like Jahiri, wondered why the gods didn't assist. It was then when she saw three elves helping at a birth. She then saw Jamilah raise the baby towards the heavens, she named her Sagal.

It was the sadness and the sense of loss on Jamilah's face that woke Oba from her sleep. She shot up, shook Jomo and pulled him close. "Jomo, wake up," she whispered. "Jamilah is alive, under a spell. She's in a long sleep, protected by the power of the elves. There's a baby! A little girl, her name is Sagal."

Jomo, half asleep, pushed her away. Seconds later his eyes fully opened, he grasped what had been said. He leapt up and went to wake Jahiri but there was no need. Jahiri was still awake and heard everything.

Chapter 12

Jahiri was in shock and had difficulty taking in what Oba had said. He left and sat beside the river, bewildered yet excited at the same time. His mind raced and he wondered how he was going to find Jamilah. He decided to backtrack to the Kingdom of Punt to begin his search there. He rejoined Jomo and Oba to tell them of his decision to leave. He said his goodbyes to begin his long walk north.

"Jahiri, hold up, wait!" cried Jomo, "Don't you think that, after all this time, we too are part of your life? Do you not think it's our place to help you? We should stay together and see where the journey takes us."

Jahiri was relieved and delighted with this offer, he didn't want to head north alone. He was used to working closely with Jomo and Oba and felt he couldn't face the loneliness this kind of search would entail. They waited for another day and then made their way back towards the Serengeti.

During their journey north they never let down their guard. They passed on the message where appropriate, so much so that they didn't realise Time was still playing tricks on them. Another five hundred years passed as they searched, they thought they were searching for only a few months.

They reached the domain of the Tuskers and were surprised to be greeted as long lost friends. The further northeast they travelled the more Oba's dreams got increasingly vivid, leading her to believe they were getting closer to finding Jamilah and Sagal.

They turned west and moved towards the land of the thousand hills where they met up with the King of all Gorillas, the one known as Khalfani. He was the oldest of the silverbacks who, along with many other silverbacks and their families, led them high into the mist covered mountains to a small crack in the cliffs concealing a tree lined lagoon.

Oba formed a bond with this silverback and together they shared a vision of the future for all mountain gorillas. It wasn't a nice prophecy but it needed to be told, "I see sad times ahead. The lowlands will become killing fields for your kind. The mountains will be a sanctuary but not for long. The possible extinction of all free gorillas will be thwarted by the efforts of environmentalists and volunteers, especially near the End Times. They are your only hope. There are good times as well. One of your descendants, one who will be known as Titus, will become the most revered silverback of all time. He will father many offspring but will be usurped by a very strong son. Even his ousting will not take away the reverence he earned throughout these sacred lands." She waited for Khalfani to absorb what she said before continuing, "I know what I showed hurts but I beg you to ensure all surviving gorillas will answer when called upon to assist Pegasus in the defence of the third age of man."

Jahiri was getting more anxious and at times irritated; the search for Jamilah was taking too long and any reassurance from Oba was wearing thin. He continuously paced and wouldn't relax; even the beauty of the surroundings was of no benefit until, after several days, everything changed. A magical light appeared highlighting another fissure in the cliff walls. The crack expanded and an Elfena appeared, inviting them through into the realm of the mountain elves, but Jahiri still wasn't happy, "Oh, for Shango's' sake, not more magic, this is ridiculous! I'm losing my patience."

Oba slapped him down, "Jahiri, have you learned nothing? All the magic we've experienced should have given you Hope. Look at the Elfena, she doesn't threaten you. She invites you in, ask yourself. Why?"

Jomo entered first, followed by Oba then Jahiri, who reluctantly made his way through. They were all in awe of the vastness of this magical place but were surprised to see an army of warrior Elves standing guard at every entrance, passageway and civic building. The army's presence showed how nervous the realm of the elves had become and this was because of the constant probing by the forces of Hell.

They continued walking deeper into the elf realm, where they were met by a familiar face. It was Kalen, whom they last met in the Temple of Olympus seventeen hundred years earlier. He greeted them and congratulated them on the completion of their task. He also acknowledged how agitated Jahiri was and suggested he follow the passageway into the next room where he would find an ornate glass pagoda.

He did what was asked and soon reached the pagoda to find it sheltered a large, and what seemed to be a very comfortable bed. When he approached he couldn't believe what was before him. Jomo and Oba joined him and they all stared at the face of a most beautiful woman who just looked to be asleep. In her arms was a baby just as Oba had seen in her dreams. Jahiri leaned in and touched her arm; he touched her face and then her hair before placing his hand on his baby's head. He moved from one side of the bed to the other, continuously and gently shaking Jamilah. His heart was racing and his breath rapid. He choked up as his head began to burst. He turned back to Oba, "I don't know what to do. How can I wake her?"

Oba shrugged as if to say, 'Work that one out for yourself, idiot.' Jahiri kept shaking her but she didn't respond. He looked at Oba again pleading for help and caught Jomo smiling as thought he knew what to do.

Jomo then took pity on him, "The great stories always include a kiss."

Without hesitation he stretched in to kiss the women be loved. He withdrew and waited, then watched her begin to waken. It was then when he felt a presence, "My friend, my amazing friend," It was Jacob. "You've become a most powerful god of Africa. You are revered among the tribes. Olympus would never have allowed anything happen to Jamilah, or Sagal, because immortality was given the moment you and her became one. Enjoy this time and be happy for your long sleep waits."

The first thing Jamilah did when she woke was check on her baby. She kissed her and she too began to stir. Jamilah looked up and couldn't believe who stood before her. Centuries of welled up tears were released just as she stretched her hand up to touch Jahiri's face. She pulled him towards her and held him so tightly he felt he had just arrived in Heaven. She whispered, "In my dreams I watched you weep. They were happy dreams because I knew you would one day find me. My dreams tell me it's been fifteen hundred years since we last met, can this be true?"

He held her tighter, "I gave up questioning Time many years ago. Just be aware another sleep awaits, then a battle, and when we defeat The Darkness, you and I will be together forever."

He took Sagal into his arms and kissed her forehead, but couldn't take his eyes from Jamilah. All he wanted was to never again let her go. When they stood together they blended into one and looked like a happy family, one always meant to be together.

Oba was by now heavily pregnant and coming close to the birth causing Jomo to become overprotective and a bit of a nuisance. The elves did what they did best and looked after her. Soon a handsome baby boy was born.

Jomo's exuberance made him think he was the only father in the world but having said that, he had the makings of a great dad. When the time came for the child to be named, it was he who held him high and called out to the gods, "I name you Zane, God of Africa and one of noble birth." He turned to Oba who nodded her approval.

After many weeks in the realm of elves the time came for them to fall into their long sleep. Jomo used his stonemason skills and assisted in creating a grotto with four ornately carved thrones. When completed he stood back and said after admiring his work, "Do you know I actually feel really tired. Is this normal?"

Kalen said, "Of course it's normal. You have been a guardian for almost eighteen hundred years and during that time, faced many challenges but most importantly you have prepared an army so powerful that when the call comes the south will answer in their millions. Sleep well Jomo, be proud. And only waken when you hear the call of the gods."

Later that day Jomo and Oba took their seats and with Zane in Oba's arms, the stone came and took them. Soon after, Jamilah and Jahiri arrived and they too took their seats. When Sagal was placed in Jamilah's arms they too turned to stone. The Elves sealed the grotto and protected it with an ancient spell.

They had begun their long sleep, destined to last two hundred years.

Mulan's Journey East

Chapter 1

Jacob turned back and saw that Mulan, Garuda and Girish were already on the steps of the temple. They were the third group destined to leave and the one group his visions showed were to suffer the most, and it concerned him. He comforted himself knowing they were a strong group and didn't have the same fear Oba and her escorts had because not only were they ancestrally of the east but they were also descended from a more enlightened people. They understood the peace and tranquillity gleaned from the teachings of Lord Buddha, and from the religious practices common in the realm of the Hindu gods.

Jacob watched Mulan approach and was in awe of her mixed western and oriental beauty. In her village she was considered a traditional Chinese beauty because of her small frame, a stature that betrayed her inner and physical strength. Her fair, almost white complexion; highlighted her almond-shaped eyes and the angular curve to her mouth. Her hair, if not bound up in a bun, was always tied into a ponytail. Her training in the art of meditation ensured she was always at peace. The cream coloured Kimono she wore was simple, straight-seamed and secured by a gem encrusted braided sash. The sleeves were long and flowing, inset with vibrant colours. Her cape was a darker shade, almost taupe. Her hair band contained an assortment of gems mined in the high mountains of the Indus peoples and when they glowed they showed that she too was a true Messenger of the Light.

Garuda stood to her left and presented as a formidable warrior of Olympus. His robes and armour didn't take away from the fact that he was of the Indus. He was good looking, tall, muscular and carried himself with confidence. His thick, coal black hair, framed his unblemished brownish-yellow complexion. His deep brown eyes and inviting smile showed his gentleness. All who met him were immediately taken, not by his looks, but by the beauty oozing from deep within his soul. There was something about his honesty, his gentleness, his simple innocence that made him stand out. His rugged good looks, especially when dressed in a traditional Indian Sherwani and Turban such as what he wore at last night's dinner attracted a lot of female attention.

Girish stood to her right and he too presented as an impressive warrior of Olympus, equally as handsome as Garuda but not as muscular. It was obvious by the way he stood that, when required, he had the strength and speed to make him equally as formidable. Like Mulan he had deep set, almond-shaped golden brown eyes. Unlike her his thick black hair was tied up in a pony tail contrasting perfectly with his sallow skin tone showing he descended from the Far East. Jacob recalled his arrival into the Great Hall for last night's dinner, how he turned heads while wearing a silk woven dragon robe elaborately embroidered with the imperial emblem of the five clawed dragon. It was a robe commonly worn by descendants of the Han.

After been greeted by Jacob all three exuded calmness as they made their way through the portal to walk along the shield towards the crossroads. They continuously glanced back, delighted by the send-off granted them by the assembled gods. They turned right and looking into the barren desert they realized the enormity of what lay ahead causing pangs of anxiety. They slowly moved into invisibility

Chapter 2

Mulan wondered what Jacob meant when he said, 'you will walk for a thousand years to become the Flowering Tree of the East. You will be my warrior queen and the gatherer of the gems of beauty'. She momentarily closed her eyes to maintain her calmness even though Jacob's words were still racing through her mind.

They walked in silence for some time before Garuda and Girish stopped to remove their armour. Never once did they feel threats, so they began to use their time wisely, visiting small villages and passing on the message, especially when travelling through Mesopotamia and Persia.

Time just drifted by and after many months had passed they reached the Indus plains where, in the distance, they saw a bright quivering light that turned out to be an old friend.

It was the wizard Apollonius, "Greetings my friends," he said reaching in to hug each in turn. "Time has treated you well. Fifty years and you haven't aged a day."

Girish went into shock. Garuda stuttered, "We only left Olympus five weeks ago, fifty years couldn't have passed."

"Over those five weeks," smiled Apollonius knowingly. "While you slept, months then years have passed."

"What about our families? Are they gone?" asked Girish. Apollonius just nodded.

The boys were shocked, Mulan wasn't. She didn't seem surprised. Apollonius allowed them grieve then enquired if they had as yet sent out the Light. "No," answered Garuda, "never once did we feel an evil presence. There's been no sightings or threats, no feelings of menace."

Apollonius looked surprised and shook his head with disappointment. "You can go no further," he said, "until you're sure the Light is your friend." He encouraged them to extract their staffs, "You should have by now taught yourselves how to control its power. My visions show you in a battle with the forces of Hell, and it's not too far away. Oh, one other thing. I'm here because there's a change to your plan."

He reached down and said while scooping a handful of sand, "Watch the sands slip through my fingers and feel the history of these lands tell its story. Much blood has been spilt, making these lands fertile hunting grounds for the serpents of Hell. Without mastering the power of the Light you will be vulnerable and will fail in your quest."

The boys felt a bit chastened, they thought the Light would come naturally. It didn't occur to them to practice for its arrival. They immediately took the guidance offered, raised their staffs and within seconds they learned a painful lesson. The Light's arrival was so powerful it sent both of them hurtling towards a close by sand dune where they suffered multiple impacts, causing injuries to their mouths, ears and noses. They also had scrapes and bruises on their legs, thighs, arms and chests. They were stunned, never thinking such pain existed.

It took several days for them to heal before making another attempt at calling the Light, and it was Girish who was first to volunteer. After removing his tunic and tightening his sandals, he positioned himself in a forward thrusting stance so as to place his full strength behind the staff. He called on the Light and when it arrived it again came with such force it sent him sliding backwards for many paces. He was covered in dust and wasn't happy, but he was more determined than ever to become its master. He held his staff firmly and for the third time called on the Light while again taking a secure stance. When the light came, he again felt its strength but this time he grasped its power. He quickly learned how to react to its arrival and after many more attempts he felt he was bringing it under control. He then assisted Garuda, and together they practiced until they were confident they had mastered its power.

Apollonius was pleased with their progress and decided it was time to tell them of their altered task. "In the southern ocean," he said pointing south east, "there's a land as yet undiscovered by the empires of the east or west. Jacob believes those who live there deserve to be ancestors of carriers."

"How are we expected to get there if it's undiscovered," Asked Garuda.

"I'm a wizard, that's why I've been sent, there are ways," replied Apollonius. From his satchel he produced a rare red crystal and as soon as it absorbed the sun's rays it sent a most beautiful light in all directions. "This is my gift to you," he said handing it to Mulan, "it's a vessel of great power, granting you the ability to travel vast distances at the blink of an eye. It'll take you to the Undiscovered Lands, then to the America's. Your journey will take you to realms controlled by gods who will assist, and others who are still angry at being made outcasts after the cosmic wars. Jacob believes your skills will convince them to support Olympus when the battle of the End Times is upon us. The crystal will then take you to the land of the Rising Sun and onwards to the empire of the Dynasties. It is from there the flowering trees will spread as you commence your unbroken walk of a thousand years. I caution you, the crystal will only assist when all three of you travel together." Mulan raised her hand with the crystal facing the sun, Garuda and Girish placed their finger tips to its side.

"In the Undiscovered Lands," said Apollonius placing his finger on the crystal, "there's a spiritual mountain. Its name is Uluru and it's the final resting place of a long gone goddess. Think of this place and the crystal will take us there."

Together all four thought of Uluru and were whisked away to arrive at the foot of an amazing natural structure, a huge, red sandstone monolith. They stood in awe of its majesty before spending the next few days exploring its many water-carved caves. They marvelled at the beauty of ancient paintings adorning the walls of this enchanted sanctuary. They drank from its waterholes and swam in its springs. In the evenings, just after twilight, they watched bats, hovered in their millions, before flying to feed out across the desert. They were also saddened to meet the malleefowl, brushed tail possum and the hare wallaby, all species their power of prophesy showed as destined to become extinct.

Circling the rock allowed them visit villages occupied by the dominant tribe of the Anangu people. When among the villagers whey witnessed the magical sleep time rituals, and listened to the ancient Aboriginal dreamtime stories. It was clear Uluru was a sacred and revered place, reserved for the spirits of the ancestral creator beings. The one story always spoken of was about the serpent wars, a war that cost the lives of countless snake species. The story spoke of how the grieving Mother Earth, Goddess of all Life, rose up and turned to stone because of the constant bloodshed. How she was to become known as Uluru cursing all those who removed anything from the mountain.

It was now time for Apollonius to depart; he had completed his task, and was satisfied Garuda and Girish were now in control and well prepared to deal with their changed circumstances. He bade farewell and returned to the Astral Plains.

Garuda found a safe location to set up home, not far from Uluru, while Mulan put in place her plans to spread the message.

Chapter 3

Mulan insisted on travelling alone among the villagers, she felt safe knowing the boys were nearby. Garuda and Girish were unhappy and decided to follow her but kept their distance, a wise decision. On arrival in the first village Mulan became aware of being watched and this unsettled her. There was no threat and Mulan quickly realized those who could see her were the wise-ones. They were the oracles and healers known as the Ngangkari. They were the storehouse, entrusted with the forty thousand year history of all Aborigines. The most senior oracle approached and offered her hand which Mulan willingly accepted. Together they shared a vision showing the future of the aboriginal peoples. Those among the Ngangkari watching saw the expression of shock, then horror, cross the oracles face and became alarmed.

Mulan fully materialised. She encouraged Garuda and Girish to do the same even though they were out of their imperial robes and armour. On materialising, they were welcomed as spirits from the 'Dreamtime', and a great festival was organised in their honour.

For many years they remained with the Anangu never interfering in their customs and traditions even when they found it difficult to watch when, year after year, seven to ten young boys set off on their traditional six month 'Walkabout', the very hazardous adventure all aboriginal boys had to endure before being accepted as men by their tribes. Those same young boys, much to the relief of their families, always arrived home and appeared to have grown in stature and confidence.

After spending almost fifty years among the Anangu, Mulan became restless. Visions of high mountains and lush rain forests appeared in her dreams and she believed the visions were telling her it was time to move on. It was also around this time when the first reports of sinister serpents became known.

The most recent sightings happened just as the latest ten boys were setting out on their Walkabout. Garuda walked with them for a short distance, shaking his head in bewilderment; even after fifty years among the tribes he still had difficulty with the idea of young boys travelling alone, especially in such a hostile desert.

When he returned to the village he found Girish in an agitated state and as the minutes passed, he too felt something sinister. They reached for their satchels and withdrew their robes and weapons, then sent out their Light. To their horror, they got their first glimpse of Hells serpents and there were hundreds. They were slithering towards the young boys.

Without much thought Garuda and Girish raced out into the outback, they were making every effort to reach the boys before the serpents, but they were too far away. Garuda felt a presence; it was Jacob, "Remember what I said that time in the lagoon, 'You will be my mythical bird and emperor of the skies.' Remember Garuda, its time you changed."

Garuda found himself soaring across the sky. He had become Jacob's mythical bird, and as emperor of the skies he sent out across the desert, a most piercing and shrill call. They answered in their thousands and the sound of their shrieking calls and flapping wings became deafening.

From a great height Garuda used his eyes to send bursts of crystalline light towards the ground, close to where the ten boys were standing. Using this light he temporarily blinded the serpents giving a now invisible Girish time to assist the boys. When Girish reached the boys he stood between them and the advancing serpents with his sword drawn, ready to unleash the full might of an Olympus warrior.

The serpents, on recovering from the blinding light, continued their advance, but from among them two expanded, then pulsated before transforming into seven foot Dark Angels. The young boys were terrified, especially when seeing the horrific faces and fiery red eyes staring back at them.

"I smell it," said one of the angels, "the warm blood of an Olympus messenger or is I a guardian. Show yourself, fool. We've been expecting your visit to this sacred place." For Girish this revelation was confusing, the visit to Uluru was set after the messengers left Olympus, therefore not in the original plans. He worried as to the possibility of a traitor in the temple.

The serpents cautiously surrounded the boys not knowing what to expect. Girish was ready and quietly reached in to whisper, "Don't be afraid; Garuda and I are close by, you are not alone," he said looking back to see how close the serpents were. "Draw your flints and form a tight circle. Prepare to defend yourselves." The boys did as asked but weren't convinced. They anxiously looked around searching for the source of the voice.

The Dark Angels noticed the boys forming a tight circle and deduced they were taking instruction from an invisible force. They concluded that the invisible force had to be a guardian and were beside themselves with excitement at the prospect of taking down a guardian of a Messenger.

The serpents attacked, and the first wave reached close to where the boys were but they were defeated within seconds by the skilful swordsmanship of the still invisible Girish. The whooshing sound and clean cut of his invisible sword was everywhere. The slaughter was so quick and precise that the Dark Angels, although taken by surprise, weren't fazed. They had a second plan, involving a two-pronged attack beginning with a far greater assault, while a hidden group of serpents tunnelled beneath the sands. This second wave was extremely difficult for Girish to deal with, the numbers were so great. Relief only came when Garuda's army attacked.

The Wedged Tailed Eagles were the first to appear followed by the Goshawks, Whistling Kites and then the Black Falcons. They swooped in their thousands and skilfully grasped the serpents, taking them high into the sky to feverishly peck at them before releasing the battered bodies, allowing the Collared Sparrow Hawks and the Nankeen Kestrels to swoop in. As the serpents fell, more birds gorged on their flesh. Although the serpents were falling in their hundreds, Hells second plan was working because the battle between the birds, serpents and Girish distracted everyone, allowing the tunnelling serpents to reach the boys.

Two boys were bitten before Girish realised what was happening, he immediately ran to their rescue. The eight remaining boys successfully used their knives to defend themselves before strategically moving onto a bank of rocks preventing more tunnelling serpents from reaching them.

The two injured boys quickly fell into what they thought was their 'Dream Time'. It was no dreamtime, it was a nightmare. They soon realised they were, in fact, in Hell, watching the continuous torture of millions of souls. Their nightmare continued with the Hounds of Hell approaching, and they braced themselves for a similar fate, but it was not to be. The tight and all embracing claws of a giant bird gripped them, and raised them high before carrying them back into the care of their village. Mulan and the village healers ran to their aid.

"I recognise the puncture marks," cried Mulan requesting alcohol. "I've seen those marks before. Alcohol will defeat the fire racing through their veins." Garuda didn't react; all he heard was the clash of steel indicating

Girish was now engaged against the Dark Angels. He flapped his wings, took to the sky and flew to rejoin the battle.

The Ngangkari healers were bewildered, a giant bird, a battle and two seriously injured boys. They put aside their confusion and tried every ancient medicine known to them, but nothing helped. They believed the boys had no hope of survival and would soon pass away, even thought Mulan insisted there was a solution. She ran to a nearby mound and grabbed a vat of the local Tabu brew, returned and administered it to both boys. Much to the surprise of the healers, the boys began to recover.

Back at the battle site Garuda arrived and took his human form before becoming invisible. He assisted Girish in dealing with the remaining serpents, the ones that skilfully evaded the attacking birds of prey and between them they destroyed every last one. All that remained to be dealt with were the Dark Angels leading to a standoff. The Dark Angels were at a disadvantage and continuously swung their swords hoping to make contact with their invisible opponents. As evening approached, the sunlight faded favouring the Dark Angels. Twilight distorted the sunlight, revealing Garuda and Girish, taking away their advantage.

The eight aboriginal boys had never seen Girish or Garuda in full armour. They were awe-struck looking at their golden armour glistening in the final beams of the now fading sun, and the first rays of the rising moon.

Hells strategy changed when the Dark Angels backed further out into the open desert seeking the upper hand. They continuously waved their swords about attempting to intimidate. Garuda and Girish followed, showing no fear. Under the light of the now bright moon Garuda and Girish saw the fiery red eyes staring back at them and weren't fazed; they just continued their slow movement out into the desert.

Each side resisted making the first move; that was until the Dark Angels began teasing then cajoling. It was as they circled each other when one of the Angels tripped and stumbled towards Girish who immediately reacted with a full force onslaught leading to a sword fight that was pure savagery. The sound of the clashing steel was heard across the desert but no one came to investigate, the tribes feared this evil was more reckless, ruthless and brutal than anything they experienced in the past. They cowered in their huts, and only the bravest peeked out to witness the sparks and flashes of steel swords making contact.

The sparing went on all night and as dawn broke Girish began to flounder. He fell to his knees from exhaustion and depended on Garuda to take on the Dark Angels alone. Garuda too was a master swordsman, and used his skills to withstand everything the angels threw at him.

While Girish rested he felt a presence, "Remember what I said all those years ago?" it was Jacob, "You will be known as Lord of the Mountains. They will open their passes, reveal their caves………' Look to the north and see the mountain's rise before you, they are magical and will soon be gone. Hurry to them and be my Lord of the Mountains." Girish got to his feet and began backing towards the mountains, much to the bemusement of Garuda. On his way and without warning he commenced a further attack, which was part of his plan - giving the Dark Angels a false sense of security.

On reaching a narrow pass leading to a steep sided gully they fought more viciously. They had drawn the Dark Angels deep into the mountains where the battle continued until they reached a flat-topped boulder, blocking their exit.

"This battle ends now!" yelled Girish after climbing the boulder, "I am known as Lord of the Mountains, they bow before me. They open their passes on my command." He raised his arms and when he brought his hands together he called on the mountains to do their worst; they did and moved as though suffering a violent earth quake. The passes closed with such speed they instantly crushed the two Dark Angels, sending them back to where they came from, and within seconds, as foretold by Jacob, the mountains disappeared.

"That was impressive," said Garuda, "did you know such power existed?" Girish rubbed his two hands together smiling from ear to ear, "I can't believe I have such power. Is it right to feel so good after what I just did?" Garuda didn't answer.

They rejoined the eight boys and escorted them back to the village, where on arrival; they were accepted back as men, the two injured boys were also given the same recognition.

Mulan summoned the Ngangkari and announced her departure; she also recommended the tribes leave and travel deeper into the desert. Her visions showed Lucifer seeking revenge. The villagers didn't need much persuasion; they too sensed the approaching danger. They took Mulan's advice and immediately left.

When the Anangu nation was out of sight, Mulan produced the crystal, preparing to leave. Before leaving she elbowed Girish and gestured towards Garuda, "I was taken aback at how majestic and handsome Garuda looked. What do you think? I always thought you were the vain one, but when I saw Garuda's golden breast feathers and the way they contrasted the pale cream ones on his wings and back, I was stunned." She turned back to Garuda, "You really looked amazing. Truly you are the Emperor of the Birds."

Garuda said trying to stifle a smile, "Enough of this nonsense, my face burns with embarrassment. Let's go." They held hands before closing their eyes and calling for the crystal to work its magic. It did and it took them across the southern ocean to arrive at a site where, in the future, the great city of Machu Picchu, spiritual home of the Inca peoples, will be built.

Chapter 4

On a plateaux set high in the mountains, Garuda lit a small and inviting fire; its glow seen across the valleys, as well as from the tops of the snow-capped peaks. Like a beacon, it attracted the attention of the many tribes and family groups inhabiting the mist shrouded forests below.

It was a restful night but Garuda was uneasy. His dreams showed him flying high among the birds, calling for their assistance many times into the future. He also saw a council, it was the 'Gods of the Americas' and they were coming together. He twisted and turned before waking and sitting up. He saw Mulan standing close to the edge of the plateau and joined her. He embraced her; said nothing and together they stood watching the sun rise.

"On looking down over the mist covered forests," said Mulan linking his arm, "the vastness of the distant peaks and the way they tower high above the clouds. I feel at peace." Girish joined them. Mulan continued, "You two boys must feel at home, one is Lord of the Mountains and the other Emperor of the Birds." They laughed, especially when Garuda began scratching,

"Don't expect me to scratch places you can't reach," quipped Girish, "or for that matter, pick the fleas." He stepped back and mockingly bowed, "my Lord and Emperor of the Birds."

Garuda wasn't amused, "I don't carry fleas but, believe it or not, I still feel the feathers stick from all over my body and I'm not sure I like it." Again they laughed.

"You two have no idea how safe you make me feel," said Mulan hugging her dearest friends. "It's strange. I have no idea what to do next."

"We will meet up with the gods of the Americas," said Garuda, "my dreams showed me a gathering but also showed gave me a warning. Some are angry, others will listen, our meeting happens somewhere in the north."

That night Garuda lit another fire and Girish sent out the Light, as usual he was happy to report there was no signs of serpents. This time the glow caused alarm in the forests prompting the tribes to call a gathering of elders where they decided to investigate.

The following morning, from below the canopy the tribes appeared. There were thousands and they were making their way up towards the plateaux. First to arrive were the warriors and they were followed by the medicine men, then by the elderly, the women and children.

Mulan stood alongside Garuda and Girish as the plateau filled. They remained invisible watching the bemused expression on the faces of the people, especially when they reached the smouldering embers and found nobody in attendance.

Mulan noticed she was being watched, it was one of the P'aqo, a medicine man; he was a most powerful seer. She walked towards him causing him to fall to his knees with his two hands firmly gripped together as though pleading for mercy. She assisted him to stand, "Be not afraid, my guardians and I are no threat to you. We are here to give you and your people a message from the gods. Tell them of me. Tell them a vision will soon appear, and not to be afraid."

The medicine man did what was asked and all waited for the vision to appear. Girish and Garuda went against Mulan's wishes and chose to remain invisible.

Mulan stepped onto a stone platform and began to materialise, causing the tribe's people to fall to their knees and adore her as a goddess. She was horrified, this was not her intention. She begged them to stand and listen to what she had to say, "I am Mulan, a traveller from a land far away. I bring you a message and hope you will answer. I also give, through your seers, prophesies I hope will help many of your descendants survive what will befall them over the next fifteen hundred years."

She moved among the people, touching each of their shoulders and to each one said, "Go now, tell your children to tell their children's children for all time, that one day, they will be called upon by the gods and they must answer."

On meeting the seers she said, "Ensure my message travels through the generations and be happy, for the next thousand years there will be many peaceful times. After that everything will change. A dark evil will show itself and you will know it has arrived when the priests on the great pyramids demand human sacrifices causing the deaths of thousands from among the forest dwellers. There will be great empires, one of which will be the 'Inca'; their spiritual home will be here on this very plateau. This empire will last no more than five generations before falling to a vast armada sailing from across the oceans." She paused for a moment before continuing, "A far more malevolent empire known as the 'Aztec' will rise. There power will last for many, many years. They will be all powerful, and lust for human blood causing it to continuously flow under the false belief that this is what their gods demand. The armada I spoke of will unleash an unfettered greed for the wealth of this land and will also be responsible for the fall of the Aztec Empire. They will bring war and pestilence and millions will die." She then advised them, "You must start preparing, go deeper into the forests and wait for the call of the gods and when the call comes, walk out and let the world see you stand proudly in defence of the Light."

The following day the tribes followed Mulan along the banks skirting the great rivers. She used her skills to teach them how to protect themselves and how to blend into the forest. She became, in their eyes, their Warrior Queen, just as Jacob had foretold. She built an army of warriors and taught them to listen to the beating heart of the forest. She developed a drum that when pounded, it sent its beat throughout the lands calling those same warriors together when needed.

The tribes loved Mulan and always ensured she was well looked after which included the building of platforms, high in the canopy for her to rest and meditate. Little did they know that there were guardians always by her side, sharing the platform ensuring she was always safe. She, just like Garuda and Girish, was of the east and understood the power of meditation, especially how it suppressed or enhanced lustful desires, how it helped bring calmness and wisdom, but most importantly, how it helped to keep them focused.

For two hundred years they lived among the tribes and were very happy until the time to move on arrived. Mulan arranged for the drums to pound calling the seers and elders together. She used this gathering to announce her departure knowing the tribes were going to be devastated even though they always knew this day would come. They were prepared, the women sat with Mulan and presented her with many gifts, one of which was a most intricate and beautiful band of white gold into which they secured precious stones of many colours. They also created a most beautiful necklace and placed it around her neck before bowing as they accepted her thanks.

The drumbeat continued calling thousands more to answer its call. They lined the forest and grieved as Mulan left. They were fascinated

212

watching the most radiant lotus flowers bloom from every step she took, the deeper she walked into the forest the brighter each flower got. What baffled the tribes was the appearance of two more lines of lotus flowers alongside those of Mulan. Only one very elderly medicine-man knew why.

Mulan stopped one last time, turned and waved; she too was surprised by the lines of Lotus flowers springing up behind her, "It's written of how the Lotus only grows in the wake of those who have reached enlightenment. Has our meditation taken us there?" she asked.

It was then when all three heard a new voice, "My children, you reached enlightenment many years ago; those nights meditating took you into my all-embracing arms. You are now under the protection of Buddha."

Chapter 5

Over the next fifty years Mulan, Garuda and Girish travelled through the darkest of jungles, crossed the widest rivers and swam in the warmest waters near the great waterfalls. They continued their meditation and never felt threatened until they reached the southern borders of the Mayan Empire where, when they crossed, they made their way towards Tikal, the capital city.

Walking through the streets was not a pleasant experience and on reaching the plaza at the base of the main pyramid they found out why. It was the constant stream of enslaved forest people being brought to face a relentless slaughter as an offering to a god they weren't aware of. Garuda and Girish found it difficult to watch the priest's abuse their power in the name of a god whom they believed should never have requested such sacrifices; they were tempted to take action. Mulan didn't say much and felt absolute contempt for these murderous executioners but knew it wasn't her place to interfere. She insisted they leave for the Hopi lands but unfortunately Girish could take no more, his temper rose and he exploded. He raced to the top of great pyramid and was so furious he intended to release the wrath of the gods. On his way he maintained his invisibility but found himself struggling with the stench of the stale blood that was spilt over many days and this fuelled his anger. Garuda caught up with, and reminded him that their job was to spread the message, not to right the wrongs of man, but

Girish was too angry to listen. On reaching the platform his anger was at boiling point. He stretched in and grabbed the high priest by the throat causing him to struggle, then fall unconscious.

As the high priest was being carried away the victim, who was due to be beheaded, leapt from the block. He took his opportunity to run down the steps and raced towards the forest. On his way he passed Mulan who quickly touched his shoulder to pass on the message. He continued his run, and ran so fast the pursuing guards had no chance of catching him. Garuda ran behind to ensure he escaped into the forest.

Back in the temple the high priest dismissed his helpers and decided to rest giving Girish his opportunity. He materialised in full armour, showing his weapons. He raised his staff and called on the Light temporarily blinding the high priest, it also showed that the priest didn't carry the mark of the serpents. When the priest recovered, he went to his knees believing he was in the presence of his god.

Girish paced back and forth, he had difficulty finding the words to express his anger. "Are you displeased my god?" asked the priest.

"I am NOT your god," replied Girish, "I am an immortal sent by the gods, and I'm so angry I'm having difficulty containing myself." He then asked, "What gives you the right to claim that a god wants human blood to appease his whims?"

"It's always been this way, we know no other," the high priest responded. "Who told you the gods wanted sacrifices?" asked Girish.

The high priest made no reply so Girish continued to pace then ask, "How many innocents have you killed?"

The high priest thought long and hard before answering, "I have no idea. How many moons have passed since the beginning of time?"

Girish was shocked and yelled, "That many?" He approached the priest with his fists clenched and yelled, "Where I come from there is a god known as Lord of the Underworld, his name is Hades. He guards a forked road, one leads to the gates of Hell and the other makes its way into the warmth of Heaven. Your time is near, which road will he usher you along?"

The priest didn't seem to care, just shrugged, "I believe he will look on me with compassion because he will know that when I offered the blood the rains came, and when I again offered the blood, the sun came. He will know how I saved the people of this wonderful city just by spilling the blood of those we deemed worthy."

Girish cried out in despair, "You fool; the weather is controlled by the seasons alone. There is no need for any blood to be spilt. What about the families of those you killed? Do you think of them? Who saves them from the pain caused by your actions?"

The high priest continued to argue, "Our god wants the blood and with it we will continue to appease him."

Girish was totally bewildered and couldn't understand how his arguments failed to sway the high priest, he then said, "I have been sent to spread a message by Jacob, a grandson of Zeus, the king of the gods. He once told me of a god who looked upon man with compassion. This god had sacred laws, one of which says, 'Thou shall not kill!' yet you just kill at will. This god is one of the most powerful and is easily angered. In the past he has sent floods, plagues and pestilence when displeased. Now do you fear?"

The priest shook his head, "I know nothing of that god. He holds no fear for me"

Girish drew his sword just as Garuda and Mulan entered the room. They watched him stretch out his left hand and cut it, allowing his blood to flow into a bowl placed next to the high priest. He shouted, "Stop the slaughter and let those people go. Use my blood and see if it will appease your god. My blood is that of an immortal and more potent than that of any man."

It was then when everything changed, a massive lightning storm developed and many bolts hit the temple. From among the lightning came the figure of an outlawed god from the Mesoamerican pantheon who was once a most powerful deity. His name was Cizin, the Mayan God of the Underworld and the bringer of death. He arrived as a dancing skeleton wearing a necklace of eyes that were still dangling from their nerve cords; they were taken from the human sacrifices performed over the previous few days.

He entered the central chambers and made his presence felt by magically expelling the high priest from the room. The foul odour accompanying him was from the congealed blood of that days victims and it intensified the smell of death filling the room. He found the light that shone around Mulan and her guardians very offensive but he also saw they were immortals and was intrigued. He then noticed the bowl containing Girish's blood and after a few sips he began to convulse then spit it out, it was too powerful.

He was curious as to where they came from and demanded an explanation. "We have come from Olympus," said Mulan, "we've been sent by Jacob, a grandson of Zeus, tasked by the gods to spread the message of the Light throughout these lands in the hope of preparing your people for the End Times battle."

She had barely finished her sentence when she felt a sinister malevolence take the room, followed by a deep guttural anger bringing a terror she had never experienced before. She sensed danger coming and began running towards Garuda but was too late. Cizin exploded into a rage so violent; Garuda and Girish had no chance to prepare a defence. He used an evil magic to raise them towards the roof and tossed them from wall to wall. In the meantime he used other powers to hold Mulan firm before beginning to choke her, on releasing her she fell to the ground in despair watching her friends pass away before her.

The sound of their breaking bones was heard throughout the heavens, wakening many of the sleeping gods and when they heard the sound of the boy's heads hitting the ground they knew that without divine help there was no coming back. With her dying breath, Mulan weakly asked, "Why?"

Cizin lifted her by the throat, yelling "I fought against the might of Zeus and the old gods during the cosmic wars. Humiliated, I swore revenge for the destruction of my realm. I waited for thousands of years to pass, and then four hundred and fifty years ago Hades locks the doors to the Underworld leaving me with no chance to reclaim my realm. His actions forced me to walk alone among man."

He swung her around, then continued, "I've rebuilt my powers using the rich blood flowing from the sacrifices carried out in this temple and I intend using those same powers to reclaim all I lost."

Mulan, although gasping, managed to say, "I was there; I saw the despair when Hades returned to Olympus to tell of the fall of the Underworld. Ares and Athena witnessed the attack. It was Lucifer, the greatest deceiver of them all. He assembled an army of serpents so vast it threatens all realms. He's working with The Darkness." Cizin wouldn't listen and raised his hand to finally smite her.

Suddenly, a very violent tremor was felt and the doors burst open allowing four colourful beams of light to enter. When the colour faded all that was left was a white light which took the form of four Archangels, the very ones who escorted Michael, Raphael and Gabriel to the council of the gods. The Archangel known as Uriel used his powers to take control. He slammed Cizin against the wall and held him there while Selaphiel, Raguel and

Barachile moved to use their powers to gently raise Mulan, Garuda and Girish into an upright position before cocooning them using their wings.

Mulan soon felt her strength return and was assisted back to the floor. She immediately thought of Girish and Garuda and feared they had gone to take their place in the tombs of Elysium. She need not have feared; the power of the Light and the assistance of the Archangels called them back. On recovering they seemed to have lost their confidence. "We were never trained for this," Girish managed to say. "I expected battles but nothing like this, such an angry god. How can anybody be expected to survive such a ruthless attack?" He didn't get an answer because the Archangels stepped back to allow the arrival of a new light, a light carrying six deities of the Mesoamerican pantheon.

First to arrive was Al Kin, Sun God of the Mayan nation who is known as the God Protector against The Darkness. He was followed by Tlaloc also known as Chaac, God of Storms to both the Mayan and Aztec empires. The colours and styles of their robes and head dresses were stunning but nothing prepared those present for the four goddesses who followed. They were the most revered of the northern tribes.

When Atira, the Pawnee sacred Earth Mother appeared, she brought a radiance long missing from this part of the world. She wore a robe of cream and white beads and a matching head band holding her long white hair in place and she was wrapped in a shawl of green and wide leaves taken from the white orchid plant. Next to arrive was Akna, Goddess of Child Birth. She was of the Inuit peoples who made the cold far north their home. Her beauty caused Girish and Garuda to be enraptured so profoundly that no amount of meditation would suppress their longings. She had the face of an angel, hair so shiny and dark that when caressed it felt like silk. She smiled at the boys and with that smile succeeded in giving back to them the will to continue their task. She brought much needed warmth back into their hearts.

Kokyan, the Hopi Creation Goddess, was the next to appear and she was mesmerising. She wore a most vivid midnight blue gown held in place by a golden belt. Her hair was held back by a feather head dress encrusted with precious stones. She had a beauty comparable only with Aphrodite.

The last goddess to enter the room was Maja, the Sioux Earth Mother. She was the most stunning. She needed no jewellery, make up or clothes to enhance her beauty. She was near naked, covered only by a silken transparent wrap leaving nothing to the imagination. Her black raven coloured hair held but one eagle feather gripped by a golden band and from her back grew the tree of life.

Uriel, at the behest of Al Kin, released Cizin into the custody of the goddess's who used their magic to contain, then clean him, so as to remove the foul odour wafting from around him. They, with the assistance of the Archangels, began to bring back the god he once was, before he became a malevolent god of the Underworld. He was still angry especially when the thoughts of his defeat at the hands of Zeus kept bouncing into his mind; that was until he faced one of the goddesses. He stared and moved closer, then said looking deep into her eyes, "My heart beats faster each time I near you. It's your face and it dwells deep in my dreams, once I walked in a magical land and you were always by my side. Do I know you?"

Akna stepped closer and broke the spell containing his powers. She reached in and touched his face; he began to remember that she was his great love and mother of his children. He then recalled how together, they once ruled as just and fair gods. He pleaded for her help, then turned and bowed to the Archangels. He pleaded for the other gods to help. They did.

He approached Garuda and Girish, "The light that offended me earlier has gotten stronger and shines brightly around both of you; it shows you to be blessed by the Ancient One. I was so blinded by my hatred of the Olympians, even Father Time couldn't take that hatred away. Mention of Olympus always brought out the violence in me and you happened to be in my path. I was wrong, I beg your forgiveness."

Girish and Garuda were about to respond when they heard a familiar voice, it was Lord Buddha, "My sons, to enter enlightenment you learned many things, and forgiveness is one of them. Look on him with compassion, he needs forgiveness and it's your duty to give it to him."

Garuda turned to Cizin, "The pain I suffered still hurts and forgiving you is difficult. We are followers of my Lord Buddha, and just now he has reminded us of how forgiveness is part of who we are. He is our teacher and has brought us into enlightenment. I know I also speak for Girish when I say, We Forgive You."

Chapter 6

Al Kin reminded all present of how when six gods from the Americas gather, a council must then be called. He suggested moving north to the sacred canyons where echoes of the beating drums are at their loudest. It was then when the Archangels bade their farewells.

Together the gods assisted Mulan, Garuda and Girish by magically taking them to the summit of one of the ancient stacks near the homeland of the Hopi nation. In the centre of the stack stood a twenty foot high totem pole engraved with symbols and etchings telling the history of all Native Americans. There were ten stone seats prepared, forming a perfect circle around the pole.

The pulsating sound of the shamanic drums pounded so loudly it punctured the veil protecting the quietness of the desert night. The continuous beat encouraged the Hopi men-folk to enter sweat lodges where they expelled negative energy responsible for creating disorder and imbalance in their lives. When happy their bodies, minds and souls were cleansed, they left to dance all night to the haunting sounds filling the air. The fire guardians ensured the camp fires burned brightly keeping the evil spirits away. The Hopi were at peace; their trances allowed them see they were being watched over by the gods.

The following morning, at the council, Al Kin was first to speak. He conveyed his annoyance at not being invited to Olympus for the gathering of the gods, and felt Zeus's isolation of the American pantheon was inappropriate considering the threat that now existed. The goddess's all agreed.

"This is not a time for anger," said Mulan in defence of Olympus. "Can't you see the Darkness is coming and it will show no mercy? The Zeus you speak of is no longer the Zeus you remember. He has mellowed, especially on discovering a daughter and two grandsons he knew nothing of. Those grandsons are our friends and one of them is Jacob. His destiny is to become the King of Kings and he has the blessing of Zeus," she waited for a response and when none came she continued, "Jacob is stubborn and strong but he is also kind and compassionate. It's written that when the End Times battle is won, Zeus will hand to him the throne of Olympus and after that we bow before him."

Girish then spoke, "It was said that on the morning of the council Zeus held Dione's hand and told her of how tired he was. He spoke of leaving. Odin, The Allfather, expressed the same desire. Both Zeus and Odin were heard to speak of two young and powerful gods. They spoke of Jacob and Odi, twins destined to form an unbreakable alliance, create two royal houses to rule as just kings."

"Does it not seem strange, us sitting here with you?" Mulan asked, "Have you not wondered why we walked into your domain especially as our visit wasn't part of the initial plan? This shows how things have changed and these changes could only have happened if Jacob made them happen. It shows how much he respects and needs you. He wants to include the American pantheons in his plans. I believe a strategy to defeat Lucifer is in place and this defeat can only happen with your help. My visions show Jacob calling for the power of the Sun Gods, even those unheard of. They will answer and come together to assist him in stopping the relentless march of The Darkness. They will play their part out in the universe but that plan can only succeed if you join us in the defence of earth. Will you assist in keeping the Light safely illuminated for all to enjoy?"

Al Kin, Tlaloc and Cizin moved away to discuss all they had heard. The goddess's remained, wanting to hear of their long missed friends, Hera, Aphrodite, Ares, Athena and Dione.

Akna requested permission to place her hand to Mulan's forehead, which was granted. She closed her eyes and searched through Mulan's mind for images of Jacob and Odi. "I see them," she said, "they rest near the lagoon and speak of their love for Eala and Panya. I see children, each will wield great power. Jacob's three are already born and are being protected by the power of the elves. Odi's two sleep soundly and will not be born for many years."

Akna opened her eyes so widely she showed her concern, "There is danger, 'HE' knows of the babies and seeks them, he has spies everywhere. What I have just seen tells me I must support Jacob." There was no more discussion; the remaining goddess's confirmed they too will support the new King of Kings.

When the council reconvened, Tlaloc spoke, "For us, it'll be very difficult to fight alongside Zeus. I, like Al Kin and to a greater degree, Cizin, suffered after choosing the losing side in the cosmic wars. But, we will assist in every way."

Just then a powerful wind developed and from its midst voices were heard prompting Mulan to ask, "Do you hear it?"

"Yes," replied Al Kin, "it's the call of the Shinto. I fear their homeland is under threat, you must leave now and travel to the Fire Islands."

Girish stood and walked to the rim of the stack and when he glanced back said, "We can't leave as yet, look below."

Mulan joined him, "So many, and among them are carriers. There are more, many more and they dwell further north. Our work here is not done."

Cizin offered to assist; he used his powers to bring her down into the valley where she spent many hours walking among the tribes passing on Jacob's message, and when she returned she said, "The tribes speak of powerful nations to the north, they speak of the Apache, Navajo and Shoshone, my visions show that among them we must walk."

For over three hundred years they travelled through the northern lands. Not only did they visit the Apache, Navajo and Shoshone nations, they also used their time to pass the message to the Arapaho, Pawnee and Shawnee nations as well as the Cherokee; in fact, they visited every Native American tribe and never once detected the presence of serpents.

They had many adventures and visited wondrous places but nothing took their breath away more than the vastness of the buffalo herds grazing on the Great Plains. They even met up with the mythical white bull who was the guardian god of the herds. This was a peaceful time; the tribes knew their place and never intruded into another's territory.

At every gathering Mulan always gave a most profound prophecy, one that was common to all tribes. It spoke of the slaughter of the great herds bringing on a great hunger. It showed the theft of their ancestral lands as well as the rampant murder of their descendants. The prophecies also showed a degree of hope where, in the distant future, wise ones would assist the tribes to preserve the old ways. It also showed how the wise ones learned to use the imposed laws of the invaders to their advantage, using the courts to reclaim their stolen land.

It was now the year 583CE and for the previous fifty years Mulan lived among the Sioux nation, immersing in their culture. During this time the voices from the Fire Islands became more persistent until they became so

226

loud Mulan had no choice but to request a meeting with the chief and inform him of her departure.

That evening, in the communal Tipi, the chief and all the tribe elders were gathered and waiting for Mulan to arrive and when she did she was surprised when he said, "I've always known you're not alone? Only I could see you. Your escorts are forever by your side, always ready and armed. Why have you never trusted us?"

"It's not about trust so please don't be offended," replied Mulan. "My guardians make their own decisions and have chosen to be permanently invisible. Believe it or not it's for your protection. They are prepared for any threat from the forces of Hell and mark my words, Hell is coming. It will be brought by the white man and will be responsible for the almost total annihilation of your way of life."

"You frighten me when you speak of annihilation," said a now very concerned chief, "will there be many of us left?"

"There will be enough to remind the world of your way of life," said Mulan trying to reassure him, "but most importantly there will be enough to carry the message and answer the call of the gods."

Mulan asked Garuda and Girish to materialise and when they did, the glow of the central fire reflecting off the golden armour created an image of pure power. To the chief and the elders they were a most awesome sight.

The Chief bowed causing Girish to say "Never bow before us; you are the Chief of this proud Sioux nation. It is us who should bow before you." Girish stepped back and with Garuda they bowed.

It was now time to go and when Mulan joined Garuda and Girish she produced the red crystal and after a slight bow to the chief they suddenly disappeared.

Chapter 7

All across the Land of Shinto, otherwise known as the Fire Islands, volcanoes were rumbling, some had already exploded. People were tense, not because of the tremors or the lava flows but because they sensed something more sinister. The fear in the people prompted Garuda to produce his staff and send out its light. His light showed the presence of a new form of evil, much different, more sinister. He wondered did the gods even know of its existence. The menace he detected emanated from deep inside Mount Fuji and it was waiting to break through. Its terror was so potent all he wanted was to leave and find a safer place. He felt an overwhelming urge to move further south, just far enough away to keep an eye on the mountain.

From a concealed cave in the outskirts of a nearby city they watched and waited and for almost sixty years they seldom revealed themselves. During this time they continued with their task, passing on the message, usually to young boys and girls who then encouraged their families to move away to the far south. Time moved on.

Between the years 749CE and 806CE, which was during the combined reigns of the Emperors Junnin, Konin and Kanmu as well as the Empresses' Koken and Shotoku, the mountain quietened, but the feelings of menace was always there. It was generally a peaceful time and many of the inhabitants prospered, especially the aristocracy, and like in the royal courts all over the world there was intrigue and conspiracy, particularly during the reign of the

Empress Koken who gave ammunition to her rivals when she conducted a clandestine and passionate affair with Doyko, a renowned Buddhist monk. That was until it was discovered he was using their romance in an attempt to overthrow her court and this wasn't to end well for him.

The intrigue didn't end there, during the twenty five year reign of the Emperor Kanmu, the growing power of the Buddhist monks, many of whom had become corrupt, prompted Kanmu to move his capital. This city eventually became known as Kyoto. From there he went to war against the surrounding clans causing many losses and the weakening of his army. It was also a time of severe famine brought on by a lengthy drought. Kanmu saw this as his chance to seek redemption, he used his remaining reserves to assist the people and as a result many survived but unfortunately for him, Mount Fuji finally erupted, unleashing thousands of serpents that slithered their way down the slopes into the surrounding towns and villages. As feared by Garuda these serpents were different. They were stronger and had the power to shape-shift. They also had the power to possess, making it difficult for the people to protect themselves. Their rampage through the surrounding lands was swift and their strategy was to rip out the souls of those who resisted while possessing those who willingly succumbed. Villagers who managed to escape carried harrowing tales of pain and torture to the capital, and when the stories reached the ears of the emperor a real fear developed. This was an onslaught no one knew how to deal with.

It was then when Mulan decided to become known to the emperor. She reached the throne room where she materialised. She didn't bow which was a major crime and a great insult, the courtiers were horrified. She wasn't interested in protocol and quickly explained who she was before offering her help. Her sudden appearance rattled the palace guards prompting them to react by lunging forward in an attempt to capture her, but they were no match for what they were up against. They were disarmed by invisible swords and sent to the floor with such force they were knocked unconscious.

"What magic is this? Why have you brought such evil into my palace?" The Emperor yelled as he leapt to his feet.

Mulan calmly replied, "There's no magic or evil. What you have witnessed is the power of my guardians," she paused waiting for a reaction, "my name is Mulan and I ask you not to be afraid. I am here to prepare your people for a battle against the forces of Hell. They are coming and will soon be here, you are going to need my assistance."

"What makes you think I can't defend my own realm?" asked the Emperor.

"You can't," said Mulan, "you or your armies don't have the knowledge or the skills but if you allow us, we can show you the way."

"What can a mere girl do?" asked the Emperor.

Mulan replied trying not to be insulted, "In my dreams I saw a Shaolin monastery. There I watched and learned the skills of the warrior monk, by adding those skills to the power of meditation I have become a powerful teacher. For some time now I have gathered from among your villages, twenty boys and twenty girls whom I secretly trained to use only their hands in battle. They have since been trained in weaponry and are now masters in the use of the Tachi sword; they know no fear. My pupils are ready to teach your armies and assist in the defence of your realm. You must accept them for there is little time." The emperor was intrigued and requested she show him her pupils in action.

Garuda left for to the parklands where he gathered the girls and brought them to the palace where on arrival they were met with gasps of disbelief. To the court they looked like twenty young unarmed girls who were too petite to be formidable.

Mulan challenged the palace guards to attack using everything they had including bows and arrows. The soldiers had barely taken up their positions when the girls suddenly moved to form a two lined circle. As the soldiers approached, the inner circle shot out between the legs of the outer circle and proceeded to use their extended legs to topple the advancing soldiers. They then used their elbows and elongated hands to knock each soldier unconscious and this was done at such speed the soldiers had no chance. The second line then attacked using spears that were not that unlike the more modern Yari, they were spears that were favoured for its reach and piercing ability. The first line of girls took the crane position and used it to leap high over the heads of the advancing soldiers, turn in mid-air to use their feet to break through the tight formation sending each one to the floor.

The final line of soldiers remained where they were and prepared to use their arrows prompting the girls to form a perfect square. Each girl identified one soldier each and waited in a forward trust position for the arrows to be released. When the arrows took flight the girls began a rapid rotational motion of their arms and used it to break the trajectory of each arrow. A second volley was launched and again each arrow was stopped. The girls then took up their original formation and bowed to their emperor.

The generals were stunned especially because this was a patriarchal society and men looked on defeat to a woman as dishonour.

Mulan then suggested the emperor allow her bring in the boys which he agreed to, and when they arrived the emperor was surprised to see they too were no more than sixteen years and looked as wretched as the girls. He was taken aback by their combat prowess as they demonstrated their skills, especially with their use of swords.

She then chose to reveal, "When I arrived you saw your guards being disarmed. That's because I'm protected by two warriors, trained by the War

Gods of Olympus." She gestured for Girish and Garuda to materialise and when they did there were gasps of disbelief. To the court their golden armour, draping capes and crafted helmets made them appear as warriors of high status, but the emperor wasn't impressed, his arrogance showed, "You have no place here. We will defend our people without your help. Leave us."

Just then numerous bolts of lightning hit the palace grounds, followed by very loud rumbles of thunder. The palace doors burst open and in walked three gods of the Kami pantheon, gods who were ancient and revered deities of the Shinto religion. The emperor, the generals, soldiers and courtiers went to their knees on recognising who was before them.

The first to speak said after acknowledging Mulan, "I am Amaterasu, the Shinto Goddess of the Sun." She then introduced the god to her right, "This is Fujin, God of the Wind, an elder who was present at the creation." She turned to her left, "And this is Hachiman. God of War, protector of those who dwell in these enchanted lands." She then spoke directly to the emperor, "I am a daughter of Izanagi and ancestress to your imperial royal family." She waited for a reaction, none came. "Your rejection of assistance alarms us. Your people are dying. Scouts carry with them horrific stories of wanton carnage. They speak of Kaido's flowing with the blood of loyal subjects and expressed their fear that within seven days the imperial city will be overrun. Can you not see you stand no chance against the forces of Hell?"

While the emperor was considering his options, Amaterasu turned to Mulan, "Lord Buddha represented the Kami at the council. On his return he asked us to watch over you. We are not to interfere."

Their conversation was interrupted when the emperor accepted he needed help. He instructed his generals to allow the pupils take control of training the imperial army. Plans were immediately put in place and over the next few days thirty of Mulan's pupils assisted as best they could. The remaining ten pupils made their way out into the forest.

Those teaching the soldiers never allowed the constant reports of serpent attacks distract them from their task. It pleased them that the soldiers were already fit making their task considerably easier. They stuck to their plans of five by forty minute regimes per day, starting with a 1.6km run, followed by squat jumps, standing jumps, push ups, jump jacks and lunges. One session per day was allocated to lower and upper body weight training. On the fifth and sixth day weapon training was the priority allowing the imperial army to become sword-masters. The soldiers learned many new skills and with this their confidence grew, their training suppressed any fear of what the future held. On the seventh day thousands of soldiers were moved into the surrounding forests.

With the army now prepared Mulan, Garuda and Girish left the palace and moved to a high ridge just outside the city. Before reaching the ridge Garuda asked, "Mulan, the ten students that left last week, you never told us why?"

"Even I don't know," said Mulan, "when I asked, all they said was something entered their heads and they needed to leave. They didn't know why. When they said it was a very bright light I knew my place was not to question it. I felt no threat."

The three gods from the Kami pantheon moved to observe the battle from a snow-capped summit on a mountain opposite.

On the eighth day a foul odour reached the city bringing a menacing terror to the populous, it was a terror that continued to build as the hours passed. The palace guards strengthened their positions along the city walls with their arrows primed and ready to launch at any movement coming from the North West.

When all was in place everything seemed to stop and the silence was almost deafening, no chirping, bellowing or howling, not a sound. Even the well trained imperial war horses disappeared, it was as though Pegasus had arrived and decided they needed protection. The eerie atmosphere added to the terror in the minds of the citizens who couldn't find solace in the power of the military. Then it began.

The serpents attacked using a stealth and speed difficult to repel. They quickly reached the walls and before the army had time to react, began climbing towards the turrets. They made their way over the walls taking the souls of many as they went. They invaded many houses ruthlessly killing all those they met. The defenders had no chance, their arrows just travelled through the serpent's slimy bodies, confirming they were protected by a new and evil magic. Lucifer gained many poor souls that day.

The emperor watched the serpents approach his palace and wished he had listened more carefully to Mulan. It was then when he ordered the release of a flaming arrow, a signal for the regular army hidden in the forests to attack. When they arrived they fought with a vengeance, quickly and swiftly destroying serpent after serpent before finally reaching the palace and securing it. There was great relief among the remaining inhabitants but the emperor wasn't happy, the defeat of the serpents in the city was too easy, things didn't feel right. He looked for answers but none came, he couldn't understand how the serpents so steadfastly reached the palace then succumbed so easily.

In the distance a portal opened, it emitted an orange glow so menacing, it could only be coming from the fires of Hell. Standing at its entrance stood a shadowy and sinister figure with his wings stretching from wall to wall. His iconic horns stood high above his head. His dark frame expanded with his pitchfork standing upright by his side for all to see who he was. It was

Lucifer and he was announcing the arrival of the Lord of Hell. His face sent out that well know image of terror all recognised, but it was his beaming smile that betrayed his delight and his belief that his ruse had worked, he could barely contain himself. His serpents distracted the imperial army long enough for his Dark Angels to materialise on the ridge behind Mulan, Garuda and Girish. He was prepared to sacrifice thousands of serpents just to capture a messenger of the gods.

There were six of them, tasked with capturing the messenger and taking her into the presence of Lucifer. They were also instructed to destroy the guardians.

Two of the six Dark Angels raced forward taking Mulan and after securing her; dragged her towards the portal. Garuda and Girish were taken by surprise but still they found the strength, and amazing speed to move towards rescuing her. Unfortunately their speed and strength was matched in every way by the new powers shown by the four remaining angels. There was now a real danger Mulan was about to be lost but the Dark Angels or Lucifer didn't reckon on the ten pupils who had, a week earlier, left the palace for reasons, that at that time no one understood.

All ten pupils levitated from the ledge below and were obviously at one with Lord Buddha. While levitating, they stretched out their arms, sending a hidden force of light to surround the whole ridge, creating an impregnable barrier preventing Mulan from being taken any further. This force also stopped the Dark Angels from escaping, leaving them to face the ruthless power of a very angry Garuda and Girish, an anger fuelled by the fact that they were so easily deceived and had failed in their task of protecting Mulan.

Lucifer, in the meantime, looked on in disbelief. Another of his plans thwarted and as the moments passed he became more furious. He couldn't step out from the portal as his presence on earth would awaken the gods. He knew a battle at this time was something for which he was still unprepared. He remained at the entrance long enough to watch Garuda and Girish use their skills to subdue; then slowly bleed their captives, extracting as much information as possible, knowing the Information would help the gods prepare for future battles.

His frustration grew, listening to his minions revealing his plan as well as his strengths and weaknesses before they were dispatched. While on view he knew it was in his interests to control his rage but when he closed the portal he shut his eyes for just a few moments before exploding and rampaging his way through the Underworld.

All was now quiet prompting Girish to raise his staff and call on the Light and this time, when it arrived, it was at its brightest. It was as though it arrived in celebration of a momentous victory and wasn't afraid to show it. Girish turned his staff, sent it out and up towards Mount Fuji where he quickly established there were no serpents in the surrounding lands. There was great relief but all three had many questions. Why did the gods on the summit opposite not come to their aid? Why did no one work out earlier how the serpent attack, although foreseen, was a distraction? How did they not detect the evil presence behind them?

Mulan looked at her guardians and for the first time she felt insecure leading her to seek solitude away from them. Garuda and Girish in turn were distressed; they had sensed her loss of confidence and for the first time didn't know what to do. They returned to invisibility and stood as far away as they could while still keeping her in their sights. They watched the gods from the ridge opposite arrive to meet with Mulan, and could see she was not impressed with their lack of action. They watched her lose her temper and lash out in anger. "Oh my," remarked Girish. "Remind me never to get on her bad side."

Garuda in a moment of weakness mumbled, "What I would do to be on any of her sides." He cringed, his face reddened, hoping Girish didn't hear. Girish was itching to comment but chose to say nothing.

After a few awkward moments they chose to move closer to Mulan but their approach was noticed by Fujin who joined them, "We are ancient and powerful gods and have learned much about interfering when things should be allowed take their own course. Have you not wondered why Zeus, Odin, Shiva or the Archangels didn't come to your aid?" he waited for a response and when none came he continued, "Let me tell you why. They didn't come to your aid for the same reason as us. We wanted to help and although distressed, we saw your future and all three of you were answering the call of the gods. The visions showed you leading the armies of the Light during the battle of the End Times. You were destined to survive this attack, it's been foretold. We are not blind and it saddens us to feel the tension between you, but you must understand it was you three who were given the task, not us." He then said, "It will always be difficult to out-smart Lucifer and today you did. You did it by training those forty boys and girls."

Garuda wasn't impressed, he shouted, "What you say doesn't help. We failed and the gods will have seen how we failed. I'm so ashamed."

Fujin responded, "I understand your anger and trust me, we intended to do battle. We know how deceptive Lucifer can be and saw the danger but as I said, we also saw your future and you were all there. We chose then to let events take their course."

Garuda stormed off and went to stand at the edge of a high cliff where he had great difficulty controlling his temper. He went to his knees and stared out over the valley below, then began to deliberately and slowly fall forward and out off the cliff. As he fell, he stretched out his arms and began to transform into Jacob's Mythical Bird and Emperor of the Skies. He used a rapid flapping of his wings to increase his speed and climb as high as he could before turning and swooping at such a speed, suggesting his intention was to slam against the mountainside.

Mulan was first to react and with Girish by her side, they both pleaded with him not to do anything stupid. He ignored their pleas and increased his speed as he approached the cliff-face. He didn't care, he wanted to end it all, but he didn't reckon on his friend, the Lord of the Mountains.

Girish, without thinking, joined his two hands together before quickly separating them, causing the mountain to part, opening a pass. Garuda entered the pass only to hit the ground with such force he painfully rolled forward and turned back into his human form. He was torn, bruised, bleeding and in agony but the worst thing was he felt like an idiot, his anger had now abated and when he looked up, he saw not only Mulan and Girish, he also saw the gods and the ten pupils staring back at him.

He composed himself, struggled and after a few moments, limped over to where the pupils were, "Forgive me," he said, lowering his head, "I haven't shown my gratitude. Only for your skills we would have lost Mulan forever. I....." he stopped and looked up at Mulan before continuing, "We will forever be in your debt."

"It's we who should be grateful," responded one of the pupils, "you took us from destitution; took away the hunger, thirst and the despair. You trained us, gave us new skills and the confidence we need to travel these ancient lands. We will fulfil our promise to be guardians and protectors of the carriers for as long as is needed."

Garuda then painfully limped towards the gods, bowed and apologised for his behaviour. He couldn't face Girish or Mulan so just ignored them, he sat on a nearby rock nursing his injuries. Mulan called the pupils together including the ones who assisted the emperor and prepared them for her departure. The three gods then bade their farewells.

From their vantage point Mulan and Girish watched the emperor's army gather the bodies of the fallen. They also gathered the shells of the serpents and Dark Angels creating numerous funeral pyres that when lit were viewed as far as the horizon. Watching the ceremonies, Mulan decided she should meet the emperor one last time. She was escorted by Girish alone. Garuda was still out of sorts.

On reaching the city the grief was palpable. Mulan used much of her time to comfort those who were bereaved before moving towards the emperor's palace. When she reached the palace, she and Girish were made very welcome and treated as heroes. They acknowledged each other's experiences and when all memories were exhausted Mulan gave a prophecy, "The deceit of Lucifer knows no bounds but I don't understand why he has spared much of this city. I fear he has other plans so beware his wrath; it will be unleashed when the earth shakes and it surely will shake," she looked directly at the emperor, "your family will rule this realm into the distant future but be aware that there will be times when your people will suffer greatly, no more so than near the End Times. Be pleased that your lands will also prosper and in years to come, your descendants will preside over what will become a powerhouse for the whole world."

The emperor was pleased with the prophecy and then presented Mulan with a gift of a most exquisite gem encrusted gown as a token of gratitude from the imperial family. Mulan was overwhelmed when she saw how the gems, on capturing the light, sent a hypnotic range of colour to all corners of the palace. It was then when she remembered Jacob's prophecy, 'You will be my warrior queen and the gatherer of the gems of beauty.'

The ladies of the court took her to an annex room and assisted her with a fitting, and when ready she walked back into the palace to gasps of amazement. Her gown was a body hugging silver grey design with white inlays, made from the finest of silks. The sleeves were a patchwork of the most beautiful gems ever mined. When she placed the golden gem filled necklace, given to her by the forest tribes, around her neck she presented as a goddess. Girish was awe struck; he couldn't take his eyes from her. He thought, 'Garuda will kick himself when he hears of this.'

She returned to the annex and changed back to her normal attire, then gently and carefully wrapped the gown before placing it into her satchel. She then made her way back to the throne room and bade her farewells to the court before making her way back to the ridge. Through all this, Girish never left her side and continuously send out the Light in search of escaped serpents and none were found. On their journey back they occasionally looked up the steep slope in the hope Garuda had come around, but he remained at the edge continuing to sulk.

It was near twilight when they reached their destination. They said nothing, but did observe Garuda turn his back, so they ignored him. Girish prepared a fire and, alongside Mulan, he sat hoping to repair the loss of trust between them, neither could forget the near disaster that happened earlier that day.

They soon became totally relaxed in each other's company but their giggling was getting on Garuda's nerves causing his moaning and grunting to get louder. His continuous groaning eventually got to Mulan and gave rise to her losing patience with him. She verbally lashed out and was so aggressive even Girish became very afraid. When Garuda's cape slipped Mulan was socked, she saw numerous pock marks on his legs and shoulders, wounds he was discreetly scratching.

She stopped shouting and gently pulled back his robe only to be shocked at the condition of his body. His feathers hadn't retracted properly and his constant scratching had torn his skin causing blood to seep from everywhere.

She opened her satchel and produced a scented oil she was sure would help, and offered him a massage. He was embarrassed and cringed at the idea of her seeing his naked and hideously pockmarked body but the itch was now so intolerable he had no choice but to accept her offer. He removed his robes and within minutes began to wallow in the soft and gentle massage he was receiving.

He continuously denied any improvement when asked how he felt such was the pleasure he was getting from Mulan's soft and sensuous touch. Her oil-drenched hands gliding across his skin caused sensations of pleasure to cascade through his body so much so he slowly drifted into bliss. Mulan's suspicions grew especially when she saw his eyes dancing behind his eyelids.

At one point he opened his eyes and caught Girish discreetly but enviously looking across and got great pleasure in showing him a sneaky smile then stuck out his tongue. He closed his eyes again savouring every moment, and then fell into a relaxing sleep.

This was Girish's chance to tease him. He silently gestured for Mulan to move aside. He took some oil and gently massaged it into Garuda's back causing a low murmuring sound of pleasure. Garuda had no idea he was responding to a massage by his closest male friend. His sleep was interrupted when all three felt a presence; it was Lord Buddha, "Come my children, it's time for enlightenment. Today you suffered, now seek peace for many more battles wait. Tomorrow you journey to the land of the Dynasties and it's there where you commence your thousand year walk."

Garuda awoke from his blissful slumber to find he was completely healed and when he turned to thank Mulan he was shocked to discover it was Girish's hands covered in oil. Girish smirked and blew him a kiss then jumped to run away. Garuda reacted by throwing his sandals but missed. Soon after, all three came back together to spend the next few hours meditating.

The following morning they prepared for their departure and when all was ready, Mulan produced the red crystal for the last time; she transported them to the grand plaza outside the great Shaolin monastery.

Chapter 8

The grand plaza was a bustling market area with thousands of pilgrims from all over China in attendance. In its centre was built a monastery set in an accessible and serene location high in the Song Mountains, surrounded by many peaks.

The sound of swishing movements coming from behind the walls particularly intrigued Mulan but it was Girish who remarked, "That sound reminds me of the one we created when training in the use of the sword back in Olympus."

Mulan agreed then said, "It's time we made our way to meet the abbot."

They reached the imposing red painted wooden doors and after knocking, a young monk presented himself. He was perplexed to see no one before him, and after stepping out to look around, he had unwittingly given Mulan and her guardians enough time to secretly enter.

The sight that met them was spectacular, consisting of sixty young novices standing in six lines facing their mentor. They were wearing the traditional black and grey robes, common during the Tang Dynasty, and they were perfecting the use of the Shaolin form of martial arts which included the use of the Dao sword.

All three silently moved along the right hand side wall, watching amazing and captivating kung Fu movements of precision and skill. They made their way to the main temple where the abbot and his senior advisers had gathered to pray before the image of a Golden Buddha. The monks took the lotus position and began a most holy ceremony. The gong of the ancient bells and the scent of aromatic incense helped bring all those in attendance into a deep meditative trance. When the bells ceased chiming all went quiet. The birds stopped chirping, the baaing of sheep and goats abated and the wind quietened down. There was now an absolute silence.

Mulan opened her eyes and watched all present sit motionless and in deep meditation. She then stood and moved towards the image of Buddha. She bowed only to be taken aback when she heard, "Welcome, my lady. I am Shi Yong, Abbot of this renowned monastery. I sense your presence and the aura surrounding you is so bright it tells me you have been touched by the calmness of my Lord Buddha."

Mulan said nothing, unsure of what to do. She looked across at Girish who placed his finger over his lips indicating she should remain quiet. He sent out the Light and established that there was no presence of Hell, but he did observe the mark of the serpent on several of the senior monks meaning they were descendants of people who were bitten in the distant past.

"It's written of how three immortals will arrive during the golden years of the Tang dynasty," said the Abbot. "Is this now that time?"

It was obvious to Mulan that the abbot was blind and unnaturally elderly. She chose to remain quiet causing the other monks to stand in alarm; the old stories spoke of an attack by serpents following the arrival of three immortals. They looked at the abbot for guidance only to hear him ask, "Why do you hide? I know there're three among us; we've been waiting, please show yourselves."

Mulan rejoined the boys who had already dressed in their robes and armour. The mark of the serpents on some of the monks troubled them and they didn't want to take any risks. The abbot again said, "Please show your-selves:"

It was then when they decided to materialise and when they did the gasps of admiration could be heard throughout the monastery. The monks had never seen a woman of such beauty or warriors of such power. They felt they were now in the presence of gods.

"We are here to start our thousand year walk," said Mulan, "it's a walk that will take us through the eastern lands before we travel to the realm of Indus where we will join Lord Shiva on Mount Kailash. We have come in peace and to learn."

Shi Yong rose and beckoned for them to join him for a stroll through the vastness of his sacred sanctum. He held on to Mulan as she struggled through the throngs of monks who had gathered.

They were taken through the forest of pagodas where the mortal remains of long gone abbots were interred. The pagodas were also the final resting places of renowned Chinese emperors spanning many dynasties.

"We are moving into troubling times," said the Abbot when satisfied they were finally alone, "I fear this most holy of places will be continuously attacked into the future. I need your assistance."

He turned to grip Garuda, "Within these walls there are traitors who will bring pain and death. My time here is coming to an end and I beg you to use your skills to train my monks in the ways of the Light. They too will become guardians of Jacob's message. Please assist those who remain loyal to the teachings, help them into enlightenment."

"You know of the message?" asked a surprised Girish.

"Of course," answered the Abbot, "I am a servant of Lord Buddha and he told me about the council of the gods. He showed me how your arrival will herald in the battle of the End Times, but that battle is not this day. The traitors will soon reveal themselves now they know you are here, they will go to the volcanoes and alert 'Him' to your presence. He will send his armies, protected by a new magic, unused and untested, but equally as destructive."

For the next ten years the monastery was filled with peace and tranquillity allowing Girish and Garuda to become masters of Kung Fu. In fact they were to become two of the greatest teachers of martial arts during their time among the monks. They did what was asked of them, they brought many of the monks into enlightenment.

It was in their tenth year when Shi Yong decided it was time to send emissaries to visit other grottoes and monasteries situated throughout Henan. This created great excitement as most of the monks, who entered the monastery in their eighth year, had never been to any other part of Henan and saw this opportunity as a great adventure. Shi Yong also knew that this was the time when the traitors would make their move.

The night before the planned departure, when all were asleep, was the night that brought a great change. There was a shadow clouding Girish's mind causing him to have a very disturbed sleep. He woke from his turbulent dreams and went to the temple to sit before the Golden Buddha. There he took the lotus position, then placed his hands upon his knees with his palms facing towards the heavens. He took shallow breaths before descending into a deep trance.

The total quietness sharpened his hearing, allowing him to hear voices that seemed to be travelling through a vast expanse of time. He wasn't afraid; he felt an affinity with the owner of the voice. His trance was disturbed when he sensed a presence beside him, it was Shi Yong. They sat together and began to share the same experiences. Both heard the voices before levitating themselves to rest mid-air. They drifted from the temple then found themselves floating through the Pagoda Forest to reach the monastery wall. On touching the wall, they magically slipped through into woodlands filled with leaf laden trees, blooming shrubs and flowers with the sweetest of scents.

They were now walking and soon found themselves in a tranquil valley filled with the sound of the many resident birds, crickets and monkeys. Another sound that reached their ears was that of cascading water flowing over many waterfalls before joining the numerous creeks and lakes. "At last I again see the beauty of creation with my own eyes," said Shi Yong, "it's been so long."

Girish was amazed at how different Shi Yong now appeared. His head was no longer shaven. He had a mop of very dark hair and looked to be much younger than the elderly man who first greeted him ten years earlier. They knelt beside a slow flowing river to drink its life-giving waters and, on seeing their reflections, in unison they said, "It seems we are of the same blood!" It was at about that time when they again heard a voice and it was calling them deeper into the valley.

They followed the course of the river to its source, all the time taking in the amazing scents of the beautiful flowers and shrubs as they passed. At times they entered tree-formed tunnels so dense no light could penetrate. Soon they reached a clearing to be met by a solitary figure dressed in the robes of a powerful Chinese warrior. They both recognised him to be Huangdi, the Yellow Emperor, a Deity of the Light and ancestor of all the Han. He appeared in his silk ceremonial dragon robes, elaborately embroidered with the emblem of the five clawed Chinese dragon.

Girish and Shi Yong both bowed before being invited to sit on the two other thrones placed in such a way as to form a semi-circle allowing a three way conversation.

Huangdi said to Girish, "You heard my call and answered, it pleases me." He turned to Shi Yong, "Your time in Shaolin has come to an end; join me and wait for the call of the gods."

Huangdi then left his throne and to stare at the sky, "It's been well over three thousand years since last I glanced across the heavens," he said. "Troubled dreams forced me to awaken. Last night I heard the dying stars scream out in pain and I know the cosmos weeps for their loss; tears bring fear because the light is dimming. The Darkness grows in strength each time it smites the Light and this cannot be allowed to continue. I'm happy you, Girish, are of my blood and using the power of my blood you walked near the Lagoon that day when Jacob left the temple. He didn't know it but the Ancient One did. You were chosen to be the eastern guardian and your destiny brought you home to prepare our people. My blood flows through millions in these lands and I promise, all will answer your call."

He paused for a moment and looked around at the beauty of the forest, "All gods agreed Jacob's messengers alone are the ones to change man by ensuring they accept his message. All this is now in jeopardy, Lucifer has evolved and is using a long forgotten and ancient magic. First he sent out the serpents, and then he created Dark Angels. He brought life to the flying demons and now, using this magic, he brings forth the Wraiths of Hell. Beware the Wraiths of Hell, they see through the messengers. They will be your biggest enemy and your greatest danger; they plan to take the Light from thousands of innocent souls and will use this Light to deceive you. They bring terror, fear, mistrust and rage into the mind of man."

Girish was about to speak when he was stopped by Huangdi raising his hand. "Shi Yong and I must leave now and await the call. Remember, beware the Wraiths." They immediately disappeared leaving Girish alone.

Meanwhile back at the temple Mulan and Garuda were awoken by the tossing and turning of Girish. They watched his rapid eye movement and saw he was in some distress. They listened to him mumble incoherently, including repeating the same word. After a few moments he shot up and leapt to his feet shouting, "They're coming, they're coming. In their thousands they're coming, they know of us and have new skills. They're coming."

He looked confused and asked how he got back to his room. "You've been here all night," said Mulan, "you never left."

"No, I was with Shi Yong and the Yellow Emperor," he said looking very distressed, "I've been warned of an imminent attack."

Garuda reached across to calm him, "I've been awake all night. You never left us." Girish got more confused

A loud scream was heard echoing around the monastery. It was a young novice who, after entering the shrine of the Golden Buddha, found the lifeless body of his abbot sitting in the lotus position with his palms facing the heavens. Girish ran to the shrine to find the abbot in the exact position he shared with him during the night but he was again shaven headed and very elderly.

He backed away and sat on the steps outside the shrine and was in turmoil, unable to make sense of what had happened. Mulan and Garuda joined him and tried to reassure him. "When asleep, you kept repeating one word, 'Phoenix'," said Garuda. "What do you mean?"

Girish looked perplexed, "I've no idea what you are talking about."

Garuda raised his hand requesting silence, he moved his head as thought trying to focus, but the commotion in the monastery was too loud. The voice he was listening too never stopped, and eventually as the monastery became more solemn and began to mourn the death of its abbot, the voice became very clear. It was Jacob, "Garuda, my mythical bird and emperor of the skies. Find the Phoenix, leave now and find the Phoenix."

Garuda looked out across the forests. He was looking for inspiration but none came. "Jacob has called," he said after rejoining Mulan and Girish. "He said I must leave. Something to do with the Phoenix, something I know nothing of."

An elderly monk was passing and heard what was said, "The Phoenix is a mythical bird, one who dies and resurrects every five hundred years."

Garuda thought to himself, 'I too am a mythical bird.' He walked to the rear of the courtyard and faced an opening out to the valley below. He raised his arms, held his cape, and then ran. His arms turned to wings, his legs developed claws and his head took the shape of an eagle. He leapt from the monastery and soared high into the sky, letting out a piercing call attracting all native birds to his side. He told them to prepare for war before circling twice and flying towards the west.

He crossed the Himalayas and flew over the Indus nations. He reached Persia and then entered Mesopotamia before turning south and crossing to the Giza plateau. He continued flying but received no inspiration and was getting very anxious. He flew across the Sahara Desert and down over the lands of the Yoruba peoples before continuing further south to rest on Table Mountain. He then flew north over the great lakes of the rift valley and it was there where, in the distance, he saw three bright auras moving south towards him.

Every now and again he saw a very powerful translucent light spread out over the land and thought, 'It can't be! It just can't be!' From his great height he focused and saw that it was Oba, Jomo and Jahiri and he became very emotional. His excitement grew and he swiftly flew towards them to land near where they were resting. Jomo and Jahiri immediately went into defensive mode and were ready for an attack. He stood before them as a seven foot tall and majestic bird prompting Oba to say, "The mythical bird? Garuda, is it you?" He quickly transformed into his human form bringing tears to her eyes.

He said while running to embrace her, "You look amazing for someone who is nine hundred years old. You haven't aged a bit."

She was confused, "Garuda, twelve hundred years have passed."

They both felt a presence; it was Jacob, "My friends, you are immortals and Time should mean nothing to you, it has moved slower for some and faster for others. It will realign near the End Times."

Oba continued to hold Garuda much to the ire of Jomo; that was until he turned and they saw who he was. They ran at him with such excitement they sent him tumbling to the ground and when their excitement waned, Garuda said, "My friends, I too am excited and can feel the tears well up but this is a fleeting visit. There is a new magic and Mulan is in great danger," he paused then asked, "On your travels, have you ever seen or heard mention of 'The Phoenix?'"

"Yes we did," said Jomo. "In Heliopolis, the City of the Sun, there were images engraved on the temple walls showing the rising of an immortal bird called the Phoenix. Go there and meet with Ra-Atum, he is a Sun God and will help."

Jahiri warned, "Be aware, he was near leaving when we were there and that was over a thousand years ago, it's possible he may have already left."

"Fear not," said Oba, "the temple may now be gone and the library burned but he will know how much he is needed and will have waited. Go now and seek the Phoenix." She went silent as though in a trance then whispered, "I see them and you are right, Mulan and Girish are in great danger, many monks have fallen. I see the Wraiths and they are near; you must hurry." Garuda quickly took to the sky and circled several times before swooping one last time. He yelled as he flew north, "Be safe!"

He flew as fast as his wings would allow and when he reached Heliopolis, he was, as predicted, greeted by Ra-Atum. He took his human form and explained the urgency of his visit. Ra-Atum said, "Welcome, Emperor of the Birds, I've waited all this time for your visit."

Garuda said as he bowed, "My Lord, time is not with us, tell me of the Phoenix!"

"I'm the guardian of the Phoenix," said Ra-Atum, "and I know exactly where to find him. Your timing is perfect, very few have witnessed the death and rebirth of this most mythical of birds."

He brought Garuda south to the Mountains of the Moon where, high on a south facing cliff was a well camouflaged cave, and they waited. Several days passed before the Phoenix arrived and when he did he bowed to his god and then turned to Garuda, "My Liege, you've come at last."

"You were expecting me?" asked a surprised Garuda.

The Phoenix replied, "I've always known that one day the emperor of the skies and king of all birds would visit me, today is that day."

Garuda explained the predicament Mulan faced and the power of the new evil that was rising in the east, then asked, "Why is it, Jacob, the future King of Kings, talks about the Phoenix?"

"The arrival of young and powerful gods into Olympus is well known about among the astrals," replied the Phoenix, "I know of Jacob and of how he will become a powerful King of Kings, destined for greatness. He is a god and a prophet. If he spoke of me then I have something he needs and I think I know what it is." He moved away and nestled near the centre of the cave, he said, "Today I die, today I turn to ash, tomorrow I rise and will fly for another five hundred years, it can only be my ashes he needs. Take a

handful and leave immediately, use my ashes, they will be your saviour."
He then passed away and turned to ash. Garuda gathered a handful, turned
to Ra-Atum, bowed and rushed back to Shaolin.

Five weeks had passed since Garuda began his search for the Phoenix
and during this time the funeral of Shi Yong had taken place. It was attended
by monks from all over Henan, as well as many local clan dignitaries. It was
a spectacle worthy of the great stories especially as one of the most powerful
emperors of the Tang dynasty attended. When the three day funeral event
climaxed, with the lighting of the funeral pyre, there was an estimated fifty
thousand people surrounding the monastery paying homage to the memory
of the blind, very elderly and most holy abbot. Soon after the funeral rites
were concluded the young monks started their delayed pilgrimage. It was
also the time and opportunity for the traitors to do their worst.

When Garuda returned all Hell had already broken loose. The traitors
Shi Yong had feared; did their evil work. They left the monastery and made
their way high into the Yellow Mountains where they alerted the Dark Angels to the fact that the messengers were staying and training in Shaolin.

From his vantage point, Garuda saw the monastery was surrounded by
serpents, and behind them were the Dark Angels. Concealed by broken
cloud cover he saw numerous flying demons. They were probing and testing
the Shaolin defences and it disturbed him to see that the forward ranks of
serpents had already broken through the first line of warrior monks and was
now moving on the second level of the monastery.

He let out a piercing call, answered immediately by the arrival of the
Pied Falconets, followed by the Japanese Falcons and the Turkey Vultures.
The Falconets were first to attack, successfully decimating the first three
formations of serpents but they took many losses. They were followed by
the Japanese Falcons who continued the aerial onslaught that eventually

destroyed all ranks of the remaining serpents. The turkey vultures then finished the job by feeding on the mound of evil bodies lying all around them.

The Falconets then turned their attention to the flying demons but this was a mistake, it allowed Dark Angels on the ground to attack the monastery without hindrance. The third level of the monastery was being defended by just over two hundred of the remaining monks and they were now on the receiving end of Hells wrath.

At the entrance to the shrine Mulan and five elderly monks solemnly stood. They were the only monks who in their 'being' held all the knowledge and history of Shaolin, they needed to be protected at all costs. Girish was standing before them as their final line of defence. He was invisible and just waited.

Garuda was horrified watching line after line of the well trained monks fall to the relentless torrent of savagery unleashed by the Dark Angels. His horror turned to despair when he saw his Falcons lose their battle against the ever growing legions of demons.

He moved higher, trying to devise a plan to rescue the remaining monks but neglected to prepare for what could come at him from behind, a weakness detected by two demons that immediately broke off from the attack and circled around the nearest mountain. They flew higher so as to put the sun behind them.

The attack on the remaining monks ended as quickly as it started with the withdrawal of the Dark Angels and this caused confusion, it flew in the face of the rules of war when one was so close to total victory. Garuda wasn't fooled; he saw the withdrawal and deduced that the final attack force was about to make its move. From his vantage point he saw Lucifer had unleashed the Wraiths of Hell. Savage off-white translucent spirits empowered to destroy everything in their path. The monks had no chance; they hadn't been trained for this form of evil. The wraiths showed no mercy, they possessed each monk they caught before showing them the torturous fires of Hell that waited. All this as their souls were being eaten from the inside out.

Mulan's anxiety showed but what helped was her belief that Jacob wouldn't send them into a battle without a chance of survival. Her fears grew when the Wraiths reached the shrine and all efforts by Girish seemed doomed to failure.

The Wraiths couldn't harm Girish as he was invisible, but they knew he was there. They followed his movements and teased as each strike passed through them causing no harm.

All seemed lost until high above, the two demons who circled the mountain came at Garuda with the sun at their backs. They hit him with such force it sent him crashing to the ground where on impact the satchel carrying the ashes of the Phoenix burst open sending its contents in all directions. The ashes were laced with a benevolent magic, a magic that brought the Light and was a force for good. As the ashes spread over the Wraiths, at first, there was an expression of pain; then screams of torture, followed by a fire that consumed them all. Another effort by Lucifer was foiled but not before it brought much death and destruction to this most revered monastery.

The battle in the sky continued for another few hours and ended with the routing of the remaining demons. Garuda, when he recovered, rejoined the exhausted birds and thanked them for their support. He also reminded them to be prepared for more calls as the End Times approached.

Back on the ground Mulan and Girish made their way through the various levels of the monastery in the hope of finding survivors. They found fifteen young monks who had been bitten and were suffering from the effects of the 'poison of fire' and this prompted Mulan to seek alcohol urgently but there was none to be found so she sent Garuda to a local village where he commandeered a barrel of a very strong Baijiu.

It was several weeks before the monks fully recovered but Girish needed to be sure so he placed them in the line and raised his staff to call on the Light. When it came, it almost sent Girish to the ground. Garuda assisted in holding the staff allowing the Light to travel through the monks and out across the mountains, only then were they satisfied all trace of evil was expelled from Shaolin.

Six months later, the travelling monks returned from their pilgrimage and were shocked at what they found. They immediately assisted the remaining monks to rebuild the monastery and its congregation. It was also around that time when Mulan became restless, knowing it was time to move on.

Saying goodbye was difficult but they had no choice, the call was getting stronger. The remaining monks solemnly stood as Mulan and her guardians passed. They waited and watched, marvelling at the colourful lotus flowers growing from the footsteps of the departing immortals. More fascinating was the flowers, growing from all trees, as Mulan passed. She was now bringing on Jacob's 'Flowering Trees of the east'

Chapter 9

Over the next few years Mulan, Garuda and Girish crisscrossed vast mountainous regions. They spent much of their time recapping the adventures, battles, escapades and tragedies that befell them, but the only topic they kept returning to was the story of the meeting Garuda had with Oba, Jomo and Jahiri.

Never once during their journeys did they neglect their duty. Travelling through village after village they ensured that the Han received the message and would be ready for the call. Their journey took them to the grottoes of Mogoo, Yingang, and Longmen. They also spent time among the giant pandas nestling in the bamboo forests. They made their way to the Forbidden City before moving north towards the Great Wall. They travelled further north east into the lands just south of the River Amur where they spent many years visiting the ancestors of the Manchu, another eastern tribe Magni spoke of as one he would call upon at the End Times.

The sweet smelling air of the Amur River basin attracted their attention. On reaching the river they realised this area would become one of their most favourite places. It was the one place so far, where they felt at one with the natural world. Its crystal clear waters fed a sea of the most colourful wild flowers, giving sustenance to an abundance of bees and butterflies of all shapes, sizes and colours. The ancient old growth forests of pine and deciduous trees helped make it one of the most diverse and temperate forest-lands known to man. It was a refuge for the musk deer and the northern brown bear; it also camouflaged the Amur tiger and its more elusive rival, the Amur leopard.

Mulan cherished her time by the water's edge, especially in the early morning. She loved watching the Oriental White Stork and the Red-Crowned Cranes feeding, preening and raising their young. Watching the wild salmon and sturgeon battle for territory and eventually spawn, beginning the circle of life all over again was her favourite pastime. All in all it was magical, but she always knew it was fleeting and they would soon have to move on.

When that time came they continued their walk by crossing into the frozen lands of Siberia before turning west to visit the plains of Mongolia. From there they witnessed the first stirrings of the Great Khan. They passed the message to as many nomadic Mongols as possible and encouraged those worthy to make their way to the far north east, out of harm's way to await the call of the gods.

Four hundred years had now passed since leaving Shaolin and a growing awareness of a need to make their way towards Indus was showing itself and it seemed to be getting more urgent. Walking south took them to the realm of the Khmer Empire where they were being drawn towards the temple complex at Angkor Wat.

It was now the year 1300CE when, one sunny morning, they arrived at the walls of this most magical complex. Mulan placed her hand on the southern wall and in her mind she read its history. She read how legend said that its construction was ordered by Indra, King of the Hindu gods, as a palace for one of his sons. She also learned that the temple was sacked by a tribe called the Chams who were in turn expelled by a young King Jayavarman VII just before he moved his capital to a new location several kilometres away, allowing the temple to slowly fall into decay. She also saw its complete transformation from a Hindu to a Buddhist temple and how Buddhist pilgrims from the Fire Islands believed that its enchanting gardens were the famed Jetavana gardens of Lord Buddha.

Her visions also showed her troubling times ahead, she saw a civil war in the distant future. A war destined to bring about the deaths of millions of innocent men, women and children as well as the partial destruction of this one off monument to man's building and artistic prowess. Her eyes squinted in disgust when she saw thieves steal its stone and art works and sell them to the highest bidder.

She became uneasy and insisted they move on towards the pagodas of Burma. "They were here," she said, "I feel their evil but I don't understand where it is. It's not in this temple but it's near." Garuda was first to arm himself, followed quickly by Girish and together they sent out the Light. Nothing showed so they climbed to the top of the temple and again sent out the Light. No serpents, Dark Angels or demons showed, so confusion became their companion, they all sensed something but the Light was not showing a presence of evil.

Entering nearby villages they remained on alert, choosing to pass the message only to those they were certain to be untouched by evil. It was only when they reached a village built near a slow flowing river, when Girish observed the mark of the serpents on many adults leaving the water. The marks were hidden on the upper thighs of the bathers, explaining why they weren't detected before now. Girish deduced that the serpents were creating their own army by biting but not killing those they attacked. These victims were allowed to pass the poison on to their children and their children's children; ensuring evil will travel through the generations eventually bringing forth murderers, rapists and villains, people fated to bring unimaginable terror in the distant future.

Girish told Mulan of his suspicions and by coincidence, her visions showed something similar, especially one image. This vision showed a young innocent boy, and then showed his descendants rising up to become warlords. Millions will be slaughtered because of them.

During their walk through the land of the Khmer towards Burma was when they stumbled across the young boy from her vision. He was playing alone, singing and humming while flicking pebbles over a tree stump lying across the road. She chose to pass the message to him in the hope of changing his path. When she materialised he showed no fear. She was drawn towards him as though by an invisible hand. Her visions became more vivid and showed her the Khmer future and the fires of Hell. Eventually she was repelled back against a nearby tree where she went into shock.

"I saw his future," she said after recovering. "Behind his eyes I saw the face of a demon. I saw him create a poisoned line destined to travel for twenty five generations and end with the birth of the most ruthless and murderous leader of the Khmer. His descendants will carry the mark and will be responsible for a horrific mass murder of Cambodian men, women and children. I saw the serpents bite and smirk knowing their poison will travel through the generations. The descendants of this boy will bring the wrath of the world onto Khmer lands and after many more deaths he will eventually be vanquished. All this will happen before the battle of the End Times when it is possible their terror will start all over again."

Garuda approached and placed his hand on the boys head, gently moving it without the boy realising his head was being eased back. He raised his sword and just as he was about to strike a young women from the village arrived and called the boy who leapt up and ran to jump into her arms. They hugged each other and entered their home. Girish asked, "Would you really have killed him?"

"I saw the pain in Mulan's face," replied Garuda, "Did you see how he didn't react when she materialised? He showed no fear. It seems he is already an ally of the serpents and yes, I would have killed him."

They walked on and travelled through the jungles of Siam before making their way into the lush and green forests of Burma. They were now in the land of the Pagodas where they were to spend the next seventy years.

They rested for a short time beside the pristine Lake Inle where they passed the message on to many local tribes. It was near there when Mulan sensed something disturbing. It was a tremor and it was coming from the realm of the dead. She soon learned that what she was feeling was the call from the Nat, the legendary Burmese spirits. She informed the boys and insisted they should answer the call. They did, and soon arrived at the foot of a massive volcanic mountain that reminded them of mount Olympus.

They joined a congregation of monks on a pilgrimage to a monastery built on the summit of a sheer sided volcanic plug called Taung Kalet in the vicinity of Mount Popa. The final part of the pilgrimage is the most difficult, seven hundred and seventy seven stairs of pure drudgery. It was then when the spirit of Buddhism gave them the strength to meet the challenge. When they reached the summit the beauty of the buildings and the colours used to decorate every corner and crevice was breath-taking.

From their vantage point they had an amazing view across the arid plains, all the way to the ancient city of Bagan. It was Bagan's famed four domes that attracted their attention, especially the one known as the Ananda temple, seat of the four standing Buddha's, all made from pure gold and each one placed to face the four cardinal points.

"Oh no," cried Garuda, "look to the horizon."

Mulan looked, "No. not again." What they saw was thousands of serpents and they were slithering towards both Bagan and the sacred mountain.

"We need to warn the abbot," said Garuda.

From behind they heard a voice, "Welcome, travellers from Olympus." They swung around and were surprised to be greeted by an elderly timid looking monk, "I am U Khandi, Time Lord and disciple of Lord Buddha," he bowed, "unlike you, I'm not immortal. For centuries I've been born and each time as my new body weakened I'd die only to be reborn again. I even know my last life begins in 1868CE and ends in 1949CE. With the blessing of Lord Buddha, I pray enlightenment will await me."

Mulan was intrigued as this was something she'd never heard of. Garuda interrupted and was showing signs of alarm, the serpents were getting closer. He asked, "The serpents of Hell. Are you aware of them? "

U Khandi replied, "In these lands the serpents of Hell have been well written about, the old stories speak about three immortals fighting the serpents on the Fire Islands, also at the most esteemed monastery of Shaolin. They speak of a beautiful goddess and two powerful warrior gods. The stories tell of a mythical bird, an Emperor of the Skies, they also speak of the Lord of the Mountains," he said as he again bowed, "I know they speak of you!"

"Your arrival means time is not on our side. I beg you to assist in the defence of this holy place," pleaded U Khandi, "see how vulnerable it is?"

"It's not our place to prepare defences," said Mulan, "our task is clear, we must pass Jacob's message to all those we find worthy, not fight battles." She then suggested, "It's you who must warn the monks and encourage them to evacuate the temple. It's you who must arrange for a message to be sent to the king and warn him of what's coming. Tell him to evacuate Bagan and the surrounding villages."

264

U Khandi said while showing his disappointment, "I understand and will do as you ask, but I will remain and stand guard on the highest step. I have friends in the spirit world and will call for their assistance. In these lands they are known as the Nats, and together we will prevent this foul and vile army from entering this most holy of places."

U Khandi pounded his staff off the top step. From cracks and crevices all around the mountain white mists rose and formed the shapes of long dead men and women who were warriors and heroes of old, they were those who had met untimely deaths. They took up positions on every fifth step as well as at the entrances to every building in the temple, and from there they watched the temple empty; they also watched the citizens of Bagan and the nearby villages move away from the path of the oncoming serpents.

Mulan felt guilty, but she knew a different path lay ahead for her. She, Garuda and Girish left and moved to a hill near a well trodden pilgrim route used to take devotees to the Great Dagon Pagoda.

From their new viewing point they observed the serpents approach and worried for the safety of U Khandi; he was the only human present. Their fears were misplaced because the Nats were ready and waiting. The most powerful protected U Khandi. They were the forest, water and rock guardians; the most ruthless spirits of all.

On reaching the lowest steps the advance party of serpents were taken aback when, as far up the plug as they could see, the Nats, in their hundreds, materialised as shimmering bright light entities that were heavily armed. The serpents instinctively knew they had no defences against the possessing powers of these ancient spirits. They couldn't retreat, the fear of their overlords, the Dark Angels, was greater.

The attack by the Nats when it came was swift and lasted no more than ten minutes. Nats arrived from nearby caves, from behind fallen trees and scattered boulders. Those on the steps showed no mercy and were the most vicious. Their attack was brutal and resulted in many serpents being destroyed leaving very few to escort the Dark Angels. When the Dark Angels arrived they found themselves defenceless against the power of the spirit world and they quickly withdrew to continue their journey towards the west.

"That was too easy," said Mulan, "too quick." She turned to Garuda, "Take to the sky and follow. Keep the sun to your back. Keep them blind to your presence." Garuda acknowledged her and left to fly high to where he had a panoramic view of a slithering mass of dark evil and it worried him as to how menacing they looked. He followed the road and from his great height he saw in the distance a colossal gilded Pagoda resting upon a hill overlooking a vast city. The main dome was plated with gold and captured the sunlight, he found this dazzling. On the surrounding stupa he saw thousands of encrusted diamonds, emeralds, rubies, sapphires and topaz, and wondered was it the wealth of the temple that the serpents were after.

He chose to land and join up with a group of pilgrims in the hope of learning more about the temple. He soon learned that the temple was the Great Dagon Pagoda and was affectionately known as the 'Crown of Burma'. He soon established why it was the most sacred shrine for all Burmese Buddhists. He listened to the monks speak of the many relics kept in its vaults, especially the reliquary holding the eight hairs of the Guatama Buddha. He now knew why Dagon was the next target of Hell's army.

After walking between two highly decorated lion faced stone Chinthes, guarding the gates to the shrine, he listened to the guides speak of what happened when the reliquary was first opened. The guides described the eight hairs emitting rays of light that terrified all around them before that same light penetrated the realms of both Heaven and Hell. He listened to them speak of the miracles that followed, how the blind could see again and the deaf hear, some for the first time. How the mute could finally talk and the lame could walk. They spoke of the mountains quaking and the coastal winds blowing with such ferociousness, never felt before. He listened to them try to describe the lightening and how it lit up the skies causing gems of beauty to fall until they were knee deep, and then how the trees all across the Himalayas unseasonably brought forth their blossoms and then their fruit.

He left the guides to stand before the main shrine where he listened to a monk speak about the building of the Pagoda and was surprised to learn it began construction in the sixth century and wasn't finished until the twelfth century. He then had an overwhelming need to meditate. And being invisible it was easy for him to find a safe location.

He emptied his mind and thought of happier times especially when with his parents, or in the lagoon with Jacob. He was now totally at peace and soon felt a presence. "My friend," said Lord Buddha, "the 'Arc of the Covenant' and its awesome power is something you already know about. In this holy shrine is a reliquary carrying eight hairs taken from my head and given by me as the foundation stone of this temple. The power channelled through these hairs is as powerful as the Arc. They are the reason the serpents are coming. You must remove them immediately without alerting the monks. I will assist by planting a seed in the mind of a young monk and he will be your guide."

"My lord, with respect," said a worried Garuda, "my duty is to protect Mulan at all costs, we were taught never to interfere except when in danger, what will Jacob say about this?"

Before he had time to express more of his worries he felt another presence, it was Jacob. "Garuda, chariots from the northern Asgard army are on their way, led by Magni. What you do today will prevent Lucifer from acquiring a very powerful weapon. Do as Lord Buddha commands."

Garuda felt his eyes welling up even though he was deep in trance, "Jacob, I think of my parents and of you. I think of the gods and Olympus and then I feel despair, sometimes I feel like a failure, why is this? Why has this task come to me?"

"My friend, no need to fret for your parents," said Jacob, "when their time came I brought them to Elysium and there they rest among the tombs of the great kings and queens of old. They share their rest with the heroes of myth and legend." He paused for a moment waiting on a reaction then said, "Be strong Garuda, by me this task was given, it was because you were chosen at the beginning of time. Our meeting, that day in the lagoon, was no coincidence. You were given special powers by the Ancient One in preparation for what is coming. The Darkness grows stronger so does your powers. Be not afraid."

Garuda then woke and he felt invigorated. He made his way into the shrine in search of the reliquary, and while there he was approached by a very young monk who excitedly said, "Your aura, my lord, it shines bright."

Garuda asked, "Do you know what's to be done?"

"No," responded the monk, "but I know what you have to do is so important it caused my Lord Buddha to visit me in my dreams and instruct me to obey your commands." He bowed, "I'm at your service."

Garuda ushered him out into the grounds and told him what was to be done. The monk was horrified, the theft of the temples most revered relic was abhorrent to him and it took some time for him to calm down. When composed he argued against the idea of stealing such an important relic but ultimately he knew his path was already set. He assisted in putting together a plan leading to a massive deception, and the possible murder of all Dagon monks but, if successful, Hells efforts to get a new and powerful weapon would be thwarted.

Meanwhile, Mulan and Girish anxiously awaited Garuda's return. They were alarmed by what sounded like rolling thunder but they knew it wasn't thunder. When the sound stopped they prepared for an attack but were pleasantly surprised when they looked up and saw it was Magni.

Girish found his arrival very emotional and on embracing him, had difficulty letting go. Mulan was equally as excited. They had been travelling for nearly fourteen hundred years and hadn't met or heard anything of either Asgard or Olympus in all that time. "How is it you are awake?" asked Mulan, "Were all gods not to sleep for two thousand years?"

"Yeah, I should be so lucky," replied Magni, "first I wake so as prevent Odi from going after Panya. She carries twins, two goddesses, soon to be born. Odi's place is to be by Jacob's side. I promised him my armies will provide Panya's protection during his sleep. Now I split my army to provide protection for you and Girish, while Garuda follows the instructions of Lord Buddha, so here I am."

"Tell me of Eala," asked Mulan, "when leaving Olympus I looked back and thought I saw something, a bump, is Eala Ok?"

Magni replied, "For Eala it has been a difficult journey, soon after she left Olympus, Jacob saw she was pregnant and lost all reason. It took the might of Zeus and Odin to prevent him breaking through the shield. He discovered there were triplets, two boys and a girl. It broke his heart not to be with them. In his grief he finally slept and went into the dream world where he found Eala. She was giving birth. He saw his children and they saw him. Poseidon used his powers to bathe Eala and the soothing waters allowed her travel into the dream world where she met with Jacob, they both found peace." He then pointed towards the sky, "Those streaks you see are part of my army. They will escort you and provide protection until you are well into the lands of Lord Shiva."

Back in the temple, Garuda's accomplice had earlier joined the congregation for evening prayers, and as time moved on he pretended to pray waiting on the remaining monks to retire. When all was clear he located a spare replica of the reliquary and brought it to Garuda who placed it in his satchel before heading to the shrine. He quickly exchanged the reliquaries then exited the temple to make his way towards a ledge where he planned to discreetly transform back to be the emperor of the skies.

He never reached the ledge because he was betrayed; he was struck on the back of his head and knocked unconscious by the young monk who retrieved the reliquary before racing north to where Lucifer had opened a portal.

It was many hours before Garuda came around, and when he did he was concussed and confused. Attempts at standing were difficult, he couldn't maintain his balance. His head pounded and his movement was sluggish. He shielded his eyes against the bright sunlight and found his vision to be foggy and blurred. When his memory returned, he quickly realised he'd been betrayed.

When he felt ready he cautiously leapt from the ledge and flew to rejoin Mulan and Girish. On arrival it was obvious he was angry, he slammed his satchel against the cliff face. Even seeing Magni didn't calm him.

"I've failed and have been deceived," he said trying to compose himself, "no serpents or demons showed themselves and yet I fell, I don't understand. The monk, sent by Lord Buddha, is a traitor. He knocked me out and took the reliquary. He's long gone."

Magni tried to reassure him, "You must understand, we are dealing with the most devious of them all. You can be sure he meticulously planned this. The serpents, Mount Popa, Bagan, they were a ruse to distract you but somehow I feel all is not what it seems."

Magni walked over to the edge of the hill, looked north and saw that a portal had opened, he called all to join him and together they watched Lucifer arrive. "Watch," he said, "see him look into the realm of man and how he fears to take those first few steps. Watch, he fears to leave Hell because he knows the gods will awaken and the battle will begin, he's not ready."

Magni continued to stare and then caught Lucifer's eye. They stared across at each other and all saw the smirk of delight cross Lucifer's face. They saw the smirk turn to a wide grin as the traitor monk stepped into Hell carrying the reliquary. All saw the legions of serpents follow and then watched the portal close as the evil stench waned.

Garuda was devastated and there was no consoling him; he felt he had let the gods down. No reassurance from Magni helped relieve the pressure he put himself under so he backed away. He placed his head in his hands and was despondent until, through the corner of his eye, he saw the small and frail figure of the Dagon Abbot walk up the hill. He was carrying another reliquary. The abbot joined him and said while sitting with him, "This is the real reliquary. Lord Buddha knew there was a traitor but wasn't sure as to who it was. He trusted me because I am a descendant of the first guardian and together we put in place a plan to deceive the traitor. Because of you, our plan succeeded."

Garuda furrowed his brow and wondered why he wasn't trusted with this plan. His unease was allayed when Magni said, "I am the supreme general of the Asgard armies and if this was my plan, I would have done exactly the same thing, you should be proud that you were chosen for this task. As the Abbot said, because of you it worked."

Magni then called on his most trusted commander and requested he take the reliquary to the vaults of Olympus. He then turned to the abbot and suggested he evacuate Dagon as quickly as possible saying that Lucifer's vengeance will be swift and ruthless and he feared it will come at dawn. As the abbot walked away he said to Garuda, "I could always see you and watched your every move. I knew the traitor would seek you out but didn't know how he planned to deceive you. Trust me when I say, Lord Buddha is very proud."

Magni requested silence, "Wait, wait!" Then it happened, a low rumble built up to what seemed like an earthquake and then again there was silence before an unmerciful scream reached out from the bowels of Hell. It was the scream of rage as Lucifer realised he had been outwitted yet again. The screams faded; then everyone heard the pitiful moans of the young monk being disembowelled. Images of Lucifer feasting on his wriggling body entered their minds. The worst sound was to come and that was when the cries of his soul being devoured echoed across the cosmos.

When all went quiet Magni said, "Enough of this evil! There is but four hundred years left before you reach Mount Kailash. Lord Shiva already prepares your resting place." He then offered to take them across the ocean to the eastern side of the Indian continent, an offer they readily accepted. Mulan joined Magni on his chariot, Garuda and Girish followed on the next and within an hour they arrived in India to begin the last leg of their thousand year walk. It was now the year 1400CE and they had entered the realm of the Indus Pantheon.

Chapter 10

The Ganges delta at this time was pristine and bountiful, and was under the watchful eye of two esteemed and powerful Hindi goddesses. Magni knew of them and was confident they'd provide protection to Mulan and her guardians.

The delta was sparsely populated at that time with very little agricultural activity. The lower plains were covered in deciduous forests with thick stands of tall cane-break grasses growing in the wetter areas. Further north were the freshwater swamp forests where, in the dryer areas, sal, teak and peepal trees grew in abundance. Nearer the coast, where the climate is more humid, vast forests of mangroves, consisting of shrubs and tall trees, have made the waterlogged soil their home. This was the lands known as the Sundarbans, home to pythons, leopards, elephants and crocodiles.

Here, Mulan, Garuda and Girish felt they were in safe hands especially when passing the many colourful shrines, set among groves of luscious trees. Many of these shrines contained images of the revered deities renowned for protecting these enchanting lands.

When moving through the mangroves they encountered a young boy who was no more than twelve years old. He was skilfully scooping honey from hives set among the trees, leaving enough for the bees not to consider him a threat.

Mulan materialised and immediately the boy fell to his knees placing his forehead close to the ground. She reached in and touched his shoulder bringing the calmness to him and when it came, a beaming smile crossed his face. "My name is Reyansh," the boy replied after being asked. Mulan then said, "Your name speaks of a ray of light. You are of the sun and part of Lord Vishnu." She stood to look around, "Tell me of these lands."

Reyansh was delighted she asked, he loved this place, "Where we now stand is known as 'The Sundarbans' and it's a special place, home to some of the world's rarest plants and animals." He was a wealth of knowledge for someone so young, and he certainly had the gift of the gab. Each time he took a breath, Girish and Garuda exhaled a sigh of relief, but only moments later they'd place their heads into their hands as Reyansh prepared for another long story. Mulan was enthralled and showed her displeasure by glaring at her invisible guardians each time they drew deep breaths of despair.

Mulan noticed Reyansh was at times looking over his shoulder and asked, "What troubles you?"

"Look into the shadows and see the face of a fearsome tiger," he said while nervously looking around, "I hear the rumbles of hunger and soon his pangs will become unbearable."

From those very same shadows the tiger began to stealthily make his move, he approached where Reyansh and Mulan were sitting. He was about to pounce when he felt the sharp edges of two magic dipped swords rest on his neck. After waiting in the shadows for so long, he couldn't believe his chance for an easy meal was taken from him.

He froze watching Mulan approach and was chastened when her light surrounded, and then forced him to bow in homage. He instinctively knew he was before one who was destined to become a Goddess of the East.

She went to her knees and placed her hand on his neck then whispered in his ear, "This boy is under my protection. Tell the forests and all who dwell here that he is not to be touched. He carries a message from the gods and is ancestor to a family from among who will come one who is destined to be a beacon for all of Indian. Do you understand?" The tiger bowed before leaping to disappear into the forest.

Mulan rejoined Reyansh, "Tell me of the statues placed throughout the forest," she asked.

"They are in honour of Bonbibi, Goddess of the Sundarbans," said Reyansh, "also the lady Manasa, Goddess of all Snakes."

"Have you ever seen them?" asked Mulan,

"No," replied Reyansh, "but it's rumoured they appear in a clearing close to the salt marshes, which are not too far from here." Mulan was curious and asked to be taken there, a request to which he willingly obliged.

He led her through the forest and after several hours they reached the clearing and found a massive grotto built among very ancient mangroves. The two goddesses were in attendance, surrounded by a very bright and translucent light. They were dressed in the most stunning gem encrusted gowns commonly worn by high ranking goddesses of the Indian pantheon.

Girish was unsettled; he sensed serpents, but what he didn't realise was, the serpents he detected were the cobra escorts of Manasa. He prepared to call on the Light only to be stopped by Bonbibi who reproached him in a not very friendly way insisting he lower his staff. He was on guard and refused, forcing Mulan to stretch across and lower his staff, an action he was not too happy about and he made his feelings known. He materialised causing Reyansh to cower, out of fear, closer to Mulan.

Girish moved to stand defiantly before Manasa, "How could a most powerful goddess of all snakes allow Lucifer use her serpents to unleash Hell and wreak havoc?"

"I can't alone stand against the power of Hell," she replied, "I'm not strong enough. If I was the daughter of Lord Shiva everything would be different." She lowered her head in despair, "I'm blessed by her and by her leave I carry her name, she bestowed on me the powers of a goddess and in her absence made me guardian of all snakes. But 'He' is too powerful, all I can do is hide my snakes and hope he never finds them."

Girish wasn't interested; he just continued his verbal onslaught, so much so, Mulan had to intervene again. He was having none of it and resented her interruption by pushing her away. He continued verbally attacking Manasa but then suddenly stopped. He was staring into her hypnotic eyes and was beginning to fall under her spell. For the first time he felt a stirring, deep within. It was so strong it took his breath, and these stirrings were something he had never experienced before. He felt himself being drawn into her very essence and was becoming besotted. His anger disappeared as her calmness relaxed him. He became aware that he was looking into the eyes of the most beautiful women he had ever seen. Those eyes had him under her spell and the strange thing was it was his eyes that had her under his spell.

Now that everything had calmed Reyansh lit a small fire and soon he fell asleep lying peacefully next to Mulan. The conversations turned to happier times but every now and again Garuda noticed a deep sadness cross Bonbibi's face, "You are unhappy, my lady; can I help?"

"This magical place is my domain and I love it," she replied. "I look around at the precious mangroves and all I see is a sinister threat and it's getting stronger. Much of this land will be drained and many species will be lost forever. When Lord Shiva is awake, his life-giving waters flow from the slopes of Mount Kailash to keep all pristine, but now he sleeps and his waters flow slower as each year passes making the waters brackish. I fear all will be lost if he doesn't wake soon. The march of decay is relentless especially with the greed that has taken the local villagers and the way they look upon these lands."

"I too am unhappy," said Manasa. "Lucifer has created an image of snakes that is evil; he uses them to put fear into the hearts of man and is responsible for the constant onslaught against my beautiful and innocent creatures. Since that time in the Garden of Eden he has created serpents in his image and they are so unlike my snakes." Mulan tried to bring comfort but failed.

"This boy is special to you?" said Manasa while looking at the sleeping Reyansh.

"He is special," replied Mulan. "I gave him the message but it was rejected because war is not part of his future, I saw his future. He will be father to a line of men who will be aware of the message. This line is strong and will become a beacon for all Indians; one of them will spread peace through meditation and poverty. He will travel the world and speak to all who will listen. Lucifer will see him as a threat and send an assassin, but it will be too late because his message of peace will have already inspired many. He will be forever revered."

The following morning when Reyansh awoke he said his goodbyes and made his way home. He was escorted through the forest by four male tigers that protected him from any threat, especially from the crocodiles.

Mulan received no callings so suggested staying with the goddesses for the next few months; a suggestion immediately accepted especially by Girish.

During this time Garuda regularly sent out the Light just to be satisfied there were no threats. Girish spent every waking hour thinking of, and getting to know Manasa. His attempts at romance were at first clumsy then, after a little advice from Mulan became more intimate.

His efforts at wooing got more romantic as the weeks passed culminating with him arranging with the Mangrove Nymphs to organise an enchanting location with overhanging trees imbued with colourful blossoms. What was organised had a seating area which included an ornate table, laden with the most sumptuous of oriental foods.

That evening, Girish prepared by wearing the robes of an eastern emperor, robes he created over the previous few days, by dying silk using the bark of a local wax tree. The colour achieved was pale brown. He spent hours embroidering images of the phoenix and a mythical dragon-headed creature into the material. He also created a black headdress and planned to use his long hair as an upright tail built into that same headdress. He crushed scented flowers to extract their oils and added small amounts of alcohol before mixing distilled water to create an intoxicating aroma he hoped would captivate Manasa.

He used every trick in the romance book to make sure all was perfect even up to persuading Garuda to once again become the mythical bird, fly high into the sky and call for a flock of canaries to assist by providing the sweet music for the evening, he also asked him to seek out birds of paradise, as many as possible, so as to provide spectacular colour.

After dressing, he made his way to the grotto and when satisfied all was perfect, he sat and waited in anticipation. He waited and waited some more until finally he saw a dim glow deep in the forest, the glow became brighter and when it reached the clearing it became so bright it could only be the arrival of a goddess. She stood before him as a most beautiful, stunning and

278

amazing vision. Her vivid figure-hugging cream sari was surrounded by the most exquisite of fine golden silks and her gems captured the shimmering rays of the setting sun. Her tiara was one created to be worn only by a goddess; it was filled with the finest of crystal clear diamonds, so bright they sent their light into every crevice in the clearing.

Girish was stumped and tried to be cool but soon found he couldn't contain himself. He leapt to his feet and ran to embrace her before gently kissing and then lifting her into his strong arms. He swung her around and as they circled they stared at the overhanging branches and watched the blossoms release their petals, giving continuous confetti creating a most romantic scene.

Over the next hour they enjoyed the sumptuous food laid on by the Nymphs and if there was one fault in his plan it was the fact he never stopped talking. After a further hour of his incessant stories Manasa decided she had had enough. She moved to sit on his lap before planting a most sensuous and erotic kiss on to his lips.

He stopped her and looked around at the birds and loudly ushered them away to their homelands, he didn't want an audience. The Nymphs bowed and indicated they too were leaving. All but one left as there was more to his plan. He turned back to Manasa, "Where were we, I mean, where were you?" She smiled and began nibbling on his ear. She slowly moved her moist lips along his outstretched neck, across his Adams apple to the other side, teasing him so much his primal instincts kicked in. He rose to his feet and lifted her into his arms and carried her across to a low grass patch where he had earlier laid out his cape.

Placing her on the ground he knelt beside her before slowly removing her sari. He bent forward and they again passionately kissed allowing her to wrap her arms around his now bare back, pulling him closer. Their unbridled passion was drifting out of control until he stopped and said, "I've one more surprise!"

Manasa threw her eyes to the heavens, finding his constant stopping and starting frustrating. He insisted and then clicked his fingers. The remaining Nymph, unscrewed a large cauldron releasing thousands of fire flies to create a mesmeric scene never to be forgotten.

They lay on their backs watching the twinkling lights flickering above their heads. Manasa had never seen such an amazing sight and was impressed, but even that amazing sight couldn't delay her desires from growing stronger.

She stretched across and placed her hand under Girish's neck and gently squeezed, forcing him to turn towards her. As he turned she saw he was now about to take control and this was what she wanted. Her breath quickened each time she felt his leg hairs gently slide along her soft and sensuous skin. They kissed, rolled and caressed for hours. For them the feelings and sensations rolling around their bodies became tantric allowing them to become one, time and time again. It was a union both physical and spiritual until finally their passion was so potent they again became one causing a subliminal light to shoot across the universe alerting those gods still awake that a new god had just been conceived.

Chapter 11

The next morning Girish and Manasa still lay together, coiled in a loving embrace and finding it difficult to separate. Not even the heat of the rising sun had the power to prise them apart. All they wanted was to make love again, but it wasn't to be.

Garuda arrived, agitated and in full armour. His light detected serpents skulking throughout the mangroves. Girish leapt to his feet and quickly prepared. He was torn until Manasa, before disappearing, placed her finger across his lips, "Now, my love, do your duty."

When ready, Girish and Garuda ran to join Mulan who was completely surrounded. The strange thing was, the serpents and angels were standing some way back and didn't seem to be in any hurry. Girish and Garuda, being invisible were able to somersault over their heads and reach Mulan. As darkness fell the menacing red eyes of the slithering serpents and demonic Dark Angels became more visible.

High in the canopy, two tiny flickering lights caught Girish's eye. They bounced about like little pixies before resting on a narrow branch. For a moment he wondered what they were but right now Mulan was his priority. He or Garuda never flinched. They paced and circled, never lowering their swords. But they were deceived.

High up, in a hollow, camouflaged by a broken branch, three serpents hid. They were waiting to pounce and when the opportunity presented itself they attacked. Dropped directly upon Mulan to bite into her with such speed her guardians had no time to react. Their poison raced through her body and instantly, her life began draining away.

Girish reacted and attacked the three serpents, and while in a murderous frenzy he decapitated them before going to Mulan's aid. He cried out in despair, praying what happened wasn't real. Through tear-filled eyes he watched Garuda fall to his knees and knowing him so well, he knew his best friend had lost the will to fight. He watched Garuda sink his sword into the moist and swampy soil, lower his head and spread his arms. He was giving himself to the serpents. The Dark Angels saw their opportunity and began moving towards him but they were in for a shock.

One of the tiny bright lights resting high in the canopy descended and transformed into the Goddess Bonbibi. She was furious and lashed out using an invisible force so lethal it sliced with ease through the Dark Angels. She was determined to defend her realm.

In the meantime, the death of Mulan travelled through the cosmos and reached Olympus causing the light film of dust covering Jacob to fall away. He woke, stepped from his plinth and blinked, taking him to the site of Mulan's demise. He landed with such force the ground shook sending tremors through the Sundarbans. He didn't wait to get his bearings, just lunged forward and brought down on the angels the wrath of the gods. During his attack he realised the Dark Angels had evolved and were more powerful than what he anticipated, some of them were able to avoid his onslaught. His concerns abated when a second god arrived causing an even stronger tremor. It was Odi. He too had awoken and followed Jacob into battle, a battle in which they were determined to teach the Dark Angels a painful lesson. Not only did they use their daggers and swords, they used lightening powers, channelled through their fingers to inflict as much pain as possible. Bonbibi was taken aback, it wasn't normal for gods to enter the domain of another without permission, let alone unleash such as what Jacob and Odi unleashed that day. Together Jacob and Odi, as a cohesive force, mirroring each other's movements, unleashed their power and showed no mercy. Their onslaught was so ruthless even those trying to escape stood no chance. Jacob discarded his well established empathy and got particular pleasure in ensuring they really suffered.

Only when he was satisfied all forces of Hell were destroyed did he calm down. He ran to take Mulan into his arms and had barely lifted her when he was sent head first towards the ground and then kicked into a pool of nearby brackish water.

It was Garuda and he was in a rage, "Where were you?" He screamed while raining down, blow after blow, upon Jacob, "How did you not see this coming?" He continued punching and found he couldn't stop.

Odi attempted to intervene but soon found himself struggling to breathe, "You're no better, Prokyon." Garuda wrapped his hand firmly around Odi's neck allowing him to somersault Odi over his shoulder and into the water alongside Jacob. Girish's face was blank, staring out into space trying to take in all that happened, he snapped out of it when he heard Garuda call Odi a Prokyon, his mouth dropped. Girish watched his best friend attack two gods of Olympus and he worried. Jacob and Odi never retaliated, they just allowed him vent but nobody was prepared for what came next.

Garuda knelt next to Mulan, his tears flowing freely. Girish joined him, cradling him in the hope of giving some comfort. "Girish, my friend, you think I'm a fool, an idiot."

Girish pulled him closer, "When it comes to love, I think you are a coward, never a fool or an idiot."

Garuda caressed, and at times slightly shook Mulan still hoping what happened wasn't real. "I've always loved you," he said moving his head closer so as to kiss her for what he believed would be his first and last time. He whispered, "For a thousand years my heart missed beats each time I was in your presence. Please, please, please come back." There was no response.

Sinking his head into Girish's chest he said, "You're right, I'm a coward. I've loved her for so long I'd lost my nerve and never found the courage to tell her. Do you think she knew?" Girish just gently rocked him.

Jacob was at a loss as to what to do; Odi on the other hand was biting his lip and was fuming. He knew by the stare he got from Jacob to say nothing. Garuda was inconsolable.

"She's not gone." It was Jacob and he repeated, "She's... not... gone. I hear a faint heartbeat, it's very faint but I still hear the beat." Just as he moved to lift Mulan the second tiny light descended and transformed into the goddess Manasa. She went to her knees and gently held Mulan. She raised her arms and extended her fingers turning them into the heads of cobras. Each cobra produced their fangs and effortlessly sank them into the teeth marks left by the serpents and began extracting the poison.

Manasa was troubled, she felt the poison leave yet Mulan wasn't responding; something else was at work. Jacob and Odi never said a word, they were afraid of another attack by Garuda and knew this time they would have to stop him before he went too far. Girish held Garuda tightly hoping to prevent any further outbursts.

Manasa was about to give up when Jacob and Odi felt a more powerful presence, "Jacob, remain with Garuda and Girish! Odi bring Mulan to Olympus, Apollo is waiting; he knows what to do." It was Zeus.

Odi moved to lift Mulan. Garuda leapt to his feet and lunged at him only to be stopped by Jacob who grabbed him by the neck, "Snap out of it, you are a God of the Indus. Zeus has spoken, we are her only hope. She will be safe in the care of Apollo."

Mulan opened her eyes just as Odi was about to blink and managed a weak smile. Looking around she saw Jacob and Girish causing a single tear to roll down her cheek. She strained to look passed them, "I see you, Garuda," she gasped, "I heard you. I too love you." He reached across to touch her cheeks then moved closer so they could kiss each other for the first time. Odi took her to Apollo and immediately returned to join Jacob.

It was awkward that night. Garuda was still angry, occasionally pacing and pounding his staff of nearby rocks and tree trunks as he passed. Girish, although still in shock, spent much of his time attempting to calm his friend. Jacob and Odi smelled obnoxious from the now congealed organic matter stuck to every part of their bodies as a result of their earlier dunking.

Jacob was very conscious of how filthy he was especially in the presence of two powerful goddesses of the Indus. His discomfort didn't go unnoticed. Bonbibi approached, "My Lord, listen for the crashing waves and soon you will reach where the Ganges meets the ocean. There the strong waves will refresh and cleanse both of you. Use the power of the rising sun to dry your wet clothes." In the afternoon, when they returned, the goddesses formally introduced themselves making their two royal visitors welcome.

Girish and Garuda moved away and when Garuda finally calmed he asked, "Did I really attack Jacob last night?"

Girish tried to suppress a laugh, "You brought down two powerful sons of the mighty Thor."

Garuda cringed while placing his head in his hands, "I can't believe my temper; I thought meditation was supposed to make us calmer."

"Love is a strange thing," said Girish. "I expressed mine over the last few months, you suppressed yours for a thousand years and when it was taken, you exploded, I understand that."

"Did you suspect?" asked Garuda. "Of course I suspected, need I remind you of the time when Mulan gave you a very gentle and sensual massage, the time when your feathers only partially retracted? I saw you trying to suppress your arousal. I saw the way you contrived to encourage her into continuing her massage even though your feathers had totally retracted. I knew then," he gently punched Garuda, "Mulan wasn't fooled. She knew you were faking it. With what I heard her say tonight, I feel she's been waiting for you to make your move for over a thousand years."

Garuda buried his head back into his hands, "It looks like I've many apologies to make. I'm wondering if Jacob and Odi will ever forgive me."

Girish laughed, "The only apology you need to give is the one to Mulan for making her wait a thousand years to hear those special three magic words. Please tell me you know what they are?"

They went quiet for a moment then Garuda asked, "Do you think Jacob would blink me to Olympus? I want to hold her and kiss her the way I've always dreamt"

Girish laughed again, "I think Jacob, when it comes to love, is a romantic. He'll gladly bring you to her. Just ask him, the worst he can say is No."

"Girish...What's it like?" Garuda asked, "I'm curious."

Girish didn't answer just turned and faced his friend. His mouth was moving, forming weird shapes, trying to put the words together. It was a case of the mouth was willing but the words weren't. "You're my best friend and I love you more than anything. You know me well, normally I wouldn't mind telling you everything that happens in my life, but this is different. She is special and everything I shared with Manasa is private and to discuss it would be wrong and unfair to her. I love her too much."

"That's not fair," said Garuda lying back to stare at the stars, "You, Jacob and Odi all know what it's like and I don't, at least give me a clue."

Girish thought for a moment and with a hint of a smile, said, "Remember when Lord Buddha was teaching us the art of true meditation?"

"Yes." answered Garuda.

"Remember when we neared enlightenment how sometimes you got these amazing sensations especially during the Tantric training?"

Garuda got more interested, "Oh yes, I still get breathless thinking of that."

Girish lay back again, "Well, it's ten times stronger and you always want more, and then you need sleep only to waken and want it all over again."

Garuda and Girish were having a very private and personal conversation forgetting there were other gods about. And those gods, with their amazing hearing, heard everything that was said. Jacob thought it was endearing, Odi just wanted to ridicule. Bonbibi got annoyed with Odi, she thought Garuda's innocence was very appealing but Manasa was mortified, she wasn't ready to reveal her feelings about Girish to anyone but it was too late.

"You're pregnant!" exclaimed Jacob.

"No, I'm not!" responded Manasa.

Jacob was certain, "Yes, you are. I see your glow, as the minutes pass it glows brighter. Even in sleep the light was bright, it shot across the cosmos. You are a goddess and carrying a god. Girish is the one you were with which means he is a god and doesn't know it yet."

"I don't understand?" said Odi.

Jacob explained, "When a god has a child with a human, the Light doesn't show because the baby is a demigod. When a god and goddess conceive a baby, the Light announces it as the conception of a new god. Remember that evening in the temple when the light shot across the universe, many saw it. Eala and I were in the dunes. The older goddesses, Zeus and Eros knew and said nothing. Only after Eala was seen to be pregnant did Eros explain to me how the light works."

Jacob, Odi and the goddesses decided to seek out Girish and Garuda and soon found them. It was still awkward but they were happy to see both of them more relaxed than expected. "Many good things have happened in the fifteen hundred years since you left Olympus," said Odi after sitting next to Girish. He was trying to lighten the mood, "Between us we have six children either born or on the way. When the battle is over and balance returns we will have much fun watching our children grow together."

Jacob and Manasa froze on the spot. Odi initially didn't realize what he said but it was too late. Girish mused, "Jacob has three, you will have two and......." It dawned on him that the only other possibility was; the sixth child was going to be his and Manasa's. He leapt to his feet and paced back and forth. The weirdest thoughts were racing through his head. He was excited yet terrified; he felt he was unprepared to look after a goddess as well as Mulan.

Jacob wanted to kill Odi but resigned himself to the new situation, he worked on the principle that the truth will always comes out. He stood and asked Garuda to join him, "Tell me how you feel now some hours have passed."

"But for the friendship of Girish I think I'd have ended it all," responded Garuda, "you have no idea how devastated I am. Did you not see her sickly grey colour, the blue veins of poison? I've failed her and let you down."

288

"I thought you knew me better than that?" said Jacob while hugging him, "I'd never allow you end it all. I'd never disown you. You were chosen not by me but by the Ancient One. I need you to finish the task. The Indus peoples need you to bring them the message so I need you to be strong."

Jacob opened a portal, "Look in and see your future. See the snow capped summit of Mount Kailash. See your throne. Lord Shiva is preparing your sanctuary. He'll be there when you arrive."

Jacob and Garuda continued talking, walking deeper into the mangroves. "Oh, by the way, Prokyon? Can't believe you called Odi a brown-noser. He's very sensitive and will never live that insult down. I love it and I loved the way you threw him into the river. Even I, in my wildest dreams, wouldn't attempt that. I can't wait to tell Magni and Modi. In fact, I can't wait to tell everybody."

"Please take me to see Mulan," Garuda pleaded. He hadn't the words fully out of his mouth when Jacob blinked and brought him one hundred years into the future.

Olympus was nestled out among the rings of Saturn, out of sight of prying eyes and away from the gaze of Hell. They landed in the great hall and as usual Jacob always took a second glance at the magnificence of the sleeping gods, even after all this time they never failed to amaze him. Garuda was awe stuck, it never crossed his mind as to what a sleeping Olympus looked or felt like. Jacob brought him to a side bedroom where they were greeted by Apollo. "Go find her," encouraged Jacob.

Garuda made his way towards the south facing window where Jacob always sat when Olympus was on earth. He saw Mulan in the distance causing his insecurities and fears to return. He was having second thoughts and wanted to run away until he felt an unmerciful kick that sent him stumbling forward. "I knew your insecurities would return, go to her," cried Jacob.

Mulan was startled and thought she was looking at a ghost. "I've been broken since you were bitten," he said as she approached, "and I died inside when I saw you fall." He hugged her and kissed her forehead, "Since Odi took you away I longed for a chance to say all the things I should have said. A thousand years? I can't believe I allowed a thousand years to pass. I've only ever loved once, and that's my love for you. Every time you were out of sight I got scared even though I knew you were safe in Girish's care. Everyday you were always on my mind, every night in my dreams. To me you are the only woman in the world and for you I want to be the only man in the world."

Mulan raised her hand to his face, "Hold, hold on a minute, I need to catch my breath. That was one long speech." He gently let his cheek rest in her palm and then slowly turned to kiss her wrist. "You stupid, stupid man," she continued, "you are the only man in the world for me and it's about time you realised it. There has never been any other on my mind. I've loved you since long before that wonderful massage. Oh, by the way, I knew you were playing me but guess what? I was also playing you. I've been waiting for this day for so long I now feel on top of the world. What took you so long?"

Jacob and Apollo were making their way towards the gardens when they saw a naked figure skulking behind a column and staring down one of the corridors. It was Eros and he had his bow raised and his arrow prepared. "They don't need your help!" yelled Jacob.

"Are you serious?" said Eros with a smile. "That guy is so slow it took him a thousand years to tell the girl he loves that he actually does love her." With that he said, "Whoops!" And off went his arrow to travel along the corridor and pass through both Garuda's and Mulan's hearts. "That's my work done," he smiled, "I'll just stay and make sure he knows what to do."

Jacob reached across and gripped Eros, "Pervert. He is quite capable of learning as he goes." Jacob blinked and placed Eros on his plinth leaving Mulan and Garuda with their deserved privacy. He waited until Eros fully returned to stone.

Jacob and Apollo continued their walk out into the gardens where they enjoyed each other's company. Jacob got great pleasure gossiping about how Garuda beat the living daylights out of him and how he had picked Odi up by the scruff of the neck and threw him into a river. When Jacob spoke of Odi been called a brown-noser by Garuda, Apollo was beside himself and spoke of how he longed to meet Odi to discuss his discoloured nostrils and unusual bath-time experience.

The following morning a very tired Garuda arrived for breakfast. He was humming to himself while filling two glasses with fruit juices, and gathering together a large platter of food. There was certainly pep in his step with a definite glow of contentment. He didn't notice Jacob sitting alone in one of the concealed alcoves and if he did he would have seen that Jacob was happy for him, but was also anxious for him to return to the task that was set.

On reaching Mulan Garuda said, "Let's hurry and eat, when gathering our food together I sensed Jacob's anxiety, I think it's time to return to the task. Best take him out of his misery." He leaned in and kissed Mulan then said his goodbyes, "I promise the seeds of your flowering trees will be planted everywhere I travel, and the gems of beauty? I'll collect all I can." On reaching the door he glanced back and waved, "I see a vision, its Mount Kailash." He blew a kiss and gently double-pounded his fist against his chest. He left and rejoined Jacob who immediately blinked them back to the Sundarbans.

Manasa had a decision to make and later that day she let her decision be known. She decided, with Jacob's approval, to take Mulan's place and assist with spreading the message among the Indus peoples. Her decision delighted Girish, but not half as much as it delighted Jacob. He suggested they leave immediately and walk towards the Eastern Ghats, then cross the Deccan plateau before travelling through the Western Ghats towards the foothills of Kailash.

Jacob offered to bring Bonbibi to Olympus but she declined, she insisted on maintaining her place as Goddess of the Sundarbans for as long as possible.

Chapter 12

Jacob and Odi remained in the Sundarbans for a while longer before returning to Olympus. They enjoyed being together especially when talking about their children and how they longed to be with them. Jacob was bemused Odi hadn't noticed something very profound that had happened, "Odi! Brother. Are you Ok?" asked Jacob.

"What do you mean?" wondered Odi, furrowing his brow and squinting before turning his head to look on Jacob suspiciously.

"Ah, nothing," shrugged Jacob, backing away so as to smile out of Odi's sight.

Odi feared Jacob was up to something and chose a pre-emptive strike. He leapt across, threw him to the ground and held him down demanding to know what he was up to.

"Odi, Odi," said Jacob while laughing loudly. "Have you not noticed?" Odi got more annoyed and demanded Jacob stop teasing. "Brother, how did you get here?"

"For Odin's sake," exclaimed Odi, "I just blinked." It dawned on him what Jacob meant, "I've got my powers. Does this mean I'm now a Time Lord? Am I now equal to you? How? When? When did it happen?"

"It doesn't matter how or when it happened," said Jacob. "It's about bloody time. Now that you've got your powers, you can carry me home."

They returned to Olympus as equals, stepped upon their plinths and drifted back into their long sleep.

࿇

For Girish and Garuda travelling through India with Manasa instead of Mulan was strange. It felt unnatural to be guardians to a goddess who didn't really need protection considering she was part of the Hindu pantheon and under the protection of Lord Shiva.

Putting his concerns aside Girish used this time to grow even closer to Manasa, regularly holding hands and at every opportunity, taking her out of sight of Garuda to spend as much time alone as possible. Even with theses distractions Manasa never neglected her duty, she spread the message to very village and town she encountered during her journey into the Eastern Gnats Mountains and across the Deccan Plateau.

Throughout this time Garuda insisted on regularly sending out his Light. Never once did he detect serpents and this should have relaxed him but it didn't. At night, his sleep was always disturbed and as the weeks passed Manasa's concern for him grew. One particularly disturbed night, while Garuda twisted and turned, Manasa reached across and placed her hand on his forehead, instantly seeing his horrendous nightmares, showing the serpents biting into Mulan. She attempted to use her powers to calm him but failed, she then felt a presence, "My lady, leave Garuda to me." It was Jacob, "There's a lake, not too far from where you are, go spend time with Girish."

Garuda woke, "Jacob, did I hear Jacob?"

"You did," replied Manasa. "He's concerned, just like I am. I think he wants to help, he's asked Girish and me to leave. Close your eyes and seek him out." She and Girish left.

Garuda lay down and closed his eyes as suggested. Immediately he felt Jacob's presence. "Garuda: My amazing friend. We know you're still hurting. Odi and I will always be there for you. We see danger, we see times when Lucifer will outsmart us, and it is during those times when you must be at your strongest. Your constant nightmares are of concern, they are draining you. Tonight I ask you to go deeper into sleep and seek the doors to the dream world. There you will find Mulan, this door will be open for as long as you need it."

"Garuda, all is not what it seems." This time it was Odi, "Evil is close by. I will send the Asgard army and they will patrol the sky for as long as you need. They will be your guardians while you sleep. Go now and find Mulan, be at peace."

Garuda briefly opened his eyes and in the sky above he saw the golden streaks of what he knew to be the chariots of the Asgard army. Feeling secure he drifted into a deep sleep. On opening his eyes he found himself racing the white horses across the Olympus realm towards the snow-capped mountains. He dismounted, knelt and glided his hands across the colourful blooms of the thick set wildflowers. He smiled watching the flower nymphs raising their fists in anger and gibbering profanities because of him damaging and disturbing their homes. He cautiously stood, trying not to do more damage, and admired the lush green leaves of the enchanted forests framing the meadows. He looked back and his heart pounded. On the raised part of the meadow he saw a lone figure sitting on a blanket, looking around as though waiting on something magical to happen. It was Mulan and he began to sprint.

"Garuda, slow down," it was Jacob. "She's not going anywhere."

"Eh. Are you going to always be in my head?" asked an appalled Garuda.

Jacob laughed, "No, buddy, I don't think I'd cope with your unleashed passion. I'll only be in your head when you need me."

"Thank Zeus for that," said Garuda, "I don't want my first time to be a threesome."

Garuda soon reached a very happy Mulan who leapt into his arms. They kissed, at first softly, then feverishly and within moments they lay on the blanket, leading to an afternoon, followed by a night of amazing passion. For two inexperienced gods they were quick learners, giving each other a pleasure they never expected. During quiet times Garuda pulled the blanket to cover their modesty.

"Tell me," said Mulan after Garuda again pulled the blanket over them, "are you ashamed of my naked body?"

"No... No...No," said a panicked Garuda. "It's Jacob."

"You're thinking of Jacob and making love to me? Thanks for that."

"There is no way I was thinking of him, trust me. He was in my head just before we met. He said he was there for me if I needed him. I just covered us in case he was around. He could be in the clouds, hiding behind a star, in the long grass. Worse still, he could be in our heads."

Mulan sniggered. "Can I just say," she stretched up and kissed him. "After the way you made me feel there's no way you need him. Trust me. He's not around, I'd have sensed him." Garuda lay back and threw the blanket off.

At times they watched the stars take over the sky to perform an amazing dance of light and for the next four nights those same stars entertained until the sun got jealous and pushed them away. As the battle between the stars and the sun continued, never once did they break their loving embrace.

During this time Garuda completely relaxed and regaining his commitment as an Olympus warrior, he again became the immortal Jacob always saw in him.

☙∽❧

With a jolt Garuda abruptly awoke. It was now night. An Asgard charioteer was kneeling beside him, "My lord, a serpent attack is in progress near the lake, and they're stronger than expected. Girish is in trouble. The main body of Asgard warriors have gone to assist."

"How long have I been asleep?" asked Garuda while leaping to his feet.

"Five hours." replied the charioteer.

"I was with Mulan for five days," said a confused Garuda, "how can this be?"

"You were in the dream world," replied the charioteer. "Did you not know? There, time means nothing."

Garuda reached for his satchel, retrieved his robes, armour and weapons and when prepared, he sprinted towards the lake where, on reaching a low ridge, he assessed what was before him. He was pleased to see Manasa use her skills as Goddess of the Snakes, especially by the way she used her Cobras to rise up and hypnotise the serpents giving Girish enough time to destroy any that came near. He saw how Girish was keeping Manasa safe from a direct attack but was very concerned when he saw the losses among the Asgard warriors. Their arrows were ineffective forcing them into closer combat with just their swords available to them.

Just as he was about to join the battle the clouds above parted allowing the moon to send its strongest beams, beams so bright they bounced off his armour sending a blinding white light across the battlefield.

Everything momentarily paused giving the combatants enough time to view an amazing sight. They knew they were looking upon a Warrior God, whose image was enhanced by the strong light of the now full moon. Girish recognised him immediately even though he had changed, he was taller, broader, bolder and ready to alone do battle.

He took two steps, stopped, and then raised his sword. Moonbeams bounced against the shining steel, sharpening its edges, making it deathlier and finer than any ever created by the sword-smiths of Olympus.

From out of nowhere came a new light. Its beams illuminated Garuda, showing his power to all those across the battlefield.

He took two more steps; then ran, tearing through the ranks of serpents by leaping and somersaulting over those he passed, decapitating many without showing any mercy. He relentlessly disembowelled others, spilling their innards onto the grass, already stained by their black blood. He showed no emotion going in for the kill.

The remaining Asgard warriors watched him destroy as many as he could and were now inspired; they recognised his skills. They knew he was trained by Magni but had never seen anybody use those skills to such devastating effect. The cobras also redoubled their efforts.

The battle was now turning and the serpents began slithering away but Garuda was determined to make them suffer. He stood in the centre of the battlefield and as Emperor of the Birds he released a piercing and shrill call, attracting the Rock Eagle Owls from all parts of the Ghats and they came as one huge flock. The cobras retreated and rushed back under the protection of Manasa.

There was a frenzy of feathers and claws as the Owls descended. They swooped, grabbed and savaged the serpents, leaving Garuda and Girish to deal with the few remaining demons. Girish was now exhausted and allowed

Garuda take the lead, he eventually just stood aside and watched Garuda destroy the remaining demons. He was despatching them like a god possessed and wasn't ready to stop until he sent all of them back to their maker.

When all demons and serpents were dispatched Garuda summoned the Asgard commander, "See how the lake runs red," he said, "It's the blood of your warriors. So many have died, this is concerning. I must insist an urgent message be sent to Magni."

Just then they all felt a presence, "We've watched the battle through your eyes and saw the valour in which Asgard fought. We're proud of their efforts." It was Odi, "We watched your skills to win out this day, but what a terrible price. Lucifer's armies are still evolving. His arrogance knows no bounds, attacking in the sacred lands of Shiva is very brave. The battle has shown how he is advancing. Prepare your warriors for their final journey."

The commander ordered his men to gather the fallen. When all bodies were gathered they were taken into the west where they were delivered into the care of the stewards of Elysium. They were placed into the tombs of the Asgard heroes of old. It was said that their funeral procession was so solemn even the trees bowed as the fallen passed. Odin, Thor and Modi woke from their long sleeps and attended, bowing as the fallen were carried into the crypt. When they were placed on their engraved slabs Odin raised his hand, closed his eyes and by his power, all slowly turned to stone.

Chapter 13

Crossing the Deccan Plateau, Manasa used every opportunity to pass on the message while Girish and Garuda remained on alert. It was now the mid sixteenth century and for India, it was the beginning of five hundred years of turmoil.

"Look at them!" said an angry Manasa, "They are the Mughals, and hail from the floodplains of the Indus River. Soldiers on horseback dressed in vivid coloured robes and tight turbans, created to intimidate. They'll soon establish a foothold before making their way across the north and taking over the remaining lands.

"Why so angry? My visions show them to be, in the main, benevolent," said a confused Garuda, "they will usher in a golden age for India."

"It won't last," replied a still irked Manasa. "Look across the plateaus. The Maratha Hindu warriors are sowing the seeds of their empire and will soon begin their attacks. War is coming."

"It saddens me to watch," continued Manasa. "How do I find those worthy of receiving the message?"

"Walk among them, let the Light be your guide," Suggested Girish.

Manasa took his advice, and day after day, she walked among both the Mughals and the Marathas, hoping to pass on the message. She travelled far and wide, walking through villages and towns dotted all across the plateau and like Mulan, she chose children, knowing they'd change, and take on an air of confidence strong enough to encourage their families to migrate to the far south.

For the next two hundred years Manasa led Garuda and Girish to many of India's most sacred sites, always arranging their visits to coincide with religious and cultural festivals. They visited the Temples of Love, the temples of Mysore and Ranakpur, the Mehrangart and Jaisalmer Forts among others, but it was their visit to the Temple of God, the most sacred site for all Sikhs that impressed them the most.

On arrival at the Temple they remained invisible as they joined the throngs of worshippers approaching one of its four entrances, "It's been many years since my last visit, and still I feel overwhelmed," said Manasa while ushering Garuda and Girish across the walkway towards the north door. "This temple was built as a place of worship for all religions; it's open to Muslims, Hindus and Sikhs. They call the lake 'The Pool of Nectar' and it was intended to be God's home, blessing those who bathe in its soothing waters."

"It surely is a wondrous place, everything's so perfect," said Garuda looking around at the majestic domed-roof buildings surrounding the lake. "Whoever designed this sanctuary is a true artist. The gold gilding, the marble work, the dome framed by four perfectly aligned Minarets. It's amazing!"

"We must be quiet and show absolute respect," whispered Manasa while bowing. "Feel the calmness and the holiness of the Gurus. See the reverence in which they are held by the pilgrims."

She pointed to an ornate pedestal surrounded by a gilded rail, "Before us is 'The First Book'. Within its covers are Sikh scriptures and devotional hymns. Its writings are the guidance for all to follow and it covers all time."

Crossing back over the walkway, Garuda remarked, "It's hard to understand when you look at them. Remove the hijab, skull cap and turbans and

302

they look to be of the same blood, all of the Indus." Manasa nodded in agreement.

For the next few weeks Manasa spent her time walking among the pilgrims spreading the message. Girish continuously sent out the Light. This went on until the time came to move on towards Delhi.

On their way they reached the Taj Mahal, tomb of the Shah Jahans and decided to stay for no more than a few hours. "Another wondrous sight, dazzling, in a way it rivals the beauty of Olympus," remarked Girish, "like the Temple of God, the ivory white marble and the four ornate minarets draw you in."

"Yes, it is wondrous, it's written that this is the pinnacle of Muslim art in India," said Manasa, "and it's said it will last until the end of time."

Garuda excused himself and took the opportunity to walk through its ornamental gardens. He admired the trees, all bulging with colourful flowers and thought of what Jacob said to his beloved Mulan, 'You will walk for a thousand years to become the flowering tree of the east.' He wondered if he was looking upon those same trees. He gathered many seeds and decided to plant them in her name, wherever he went.

☙❧

The call of Mount Kailash became so persistent Manasa decided to change their plans and begin the final part of their journey. On their way they encountered a new threat, a vast army.

"Look at them, vicious thugs, loyal to a new conqueror," said Manasa while covering her mouth in horror. "My visions show me their true intentions. There's no discipline; no empathy. Those murderers will ravish these lands and crimes against humanity will be their legacy. The wealth and prosperity that once dwelt in this beautiful realm will be pillaged and brought to the crown of a far off empire. I see famine stalk the descendants of the Indus. I see savage taxes forcibly collected by corrupt administrators. Peace will not return for many years if at all. There's nothing we can do. We must leave." Thinking of this broke her heart.

The devastation felt by Manasa as a result of her visions was soon replaced by images of a tranquil and free flowing Indus River. As the days passed and they approached the river her mind drifted towards the birth of her baby. She was now heavily pregnant and struggling to walk. Girish made many efforts to assist but each attempt was met with a rebuff. Garuda sniggered.

"Nothing worse than a snarky goddess," grunted Girish after another failed attempt.

"I heard that," yelled Manasa before firing her satchel towards him, "you try carrying a baby who enjoys kicking and seems to get pleasure in making my life miserable." Garuda picked up the satchel but this time sniggered out of sight. Girish was at a loss as to what to do, that was until they reached treacherous and bumpy scree slopes. The pace slowed forcing Manasa to finally accept she needed assistance. Girish cautiously moved closer, using his arm to support her and was pleased when he felt her hand rest on his hip.

Manasa's breathing became more laboured as she climbed a small hillock to the right of the river, and as the hours passed her contractions began. Girish had difficulty suppressing his pain as Manasa's fingers dug deep into his side while each contraction intensified.

There was a degree of relief when the renowned Thikse Monastery came into view, "We must materialise," gasped Manasa. "Always show yourself when in the presence of the Panchen Llama." They materialised.

304

On reaching the crimson red painted gates, it was as though they were expected. They were greeted by the Llama and his congregation of monks and nuns who bowed before them. Girish was taken aback and asked them not to bow.

"Young warriors, so humble, so innocent, do you not know?" said the llama, "We bow because you are now powerful gods, one born into the Indus and the other the Shinto. Both chosen at the beginning of time and blessed by the Ancient One before being placed for Jacob to find."

"How can this be?" reacted Garuda, "Powerful gods? I feel no different,"

"I too feel no different," said Girish. "We haven't changed; we are as we were when leaving Olympus."

"Trust me, you are gods," said the Llama. He turned back to Garuda, "Remember what Jacob asked after Mulan was taken to Olympus, 'is there a gift I can give?'" Garuda nodded. "You thought the gift was the dream world, it wasn't. It was your elevation into the pantheon of gods; your humility prevented you from realising it. When you returned to fight the serpents, those watching knew they were in the presence of a God of the Light. They recognised your skills to be those of a God of War. Even the moon sent its brightest beams to guide your way."

He turned back to Girish, "That night when you and Manasa conceived your baby was the moment you became a god, which for your sake is a good thing. Lord Shiva would never accept a demigod as his grandchild."

Girish was taken aback, causing him to stutter, "Shi.., Shiva... is your father?"

"You never asked," she replied shrugging her shoulders. She placed her hand on his cheek, "Remember when I told you about his daughter, also called Manasa? She's my friend and mentor. She blessed me with her name and granted me her powers, elevating me to be an adopted daughter of Lord Shiva. This made me a goddess, under his protection." She then puckered her lips and grimaced holding her side and bending slightly forward. Girish leaned in to give her much needed support.

Manasa grimaced again but this time, after taking another very deep breath, she exhaled in rapid bursts. She let out a scream; her baby's birth was very close. After being taken to a side room her labour intensified and lasted several more hours before the loud cries of a healthy baby boy echoed throughout the monastery. For Girish, holding a baby that was his was something he hadn't seen in his future. He was awestruck, beaming, his eyes filled with tears of joy. He asked Manasa if Hemish was acceptable as their sons name and she agreed. He kissed her then took his son outdoors. He looked towards the heavens, and thinking of his mother and father, he wished they were there to put their arms around him. He raised his son above his head and called on the gods "Look upon my son and let it be known his name is Hemish. Bless him for he will be forever known as 'Lord of the Earth' and a beacon of light for all of India.

On returning to the room he was greeted by the Llama who said while rubbing holy oil on the baby's forehead, "You have been given the name, 'Lord of the Earth', a good and wise name for one who will be called upon to protect the people of these sacred lands."

The following morning the last leg of the journey to Mount Kailash began and after securing Hemish in a baby sling Girish, Manasa and Garuda said their farewells and moved to continue their walk along the barren and rock strewn banks of the Indus River.

Five hours later they reached the foothills where they joined thousands of pilgrims who had gathered to walk the twenty three leagues around the base of the mountain. Garuda looked towards the summit hoping to see his beloved but she wasn't there. "Garuda, relax," said Manasa, "if Jacob said she'll be waiting, trust him. She'll be waiting."

Garuda couldn't relax. He moved towards a narrow walkway winding its way up the mountain with Girish and Manasa following close behind. On reaching the first ledge there was no sign of Mulan so he rushed to the second ledge. This time a heavier snow covering made the ground more treacherous. By now Garuda had lost his patience, he continued up to the next ledge to reach the entrance of a large cave. His heart pounded when he saw the first signs of life but his anticipation turned to anger when he saw it wasn't Mulan. It was Lord Shiva who appeared.

Shiva sat in his usual yogic position as he floated from the cave to rest outside the entrance. This day he presented, not as half man and half woman, but as a powerful male deity, his face and throat blue and his body white. His third eye was covered by three horizontal lines drawn in white ash. "Beware his eye," cautioned Garuda while turning to Girish, "it might represent wisdom and insight but you're the one who got his daughter pregnant, if he opens it in anger, you'll be smothered by fire and even your immortality won't protect you."

"Thanks, friend," said Girish, "can you make me any more nervous?"

Shiva stood, revealing his powerful muscular body. He was wearing the full ceremonial dress of a Hindu God. Around his neck he wore his renowned cobra necklace signifying his power over the most dangerous creatures ever created. He was wearing a well trimmed leopard skin. In his right hand he held his three pronged trident. "Hard to believe he is known as Shiva the destroyer," said Garuda, "see how he smiles and looks so tranquil. I think you're safe."

Garuda strained his neck to see passed Shiva, watching and hoping. He kept staring and then a vision appeared. She was stunning. Mulan presented as a Goddess of the Light, wearing the shimmering silver, gem encrusted gown, given to her by the Emperor of the Fire Islands. The jewels bestowed on her by the forest peoples of the southern tribes served to enhance her beauty. He ran to embrace her, "Everywhere I travelled I planted the seeds; your trees are flowering all over the east." He reached into his satchel and said while extracting a handful of gems, "Look, I collected so many but now I see you don't need them. You are the jewel, the real jewel; you are the gem of beauty."

She placed her fingers across his lips, "Here on Mount Kailash is not the dream world. Here everything is real. You are certainly saying all the right things even if it has taken eighteen hundred years. I need to hear you say those three little words again."

"The ones I said many times when in the Dream World? But if you insist." He bent forward, kissed her and said, "I love you."

Shiva joined Manasa who bowed. He gently touched her cheek. He then turned to Girish causing his heart to skip a beat. He leaned in and took Hemish in his arms. "It's good to see my beautiful and handsome grandson, one who is destined to be a Lord of the Earth." He turned back to Girish, "For one so terrified of me, brave of you, father of my daughter's child." Girish gulped.

Garuda after rejoining Girish, whispered, "My friend, relax. Look at him, the great Shiva, remember what I said a few minutes ago, 'The Destroyer'. He holds your son so gently, who would have thought?"

"I'm saying nothing," said Girish. "Not a word."

Shiva smiled, "Now, now boys, I hear everything. See and feel how contented I am? Manasa has returned, she brings me a grandson, and into my family a most powerful god of the east. There's nothing to fear."

Garuda and Mulan sat next to Shiva but Garuda couldn't stop staring; he was watching a steady flow of water-drops dripping from Shiva's matted hair. Mulan nudged him, "Stop staring, those droplets are the source of the great river Ganges. If they ever cease, India dies."

❧

The following morning in a cave higher up the mountain a fourth throne was made ready. From its entrance the plateaus of India were visible, "Who would have thought that a messenger and her guardians would travel for so long and touch so many," said Shiva pointing into the distance. "Look out over India and see the light of all those who have received your message. Because of you many millions will answer the call of the gods. Jacob's army grows as each year passes."

Girish was slightly subdued until he looked into the cave and saw there were four thrones. "You didn't think I'd let you sleep for hundreds of years without me by your side?" said Manasa reaching in to take his hand.

"My prayers are answered," he said in disbelief, "I didn't think your father would allow you sleep,"

Together they took their seats. Shiva placed Hemish in Manasa's arms and kissed both of them. He bowed to Girish just as the ice came. Mulan said hugging Garuda, "It's nice to think that you and I will also be stuck together for hundreds of years."

"Hundreds of years! I plan to be stuck to you for eternity." They kissed for the last time and the ice came.

Before sealing the cave Shiva looked back at a most wondrous sight. The ice image of powerful immortals, all frozen in time, and it worried him. "What future awaits you, Lord of the Earth," he said staring at his now frozen grandson. "You're shielded from me and I wonder why? I pray Jacob's plans prevail." He checked again to ensure the cave was totally secure, inaccessible to climbers or prying eyes. He then sealed the entrance using an ancient magic known only to the Hindu gods, a magic so potent no evil force could undo its power.

They had completed their task,

their work was done.

They had gone into their long sleep.

Eala's Journey West

Chapter 1

This was the worst moment for Jacob, anguish showing as he opened the shield for the last time. With his muscles tense and his breathing erratic, he feared for his, and Eala's future, knowing she was to travel through some of the most dangerous lands without his protection.

While watching her approach his heart raced and he had difficulty preventing his tears from gathering. Eala presented as a beautiful, statuesque vision, wearing a fitted silky white full length gown, covered by a gold braided cape. The softness of her gown accentuated her curves making it difficult for Jacob to avert his eyes. Each step she took encouraged her slightly curled fair hair to dance in the light wind. The diamonds in her necklace and earrings sparkled, capturing sunrays before beaming them in all directions. To Jacob she was captivating but not just in a physical way. He loved her so much he saw into her soul and knew she was the one to keep him grounded, to protect the power of the Light, to wrap her arms around the realm of the gods and that of man.

He reached out and took her into his arms, holding her firmly, yet kissing her gently. He closed his eyes taking in the beautiful feeling of her body resting against his, one last time.

When Fafner stepped forward to take her arm Jacob wanted to break his neck, but he knew Fafner was only doing what was asked of him. Faer patiently waited at the crossroads.

Fafner and Faer both looked formidable dressed in their armour, helmets and capes. Both met when they were toddlers and although tough and strong they were scared at being tasked with protecting Jacobs's partner.

Faer was the son of a fisherman and Fafner seemed to come out of nowhere. Nobody questioned where he came from or where he went at the end of each day, they just knew he was to be looked after. He stood over six feet tall, very muscular and handsome. His hair was thick, dark and wavy, split in the centre framing a sun drenched face. His deep blue eyes were such that they seemed to penetrate all he looked at, and his smile disarmed those he met. He didn't suffer fools lightly but he'd defend those he loved with his life.

Faer too was handsome but in a different way. He also stood over six feet tall but wasn't as broad or muscular. His face was equally as sun kissed but his eyes were a paler shade of blue. His hair was cropped shorter and parted to his left. He was known to be grumpy but when motivated he was considered difficult to beat.

Eala, on exiting Olympus, moved along the outside of the shield and quickly went out of sight forcing Jacob to run along the inside just to keep up. They'd both forgotten how 'Time' moves faster in the realm of man. The further she moved away the faster the weeks passed. When she went out of sight Jacob never took his eyes off the road hoping to see her one more time. He continuously called after her until she finally heard him and turned, revealing a pregnancy he was unaware of. He went into shock and attempted to follow, but the shield was being held firm by the senior gods, preventing him from leaving. When told there were three babies, he went into a rage, and only relaxed when shown his future, he knew then Eala and his babies were safe.

That night while sleeping Jacob drifted into the Dream World and used his powers to search for Eala. He reached her just in time to witness the birth of his babies. He watched in despair as his babies were taken into the Realm of the Elves for their protection, and then he watched Eala sit in the warm waters before drifting into sleep. He prayed the Dream World would open its doors and allow her in, it did and he was ecstatic, but their time together was fleeting and soon Eala was awoken by a gentle prod; it was Faer insisting they leave immediately.

Chapter 2

Walking along a dusty road took Eala, Faer and Fafner into a mountain pass leading up to Mount Olympus where, on arrival, they became alarmed on seeing the condition of the temple. Fafner couldn't understand how Zeus allowed it fall into such disrepair. He only relaxed when Eala assured him nothing sinister was afoot; she concluded that the destruction was due to earthquakes and years of natural decay.

There they used their time honing their combat skills and learning to master the arrival of the light. As the nights passed their sleep became more broken especially for Fafner, his twisting and turning became disruptive. At times wisps of smoke drifted from his nostrils. A vision showed Eala what was coming. It showed her and Faer continuing the journey alone; it also showed the city of Rome. She knew then where their next destination lay.

The journey to Rome was uneventful and while making their way towards the west coast of Greece Eala used every opportunity to pass on the message but she was distracted by changes happening to Fafner. She never took her eyes from him, concerned by the lumps that occasionally appeared on his back and then disappeared. She had difficulty suppressing a laugh when his legs buckled and then strengthened or when his arms involuntarily rose and then fell.

She never said a word but on reaching the western beaches she had a choice, a long walk or a short flight. "Now, Dragon Lord," she said, "it's time you spread your wings and carried us to Italy." Her suggestion was met by howls of laughter from Faer.

Fafner wasn't amused; he was furious with Faer for questioning his abilities but, in reality, he had no idea what to do. He thought of Jacob's prophecy and surmised that it must be time for him to become a dragon. He climbed a high cliff, raised his arms and jumped, only to plummet to the beach below. He wasn't injured; he felt the assistance of an invisible hand and knew then he was being protected by the gods.

Faer's laughter got louder and almost derisive making Fafner more determined to prove himself. He repeatedly climbed the cliff and jumped. Faer couldn't contain himself each time Fafner hit the ground. Eala never laughed; she knew Fafner's efforts were soon to pay off.

The tide had returned when Fafner decided to take one last leap. This time he plunged into a very deep pool where out of frustration he settled on the sea floor, wallowing in his annoyance and questioning why he was called a Mythical Dragon.

He was about to give up and swim to the surface when he felt a presence, "Fafner, my friend, trust me, you are the Mythical Dragon," It was Jacob, fulfilling his promise to always be there for them. "Raise your arms, let your throat feel the heat of the smouldering fire, release the flame and watch the waters part. Use your wings and take to the sky, be the god you are meant to be. Be my Mythical Dragon."

Faer was astonished, Eala delighted. They watched the amazing sight of Fafner release his flame before flying across the sky where it didn't take long for him to master the flight. He flew high before turning to descend at such speed he raised millions of sand grains, forming a magical cloud. After one more flypast, he turned and came back into view through that same cloud. When he landed, he said while sarcastically staring at Faer, "You were saying?"

He turned to Eala, "Jacob came to me and told me to be the god I was meant to be. What could he possibly mean?"

"I too felt his presence but I don't know what he means." She whispered and hugged him, "It's time you carried us across the sea."

"Climb up," he said without hesitation.

"No way!" reacted Faer in horror, "Your back and I are not meant to get along."

Eala laughed while lovingly slapping Faer across the back of his head, and then she climbed up. She insisted he join her which he reluctantly did. Fafner then flapped his wings and soon they were flying.

It was an incredible flight. Faer stretched out his arms, taking in the wild wind and as Fafner swooped, Faer shrieked his delight. On their journey towards the southern shores of Italy the views of Sicily were breathtaking, especially when flying close to Mount Etna, who was angry that day.

It was now the year 98CE and the visions of Rome were getting more vivid, they were showing a new Emperor. It was Trajan, and he was making

Chapter 3

Trajan's political skills and his awareness of the power the Praetorian Guard wielded prompted him to remain in the northern parts of the empire until the year 99CE. He wanted to ensure he had the loyalty of the army before making his grand entrance into Rome to meet with the senate.

Eala sensed something special about Trajan and insisted they make their way to witness his triumphant arrival. While waving at the crowds Trajan, at times, stared directly at Eala, making her feel compromised. She withdrew and waited for darkness.

That night they located Trajan's chambers and when sure he was alone, they entered his room and quickly established he could only see Eala. He reacted by calling for his guards and when they arrived he ordered them to seize her but the guards were bewildered. To them Trajan was alone.

"You've nothing to fear," Eala said trying to reassure him, "I'm only here to give you a message." Trajan had difficulty relaxing but when he did he dismissed the guards.

"My Lord," she said, "In you I sense the hand of an immortal, a very close friend of mine." She requested permission to touch his shoulder which he cautiously granted. Immediately she saw Panya, Thanases and Baldor. She saw the massed armies withdrawing after their sack of Jerusalem. She also saw serpents biting their way through the ranks of soldiers, but not killing them confirming Hell's strategy was indeed to allow their poison pass through generations of Roman families ensuring the evil of Lucifer would always be present. Trajan also saw everything Eala witnessed; it was one of the gifts granted him when Panya touched his shoulder.

"I've been sent by the gods to pass on a message," she said after withdrawing her hand, "a message calling on all those touched, to be ready for a battle to be fought between man, the gods, and what is known as The Darkness. This Darkness is being assisted by the Archangel Lucifer, the most devious of the fallen angels. Lucifer's spies already walk in the realm of man."

"I remember a strange feeling," said Trajan. "It happened close to Masada, just as I was being redeployed to Hispania to take command of the western armies. When there I ordered assault after assault on Spanish cities but only after I heard the voice of an angel encouraging me to order my troops to be triumphant but respectful. The conquered peoples never rebelled against Rome while I was in command. Your friend, not only did she touch me, she showed me my destiny but never did I imagine it would lead to me being Emperor."

Trajan exited his room on to a patio giving him a view across the torch lit streets of Rome. "It disturbs me to see the living conditions of my citizens and how dilapidated this once beautiful city has become, nothing has been done since Nero fiddled while the city burned. I'm surprised and disappointed that mountains of ash, from the eruption of Mount Vesuvius, still choke many parts of the city."

"Yes, it does look bad;" said Eala, "Now listen carefully to what I have to say!" She leaned against a balustrade, "You will be remembered in all writings as second of the five greatest Roman Emperors of all time. You will preside over a long sought after peaceful time for this empire. You will begin the most feverish building program Rome has ever seen, and you will be revered because of your welfare supports for the children of all Italy." Her demeanour then changed, "Be aware of stains on your reputation. Your attack on Dacia and the theft of their treasury is bad enough but the most damning one will be your continuous attendance at the Colosseum and your refusal to stop the senseless slaughter of Christians, slaves and animals."

"What am I to do?" he asked, "If I stop that part of the games, people will become restless and rise up causing great difficulties for Rome, I need time to think."

Eala left, and with Faer and Fafner, they made their way into the catacombs, where they located an isolated crypt that was to become their home for the next four hundred years.

Over the next few nights Trajan had very troubled sleeps, waking many times. He spent his waking hours mulling over what Eala had said until finally he decided to call for a special sitting of the senate. He requested finance to begin important building projects, including the repair and restoration of the dilapidated private and public buildings throughout the city. He succeeded and used some of his new resources to employ the best architects and craftsmen to begin the construction of public works such as Trajan's Market, Trajan's Column, the Via Traiana and a Forum. He kept the citizens on side by instituting a form of social welfare for the children of all of Italy.

All this needed to be financed and although very aware of Eala's prophecy he still chose to stand at the head of the army in two major battles leading to the ruthless conquest of Dacia. He tried to suppress his guilt while watching the continuous flow of carts carrying the confiscated wealth of the defeated nation. He got solace from the fact that his actions ushered in the most peaceful and prosperous times for the empire, his actions so impressed the senate that they included in his titles the word, 'Optimus'.

Towards the end of his reign Eala warned him his remaining time was limited and as a result he never feared death which came in the year 117CE. He took ill and passed away, to be succeeded by Hadrian who went on to become third of the five greatest Emperors of Rome.

Through all this time Faer and Fafner never shirked in their duties. They continuously sent out the Light, checking for serpents.

Chapter 4

It was now the year 122CE and all was quiet, it was also the time when Fafner's restlessness became unbearable. He was itching to fly again and when word arrived from the far west that Hadrian had completed a wall across the ancient lands of Britannia he used this as an opportunity to go and witness this major engineering feat. His instincts also told him he was about to fulfil his true destiny. He made his intentions known to Eala and Faer, and after saying his farewells he found a secure place to prepare for his flight. He was excited, but his youthful insecurities caused him to wonder if he was doing the right thing; that was until he realised his need to fly was much stronger. He ran forward, gathered speed and within seconds, he was airborne, flying towards the west.

With the sun at his back he crossed the Mediterranean and soon reached Gaul. He didn't rest until he reached Britannia. He knew this was the realm of Merlin and wondered if they would meet. They didn't, so he flew north and the wall came into view. It was as impressive as Rome was led to believe and it successfully separated the tribes of the north from the towns and cities of the south securing peace in this once war-ravished land.

He landed on one of the unmanned towers and faced south causing panic among those who saw him. The people of the south thought the tribes of the north had a new ally but they need not have feared because within seconds Merlin materialized and he was furious, "What are you doing? Why are you here? His eyes are everywhere and he will already know of your presence. This is a disaster and very careless of you, you must leave."

Fafner, while in his dragon form, looked majestic but when he took his human form he looked very powerful, especially when dressed as a warrior of Olympus. When he transformed, he pleaded with Merlin to listen and insisted on being heard, "I woke this morning with an insatiable urge to fly. I discussed my plans with Eala and Faer before taking flight. The urge is still strong, it's as though my future is being rewritten. I don't understand."

Merlin was no longer as angry; he kept looking around showing his nervousness. He felt another presence, one that was strong and evil. Suddenly, he was struck by a bolt of lightning that seemed to come out of nowhere sending him tumbling to the ground. Fafner was taken by surprise; he raised his shield and drew his sword. The next bolt came hurdling towards him but his skills as a swordsman kicked in and he deflected it towards a bank of rocks.

At the distant tree line he saw the figure of a beautiful women and she was walking towards him. Her eyes drew him in causing him to lower his defences. Merlin quickly recovered and yelled, "I wondered when you would again show your face, mistress of evil." It was Morgana.

"Sorcerer, you are still a gift that keeps giving? I see you bring me a new plaything." She went quiet for a moment then sniffed, "I smell a dragon, a powerful one; this one flies in the Light." She looked around in confusion but still couldn't see any dragons, then hissed, "What trickery is this? How is it a mere wizard can conceal a dragon?"

Fafner was still staring and becoming more besotted by her beauty. He had fallen under her spell and failed to detect the pure evil dwelling within her. As the moments passed he got more listless not realising she was using her power to beguile him.

326

He then felt a presence that jolted him from his trance, "Fafner, my friend, close your eyes, close them now," it was Jacob, "she is a mistress of Lucifer, an enchantress that walks in Darkness, and she is the most powerful of them all. She detects the dragon but cannot see him. Don't allow the dragon show itself. Prepare for battle while Merlin calls for allies. Prepare for battle." Fafner snapped from her grip and did as Jacob asked.

Morgana was furious watching Fafner move his hand towards his sword. She couldn't understand how her charms had failed. She exploded, and released a continuous flow of fearsome lightning bolts. Merlin used his magic to protect Fafner as best he could by taking the full force of the lightening. He found her power difficult to deal with suggesting she was receiving assistance from The Darkness. He had no choice but to leave and seek help. When Merlin disappeared Morgana used her magic to rapidly approach Fafner but before she could attack he saw an opportunity and lunged forward with a swiftness that took Morgana by surprise, but he too was unable for the power of The Darkness.

She ripped his armour from him with an ease that left him very vulnerable and he wondering how armour forged in Olympus could so easily fall away. He quickly refocused and due to his speed he was able to deflect bolt after bolt of jagged lightening but his training wasn't enough. The bolts soon got through and tore into his arms and legs leaving a stench of burning flesh to fill the air.

Showing smiles of evil pleasure Morgana used hand motions as though they were claws to tear into his flesh and deliver the most excruciating pain he ever experienced. Her invisible claws left open wounds across his chest, arms and legs. Most cruelly, she disfigured his face, leaving him blinded in one eye. His piercing screams and pitiful cries of pain reached the ears of those gods who were still awake, they didn't react; they knew help was on the way.

Morgana was moving towards ending Fafner's life when in the south west a loud and full-throated roar was heard, it distracted her enough for Fafner to extract his dagger and plunge it into her foot, impaling her to the tree stump she was standing on. This distraction gave him enough time to find the strength to roll behind a nearby fallen tree.

The sound of flapping wings became more audible as a thunder of dragons from the Welsh realm came into view. They were Morgana's arch enemies and their arrival meant she was in real trouble, especially while still impaled.

She hissed when raising her arm in one last attempt to kill Fafner but she was too late. The first of the dragons had reached her, gripped her and dragged her kicking and screaming into the sky. She had being grabbed by the powerful claws of the dragon leader and he knew what he was doing, he intended inflicting the greatest level of pain imaginable. He saw the dagger handle and intended for it to travel through her foot to tear her flesh from her bone. It did, and her screams echoed along the full length of Hadrian's Wall and into the bowels of Hell.

The dragons used her live body, by one gripping her and then releasing her, another then uses its claws to impale her. This went on until all dragons had their turn; they tore her asunder and were determined to eliminate their most lethal adversary once and for all.

After destroying Morgana the dragons landed and took their human form. There were twelve and they were a group of the most handsome people Fafner had ever seen. They were over six feet tall, slim yet muscular. They resembled Fafner in many ways. Their hair was thick, dark and wavy, split in the centre just like his. Their deep blue eyes were such that they too seemed to have the ability to penetrate deep into the souls of all they looked at. They reminded him of the elves.

Fafner managed a smile when one of the lady dragons knelt beside him and said, "I'm Heulwyn, a guardian of the dragon realm. For a thousand years we've been waiting for you, my Emperor."

Fafner, although in terrible pain and only able to see through one eye felt something pleasant travel through his body. He also felt confused by what she said about him being her emperor. He was now really suffering and fell unconsciousness.

Chapter 5

Fafner life was draining away and the guardians knew they hadn't much time. They retook their dragon form and one after another took to the sky. Andras, the dragon leader, used his claws to cradle Fafner before lifting him to join the others. Instinctively they knew to travel east and seek out the Light of a messenger. They crossed the seas into France, and soon reached the Mediterranean Sea where they watched out for the Light. On approaching Rome they saw its power. It was Faer and he was using it to search for serpents but little did he know it was also acting as a beacon for the dragons. They reached the outskirts of the city and one by one they took their human form as they landed. Andras gently placed Fafner on the ground before he too landed.

Faer knew of dragons and wasn't afraid but when he saw what he thought was the body of his closest friend he went into shock. He froze for a moment before going to his knees to take Fafner into his arms.

He carried Fafner into the catacombs to where Eala was sleeping. The commotion woke her and when she saw Fafner her heart sunk. She looked around at all the elf-like people and was surprised when they bowed to her. She for a moment thought that strange but immediately turned her attention to saving Fafner.

She removed his torn tunic only to be horrified by the damage done. His glistening red flesh sickened her, especially where it was seeping the last of his blood. She retched when she saw his white rib bones protruding through his torn muscle and cartilage.

She closed her eyes to call for assistance from the Light and it quickly came. Its power illuminated her body and when she raised her arms it got even brighter. She placed her hands on his chest and waited for the Light to sew his wounds, she then moved her hand around his body encouraging wound after wound to heal. Through all this Fafner remained unconscious making it difficult for her to begin healing his eye.

Faer bent forward and whispered in his ear hoping to call him back but it was to no avail, there was no response. It was then a voice was heard, it was Jacob, "Faer, my friend, you are the traveller, a God of Travel. Enter his head and find him, walk with him, travel through time and escort him back, do this for him, you are the traveller."

Faer moved so close to Fafner that they looked as though they were glued together, he then closed his eyes. He entered Fafner's head and walked around opening many doors but only one allowed him in; it brought him back to a village, set high in the mountains, where he saw Fafner sitting with two, who looked to be his parents. He said while running to embrace him, "You must come with me. We are waiting. You're needed; your task isn't over."

"No!" Fafner replied, "This is my happy place. Meet my mother and father, its time I got to know them. Faer, I've no memory of them yet see how they love me."

Faer pleaded, "This is not real, you are hiding in your memories; you must come with me."

Fafner moved back towards his parents just as they were fading; he looked back at Faer and asked, "Are you sure? They look real."

Faer replied, "No, you are traumatised, you've gone to the one place you knew you would always feel safe but friend, it's not real."

Fafner thought for a moment. He remembered been shown two spirits when he first met Jacob in the lagoon, then remembered they were dead. He said when Faer took his hand, "Help me to find my way, friend. Take me back."

Fafner slightly moved his head. Behind his eye lids his eyes began to dance. After struggling to sit he found he couldn't open his eyes and began to panic. He got more distressed while reaching out for Faer, "Faer, Faer, I'm blind." Eala leaned in and with Faer's help tried to comfort him.

Eala bathed his right eye, removing the congealed blood allowing Fafner to partially see his saviours. It was his left eye that was severely damaged. Eala placed her palm across it hoping her power would help, it did help but Fafner couldn't tolerate the pain, he fell into a deep sleep and didn't wake for many hours.

While Fafner slept Eala and Faer used this time to get to know their visitors. The first thing they needed to establish was - what were they to call them, Elves or Dragons? It was agreed that they were to be called dragons.

Faer was intrigued as to how they knew to come to Fafner's aid. "It was Merlin," said Andras, "he reached us and spoke of the rise of a dragon lord. He told us of a battle between a dragon and a sorceress, it was then when we knew our time had come. For a thousand years our oracles spoke of this battle and told us to be prepared. We know of him, we know he is the god of all dragons and we will follow him into battle against the forces of Hell. We know he is Fafner, one of royal blood: He is to be our Emperor."

When Andras said, 'He is to be our Emperor', a new light entered the crypt and illuminated Fafner causing him to open his eyes. He stood and all present, except Faer and Eala, bowed. He individually acknowledged his twelve saviours but avoided Eala and Faer. Eala wasn't fazed; she sensed a change and knew the time was coming for him to permanently leave. Eala always knew his true destiny and was happy for him.

Fafner requested some time alone and left the crypt to sit looking out over the city. He was eventually joined by Andras, "For millennia we waited for your arrival. Throughout this time many slept, there was no desire to waken, feed or fly. Occasionally one or two of us travelled to the realm of man and inadvertently caused panic so we chose to stay hidden. We have been leaderless for so long we wondered if we had a future."

Fafner asked, "How many dragons are there?"

"Thousands," replied Andras, "we twelve are the guardians of the three gates, always watching, always checking. When Merlin alerted us we immediately flew to your rescue."

Fafner stood and with signs of concern asked, "Tell me gatekeeper, if all gate-watchers are here, who protects our realm?"

Andras was quick to respond, "You said 'Our Realm'. Does this mean you will lead us?"

Fafner asked again, "Who protects our realm?"

Andras continued, "As I said, when Merlin arrived he alerted us to the attack on you. After discussion, he sealed two of the entrances and placed a magic over the third, his spell is what conceals our realm from gods and men." Fafner just nodded, and Andras said no more.

In the distance a slow moving and very bright light grew larger as it approached. Andras leapt to his feet and drew his sword only to be held back, "There is no danger," said Fafner, "Feel the calmness." They were joined by Eala and Faer along with the remaining dragons. All fifteen watched the light arrive and soon recognised it to be an angel. It was Michael and he was fully armed. The dragons had never seen an angel in real life, let alone an Archangel and were awe struck. Eala stepped forward, bowed and all others followed her lead.

"I bring a request from the Ancient One," said Michael, he stared directly at Eala. She bowed again. He turned to Faer, "A new task is set. You and Eala are two most powerful gods and will travel a different path. Go deep into the bowels of Hell and seek the fair goddess; she was there at the creation and is a favourite of the Ancient One. Dark Angels delivered her into the hands of Lucifer. Her death light hasn't crossed the cosmos so we know she still lives. Her name is Danu, Goddess of the Celts and she is a mistress of the Light. Her power will be needed when The Darkness arrives."

Faer was suspicious and moved to stand between Michael and Eala. "How do we know you don't walk with The Darkness?" he said extracting his sword. "Strange how Jacob never mentioned changes to his plan. Mounting a rescue was never something we were trained for so forgive me if I seem concerned."

Eala lowered Faer's arm, "Look at him Faer. It's Michael, we met him before. See how the light surrounds him. Do what is asked and seek an entrance into the Underworld."

Fafner looked confused, "You said 'two most powerful gods'. What did you mean? Why did you not refer to me?" Michael joined him, "Your fate was sealed when you walked into the lagoon that faithful day. Since the beginning of time your destiny was set. First you were to become an immortal, Zeus saw to that; then you were to become a powerful god. Remove your fears, you are the Dragon Lord; Emperor of their vast and magical realm. The day you sat on the seabed and stretched out your arms was when everything changed. Remember how you parted the waters and took to the sky; that was when you became a god. Be the god you are destined to be," he placed his hand on his shoulder and continued, "Fafner, it's time for you to leave, the dragon realm needs their emperor. Eala and Faer will continue alone. You will return and as planned, together all three of you will enter your long rest."

Eala's eyes welled up; she reached across and hugged her friend. She had learned to love Fafner as a brother and was already missing him. Her visions showed her a thousand years passing before they'd meet again. Faer joined them and was distraught at the thought of losing his closest friend. All three had trouble letting go but they knew they must obey a request from the Ancient One.

The dragons took to the sky and waited for Fafner to transform and when he did all thirteen dragons circled Rome and then flew over the heads of Eala and Faer before they made their way towards the west. A small amount of droplets fell and landed on Eala's and Faer's cheeks, they instinctively tasted them and realized they were Fafner's tears. They were devastated watching the dragons disappear over the horizon.

Michael turned to Faer, "When you left Olympus as an immortal was when you became a god. Across the universe you are known as the God of Travel. Roads, lanes, walkways, mountains and rivers, even the oceans cannot hide from your gaze all what has travelled across them. Now, clear your mind and find the entrance to Hell. It's time to use the power of the God of Travel."

Michael saw how upset they were and felt for their loss but had no choice but to remind them of how urgent the task was. He insisted Faer start looking for the way. He turned to Eala, "You became a goddess that day when you conceived Jacob's children. You are a Goddess of the Light and a guardian of the old ways. Your powers will grow as the years pass but today they are needed to enhance the Light of a goddess in need." Michael then disappeared.

The sense of loss weighed heavy and they felt very lonely. Faer was devastated and moved away to sit on a low wall, he was distraught and bewildered. Something caught his eye, and as he lifted his head he noticed a shard of light, indicating there was something behind a minute crack in the wall opposite. He walked over and using his dagger he scraped and pulled at the crack until a wide entrance exploded open, sending masonry in all directions. He looked through and saw a long, dank and dark passageway, and from the passageway he felt the dead heat of Hell. He retched on smelling the putrid stench of decay. He turned to Eala, "They came through here; I sense the presence of a proud Light being dragged into the abyss. We go this way."

Chapter 6

Walking into the narrow tunnel was unsettling; it was a tunnel so sinister it played tricks on their minds. Shadows appeared from, and disappeared into every crack and crevice. Never once did Faer or Eala feel threatened.

Faer used his powers as the God of Travel to quickly establish that the tunnel was only ever used once, and that was by the forces of evil dragging a Goddess of the Light into the darkness of Hell.

On reaching the end of the tunnel they turned right into a large gaping hole that opened into a vast underground chamber. The cavern walls were strange; they comprised a shiny black flowstone that over the centuries had formed sheets of mirror-like crystal. Looking at their reflection they saw behind them the dim orange glow of the fires of Hell and this gave the only light for them to continue their journey. Although the temperature was increasing it had no effect, all they felt was an eerie chill coming from the misery in the torture chambers below. The true image of Hell had reached their minds and made their skin crawl.

The orange glow, although quite dim, was enough to allow them see a walkway meandering down ten levels to thousands of bubbling cauldrons filled with simmering oil. They cautiously moved along the walkway and reached a new tunnel that took them into another chamber, much bigger than the last. This one had another four tunnels feeding into it from the ceiling.

They watched in horror as four trapdoors opened pouring thousands of lost souls into the serpent filled pits. Eala surmised they were the souls of Jacob's carriers from all corners of the world, she recognised their diminishing Light. She was now beginning to understand why Jacob wanted the message passed to as many as possible, the carriers would become targets of Hell.

From grottoes placed around the cavern thousands of flying demons arrived, each one carrying weapons of torture used to bring forth an unimaginable reign of terror on the lost souls. Eala's heart broke listening to their symphony of pain.

While passing through a nearby tunnel Eala followed a Dark Angel. This one was taller than the others and wore a purple sash indicating he was of high status. They had to step aside to avoid the numerous demons using meat hooks to drag beaten souls into the torture chambers. Occasionally when Dark Angels approached, they'd stop; look around as though sensing a presence. Throughout this ordeal Eala's and Faer's invisibility continued to provide protection.

The most dangerous incident happened when Faer inadvertently scraped his sword against the wall alerting the Dark Angels. The investigating Angel sniffed the air and checked into shadows never realising he was face to face with a guardian who had the tip of his sword ready to plunge. His dead eyes and putrid breath caused beads of sweat to gather across Faer's forehead but he held his nerve and only relaxed when the demon moved away. They continued their journey and reached the end of the tunnel giving them a panoramic view across another chamber that was so vast it seemed to have no end.

They climbed towards a ridge where they saw a wide circular platform joined to the outer wall by a causeway. The platform was surrounded by lapping flames rising from the lava flows below. At its centre were seven stone thrones of which six were occupied.

A figure crossing the causeway caught their eye and they watched him take his place sitting on the vacant throne. Eala knew she was now looking at the seven Princes of Hell and the latest arrival could only be 'Him' and what surprised her was he was staring directly at her. She knew it was Lucifer and was startled by how handsome he was but soon put that image from her mind. "I think he sees me?" she whispered.

Faer shook his head, "Relax, no, I don't think so. Granted he's staring, suggesting he senses something. My instincts tell me he isn't sure."

Lucifer's attention was drawn by the arrival of several high ranking Dark Angels, all identified by their purple sashes. They were escorted by the infamous two-headed Hounds of Hell. A very deep conversation ensued.

Faer strained to hear what was being said but the lashing of the whips, and the screams of tortured souls drowned out everything Lucifer and his generals were discussing. He suggested they move closer.

On reaching hearing distance they were shocked when they heard Lucifer ask, "Have you located the resting place of the boy king? Where is he?"

They partially heard the generals reply, "No, my liege .... under the protection of Olympus .... floats out .... Cosmos. Hidden from our gaze." Lucifer twitched and tried to contain himself, he didn't like bad news.

The general spoke again, "We've located three groups of messengers and expect to capture them .... days; they're getting careless. They're showing themselves to more of man than what was intended."

"I will witness their capture," said a more relaxed Lucifer, "make sure of it."

Lucifer left his throne and walked to the edge of the platform giving him a clear view over to where Faer and Eala where standing. He raised his hands and said while bringing his fingers together, "Two faint glimmers of white light, interesting." He made his way towards the causeway and bellowed in a deep and rasping voice, "I know who you are. I sense your essence, emissaries of the Light. You will be my dinner this day."

Eala and Faer had heard enough. They saw a dim white light emanating from a grotto two levels above and assumed it was an exit but they were wrong. They had inadvertently stumbled upon the location of the missing goddess. Faer raced in and was shocked to find Danu, ancestress of the Tuatha De Danann and Earth Mother to the Celtic peoples, bound to a pillar of pain. She was barely alive, and on reaching her, he knew he had very little time. He cut her binds, allowing her fall into his arms. He placed her on the ground and asked Eala to call on the Light. When it came, it was so powerful it took away their invisibility. It also ensured that when Danu recovered Lucifer would now have two very powerful goddess's aligned against him.

Danu was recovering when Faer was dealing with scores of winged demons who had arrived and were preparing their attack. This was Faer's first real battle and he couldn't rely on the support of Eala or Danu as they were still deep in the healing process. He was alone and his nerves showed until he felt a presence, it was Athena, the Goddess of War, "Guardian of Olympus, I'm with you, raise your staff and sword, close your eyes and Let … Me … In."

Faer thought he was imagining things but something was guiding his hand towards his satchel. He extracted his staff and immediately raised it to call on the Light. His confidence returned and he was ready to do battle until he looked up at what he was up against. There were hundreds of them and they were everywhere. It was then when he felt another presence, and this time it was the God of War, "Relax, young warrior. Remember how I trained you, allow … Athena … in."

He closed his eyes allowing his other senses to take over. The demons were now so close he heard their thoughts, smelt their stench and felt their breath. He even heard Lucifer enter their dim minds and say, "I'm warning you, harm the goddesses and you will pay. Feed on the corpse of the guardian."

Faer instinctively moved to protect both Eala and Danu and prayed for Danu's quick recovery. His kept his eyes closed hoping to lure the demons into a false sense of security.

When the first demon was within striking distance, was when the full power of the Goddess of War was unleashed. Faer felt her strength and tactics as he brought down demon after demon. Heads rolled and innards dangled. Blood oozed as bodies mounted. It was carnage and a major defeat for Hell. That was until the entrance to the grotto darkened. Lucifer had arrived and showed his fury by transforming into a winged demon. Seeing Danu released didn't really bother him, he captured her once and knew he'd capture her again. It was seeing his demons destroyed when he got more incandescent with rage, that was until he saw Eala, he smirked and his face lit up, "Ah, consort of the boy king and mother of his children. This day gets better. I wondered who the other goddess was."

He then widened his eyes and gazed at Faer with a glare that meant his wrath was about to be released. He raised his arms, and using an invisible force, he sent Faer hurtling against the wall, seriously injuring him. His legs breaking and his skull cracking sent echoes around the grotto. Faer was in so much pain he no longer thought of Eala or Danu, he prepared himself to be slaughtered.

Just then the grotto lit up with a light so powerful it sent Lucifer back through the entrance. Danu had regained her full strength and joined forces with Eala. They used their combined power to send a more powerful burst that was so bright it sent Lucifer deeper into the recesses of Hell allowing time for Faer to be rescued. His rescue wasn't easy, his injuries were so catastrophic. Danu and Eala called on all their powers to assist by gently floating his body through the tunnels to reach Rome.

Faer remained unconscious for almost a week. He had lost a lot of blood making his recovery a lot slower than expected. Eala's light assisted in repairing his broken bones but not his broken spirit. When he finally came around it was obvious he had lost his confidence. He raised his hand and placed his palm against Eala's cheek, "My first battle and I failed, only for Athena you would be a plaything of Lucifer; you can no longer trust me."

Eala was taken aback, "No longer trust you? You are so wrong. You fought as you were taught and you fought alone. Athena wasn't there, you definitely fought alone."

"I don't understand?" said Faer, "I heard Athena say, 'Let me in' and I heard Ares say, 'let Athena in'. How can this be?" He was about to speak again when Danu stepped from behind Eala,

"Remember me, my hero?"

"I do," said Faer trying to sit up, "I remember you so helpless and weak, now I see you as a goddess. Forgive me, I can't bow. The pain.... it still hurts."

Danu leaned forward and kissed his cheek, "Only for you my light would be extinguished and the Elysian Fields would never bear my name," she wiped away a tear, "the Fair Lands will forever be in your debt and one day will show its gratitude." She kissed his forehead, "When I looked up it wasn't an Olympus god I saw before me, it was one who has occupied my dreams for millennia."

Danu began to fade, "Seek the Fair Land, there you'll find me."

Faer struggled to stand, "Wait!" he said while limping towards the door, "And I too saw your face. In my dreams we shared a happy place." He stumbled and was rescued by Eala. He reached across to take Danu in his arms, "I've never held a woman and always longed for such an embrace." He gently caressed her hair, "Hold me. Give me a memory worth living for? Let me feel you wrapped around me; only then I will know.............." He didn't get to finish his sentence. Danu took him into her arms and allowed him rest his head on her shoulder. He slowly inhaled her scent and relished the moment as she pulled him into a tighter grip. He now had the memories he sought and something to look forward to. He called after her as she again began to fade, "I've just received a vision and it shows us meeting sooner than you expect."

Eala was happy for him and said as she assisted him back to his bed, "So, now we are a prophet?"

He laughed, "Well. If you can be, why can't I?" he paused, thought for a moment then asked, "Did I really unleash the power of Olympus? Was it really me?"

Eala pulled him closer, giving him his second female embrace in as many minutes, "I've never seen such power. You bear the seeds of greatness and are one of the fiercest warrior gods. Jacob knew what he was doing when he picked you."

"There's something bothering me," said Faer, "Lucifer knows there is more than one baby; does he know there are three? How did he find out? Is there a traitor among us?"

"While you slept Danu and I discussed those concerns," replied Eala. "She assured me my babies are safe, she has absolute faith in Lord Kalen and knows he will move Heaven and Earth to protect them."

Eala held Faer tightly that night and when she moved her hand to hold his he got very uneasy. His mind was racing and the only thought crossing his mind was, 'Jacob is going to kill me.' He got really worried when Eala said, "I'm going to take you to a special place, you will need to close your eyes and relax."

Sleep quickly came and soon they were in the dream world. They reached a thick white mist and as it began to clear, they saw the outline of high mountains. They kept walking and reached the meadows of Olympus. They continued walking and soon the ornamental gardens came into view. "You better let go," said a very nervous Faer, "Jacob is there, look. I don't think I'd survive another beating."

"Don't worry. Jacob is putty in my hands," said Eala enjoying his un-easiness. "We need to hold hands for a little while longer. You're still suffering and you need the calmness of Olympus. If we let go too soon you will drift into the nightmare world and you don't want that, do you?" Faer just shook his head.

They soon reached Jacob who was delighted to see them. He greeted Faer by playfully flicking his hand away from Eala. "It's not what it looks like," said a rattled Faer.

"No worries my friend, welcome to the Dream World."

Jacob lifted Eala high and swung her around prompting Faer to say, "Yours is a love I envy."

Jacob replied, "You may not believe this but you've found yours, she's just a little bit hidden," he hugged Faer and continued, "I'm so happy to see you again, you and Fafner have been a constant reassurance for me. How you fought off the demons in their own domain was amazing to watch. Your skills will be remembered in the great stories."

Faer said while furrowing his brow, "You watched?"

"Yes. Our visions told us it was you destined to find Danu. For many years Lucifer kept her shielded, and you broke through that shield."

Faer flinched, prompting Jacob to say, "My friend, you are battered and bruised, go and see Apollo, no better god to take your pain away."

Faer left and walked towards the temple to be met by Athena who said, "Speechless. I'm speechless. You used skills unheard of along with those taught to you. I'd hate to be your adversary in any future battle."

Faer was chuffed, not only has he been endorsed by Jacob but being endorsed by the Goddess of War is special. As he was leaving he said, "I'm confused, how come so many gods are awake? I thought you were all asleep."

Athena replied, "We are asleep, this is the Dream World. This is from where we keep watch."

Faer soon met up with Apollo, who said, "It seems Jacob knew what he was doing when he chose you. Never before has a novice used his untested skills to prevail against such overwhelming odds. When Lucifer arrived we prayed for the Light to assist and when it did, we never seen it use such force. It announced to the Cosmos how you are a favourite of the Ancient One. It also showed us the spark of true love, Danu will wait for you."

Apollo placed his hands on Faer's shoulders and saw he was still hurting. He left to fetch healing oils and on his return rubbed the oils into Faer's shoulders, back and arms as well as his left leg. It took several hours but the oils did work their magic, all scars healed and all bruises faded. Faer now had no pain and was completely healed.

Meanwhile Jacob and Eala sat by the ornamental pool where they held each other in a loving embrace. He sensed she was troubled and asked as to what was bothering her. "Lucifer knows we have more than one baby," she said, "and knows I'm their mother, he calls me the consort and you the boy king."

Jacob was taken aback, "I can't detect the work of a traitor so I can only conclude that Lucifer has gained new powers allowing him work things out, without any real evidence."

Eala felt a little happier and snuggled closer, she than started whispering causing a chill of excitement to travel down his spine. When she nibbled on his ear his breath quickened. She whispered again but this time all he could do was gasp, "What? Now! No Way!"

She wasn't giving up; her fingers gently and sensually massaged his shoulders bringing him to a point where he had no choice but to pull her closer. She continued teasing by using her index finger-nail to travel from his knee to his inner thigh. She moved her mouth from his ear, across his mouth to his other ear, all the time using her nail to send sensations of pleasure throughout his body. Although he was playing hard to get, her playfully seductive and flirtatious ways began to break his resolve. She knew she had him when his hand drifted towards her hips so she lay back and waited, knowing her work was done and he was about to take control. When his chiselled and god carved chest rested against hers she knew that he was going to take her to Heaven. Her body softly trembled as his hands found those places reserved only for those in true love. He nuzzled into her neck bringing her close to ecstasy before moving to press his lips against hers leading to them becoming one. Their love for each other was so strong they got lost in time and their passion was so intense it sent ripples across the cosmos. When finished they lay together in an embrace of love so pure they couldn't part.

Back in Rome Faer was first to waken, he lay on his side with his head resting on his upright wrist, he was chewing a straw and grinning while watching Eala writhing and moaning in her sleep. She eventually woke to a smiling Faer who couldn't resist saying, "Was it good for you?"

She said as she gave him an affectionate thump, "How long have you been awake?"

"Long enough." he replied.

He leapt up and danced around the crypt. "Look, no pain. I thank you and Danu, your powers helped me but Apollo used magic oil." He sat back beside Eala, "You and Jacob have something that's amazing; I hope one day I will be as lucky."

"It's not about luck," said Eala hugging him, "it's written in the stars. Your future is already set and it's with Danu. Seek again the Dream World before we leave Rome, travel back to where I know she will be waiting. You are the God of Travel, its time you used your powers for yourself."

He thought for a moment, "I saw how the Dream World made you so happy. You were with the one you love. For me, I don't want my first time to be a dream. I want it to be real."

"Faer, Faer, my amazing friend, go find her. Seek the Fair Land. She's waiting, so go."

He leapt to his feet and moved towards the door but then hesitated, "I'm tempted, but no, my part in this task is to be your guardian. I promised to protect you. I'll use the Dream World some other time, right now I'm happy."

There was no more to say so they left the crypt, remained invisible and walked the streets of Rome. They had great difficulty locating those they felt were worthy of the message and this troubled them. Faer continuously sent out the Light and the more Romans he met the more upset he got, it seems Rome was infested with descendants of those bitten in the past. For him the worst thing was the constant bloodshed flowing from the actions of the gladiators in the colosseum. He remarked at how many were carrying the mark and dreaded the damage their descendants would inflict on the world when called upon by Lucifer.

Chapter 7

Eala and Faer remained close to Rome for the next three hundred years and witnessed the rise and fall of many Emperors. For them, the one that stood out the most was the Emperor, Constantine the Great. They were present when he decreed that Rome was to be a Christian state.

They found him fascinating and even headed back east, almost to the place from where they started; to witness the council of Nicaea which he instigated. They watched the proceedings from a chamber high in the rafters of the council hall and listened to the bishops argue about text after text of what was to become the Bible for all Christians.

Towards the end of the council they were furious, "Will I say it or do you want to say it?" asked Faer.

"I want to say more than just one thing," replied Eala. "This is a disgrace!"

"What do you mean?" asked Faer.

"How many do you see below us?" she replied

Faer glanced, "Three hundred and eighteen."

She then asked, "And? Do you notice anything?"

"I know what you want me to say. Where are the women?" he said as he bent forward, "It's the first thing I noticed when we arrived." He shook his head in disgust, "Last night I dreamt of Panya, she came to me. She spoke of a cave near Jerusalem where she met up with a very aged and lonely woman.

The lady's name was Mary. Mary knew the 'Man' those bishops speak of, she was there. She travelled with him and was there at his execution, on a cross. She was also there, three days later, when he left his tomb. She knew everything and here at this council they have discarded her story to be lost to all memory. That...is...a...Mistake."

Eala then said, "Worse is to come, they will destroy all engravings and all the old codices. The fools, do they not know that in those texts is written the truth. Fear not, for little do they know that, all over the world, there are those who will save, hide and protect those writings. The truth, her truth will eventually be found, hidden in urns near the Dead Sea, and many will believe. Still they will try to discredit her. Those we see before us and those who will come after them will, over the centuries, become very powerful and in many cases, they will forget his message."

Faer went very quiet and slowly descended into a trance, when he returned he said, "She will be back, I've seen it. I saw the last day. I saw the gates of Hell open and Hades stands there in total command. On a hill above the fires I saw the greatest of the gods, they stand in despair while watching the souls of the damned falling into the abyss, and they grieve for them. My visions allowed me hear his steps, he is there and she is by his side. It's over. The fourth age of man begins."

Eala reached across and took his hand, "My friend, truly you are the God of Travel, your powers; they grow stronger as each day passes." They returned to Rome and continued their walk through the city hoping to find more souls worthy of the message.

They remained to watch the beginnings of the fall of Rome and were there in 410CE to witness the arrival of the Goths followed in 451CE by the constant probing by the armies of Attila, the Hun. It was in that year when Eala decided to become known in the Holy See. She knew that if Rome fell it would be the end of Christianity and she believed this to be a bad thing. She needed inspiration and decided to seek help.

She left and made her way deeper into the catacombs to where the tomb of the fisherman lay. His tomb was the only one emitting a low, yet powerful light showing that Peter too was a carrier of the Light. On touching his tomb they were whisked back to the time when he walked with, talked with, and then denied the 'Man'. They watched him grieve and then follow the ways of the 'Man' before going on to found a new religion, they then watched his capture. They watched his upside down crucifixion and then him being laid to rest. The devotion shown by the followers of Peter gave them the inspiration they sought. They left the catacombs and made their way back to listen to Pope Leo 1st preach about the true message and were impressed.

Over the years they had learned of Leo's ability as a negotiator, garnered since his early days in the priesthood. They hoped those skills could be used to save Rome. They were impressed by how he used his skills to fight the cowardly actions of the senior clerics, who wanted to evacuate St Peters and leave the library and all its treasures of Christendom to the mercy of the advancing Huns. They were there when he yelled, "We will not evacuate, we will negotiate, and I alone will meet the Hun."

This decisive action by Leo prompted Eala to materialise causing consternation among those gathered. She immediately moved to reassure Leo, "Be not afraid, I'm a carrier of the Light and here to help."

Leo asked, "Are you an angel?"

And Eala replied, "No, I'm Ealasaid, my friends call me Eala. I'm travelling to the far west carrying a message from Jacob."

Leo queried, "Jacob? Grandson of Abraham?"

Eala smiled then shook her head, "No! Jacob, grandson of Zeus."

The word 'heretic' was heard coming from among the clerics; 'blasphemer' was also heard. Witch and sorcerer were other words uttered. Several bishops reacted and lunged forward to expel Eala from St Peters but were stopped in their tracks by the appearance of Faer in full armour. He said as he rested the tip of his sword against the neck of the nearest bishop, "Are you that brave? Touch her and see what happens."

Eala gestured for Faer to lower his sword and return to invisibility. She turned to the bishops and questioned, "Why react like this? Why insult me? You who believe in the resurrection and the turning of bread and wine into the body and blood of one whom you follow. You believe in one who walked on water and raised the dead. Need I go on? Why can't you accept that I too have special powers?" She turned back to Leo, "There is much to tell but first you must meet with Attila before it's too late. We will assist and show you the way but we must leave now."

Leo agreed and called for his carriage. He, at the insistence of the emperor, Valentinian 3rd, was joined by two state senators and together they left for the Hun encampment, which was set up just north of Rome. Safe passage was arranged and Leo was escorted into the presence of Attila.

On arrival they were greeted by Attila who was surrounded by ten imposing generals who seemed to be very nervous. Leo sensed a betrayal and quickly moved to calm the atmosphere; he began by acknowledging the greatness of Attila and the prowess of his armies. He also made it clear that he follows a god who only speaks of peace and justice; he then put in his plea for the preservation of Rome but this was rebuked. Attila insisted, "I will take Rome and all its wealth. I will enslave its people and bring down on the new religion the wrath of the Hun." He raised his sword and said while waving it about, "I will destroy Rome, brick by brick, and remove it from all memory. My revenge for the constant attacks on our ancestors will be forever remembered."

It was then when Eala materialised causing the generals to draw their swords and move to attack. Needless to say, no attack happened, the generals were disarmed by the skilful use of an invisible sword. Faer then materialised causing the generals to go to their knees and bow when they recognised the etchings on his armour to be those of Asgard and of Olympus.

Attila was furious, "This changes nothing," he shouted, "Rome must fall." He hadn't reckoned on what was to happen next. Faer's patience gave in and he swiftly grabbed Attila by the neck forcing his head into a vat of water where he held him until his struggle waned. The generals were stumped watching Faer hold Attila's head below the water using his left hand, and threatening them using the rapid motion of his sword in his right hand.

"This lady is under my protection; she is a messenger of the gods and is of the Light," he said raising Attila from the vat. He threatened him further, "You will listen and watch me show you your future. When I'm finished you will be given two choices, live or die."

Faer pushed Attila's head back into the vat and immediately he saw what was coming. He saw disease spread through Rome and watched his soldiers succumb to plague and pestilence. He saw those who managed to leave the city, fall and never get to enjoy the spoils of war. He watched the remnants of his once powerful army fall into madness. He saw fear and terror in the faces of the women and children of his homeland as they became slaves to the once vanquished of Europe who returned seeking revenge.

Attila was then released. He backed away and was obviously in turmoil, within minutes he ordered a total retreat leaving Rome safe.

"Remind me never to ruffle your feathers," whispered Eala.

"He really got on my nerves," was Faer's reply.

They returned to invisibility and took the opportunity to walk among the Hun army where Eala found many young soldiers who had only recently been conscripted. These soldiers didn't have blood on their hands suggesting they had to be the Huns Magni spoke of as those who would be called upon to fight in the End Times battle. She said as she moved among them, "Go now, tell your children to tell their children's children for all time, that one day, they will be called upon by the gods and they must answer."

In the meantime Leo arrived back into Rome to be greeted as a hero by the Emperor who bestowed on him a new title. He became the first Pope to be referred to as 'The Great'.

The relief felt by the people of Rome was not to last. Within five years a new army gathered at its gates. They were the Vandals and this time Leo's negotiating efforts only secured the protection of the sacred buildings but not the many wonderful ancient monuments. These priceless works were destroyed giving the world, a new word, 'Vandalism'. The Vandals robbed all the riches and wealth they found before leaving a devastated city with no resources to rebuild itself.

What surprised Eala was the fact that there were many young Vandal soldiers untested in war, still innocent, and again she remembered Magni's words, 'I will call on the Huns and the Vandals'. She walked among them before they entered the city and identified many she believed were destined to carry, and pass on the message. These Vandal soldiers then used their influence to prevent the worst excesses of their army by ensuring they stuck by their agreement not to kill citizens or destroy any of the sacred buildings.

It was now the year 455CE and Eala decided to speak to Leo one last time. When she materialised she said, "Before I leave I must warn you of troubling times soon to arrive, you must prepare Rome for sadness and turmoil."

Leo pondered, "This was once a great city. See now how it is so poor and impoverished. Why has our god forsaken us?"

Eala saw how traumatised he was by the constant attacks on his beloved city and felt pity, "Walk with me through the vastness of this most holy of places and listen carefully to what I say," she linked his arm then began.

"Soon Rome will be attacked by the Ostrogoths and history will write of this year as the year that begins the fall of the Roman Empire. Your once proud city will begin its decline. The Armies of Rome, though devastated will successfully drive your enemy away only for that enemy to return in the year 547CE. Where once there were a million souls; there will be but a few hundred left. History will write of the savagery. It will speak of the torture and murder of the men and children and the rape of the women. Survivors will be sold into slavery and then, for many years, it will become a barren waste land."

Leo was devastated but Eala wasn't finished, "The next assault will be at the behest of the Normans. They will be invited by a future Pope, as Rome's saviours, but not by the citizenry who will turn on them. The Norman retribution will be swift and ruthless and again the population will be devastated," she paused as Leo placed his head in his hands. "Worse is to come. Descendants of those bitten by the serpents will become soldiers under Charles V, who will be known as the Holy Roman Emperor, and in 1527CE they will raid Rome. They will be leaderless and will bring forth the fires of Hell and will get great pleasure in attacking this most holy of places. They will annihilate the Papal Guards before entering the newly built Basilica. The Pope of that time will escape through secret tunnels. This blood thirsty rampage, bringing Hells induced horror, will result in half of the 55,000 inhabitants left either dead or homeless. Many artists who created the greatest and priceless artworks will be killed and much of their art destroyed, the attack will be forever known as the end of the Italian Renaissance."

Pope Leo was horrified and asked, "Can it get worse?"

Eala replied, "Yes, much worse. There will be evil Popes who will have forgotten the message; many will be responsible for church sponsored wars. There will be inquisitions and much pain. But for those who remember the message, there will always be hope."

Leo went very quiet, trying to absorb all Eala foresaw; then said, "Enough, such pain and terror, it's too much to bear." He moved to sit on a bench placed near the high alter where he clasped his hands and went into prayer. He then surprisingly asked, "Tell me about your Jacob."

Eala lit up showing how much she really loved him, "Jacob is the father of my children and is a most loving and caring god who is full of compassion. He will soon wear the crown of Olympus, and with his brothers he will lead the forces of the Light in the battle of the End Times," she held Leo's hand before continuing, "I fear for him, he is the one to stand alone against Lucifer and he alone is tasked by the Ancient One to lead the defeat of The Darkness."

Leo asked, "Who is the Ancient One?"

"Do you not know?" said a very surprised Eala, "He is The Creator." Leo and Eala both bowed,

"Is there anything I can do?" asked Leo.

Eala touched his arm, "Be the great Pope you're meant to be. Lead and remember his message, for it is the truth," she stood and said as Faer materialised, "it's time for us to leave; Your Holiness, watch Faer send out the Light."

Leo watched the Light travel across Rome and saw Faer's delight when he confirmed no serpents were detected, but he also noted a degree of concern when Faer said, "It troubles me seeing the mark of the serpent on so many of Rome's citizens, especially on a number of your most senior bishops."

Leo nodded, "I too saw the mark and now know that within my inner circle I have many enemies. It seems I must keep my enemies close and those I thought were my friends even closer." Eala agreed.

358

Chapter 8

Eala and Faer left Rome and walked north before turning left into the land of the Franks, and after many years passing on the message they eventually reached the Kingdom of Childeric 1st.

Never once during this long walk did Faer lower his guard. Day after day he sent out the Light and was always happy to report the absence of serpents. Eala loved him, he was her constant companion and she was always sensitive to his moments of loneliness, she knew how to motivate him by just saying, "Danu is lovely, I can't wait to meet her again," or "Tell me about your time with Danu." Just the mention of her name and Faer would always react with excitement and was happy again.

It was now the year 481CE and they had reached the city of Doornik just as Childeric had died. His funeral procession was vast and attended by thousands of mourners. There they watched his son, Clovis, the as yet uncrowned young king, walking behind the coffin. The prince was but a boy of just fifteen years and was well tutored by his father in the ways of the court. He was easy to identify because from him emanated a light that showed he was once touched by the gods. It was obvious to them that he was the successor and they could see how he was regal, proud and the true heir to the throne.

It was during the funeral procession when Eala made her way to be with him; she whispered, "Be not afraid, I'm by your side. Beware the court! They plan to take the throne."

Clovis said as he looked around, "Show yourself; what magic is this? I hear you yet I can't see you, who are you?"

Eala replied, "I am Eala and I'm a friend, you walk in the Light as do I. We will speak tonight."

She turned to Faer, "I'm not happy, look at the faces of the lords and knights; they show their resentment."

Faer promised, "He will have my sword until he becomes king."

After the funeral, Clovis was declared king, and he became known as Clovis 1st. He was nervous and felt he had no allies, although just a boy he was astute enough to recognise that the court was already scheming against him. He thought, that for him to survive, he would have to convince the court to use its power to unite, under his kingship, all the tribes from the northern Germanic lands to the western seaboard, and as far south as the Pyrenees. His nerves were showing until he felt a hand rest on his shoulder. This time he heard a male voice, "I am Faer, a friend and a Warrior God of Olympus, be not afraid. I have a plan," he tightened his grip on Clovis's shoulder then said, "stay with this gathering a little while longer, study their faces and soon you'll see who's an ally or who is a foe."

As suggested Clovis remain with the gathering for several more hours before making his excuses and leaving for his room.

That night, his bedroom door opened and then closed as though an assassin had entered. He sensed a presence and in the dim light found it difficult to focus. He heard Eala's voice and leapt up as she said, "Do not be afraid."

It wasn't Eala who materialised; it was Faer in full armour, with his sword in hand, and to Clovis he looked like a god. He studied the emblems on the armour and recognised the mark of Asgard as well as the emblem of Olympus. He tried not to panic but fear was written all over his face prompting Faer to again try to reassure him. He said after placing his sword back in its scabbard, "I'm guardian to a Goddess of the Light and our task is to prepare the world for the coming of The Darkness. We have a message for the Frankish peoples and it's simple, when the gods call they must answer."

Eala then appeared and Clovis immediately bowed. She walked towards him and said after placing her hand on his shoulder, "Go now, tell your children to tell their children's children for all time, that one day, they will be called upon by the gods and they must answer."

Clovis asked, "How will our descendants recognise the call?"

"All touched by a messenger will know," replied Eala. "The Light will be visible to them and them alone." She then imparted a prophecy, "It's written that you will become a great king, known for all time as the first king of the Franks. You will be the one to unite the tribes ensuring the kingship passes down through your heirs, and between them they will rule for two centuries. In the next five years you will conquer the last of the Western Roman Empire and before your death, you will have brought all of Roman Gaul under your rule. One day your lands will be known as France, destined to become a great nation. Your name will be borne by eighteen future Kings and that name, in its French form, is Louis."

Clovis was daunted; he felt too young for such a task and asked to be left alone to think. Just as Faer was leaving, Clovis asked, "Will I see you again?"

Faer replied, "You may not see us but you will know we are near. You are a descendant of the Trojans and your royal blood will continue the rule of the long haired kings. We will be spreading the message throughout your realm and will be by your side as long as you are king."

The next morning, on his way to breakfast, Clovis met his mother who bowed and he was horrified, he requested she never bow to him again. "All must see that you are our king," she said while hugging him. "When they see me bow they will know they must obey your commands and do your will. In private, I promise I won't bow."

Clovis took his seat at the head of the table and gestured for his stewards to allow the visiting dignitaries enter his hall, and when all were seated Eala took the opportunity to guide him and suggested he repeat everything she said. He stood and repeated her words, "Last night I received a message that must be passed on through the generations and as the centuries drift by more and more Franks will receive that same message. Mark my words," he began pacing before continuing, "let all here present bear witness and recognise me to be King Clovis 1st and be assured I will rule as a just king who will bring unity to all Franks, a unity never before seen in our history. Over the next five years the remnants of the Western Roman Empire will be part of my domain. Remember today, for today is the day when I move to unite, under my kingship, all tribes in the northern Germanic lands as well as those who dwell in the lands along the western seaboard, and those who rule the foothills of the Pyrenees. I say again all will be part of my domain. Nothing stands in the way of the rising Franks."

There were gasps of disbelief, murmurs of dissent but all were silenced when Faer, while standing on the table, materialised. No one could miss him, and all heard him say, "Clovis has been chosen as King of the Franks and he is under my protection." He, as quickly as he came, disappeared. Rumours then spread throughout the kingdom and beyond speaking of a new 'Boy King' who had the blessing and protection of an unknown warrior god.

362

A week later Clovis, who was already a brave and skilful horseman, led an army of over a thousand knights and marched south into the land of the Gaul's where he convinced village after village, as well as the nobility in every district, to support him as their king. He moved west and headed towards the borders of the Ostrogoths and again convinced all the smaller Frankish kingdoms to recognise him as their absolute Monarch. His greatest challenge was convincing the tribes of the north east to bow before him and when he succeeded in receiving their support, occasionally using strong arm tactics, he became unbeatable.

It was during his many campaigns when Clovis met and became besotted with a young princess called Evochildis, who was from a neighbouring tribe. He made her his queen and together they had a son but unfortunately this marriage was not to last and for the three years since his separation he spent most of his time looking after the young prince. It was now the year 492CE and he was finding the loneliness very difficult to handle which was beginning to affect his reign. Eala saw he was struggling and resolved to find someone she believed would bring him happiness.

It was from among the tribes of Burgundy where a princess was found, and in the year 493CE that princess became his queen. Her name was Clotilde and she brought Clovis great happiness, together they had a daughter and four sons. Although the marriage was successful it didn't stop him from going to war against Clotilde's people when, in the year 500CE, he initiated a war leading to the defeat of the Burgundians. He now had complete control of what was to become France. Clotilde accepted his efforts and supported him.

Clotilde was a devout Catholic and made it her mission to convert Clovis to Christianity. She succeeded when, in the year 508CE, he agreed to convert into the Catholic faith. She stood by his side when, on Christmas day he was baptised in the cathedral of Notre Dame, in the city of Rheims. Thousands, loyal to Clovis, also converted and were baptised that day. This began the long and sometimes vicious dealings between the Roman church and the monarchy of France.

Eala and Faer used this now very peaceful time to continue spreading Jacob's message. They remained close by to witness the end of Clovis's reign and followed his funeral procession through the streets of Paris to the church of St Genevieve. They also remained in Paris for the funeral procession of Queen Clotilde. When the cortege arrived at the Church they were pleased the see the spirit of Clovis was waiting to greet his beloved queen.

Chapter 9

For the next two hundred years Eala and Faer continued to spread the message throughout France. Never once were serpents detected but occasionally they encountered descendants of those who were bitten in the distant past. The mark of the serpent was certainly travelling through the generations, never fading.

One particular day while resting near the mouth of a cave situated on the slopes of the Alps, Eala saw a group of travellers making their way north. Among them was a teenage girl who she felt was destined for something special. The girls name was Bertrada. Eala waited until she was alone before approaching her and saying, "Do not be afraid."

Bertrada was used to hearing voices and wasn't afraid. It was as though she expected something strange to happen but never expected it to be the appearance of a goddess. Eala materialised and again said, "Please don't be afraid."

Bertrada responded, "I'm not, are you an angel?" And as usual Eala said,

"No. I'm Eala and I have come to offer you a prophecy."

She sat and began, "I see you as a queen, mother of an emperor. For this to happen you must travel west towards Paris where you will meet he who is known as 'Pepin the short'. He is destined to become king and you his queen. From you will come eight children, one of whom will be known as 'The Father of Europe', a most powerful emperor who will reign for many years. His name is Charles and he will be remembered for all time as Charlemagne."

"No one but the gods could have known my inner most thoughts," said Bertrada, "in my dreams I've seen this day, the crown and many children. How can this be?"

Eala replied, "For many there are several paths. For you, yours was set at the beginning of time. Go now and become queen, fulfil your destiny."

Bertrada bowed and returned to her companions, "We are travelling in the wrong direction," she said, "we go to Paris."

Out walking one fine summer's day, Bertrada caught the eye of Pepin. He saw her and was instantly taken by her beauty; he stopped his coach and called for her to join him. Their courtship began and went on for several months when finally he asked for her hand. She was of royal blood so the nobles and courtiers saw no reason for a wedding not to take place.

Within a year Bertrada gave birth to her first son who was known as both Karl and Charles. He grew to be a gentle child but always had his eye on the crown. He was present when his father was anointed as King of the Franks for the second time; this occasion was in the basilica of St Denis and was presided over by Pope Stephen 2nd. Charles was only twelve and his younger brother was three and for the sake of continuity they too were anointed as successors to their father. These crownings were the first known anointing of a civil power by a Pope.

Eala watched Charles throughout his teenage years and used her powers to influence him in preparing to be a good and wise king. She at first appeared in his dreams and then materialised to give him many prophecies. The prophecies showed what he had to do and how he would have to be ruthless to hold on to his power. She told him she had a powerful warrior god as her protector and suggested he ask for his assistance. It was then when Faer became visible and immediately began sharing his counsel.

In 768CE, when Charles assumed the throne, he made known his plans to the court. His main ambition was to reunite all the Germanic peoples under one rule and convert them to Christianity. He was determined to achieve his goals and as a result much of his reign was taken up in warfare. Eala and Faer watched in awe as his skills allowed him to succeed in uniting all of Europe. In 800CE he was crowned by Pope Leo 3rd as Charlemagne, Emperor of the Romans.

Eala and Faer followed Charlemagne on many of his campaigns and continued to provide him with counsel but never interfered. They used this time to spread the message even though it was well secured in the minds of many Franks since the time of Clovis.

The only issue bothering Eala and Faer was watching him lead his armies in a thirty two year war against the Saxons, a war that ended with the execution of several thousand prisoners and the brutal forced conversion of the remaining survivors into the Roman Catholic faith. This was not the way of the gods and they made their unhappiness known but their disappointment was set aside when they saw him become the greatest tactical Emperor of all time who did succeed in uniting a vast territory and maintaining a high degree of peace. They were happy to see his administrative skills bring a new prosperity and a cultural revival that was to last for many years after his death. What pleased them the most was when he used their suggestion to get the upper classes to set up scholarships in literature, art, music, dance and architecture. They knew their suggestion would bring on what was to become known as the Carolingian Renaissance.

In 810CE Charlemagne showed the first signs of illness prompting Eala to use her powers to lessen the pain making him more comfortable. This went on for four years until the 28th January 814CE when Charlemagne drew his last breath. His funeral procession took his body to the Cathedral of Aachen for internment, and it was so vast nothing like it has ever been seen since.

Charlemagne was no sooner in his tomb when Eala sensed a new calling, it was faint but as the hours passed it was getting louder. "I don't believe it, its timing is terrible," Eala said turning to Faer, "for over seven hundred and fifty years we visited many places, we witnessed many great events. Remember the rise of Trajan? Remember the fall of the Roman Empire and the power of Pope Leo? We were there for the crowning of our friend, King Clovis, and the reign of the Emperor Charlemagne. There is no way I am missing the crowning of Charlemagne's son! We will answer the call after the coronation."

Faer threw his arms towards the heavens and said while walking away, "Women!" he shook his head, "Clothes, fashion and spectacle. You will be the death of me."

Eala enquired, "What was that?" She got no reply.

Chapter 10

During the spring of 815CE Eala felt the need to travel towards the Alps and with Faer by her side they soon reached a land destined to become known as Switzerland. Their journey took them deeper into the mountains where they followed pine-pin covered trails to reach the snowline. The higher they climbed the mountain-scape changed from a dusting of snow to a blanket so thick it became a struggle, "That's strange," said Faer glancing back, "I felt something, a change, it's as though we've left the realm of man and entered the domain of the astrals. See how our footprints fade."

"Yes," said Eala resting her hand on his arm, "I too sensed it, but there's nothing to fear. Once before I felt such a change, it was when Jacob brought me into the domain of the Yeti."

Faer quietened and went on alert. He slightly lowered his head discreetly glancing through the now sparse trees. From the corner of his eye he caught glimpses of movement. On checking, he found no footprints, no damaged branches or no scent marks. He wondered if there was a new magic at play so he sent out his Light only to find there was no threat.

"Relax, my friend," said Eala after sensing his anxiety, "feel the calmness, feel the love. I think we've entered the domain of the Mountain Elves." Faer didn't lower his guard.

In the distance they saw what looked like the figure of a man and as they got closer Eala recognised him. It was Yaz, Lord and God of the Yeti

Nation. She got excited and ran to him. It was then when the Yeti army materialised, there were hundreds of them and they were armed with the swords of Olympus. They manoeuvred to provide a protective shield around Eala and Faer. Eala enquired, "How can this be?"

Yaz replied, "We've been summoned by Kalen, lord of all the Elves. He's helping with the migration of the Yeti nation. Let's walk together."

"How did you travel so far without being detected?" asked Eala.

"We waited for the late winter snows," replied Yaz, "then crossed the highest mountains and the least inhabited plains. Our whiteness and an ancient magic camouflaged us. Kalen foresaw your arrival into his domain and needed our magic to hide you from Lucifer. My armies surround you because it seems as each year passes your Light grows brighter, making it easier for you to be detected by the forces of Hell."

He turned to Faer, "I see your powers have grown. You've a power unknown to us, no warrior has ever detected our presence, you may not have seen us but you knew; I see it as a gift that will only get stronger as you continue your journey."

"I'm known as the God of Travel," replied Faer. "No footsteps can be hidden from me."

Yaz turned back to Eala, "Since we last met you've become a Goddess of the Light and the consort to the one who will become King of Kings. Be happy in this enchanted sanctum of the elves. I feel Kalen has much to show you, one which will be a most pleasant surprise and will ease you on your journey. Six moons will pass and then you walk towards the home of the Medici's."

They climbed higher and deeper into the mountains and reached a stone bridge that to them seemed to be frozen in time, icicles' hung from the crafted guardrail running along both sides, and frosted moss covered the full length of the bridge. After crossing they were met by a colonnade of ice sculptures depicting twenty elf Lords of old, heroes and warriors long gone to the Elysian Fields. They walked through the colonnade in awe of the skilled craftsmanship.

They soon reached the ice columned grand entrance to the Realm of the Elves. On walking through they were greeted by the sight of a vast palace with seven high towers, each connected by a wall topped off with many turrets. Between each turret fully armed warrior elves had gathered.

They reached the main door and waited as it slowly opened to allow them enter into a bright and warm wonderland of lush greenery, colourful flowers and soothing music.

After climbing the steps to the main entrance they were greeted by Kalen who was pleased to meet them after such a long time. He greeted Yaz as an old friend and then ushered them through to the central hall. Faer was uneasy, especially after seeing so many armed elves. He walked closer to Eala ensuring her safety until Kalen said, "Relax; Warrior of Olympus. Eala is safe here."

"Tell that to Jacob!" replied Faer

"I'll let you tell him yourself," responded Kalen. Faer furrowed his brow and wondered, 'What did he mean by that?'

Kalen guided Eala through nearby doors taking her into a bright and colourful annex that was shielded by elf magic. When she walked through she momentarily froze before releasing tears of joy as she ran to three small cribs she hoped contained her babies. They did, all three were frozen in time and looked exactly as they did when they were born. She raised her hand and called on the Light and when it came she used her hand to wave its power across each baby bringing on the first signs of an awakening.

First to waken was Helena, the little princess, she opened her eyes, strained to look around then smiled. Prince Demetrius then woke and he too smiled. Obelius, the second prince, refused to waken and took a longer sleep. Faer remembered the stories of when they were born and was pleased to see they were still babies. He watched Obelius stir and waited for see him open his eyes.

Eala took Helena into her arms and sat on a small sofa style bed with her back resting against the wall. She had waited for this moment for so long and was speechless. She kissed, hugged and held her daughter tightly while watching Faer lean into the next crib. "Wow, I've forgotten how lovely it is to hold a baby," he said taking Demetrius into his arms, "the last I held was my baby sister all those years ago."

He brought Demetrius to rest in Eala's free arm. He then went and took Obelius in his arms before placing him on Eala's lap. He stood back and said while slowly shaking his head, "There's only one thing missing from this beautiful image." It was then when he heard a familiar voice, "And that thing missing is me."

It was Jacob and he gasped while being grabbed in a strong embrace, "Faer, Faer, you're squeezing the life from me."

Faer wouldn't let go, he was overwhelmed: It was almost eight hundred years since they last met in real time. Jacob instinctively knew that all Faer needed was reassurance and said, "Friend, you did good, I'd trust you with my life."

Faer slowly let go, backed away to leave Jacob and Eala to be alone with their children.

Jacob seen his babies a few days earlier but wouldn't wake them until Eala had arrived. He was also warned by Kalen not to show too much emotion for fear it would attract the Light alerting the armies of Hell to the location of the elf realm.

"Is this a dream?" asked Eala.

Jacob shook his head as he took Obelius into his arms. "No," he replied, "this is meant to be. It's real." He fell to his knees, stretched across and after giving Eala a long missed kiss, he whispered, "I've had a restless sleep and felt every threat that came your way. Every time I woke my first thoughts were always of you and my babies," he looked around at the three wide awake sets of eyes looking up at him and his heart felt like it was bursting, "I prayed the Light would help. It did, and now we're together." Kissing her for the second time lessened the pain and loss of the last eight hundred years, especially when the Light came to surround all five of them. As feared, it was so strong it shot out across the universe.

Kalen rushed to the annex and he was furious, barging through the door yelling, "I warned you not to show emotion." He separated Jacob and Eala showing a real fear that his domain may have been compromised, "The love between you has called on the Light and when it came it announced to the cosmos how you have come together. It was such a powerful light it will have penetrated the depths of Hell and 'He' will have seen it. He will fear this power and know your babies are here. No stone will be left unturned until he finds them." Faer arrived and he too sensed danger.

Jacob fell back against the wall, holding Obelius even tighter, "Surely you understand, it's not the same only ever seeing my babies in the dream world. I needed to see and touch them and prayed the Ancient One would allow it. I swore that what happened to me and Odi would never happen to my children. Remember, I never knew my father."

"You fool, your babies are destined to be true and powerful gods!" yelled a still angry Kalen, "They'll always know you are their father, it's something they will have known from the moment they were conceived."

Kalen was seriously agitated fearing Hell was already close by. It was then when Merlin arrived. "Too easy, it was, for me to follow the Light and what do I find? The triplets, together with their parents. This is now a time of great peril." He paced and paced and then called Kalen to join him in the gardens.

Jacob was in shock and furious for allowing his heart to overrule his head. Eala was frozen watching his confidence drain from him. Obelius gurgled and as the seconds passed his gurgling began forming words Jacob soon understood. He kept repeating, "Magni, Magni, Magni." Jacob looked across at Helena and Demetrius and they too repeated the same thing, "Magni, Magni, Magni."

Jacob handed Obelius to Faer and ran out into the meadows. He looked towards the cloud-filled sky and found a spot which had the smallest opening allowing him to see the stars in the northern skies. He sought the golden streaks of the Asgard army and when he found them, he raised his hands to his forehead and continuously called until finally he heard the loud and thunderous sound of his brother's golden chariot. When Magni landed he leapt from his chariot with his fists clenched and a walking pace that indicated he meant business. Jacob knew he was in for another tongue lashing. "Magni," said a panicking Jacob as he backed away, "I've blown it. I've allowed The Darkness in, my babies are in danger and I don't know what to do."

Magni was having none of it; he showed no sympathy and lashed out by grabbing Jacob by the scruff of the neck and lifting him so high the tightening grip caused him to choke. Faer arrived; fearing something like this would happen and drew his sword to go to Jacob's aid only to be stopped

374

when Magni pointed with his free hand and said; "Don't even think about it." Faer knew better and froze on the spot.

"You idiot," raged Magni, "I saw the Light, we all did. I just knew it was you. Your time living among man has made you too emotional. If it was Odi or Modi I would be kicking them half way across the universe. Were you not soon to become King of Kings I would be kicking you from one end of Asgard to the other."

Jacob knew all he had to do was blink to escape but he also knew he had made a serious mistake and was prepared for the humiliation being meted out. He continued to try and explain but Magni just wouldn't listen.

Magni was so mad he dragged Jacob towards the great hall in the full gaze of the elves but was stopped by a calling for mercy. "Magni," said Faer, "he's your brother, soon to be King of Kings. He knows he's made a mistake and needs your help to fix it. You are humiliating him before the elves, show some mercy."

Magni was horrified that his temper caused him to humiliate his brother so much that mercy was called for. He let Jacob go and when he calmed said, "I'm sorry, I don't think I could really hurt you but you do need to be taught a lesson. You've endangered everything and this is now a life or death situation."

"I've lived among man for the first sixteen years of my life," interrupted Jacob, "I've watched them love and grieve, have fun and also fight. I've experienced friendship and compassion as well as jealously and fear, that's from where I get all this emotion. I always swore never to allow any child of mine grow without both parents and then what happens? Eala gets pregnant and our children are taken from us. It's exactly what I swore never to allow. You have to find a way."

"You and Eala are immortals," said Magni, "time should mean nothing to either of you...." He was interrupted again by Jacob,

"Something or someone brought us back together and it can only be...." Magni answered for him, "The Ancient One."

"The babies," continued Jacob, "they know nothing, and the first words they speak are, Magni, Magni, Magni. Do you think they called on you because they must feel safe in your hands?"

Magni threw his hands to the heavens, "That idiot brother of yours is responsible for me patrolling the northern skies because he couldn't keep his hands off Panya, now I'm expected to protect your three. I am the Asgard God of War and to you two low life's I am just a baby sitter. You do realise there is a major battle coming?"

"Wait until you meet them," pleaded Jacob, "wait 'til you see them; tell me then how you feel." Magni walked away then shouted back at Jacob, "Bring me to them."

Magni walked into the annex where his bulk brought a shadow across the whole room. He immediately went across to where Eala was sitting, "You look as beautiful as ever, how did you end up with that idiot?"

"I love him." replied Eala.

"I can see that," said Magni shrugging his shoulders. When he looked down at the three sets of eyes staring up at him and saw their total helplessness he began to melt. "Hi, little one," he said bending forward to take one of his nephews into his huge hand, "what's your name?"

"We named him Obelius, God of Olympus," said Eala,

"A War God, just like me, this should be fun," he continued as Obelius snuggled closer to him, "the last time I held a baby like this was when your uncle Odi was but a few weeks old," he thought for a moment then shook his head, "now look at him. An insolent prick and a holy terror." Jacob nervously laughed.

Magni brought his other nephew into his arms and got very protective. He passed the boys to Jacob then took his niece into his arms only to become besotted with her. "Never before have I felt like this," he said while pacing back and forth across the room. "You and your brothers will forever be under the protection of the War God of Asgard."

Eala and Jacob held each other and were relieved to know their babies not only had the protection of the elves but were now even safer under the watchful eye of one of the mightiest War Gods of them all.

"Now, how do we sort this mess?" asked Magni before turning to Faer, "God of Travel, from the highest turrets send out the Light and tell me what you find."

Faer, escorted by four warrior elves climbed the highest tower and sent out the Light. Nothing showed so he left the palace and climbed a steep cliff to reach the summit of one of the snow-capped peaks. He balanced himself, assisted by the elves, and again sent out the Light. This time to his horror he caught two serpents slithering down the slopes of a mountain at the far side of the valley. The elves, with the help of the Light, also saw the serpents and were the fastest to react. They leapt from the summit, jumped from rock to rock across glacier after glacier until they reached the tree line. They were then assisted by a column of patrolling Yeti warriors. Unfortunately it was as they reached the tree line when they lost sight of the serpents but Faer was watching and was not to be deceived. He called on the assistance of the tree nymphs who sprinkled him with their magic allowing him to travel across the sky at a speed that helped him to land at the far side of the valley. He used his staff to penetrate the deep snow forcing the serpents to reveal themselves; they were cornered and quickly transformed into armed Dark Angels.

High in the mountains Magni was observing, he turned to a very anxious Kalen, "I asked him to tell me what he found. Now I am watching a stand-off. Do these young gods not listen?"

"Can you not see that Faer is a master? My elves have backed away as have the Yeti warriors," said Kalen, "it tells me they believe the serpents to be scouts and not part of any army. It is a wise move on the part for Faer to fight alone because Lucifer would be sensitive to a large scale battle and would send his forces to investigate."

Jacob and Yaz then joined them. Jacob chose to say nothing while in the presence of Kalen; he was also terrified of opening his mouth as Magni again looked to be angry enough to send him flying across the cosmos. The only comfort he got was the soothing words from Yaz, "Don't be too hard on yourself," he whispered, "once I knew a god who made many mistakes, he listened to counsel and then did the opposite. Now he is King of the Gods.

"I'll never be as powerful as him," replied Jacob

"Zeus looks on you and sees himself," continued Yaz still trying to reassure him, "you are his grandson and still very young, he knows you will make mistakes, just don't make too many. He also knows Olympus will be safe in your hands."

They watched Faer take on the Dark Angels and remarked on his bravery as he lunged forward to make contact with his enemy. Through the silence of the snow covered valley they could hear the clash of steel, and the continuous grunts of exertion. At times they saw the sparks fly as sword met sword. They heard the yelps of pain as skin was penetrated and were satisfied it was Faer who was causing the pain. Never once did the Dark Angels make contact with Faer, he was too fast, too agile, too well trained, he was in control.

Magni grew concerned as the battle was taking too long to conclude, it bothered him how the Dark Angels were evolving even as Faer held them off, and he feared they were playing for time, sometimes getting the better of Faer. He had seen enough and turned to Jacob, "It's time for you to redeem yourself. Wear the imperial armour of an Olympus god and take yourself down to assist Faer. End this battle now."

Jacob just nodded, still afraid to say anything. He was ready in seconds. He blinked, then materialised alongside Faer, "Do we keep playing or do we finish this?" he asked.

"That's a bit cheeky," responded Faer, "I've been playing with them for the last hour. Drawing them out just to see how they are evolving. I want to learn more of their ways."

The Dark Angel's were ecstatic when they realised Jacob had arrived, "It's a pleasure to be the one to fight the 'Boy King'," said the nearest one, "our hunch was right, for you to be here means your babies must be close by."

Jacob's heart nearly missed a beat especially as at that very time the Dark Angels were moving into invisibility. It terrified him to think they were on their way to carry this news to Lucifer.

No one could have foreseen what was to come next. Faer travelled at such speed, he leapt forward with a determination that took out the Dark Angels. He decapitated both of them in one foul swoop preventing them from making their way back to Hell. They fell and then slowly turned to dust. "Remind me never to get on your wrong side," said an awestruck Jacob.

"Eala always says that to me," smiled Faer.

Jacob then placed his hand on Faer's shoulder, blinked and took them both back into the elf realm which was now totally safe again.

On arrival in the palace Faer asked, "Jacob, don't you trust me? Why did you come to my aid?"

"Faer, Faer," said Jacob. "I told you earlier of how I trusted you with my life. Why do you always doubt yourself? Magni wanted the battle to end and sent me to join you so as to redeem myself, but you ended the battle with a ferociousness they would never have expected."

"I ended the battle because of the threat made against your babies," said Faer removing his cape, "you gave me a task which was to protect Eala, a threat against her babies is a threat against her and that I will not tolerate."

"I've created a monster," said a proud Jacob. They both laughed.

Over the next six months Jacob and Eala spent as much time as they could with their babies. During that time, almost without noticing, their babies grew to be toddlers and even began to walk. They were funny, boisterous, and prone to the odd tantrum but most importantly they were very protective of each other. Obelius in particular, and even at such a young age, was always keeping an eye on his brother and sister. Poor Faer was pestered by them and soon became the uncle that all toddlers should have. He brought them everywhere and always found new ways to spoil them. Their time with Faer gave Jacob and Eala space to be alone but their children were never far from their thoughts.

The six months seemed to pass rapidly and the time soon came for Eala to continue her journey, she could hear the call of the south east and it was getting louder. Jacob felt the loneliness of his plinth calling and knew he had no choice but to answer. The elves also sensed the time was approaching for Eala to leave so they prepared three comfortable beds for the toddlers.

Jacob and Eala were unable to hide their upset trying to find the words to explain to their children what was about to happen and why? They needn't have worried, Demetrius just walked over and climbed on Jacob's lap, pulled at his head so that he could hug and kiss him. He then went over to his bed and made himself comfortable. Within seconds the stone came and he entered his long sleep. Eala tried not to cry; she felt her tears well up and did everything in her power to prevent them from flowing. Helena then hugged both her parents, went to her bed and again within seconds the stone came. Obelius was more obstinate; he refused to move and demanded more time with his parents. He was showing an early streak of independence similar to that of his father, but he also recognised the pain showing in their faces. He pulled them together and snuggled before kissing each of them in turn. He placed his little head between theirs and said while moving his lips closer to Jacob, "Father, I see you wake and wear a golden crown. You will walk alone, at the barricades and the old women will bow before you. I see you create the water bridge to cross the sea. The metal birds, they follow you. You will stand proud and wait, then send out the Light. There is another, a warrior, he stands beside you. Soon after, the battle begins."

He hugged and kissed his mother then crossed to his bed, climbed in for the stone to come and take him. It was then when Eala released her tears and she was inconsolable. Faer arrived, held her and tried to comfort her, he didn't care that Jacob was watching. He placed both his hands to her face and said trying to get her attention, "We've been to Hell and back and there will be many more travails ahead, let your tears flow and then reclaim your strength for we need to go.

"Look at my children," she cried, "they've turned to stone, it's killing me." "They're safe," he said pulling her closer, trying to reassure her, "when the elves are finished they'll never be detected. You must trust the magic of the elves."

Jacob watched and wondered did Faer love Eala more than he pretended, a thought he quickly dismissed. Faer parted and while making his way from the room said, "I do love Eala but not in the way you are thinking. There's someone I love and will be seeking her in the not too distant future."

"I wasn't thinking that," said Jacob.

"Your face says different," responded Faer sarcastically.

Magni, Kalen, Merlin and the Elfena arrived and together they called on an ancient magic, it surrounded the beds and quickly grew from the floor to the ceiling. It formed a dome and then the beds faded into invisibility. The children were safe, protected and concealed from the gaze of Hell. Jacob, Eala and Faer then left to meet out in the main hall.

After some time passed Faer took Eala's arm, "It's time for us to go," he turned to Jacob, "Eala will be safe with me. The call is now so loud even I can hear it."

"Promise me you will protect her; promise me," Jacob pleaded.

"You really don't trust me, do you?" said an annoyed Faer, "What do I have to do? I promised to protect her with my life."

"I didn't mean it to sound like that," apologised Jacob, "I do trust you. I trust you with my life but the pain is too much; I'm distraught at leaving Eala yet again and am just looking for reassurance. It's only my friends who can give me that." He blinked and was gone.

Eala walked back to the annex and to those watching she seemed listless, she wanted to set her eyes one last time on the stone images of her babies but they too were gone, hidden from all gazes. She wept some more, took a deep breath and turned to rejoin Faer.

When she arrived back into the hall she was taken aback to find Faer was involved in a full-on argument with Magni, strongly objecting to the posting of a battalion of Asgard warriors above the Alps. He believed their presence would attract the attention of Lucifer and his spies. Everybody knew Magni didn't like being questioned and they could see his temper rising as he reminded Faer of his place, but Faer was having none of it.

Magni turned his back and walked towards the door which really infuriated Faer who went after him, he placed his hand on Magni's shoulder and roughly turned him back, "I will say this only once, don't ever turn your back on me. I am Eala's protector and if there is a danger to her babies, there's a danger to her. Your decision is flawed and will attract the attention of Lucifer."

Eala stood with her mouth open, Kalen didn't know where to turn and Merlin just smiled. Magni and Faer stood chests out, almost nose to nose, their foreheads touching.

Magni smiled and while pulling away said, "Well done, you passed!" Faer's temper was now at breaking point, "I don't like being constantly tested; I've proven myself and will not have my loyalty questioned."

Merlin stepped between them and counselled, "My friend Faer, you will always be tested and that's because Eala is destined to be Queen of Olympus. You just have to accept this. Magni never had intentions of leaving warriors here, he's not a fool. He knows they would be a beacon for the allies of Lucifer and would never make a mistake like that. You are a most powerful god but your weakness is your constant need for reassurance. We too need reassurance."

"I'm sorry for disrespecting you," said Faer after calming down, "it's just that I feel at times very lonely. Fafner was always the strongest, and I liked following his lead. Since he left this task has become a huge burden and that's why I'm always seeking validation and reassurance."

"Fafner will always be part of this story," said Merlin before closing his eyes to seek him out, "I see him, he will rejoin you in the not too distant future. His task was always to prepare the dragons. He has become their emperor."

Faer finally accepted this and then bowed to Magni who nodded his approval before heading for his chariot and disappearing over the horizon. "Faer," said Merlin, "before I leave, promise me you will seek me out if you are troubled again. Find me in the Dream World; I'll be there for you."

The following morning Eala and Faer joined Yaz, Kalen and the Elfena for breakfast before bidding their farewells and beginning their walk back towards the north of Italy.

What surprised Eala and Faer was the six months they spent in the realm of the elves actually equated to almost five hundred and thirty years in the realm of man. It was now the year 1347CE and they were about to arrive in the city of Florence for the beginning of the Italian Renaissance.

Chapter 11

On Arrival in Florence Eala and Faer were captivated by the beauty and vibrancy of this very busy city. They especially loved walking through the workshops of the great artists and sculptors but it was the bookbinders who caught Eala's eye. She watched them work, and knew that from the books would come a wealth of knowledge put together so as to usher in a golden age of learning, destined to last for the next four hundred years.

Visiting a small workshop Eala said, "One of the greatest artists of all time will, in this place, create some of the world's most renowned paintings and sculptures. This is the studio Jacob and Odi will visit. Remember the statue of David, the one Jacob brought back to Olympus, the mould will be made over there and a naked Odi will stand upon that very plinth." Faer sniggered, remembering the teasing of Odi when the gods first viewed the statue.

Faer face suddenly changed, he felt an overwhelming threat. Reaching into his satchel to extract his staff, he sent out the Light and to his shock he saw two Dark Angels making their way through the city. He immediately dressed in his robes and armour and insisted Eala walk behind him.

Approaching the Dark Angels was nerve wrecking, what they were up to wasn't obvious, until rats were seen scurrying into every available crevice. "The Dark Angels aren't targeting the people, it's the rats," observed Faer. "They've done something to the rats." He again sent out the Light and this time saw that the rats were carrying something strange and sinister. He turned to Eala and with a puzzled look said, "I don't understand, the Dark Angels have disappeared but the rats, they're everywhere."

Eala was equally confused and used her powers trying to understand. She closed her eyes and slipped into a trance calling on the Light for help. When the Light came it showed her the depths of Hell where she saw Lucifer sitting on his throne looking very pleased. The light brought her back by one day and again showed her Lucifer and this time he was passing a small urn to each of the generals who were present. She heard him issue and instruction for them to use the contents of the urn and infect every city and town in the realm of man, it was then she realised he was responsible for spreading a great pestilence. She remained in her trance and travelled all over the world to witness the Dark Angels let loose the plague. She was horrified, this time she knew there was no defence.

"There's nothing we can do, it's too late," she said in despair, "the infection is everywhere and millions will die. It is the Black Death."

"Why would the Ancient One allow this? Why have we been sent out with a message when millions of those carrying that same message will die before they pass it on?" asked Faer.

"We need to wait and see what happens," said a very confused Eala, "always remember, the Ancient One works in strange ways so there must be a reason."

They watched the citizens of Florence succumb and felt the grief as family after family lost their loved ones. They were horrified when the burial pits became mass graves for bodies given no dignity.

"The sense of despair is overwhelming," said an exasperated Faer, "there must be something we can do." It was then when he felt a familiar presence, it was Jacob,

386

"The Goddess of the Snows, Chione is her name, and you must call on her. Ask her to bring her wrath, it will help."

Faer used his powers as the God of Travel to journey back through time. He arrived in a temple not too far from the Parthenon, there he sought out Chione and on finding her, requested her help. She agreed to assist and promised to watch out for his Light. Faer rejoined Eala and this time directed his Light back through time to create a pathway for Chione.

Chione sent three consecutive severe winters, each one with a ferocity that affected the whole world, killing off the pestilence, but not before over half the world's population had succumbed. Unfortunately Lucifer wasn't finished; he sent his demons to create more panic, planting the seeds of dissent ensuring survivors would blame smaller minority groups, bringing on further civil unrest.

Towards the end of the third year, after a particularly tough winter, the snows began a slow melt revealing mounds of bodies everywhere. Faer continued sending out his Light, always checking, always on alert, especially the night he thought he heard the sound of flapping wings. It was a once familiar sound and one he hadn't heard in a thousand years. Within moments his excitement grew and his tears gathered. It was Fafner and when he landed, he said after taking his human form, "I'm back!"

"About bloody time," said Faer trying to be cool.

They momentarily paused and then ran to hug each other. Fafner asked, "Where's Eala?"

"She sleeps." replied Faer, but he was wrong. Eala heard the commotion and ran out to investigate. Just like Faer, she momentarily froze before joining them in a loving embrace.

"I've much to tell you but before I do," said Fafner, as he pulled away. "The stench of decay is everywhere, humanity has been devastated. I've been sending out the Light and all I see is microscopic balls of a poisoned light and it seems to be the cause of the pestilence. I challenged them and was able to use my Light to vanquish those I caught. They're alive and seem to be balls of pure evil. They show no mercy."

"The Goddess of the Snows assisted us by sending her wrath," said Eala, "the freeze came and it seems to have worked. We are now dealing with those spreading false rumours and they are making it very difficult to bring back peace." She looked across the city and wondered, "I hope out friends have discovered how to destroy this plague."

All three joined forces, sending out their Light. Each new burst travelled further, ridding Europe of the greatest pestilence ever to menace man. When they were satisfied the plague was defeated they relaxed and talked about all that had happened since beginning their walk.

"I've got so used to being alone with Faer, I find it strange that three of us will be travelling together again, it's going to take some getting used to," said Eala.

They laughed then Fafner asked, "Do you want me to leave?"

Faer was quick to respond, "Absolutely not, you can take over; my nerves can't take much more."

"We really missed you," said Eala while hugging Fafner again, "you also missed meeting Jacob, Magni, Kalen and Merlin," she paused thinking of her babies, then continued, "you missed meeting my babies; they are now toddlers, but wait until I tell you this. You missed Faer unleashing a frenzy of blows on an army of flying demons in the bowels of Hell. He was like a god possessed. He also attacked two powerful Dark Angels, an attack that was witnessed by Jacob and Magni."

"Jacob said to me, 'remind me never to get on your wrong side'," said a smug Faer, "it felt so good."

388

"Oh, he also attacked Magni," continued Eala, "I was shocked, I think Magni was taken aback and will bide his time to put him back in his place."

Faer said after letting out a nervous snigger, "When I grabbed him from behind, I felt my life drain away. Only for Merlin I think I'd still be travelling out across the cosmos." All laughed again.

"What about you," asked Eala, "tell us of your time in the dragon realm."

"As soon as I arrived," said Fafner, "I asserted my authority and became Emperor of the Dragons. They respected my power and looked on me as their one true god. One after another they bowed before me. Remember the twelve guardians, the ones who rescued me from Morgana? They became my counsel and together we brought hope and peace to our realm," sadness crossed his face. "My peace was shattered when my eldest son rebelled against me. He ran away and I've no idea where he is. I searched but never found him, now the time has come for me to rejoin you. The good thing is, his mother is continuing the search, and she's gone to the deserts convinced she will find him. He has broken our hearts and the hearts of his brothers and sisters."

Fafner's distress showed in the worry lines across his face. Faer promised to help with his search.

Eala was enthralled, it never dawned on her that Fafner would have found a partner and had a family of his own. She had difficulty trying to find the words but when she did she suggested, "You had better start at the beginning."

"Do you remember the lady dragon who nursed me after the attack near Hadrian's Wall?" asked Fafner. They both nodded then he continued, "Her name is Heulwyn, it means 'Sunshine' and she became my partner. She is my queen and empress. We travelled everywhere together and soon fell in love. We couldn't get enough of each other and it wasn't long before she was pregnant and ….."

He was interrupted by Faer who couldn't resist asking, "How do dragons do it?"

Eala punched him and Fafner slowly turned to give him one of his well-known stares. "How am I supposed to know if I don't ask?" continued Faer.

Fafner maintained his stare and then said, "We are dragons only when we fly, we take our human form at all other times, now have you worked it out?"

Faer responded, "That's disappointing, I was expecting something like claws and fire and a raging passion, at least make it interesting."

Fafner was getting snarky, "Let me assure you that there are no claws or fire but there would always be a raging passion and whoever is with me will always find it interesting." They all laughed again.

Faer then asked, "How many children, or little dragons do you have?"

Fafner smiled and said with pride, "I have three sons and two daughters."

Faer couldn't help himself and jokingly said, "You've been busy, I didn't realise you'd been gone that long."

Eala asked, "May I put my hands on your forehead?"

Fafner was taken aback but was also curious. She entered his head and immediately saw the great love he had for his family. She searched and eventually found where his son had gone. She kept her eyes closed and said, "Your son, his name is Derwyn; he is of the oak tree and they will be his protectors. He is alive and is in his human form. He lives in a small village in the midlands of Spain. You have no need to worry; he walks in the Light and has become a protector of the village. He also has a companion and he seems to be very happy. Heulwyn has found him."

"I guess we're going to Spain!" said Faer.

"No!" disagreed Fafner, "I remember how we chose our destination, only Eala knows the path we follow."

Eala shook her head, "Right now I feel nothing, so we should go to Spain. If I receive any callings we'll decide then on what to do."

The following morning they made their way to the Port of Livorno and after establishing that ships left Italy for Spain on a daily basis they sailed to the Port city of Barcelona before quickly making their way to find Derwyn.

Chapter 12

The journey from Barcelona to central Spain took almost a week and was uneventful. Arriving at a hillock on the outskirts of the village was nerve-racking for Fafner, until he saw his son leaving one of the small chalets. Derwyn looked happy, especially when joined by a young girl who occasionally kissed him. A few moments later Heulwyn arrived carrying a new born baby. Fafner watched them gather near where Derwyn drew water from a deep well and was happy to see how he seemed to have made his peace with his mother.

It was one of those really hot days common to central Spain and not much work was being done due to the incessant heat. Derwyn took many water breaks and it was during one of those breaks when he looked up at the crest of the hill, shielded his eyes and thought he was seeing things. He thought he saw two warriors and a beautiful woman staring back at him. He wasn't alarmed but did ask his mother if she could see what he saw and she denied seeing anything.

Fafner watched more villagers arrive. They seemed to be congratulating the young couple and admiring the new baby. When Derwyn asked if anybody could see the figures on the crest of the hill, they all said no. They teased him, saying he was seeing things, putting his vision down to his baby causing sleepless nights.

Derwyn got more unsettled. It was bothering him that he alone could see the figures so he decided to investigate. Heulwyn joined him, "My boy, I too can see them. I didn't want the villagers to panic so I said nothing. You must prepare yourself for a shock."

"Why," asked Derwyn. "The closer I get I see they look like gods of old, two warriors and a goddess, I feel no threat."

Heulwyn replied, "The warriors are trained War Gods, they are her guardians, she is a Goddess of the Light."

"You act as though you know exactly who they are," said an intrigued Derwyn.

"I do know exactly who they are; one of them is very special to me. I met them in the past and married one of them."

"You were married before father?" he said while trying to compose himself. "How come you never told us?"

Heulwyn quickening her pace, "Be patient, I'll tell you everything but not just yet. You are safe with these gods and they'll welcome you. I must warn you, prepare yourself for a shock. I didn't expect, or know this meeting was going to happen, but I'm happy it's happening now." She then stretched across and linked his arm.

When they reached the crest of the hill Heulwyn bowed before Eala. "Mother, why are you bowing to her, she's nothing to us."

"My son," said Heulwyn while gripping him tighter, "she is a most powerful Goddess of the Light and is destined to become consort to the King of Kings. Together they will rule the universe."

"Mother," snapped Derwyn, "I left the pomp and ceremony of a royal court and just want to enjoy a peaceful existence with my wife and daughter; I'll bow to no one."

"There's no need to bow to us," said Eala, "but I'm curious, why so much anger?"

"Too right there isn't," he replied, "I still have a rage that's hard to control."

Derwyn was tall and strong, definitely his father's son. His eyes were drawn to one of the warriors; there was something about him he couldn't put his finger on. He demanded the warriors remove their helmets. Faer obliged and said as he turned towards Fafner, "That old saying about the apple not falling too far from the tree certainly applies here." He then said as he turned back to Derwyn, "You remind me of someone, my closest friend and my greatest ally. He is a warrior of legendary prowess and a guardian to a Goddess of the Light. He is here with us, he's your father."

Fafner then removed his helmet and waited for an adverse reaction. He didn't have to wait or too long, the force at which Derwyn lunged forward sent Fafner stumbling back and down the hill. Derwyn went after him and pounded his fists off his father's armoured chest until they started to bleed. It took some time for Derwyn to weaken and lose his strength, allowing Fafner to say after catching his breath, "I love you, son." He paused for a few moments then continued, "I don't understand why you hate me. I never treated you badly. I supported you and was always there for you, why?"

There was a lengthy pause and then Derwyn shouted, "I saw you! I saw you! I was walking through the forest and when I reached the high ledge, I saw you!" He was in a rage, and through his now flowing tears yelled, "I saw you turn into a demon and spread your wings. I saw you breathe fire and take to the sky."

"Your father is no demon," said Eala while helping Derwyn to stand. "He's an ally of the gods, a dragon lord, and Emperor of all Dragons. For a thousand years he's been building his armies in preparation for the End Times battle."

Derwyn had difficulty calming but he did. The light flowing from Eala's touch had entered him and was helping him relax. Eala continued, "I've known your father for fourteen hundred years. He's my guardian and a favourite of the gods. He's a Warrior of the Light, charged with preparing the dragons for the defence of earth and he needs you by his side."

"I don't understand," said Derwyn, "in school our teachers spoke of flying demons with fire as an ally. I saw you fly, I saw you breathe fire, what I saw was what was taught."

Fafner pleaded, "Look at me son, do I look like a demon? I'm a dragon lord and I walk in the Light. You too are a dragon but for some reason, it hasn't shown itself."

Derwyn hissed, "I'm no dragon, I'm a man, a husband and a father."

Heulwyn intervened, "My beautiful boy, of course you are a man but all born of a dragon will eventually become a dragon when the time is right, some early in life, most late in life. We never tell our children of their powers until we sense the change is coming. We never let our children see a dragon until it is near their time to become one. That's why you never knew the truth. I found you because a dragon mother's love is so strong and because dragon mothers are first to sense the change and have the ability to find their children no matter where they might hide."

"Mother! Not you as well? You can't be a dragon."

Eala intervened again, "Derwyn, I see your father in you, you are so alike it's uncanny. Walk with him and learn to rekindle your love for him. We cannot have him worrying and despairing as the battle approaches." She gently touched him again and the calmness was now complete.

Derwyn agreed to walk with Fafner and they made their way towards a calm lake that was surrounded by blooming wild fruit trees. It was a steady and silent walk that was soon interrupted when Fafner placed his hand on Derwyn's arm, "Stop! Something's wrong! I smell burning and can hear screams of terror."

Derwyn concurred, "Father, my heart is racing, I have a strange feeling; I too can hear screams."

Back on the hill Faer asked, "Does anybody smell burning?"

Heulwyn said as she moved back up the hill, "Yes, I too smell burning. I fear all is not right." It was then when Eala and Faer saw her fall to her knees, holding her hands to her head and screaming in despair. They watched her stand and raise her arms towards the heavens before transforming into a powerful and regal dragon. She took to the sky and flew down towards the village. Faer and Eala ran back up the hill and were horrified at what was before them, the village was ablaze and there were many bodies strewn across the fields. Faer extracted his sword and ran to rescue those he could hear screaming in the burning houses. His efforts managed to save roughly twenty of what was once a village of two hundred souls. Eala used her powers and saw nothing, this troubled her. It meant the attackers were shielded.

Fafner and Derwyn quickly reached the hilltop and were met with scenes that horrified them. Derwyn attempted to continue running but was held back by Fafner who insisted he wait. He held him tightly and at the same time he removed his staff from his satchel. He sent out his Light and it was then when he detected a convoy of evil slavers, bitten in times past by the serpents. They were heading east. It was a forced march of innocents who were about to be sold into slavery. They were being taken to Granada, the last stronghold of the Moors.

Fafner sent out a loud and shrill call that Heulwyn knew meant she was to return and join him. When she took her human form she immediately sensed Derwyn's change was coming. She and Fafner stepped back and watched.

Derwyn was still so devastated he couldn't find the strength to move. It was when beads of sweat formed on his forehead, he started breathing erratically. He fell to his knees then rolled around in the dust before landing on to his back. He ripped off his clothes and tore at his skin but no relief came. His legs and head expanded, his torso widened and his arms shrunk. His transformation was well underway. He was in agony but had to go through this alone. His skin hardened and became scaly before changing to a gunmetal grey; then his wings appeared. They sprouted from his back through his ripping skin. Through all this his parents watched and had great difficulty listening to his pitiful screaming, they knew they couldn't interfere. When he finally took his form, he stood as a young dragon, smaller than his father but looked just as powerful. He spread his wings and waited to feel the warm air lift him.

Fafner and Heulwyn had already transformed and together they all took to the sky where they circled for long enough to allow Derwyn master his flight skills. In the distance Fafner saw the tail end of the convoy and watched it attack village after village, enslaving the occupants. He was about to pursue when he sensed a presence, it was Odi, "Fafner, my friend. Don't pursue, wait until you are in control, fly south to a narrow gorge and wait for the convoy, then attack. Be aware there is something we cannot see and it worries us."

Fafner and Heulwyn returned and landed alongside Faer then transformed back into their human form. They were quickly joined by Derwyn, who wasn't happy, "What are you playing at, my wife is in that convoy and so is your granddaughter."

Fafner tried to reassure him, "Odi, an Asgard God of War, came to me and said we should wait. When a god of Asgard speaks I'll always listen."

"Derwyn, if you need to do something," said Faer trying to reassure him, "take me to the sky and let me see the convoy. We will prepare a plan, trust us."

Fafner intervened, "No! While flying high I saw a narrow gorge, it's to our south and looks to be the gorge Odi spoke of."

Derwyn got more confused, "But the convoy is moving east! It's going in a different direction."

Fafner said, "What I saw was a convoy of Moor slavers, they will move east and then turn south to where they must pass through the gorge. Odi is a master tactician and I believe he is guiding us to save the villagers."

"My powers are failing me, something's not right," said Eala, "I cannot see what lies ahead. This convoy is hidden from me, protected by an evil force. We must do as Odi suggested."

Heulwyn placed her arm around Derwyn and said, "My son, I feel your pain and sense your terror, but you must trust us. We'll take to the sky as a family and wait at the gorge. Like lord Odi, your father and I are also master tacticians and we will rescue Isabella and your baby."

He said as he rested his head on her shoulder, "Mother, nothing feels right."

It was time to leave and they swiftly flew towards the gorge, Fafner carried Faer and Heulwyn carried Eala. When they reached the gorge they landed and put in place their plans. Heulwyn hid on a high ledge near the entrance, Derwyn was told to take up a position further south and wait for instruction while Faer took control of the whole valley for fear Fafner's judgement might be clouded.

Fafner took his human form and was obviously very agitated as he paced back and forth. "Our invisibility is supposed to be an asset," said Faer, "your constant pacing is raising so much dust you will alert any scout who happens to be close by. Relax! Otherwise you are no use to me."

"Do not fear for me, friend," replied Fafner, "I remember Eala speak of how you, in the bowels of Hell, fought like a god possessed. Trust me, I am totally focused, watch me bring down the wrath of the gods on these slavers."

Eala intervened, "Fafner, please listen to Faer, I fear all is not what it seems. I sense this day will not end well but I can't see who falls." Fafner accepted what was being said and took the 'at ease' position alongside Faer and they waited. It took another twenty four hours before the first signs of the convoy appeared.

High in the mountains Heulwyn maintained her vigil and watched the convoy finally reach the valley and pass below her. While watching she was horrified at the treatment being meted out on the young men and was shocked by the condition of the girls and young women. It was obvious terrible things had happened to them during their journey of just one day.

She searched for her granddaughter and was devastated when she saw her being wrenched from Isabella before being tossed into a cart along with all the other babies and toddlers. Her anger was growing and reaching breaking point, it took all her strength to stop herself from unleashing her wrath.

She was also very concerned because at the far end of the gorge she saw Derwyn straining his neck trying to see if Isabella was in the convoy. She knew her son well, and feared if he saw the condition Isabella was in, and the treatment meted out on his baby, he would explode into a rage ruining any plan Faer and Fafner had put together.

Derwyn was agitated and trying to control his temper. He could hear a low subliminal sound, similar to the rumblings of elephants, and didn't realise that his mother and father were communicating in an ancient dragon language so as to prevent him knowing what was happening. Fafner's rage was again showing itself and he had great difficulty maintaining control. "They've done things to Isabella and the girls," he said through gritted teeth, "they've carelessly thrown my granddaughter into a cart. The boys and young men have been savagely beaten. Who are these people?" He looked back at his son and saw he was still straining his neck, "I worry for Derwyn, I fear his temper."

It was all too late; Derwyn had caught a glimpse of Isabella and saw how she was now a torn and broken woman. He also saw the condition of the babies and toddlers, he could take no more. He expanded his wings and took to the sky. On reaching the convoy he landed just before the lead slaver.

Fafner was furious until Derwyn looked back at him and somehow he knew there was a new plan. Derwyn whimpered and coyly played up to the slavers by acting like a puppy dog, giving them a false sense of security. In the meantime, while he was distracting them, Heulwyn took to the air and flew towards the unguarded cart carrying the youngsters. She used her claws to firmly grip the cart, taking it into the sky to set it down high in the mountains. The toddlers were terrified when they saw the dragon so Heulwyn immediately took off, but landed just behind a large boulder where out of sight, she transformed back into her human form. She ran back to the children to sooth and reassure them, particularly checking on her granddaughter only to find that her arm was broken. She promised to return as soon as she rescued their parents. When she was again out of sight she left her dragon scent in the immediate area ensuring no wolves or bears would come near.

The slavers held their captives near the rear of the convoy with very little security giving Eala and Heulwyn an opportunity to prepare a rescue. Eala tapped into her powers to raise a shield of light around the captives, giving Heulwyn time to arrange their escape and guide them up to where the children were hidden.

In the meantime Fafner was sending out his Light and found it was having difficulty reaching the carriage at the centre of the convoy, and this bothered him. He concluded that it was protected and they were dealing with some new form of evil. Although he was bothered he never took his eyes from his son and was trying to understand what he was up to. Eala, by now, had rejoined Faer and Fafner and was waiting for Derwyn to make his move.

When Derwyn was certain his mother had secured the prisoners safely on the mountain he stopped acting and took on the appearance of an imperial dragon. He had used his time to separate the subliminal sounds and began to understand how to communicate using them, he also found he had developed the ability to telepathically communicate with his parents and together they began to make their move.

Heulwyn retook her dragon form and hovered near the rear of the convoy where she prepared to attack. Wisps of coloured air began to waft from her nostrils before turning to a mass of bellowing smoke and then she released her fury. She sent intense and burning flames so far along the convoy that she succeeded in turning all the carts and their slaver occupiers to ash. What surprised her was her effort stopped at the sinister carriage.

Derwyn then prepared to release a molten and intense shaft of flame but forgot he was still learning to be a dragon, and hadn't mastered the art as yet. The slavers saw this as a sign of weakness and took their chance.

They released volley after volley of arrows but were dumbfounded as each arrow was sliced in two and fell to the ground without making contact with him. They couldn't understand what happened until Fafner and Faer materialised showing them what they were dealing with. The slavers released another volley and as before the swiftness and the power of the warriors showed when that volley was also destroyed. Derwyn moved forward and again tried to unleash his flame but found he couldn't so Fafner stood before him and retook his dragon form before releasing his fury, incinerating all before him, including their belongings. It hurt him when his actions also killed all the horses, but there was no choice. When he was finished what was left was the sinister carriage and piles of black ash running for hundreds of meters each side of it. Faer joined him and together they used their combined Light power, but even its strength couldn't penetrate the carriage causing Fafner to cry out, "What evil is this? How can it be so powerful it resists the Light?"

High on the hills above the valley, unnoticed by Eala and the boy's, was a line of knights who had just arrived, they were escorting Ferdinand 2nd, the King of Spain. The king and the knights watched the destruction of the slavers and the rescue of the villagers; they were in awe of what unfolded before them. They stood in silence as the stand-off between the warriors, dragons and whoever it was hiding in the carriage continued.

It was then when everything changed. There was an eerie silence. The wind ceased and the relentless heat of the now high sun seemed to intensify.

Out of the silence came the sound of heavy steel doors unlocking and the creaking sound of them opening. As they slowly opened, they grated on everyone's nerves. Metal steps descended and after a few moments, they alighted. There were five of them, one being protected by the other four. They were taller, darker and more sinister looking and they didn't wear the black of the Dark Angels met in the past. These ones were wearing dark navy cassocks with deep purple capes, and on their heads sat a crown of skulls placed between two horns creating the ancient image of Hells demons. They bore black steel swords and a staff with rare black crystals embedded in its crown. They oozed an unseen evil that was very different.

Fafner turned to Eala and was about to speak when the first demon said, "Today you meet your doom, consort of the 'Boy King'. Capture you; we get your children........"

Faer interrupted, "There'll be no doom for us today, we travel in the Light and trust me; we will smother The Darkness."

The demons laughed and then two of them transformed into gladiator style warriors. They inched forward, battle ready. They then lunged to commence an epic battle, fought with such viciousness it was destined to go to the death.

Faer and Fafner called on all the skills given to them by the War Gods and fought valiantly. They struggled because the demons seemed to have the advantage, they were able to anticipate every move made and used this to inflict a great deal of pain.

Faer fell and Eala ran to his aid but something stopped her, it was Jacob and he whispered in her ear, "Wait!" A loud thunderous sound could be heard and it was coming from the north. Fafner immediately recognised it as the sound of chariots from the Asgard army and when they arrived they immediately unleashed their might. Their arrows quickly destroyed the gladiators but failed to reach the three remaining caped demons.

These demons were very swift; they raised their staffs and released thousands of black crystals which transformed into devastatingly sharp micro spears that, when targeted, had the power to penetrate the shields protecting Faer and Fafner. The spears did pierce their armour, seriously wounding both of them. Fafner then collapsed and fell unconscious.

Derwyn was devastated with this turn of events and took to the sky, his anger was growing as he increased his speed and then the fire came. He felt his throat burning and had an overwhelming urge to release its power, which he did and succeeded in taking out two more of the demons leaving what looked like the most powerful one still standing.

This demon was certainly more resilient and had the ability to withstand the fire of a dragon. He retaliated by targeting Heulwyn who unfortunately wasn't fast enough to protect herself from a cluster of micro-spears. She collapsed and fell into sleep releasing her white mist towards the heavens. Her spirit was now on its way to the tombs of the dragons.

Eala ran to her aid but all she could do was cradle Heulwyn's body and when she looked across at the seriously wounded Fafner who was now awake, she was totally distraught. She called on the Light and when it came she released its full power towards the demon and it too had no effect. She increased its intensity and all it did was erase the last vestiges of the already fallen demons by turning them to dust and sending them back to the depths of Hell. It was now obvious this demon was different, more powerful and heavily protected. He looked at her and then she knew; he wasn't Lucifer but was of him; he sneered and then said, "My work here today is complete. The Dragon Lord will now know what real pain is."

Eala asked, "What do you mean?" The demon sneered again and then showed he had the power of invisibility and was gone. She wondered who he was.

Derwyn took to the sky again and swooped down towards the carriage, he sent out his new and more intense flame, incinerating the carriage and watched it turn to ash. He then landed alongside Eala and after taking his human form he fell to his knees in grief. He held his mother and just kept repeating, "I'm sorry, I'm sorry. Forgive me mother."

Fafner eventually dragged himself over to where Heulwyn lay, his heart was broken and he had great difficulty watching his weeping son rocking back and forth, cradling his fallen mother. Eala and Faer stepped away and watched a broken family slowly fall into mourning.

The villagers had been watching these sad, yet amazing events and as soon as it was safe they made their way down to be with Derwyn. The psychological trauma, especially among the women, was so bad they seemed to be listless; it manifested itself when Isabella arrived and walked up to Derwyn carrying her injured baby. She was catatonic and said nothing, just handed him the baby, turned and walked away. Derwyn cradled his baby in one arm while rocking his dead mother in the other, and when he finally looked up, Isabella was gone out of view. Eala approached him and said, "I know you are grieving but Isabella is you wife and you must go after her. Derwyn, she needs you." He said nothing.

Eala continued, "Remember her, remember the happiness, she needs you."

He still said nothing forcing Fafner to intervene, "Go after her son, what happened was not of her doing, she needs you and your daughter will always need her mother."

Derwyn's mind was in turmoil and all he could do was stand up and walk in circles, he still said nothing. Eala then placed her hand on his forehead and used her powers, forcing him to remember his love for Isabelle. He might have taken his time but when the memories came back he handed his baby to Fafner and began to run. As he ran he found himself taking to the sky, giving him a wider view of the search area.

His search took him near a small lake where he observed ripples rolling across its glass-like surface and thought that was odd. He decided to investigate and when he landed he transformed back into his human form. He searched along the lake shore and soon reached an entrance to a large cave from where he heard a splashing sound. He swam into the semi darkness and after searching some more he found Isabella. She was scrubbing as though she felt a permanent dirtiness. He joined her and said while placing his arms around her, "This pain can be taken away," to which she replied,

"But you will always know and I can't live with that."

He said, "I too can have those memories taken away." She said as she snuggled closer to him,

"You would do that for me?"

He nodded, "I would do anything for you."

Derwyn said as they left the cave, "I take it you now know what I am?"

She replied, "I've always known you were special but never in my wildest dreams did I imagine you to be a dragon."

He said as he pulled her closer, "My father came looking for me and that's when I discovered I too was a dragon."

She enquired, "Why have you never spoken of him?"

He lowered his head showing his shame, "I hated him, I thought he was a demon when all the time he was a dragon, I've now discovered he's not only Emperor of the Dragons he's also a God of Olympus."

Isabella asked, "Now that you know who and what you are, will you be leaving me?"

He was taken aback and moved to reassure her, "Trust me, if I am leaving, it will only happen with you by my side. My homeland is a place that is most enchanting. It's protected by the Light and it's full of music. Its forests, lakes and meadows make it the most magical place in the universe, but most importantly, it's safe." He then transformed into a dragon and asked her to climb up.

While Derwyn was away Eala used her powers to heal those who were injured including Fafner who when fully recovered, flew to one of the highest peaks and let out a piercing and heart wrenching call that awoke the dragon realm. Soon the sound of flapping wings was heard and hundreds of dragons appeared across the horizon. They had come to escort the body of their empress back to her homeland.

Fafner, in the meantime, landed beside Eala and was joined by Derwyn and Isabella. He turned to his son and said, "I need you to escort your mother's body home. When there, you must lead the dragon armies and learn to be a warrior king. I will continue with the task set by Jacob so I ask you to look after your brothers and sisters, help them grieve for their mother. Tell them I love them and will see them soon," he looked at Eala and she nodded in agreement then he continued. "You're my son and heir and will rule in my stead. Be a wise ruler and continue my preparations for the End Times battle."

Fafner then knelt by Heulwyn's body and raised her head to rest on his lap. He kissed her softly as he descended deeper and deeper into grief. When he composed himself he whispered in her ear but everyone present heard him say, "You are the only one I've ever loved and I thought us being immortals meant we'd forever be together. It seems a thousand years is all we've been given but when I look at our son and think of his brothers and his sisters I know that you, through them, will always be near me. Farewell my love, rest in peace."

A hastily made flat board was prepared and it was covered in the most colourful of flowers. When Heulwyn was laid out a floral headdress, created by the villagers, was placed on her head. Four elderly dragons then arrived and using handles placed at each end of the cart slowly raised it into the sky. They joined a formation of hundreds of dragons and where escorted by the chariots from the Asgard army. Derwyn, Isabella and their baby joined the procession as it flew south before turning back to fly above where Fafner, Faer, Eala and the villagers were watching.

Eala entered Isabella's head and said, "I've taken away the bad memories for both you and King Derwyn and have given you the gift of immortality."

Fafner was heartbroken watching the dragons leave then remembered he never learned his granddaughter's name. His last happy memory of Heulwyn was watching her carry the baby out to the yard where Derwyn was drawing water. He called after his son, "What's my granddaughter's name?"

Isabella answered, "We named her Isidra, she is a Gift of the Gods and one day will wield great power. She will be a Queen of the Dragons and, alongside an Asgard War God she will walk in the Light and bring the sunrise when Shadow is at its strongest." Fafner just nodded.

Eala wondered, "What is this Shadow she speaks of?"

It was then when King Ferdinand rode down from the hill and said when he reached Eala, "I always knew evil was everywhere but never before have I seen such malice, fiendish and diabolical foulness. For five days we have travelled through village after village to find devastation on a scale never before seen in my realm. I saw what you did and how you fought the demons from Hell. I will forever be grateful for how you showed compassion and love towards my subjects. Is there anything I can do for you?"

Eala acknowledged his comments then said, "I need you to escort these people back to their villages, help them rebuild. I have given a message to each of them and they will carry that message through the generations for their descendants to answer the call of the gods near the battle of the End Times."

Ferdinand ordered his knights to set up camp for the night and instructed them to ensure the villagers were well cared for. He then asked Eala to walk with him and when out of earshot he said, "Through the royal houses of Europe I have heard that since the time of Rome messengers have been travelling around the world. I have always wondered was Spain visited and now I know," he paused for a moment and then asked, "these End Times you speak of; are they close?"

Eala shook her head, "The End Times are coming but you will be long gone. When your descendents hear I am in the Western Isles they will know it will be but two hundred years away."

Ferdinand asked, "Is my realm safe?"

Eala replied, "I have the power of prophecy but as yet I cannot see the End Times. You and Queen Isabella will be remembered as a strong and wise royal family. You will herald in the golden age of discovery for all of Spain and will be instrumental in sending a voyage to lands that will one day be called the America's. There will be good things about your reign but there will also be bad things. You will unite all of Spain but you will break treaties that were so carefully agreed. At the behest of others, ones whose ancestors were bitten by the serpents, you will usher in the expulsion of the Jews and you will bring on the terror of the inquisition."

Ferdinand was taken aback. He chose to back away and left Eala alone. He fulfilled his promise to assist the villagers and then returned to his palace.

Chapter 13

Eala, Fafner and Faer remained in Spain for another twenty years before embarking on a voyage that took them to the great city of London. It was the year 1502CE and the death of Arthur, Prince of Wales had just occurred. On arrival they watched the funeral procession and felt for Catherine, his grieving wife. She was the daughter of Ferdinand and Isabella of Spain and a most stunningly beautiful girl of seventeen years. Her grief was exasperated when she fell under the control of her father-in-law, Henry VII.

After the funeral Catherine returned temporarily to Ludlow castle on the borders of England and Wales, where she had originally gone to live with Arthur after their marriage. It was there where her stoic personality became obvious to all especially by the way she made the best of a bad situation.

She was summoned back to London where for the next five years she was subjected to many humiliations under the gleeful eye of Henry. He held her finances so tightly she became impoverished, but her pain was not to last. In 1509CE, Henry VII died, bringing on the reign of his son Henry VIII.

Henry VIII, a young man of eighteen years was, since the age of ten, infatuated by the beauty and charm of his sister-in-law. He petitioned the Pope for the right to marry her: A petition that was granted.

Henry was over six feet tall, extremely handsome and proud. He was considered at that time a most eligible bachelor but he only had eyes for one woman. His love for Catherine was obvious to all and their public displays of affection, and regular kissing sessions, were to become the talk of the royal courts throughout Europe.

Catherine was popular in court as well as among the people; the clergy loved her because she was a devout Catholic just like her mother. She became a true consort for Henry even to the point that when he travelled she was appointed regent and defended the realm especially when Scotland used every opportunity to attack England while Henry was away.

Unfortunately for her there was to be much personal tragedy in her life, she was pregnant six times with only one child reaching adulthood and it was in 1518CE when, after the still birth of the sixth child, that Henry became anxious about the succession. He knew Catherine was getting close to the end of her child bearing days and he was determined to have a son. He began to take mistresses and even fathered a son by one, but this son would never be accepted as king because of being born outside of marriage.

It was around then when he met and became infatuated with Anne Boleyn, a young courtier, and together they conducted a clandestine affair. It is said that he even secretly married her as he considered himself divorced from Catherine since 1527CE. He informed Catherine that she would now be known as the Dowager Princess of Wales as she was the widow of his brother. It was in 1533CE during a dispute with The Pope when Henry finally lost patience and declared himself to be head of the Church of England, allowing him to officially marry Anne. He had, three years previously, banished Catherine to Kimbolton castle, some miles north of London, where she retreated into prayer and was known to wear only sack cloth. Henry also banned his daughter, Mary, from visiting her mother which intensified the pain of loneliness she suffered. She wrote to her nephew, Charles V, who was Holy Roman Emperor and told him of her pain.

In 1531CE she wrote: *'My tribulations are so great, my life so disturbed by the plans daily invented to further the Kings intentions, the surprises which the King gives me, with certain persons of the council, are so mortal, and my treatment is what god knows, that it is enough to shorten ten lives, much more mine.'*

Eala had had enough. She made herself known to Catherine and as always happens when she first appears the opening question is, "Are you an Angel?" And Eala's answer always is, "I'm not an angel, I'm Eala," she sat beside Catherine and continued, "when once I met your father I showed him the Light and he has, as foretold, become a great king. I didn't meet your mother, Queen Isabella."

Eala placed her arms around Catherine, "My heart breaks for you. To lose so many children is too much for one woman to bear but to lose the man you have loved so unconditionally the way you have is insufferable."

"I have my faith and no one can take that from me," said Catherine, "I will defend it with my life."

Eala then said, "In deference to your father I'll stay by your side until it's your time to pass."

For the next five years Eala remained by her side. She gave her companionship and counsel which was a great relief for Catherine. She provided comfort as each year brought more demands from the palace, especially the constant requests for the crown jewels to be returned for use by Anne. Eala assisted Catherine when in 1532CE she spoke of her status and said,

"In this world I will confess myself to be the Kings true wife, and in the next they will know how unreasonably I am afflicted."

Eala was crafty and decided to visit Henry. On arrival she was shocked to see he was no longer the handsome and fair king he once was. She watched him scheme and plan the dissolution of the monasteries then bided her time. When he was alone she planted an idea in his head by repeatedly whispering, 'Allow Mary visit her mother.' She repeated her words until he sent out a decree that Mary was to be brought to see her mother.

Within days a royal carriage, bearing the emblem of the Princess of Wales, arrived at the gates of the Castle. Catherine got very excited when she realised it was her daughter, and although her health had deteriorated, she raced to greet Mary and they spend several happy weeks together. Catherine cherished what time they had but it was not to last as spies were reporting back to the palace causing Henry to again ban them from meeting up. When Mary was leaving, Catherine whispered, "Always be obstinate in protecting your rights as Princess of Wales."

Mary left and Catherine continued her decline, only lasting for two more years. It was now 1536CE and Catherine sensed her time was coming to an end. She and Eala spoke for what was to be her last time. Eala assisted her in writing her final letter to Henry, in which she said,

'My most dear lord, King and husband, The hour of my death now drawing on, the tender love I owe you forceth me, my case being such, to commend myself to you, and to put you in remembrance with a few words of the health and safeguard of your soul which you ought to prefer before all worldly matters, and before the care and pampering of your body, for the which you have cast me into many calamities and yourself into many troubles. For my part, I pardon you everything, and I wish to devoutly pray god that he will pardon you also. For the rest, I commend unto you our daughter Mary, beseeching you to be a good father unto her, as I have heretofore

desired. I entreat you also, on behalf of my maids, to give them marriage portions, which is not much, they being but three. For all my other servants I solicit the wages due them, and a year more, lest they be unprovided for. Lastly, I make this vow, that mine eyes desire you above all things.' - Katherine the Quene

When Eala read the words of the finished letter she whispered a prophecy into Catherine's ear. "You are too generous. Henry will rue the day he forsook you. He will never again be happy in love and will not get his wish, for his line will end in 1603CE with the death of Elizabeth." Late that fateful night Catherine peacefully passed away.

Eala was devastated and remained by her side for many more hours. In the meantime Fafner took his dragon form, maintained his invisibility and followed a messenger who was riding to the palace to bring the news to Henry, only to be shocked by the glee and delight that greeted the news.

Henry and Queen Anne decided not to attend the funeral but didn't object to other dignitaries attending. The funeral was treated as a state occasion and the pomp and ceremony was spoken about for many years after. Catherine was buried in Peterborough Abbey and a plaque was engraved with the title 'Queen Catherine'. It was written that she was 'A Queen cherished by the English people for her loyalty, piety, courage and compassion'

For the next one hundred and thirty years Eala remained in or near London and during all this time either Faer or Fafner would send out the Light and were always pleased to report no sign of serpents. Eala used this time to spread the message and fulfil Magni's prophecy about calling on the Saxons for the End Time battle. This part of England was home to thousands of descendants of the Saxons who became known as the Anglo Saxons and many were deemed to be worthy of receiving the message.

Although there were no signs of serpents, there were many in the palaces carrying the mark. On some, the mark showed itself publicly, resting on the necks of those carrying out the most devious, ruthless and cruel deeds. These were the very people who had an unnatural ability to manipulate Mary and Elizabeth into causing the most draconian of decrees to be issued, bringing on pain and misery during each of their reigns.

Chapter 14

Eala never allowed Faer or Fafner to interfere in royal issues no matter how unjust they were. She concentrated on spreading the message and was always pleased to see the reaction of those who went on to be ancestors of all that was great about the realm of the English.

Unfortunately, in the year 1665CE the first signs of serpents appeared. They were slithering through the streets of the old city and had evolved; they were more cunning and never to be found in the same place for more than two nights in a row. The tightness of the streets and the wooden structures of the buildings provided them with the safest hiding places.

Faer and Fafner maintained their alertness while travelling through the streets and no matter how hard they tried they never found the serpent's lair. They knew the wretchedness, and the overcrowding in the city was a recipe for disaster, and worried that the stench, as well as the lack of hygiene, would lead to a rat infestation similar to what happened in Italy. They knew that wherever there are rats, fleas would follow, spreading the seeds of plague.

Their fears were not ill-founded, for soon the first signs of disease appeared. People were beginning to stay off the streets and remain in their homes. An odour of decay rose and people didn't seek help for fear of the shunning, or more direct threats from their neighbours. Within days panic spread to the wealthier parts of the city causing the rich, and the upper classes, to move to their country estates, leaving the poor to suffer alone.

While patrolling near St Paul's cathedral Fafner stumbled upon two serpents releasing infected fleas into the surrounding streets. He materialised and challenged them. They instantly transformed into Dark Angels and within minutes, serpents seemed to come from everywhere. They too transformed as they arrived, leaving Fafner very vulnerable. He used his Light and quickly established that the serpents were centred on St Paul's. He wasn't fazed because he knew Faer would soon see the troubled Light and come to his aid. The Light did alert Faer who immediately made his way towards the cathedral.

Eala in the meantime was outside the city spreading the message to people escaping to the country and was in no danger.

When Faer arrived he climbed upon the roof of a nearby townhouse giving him a panoramic view of the surrounding streets. He remained invisible and waited to see what the Dark Angels were planning.

The people watching from their homes were awestruck by the sight of a fully armed warrior, dressed in golden armour, who seemed prepared to stand alone against an army of demon angels. Some people left their houses for a better view and were instantly attacked. Their white mists never rose indicating their souls were mercilessly taken and sent to Hell to be the playthings of Lucifer.

The doors of the cathedral opened and the Bishop of London, as well as a number of his clergy appeared. Faer saw they were carrying the mark of the serpent and that the marks weren't recent. The Dark Angels at the base of the steps all bowed before them. This meant that Fafner was surrounded. It also meant the serpents not only penetrated Rome, they had also taken the churches of the far west.

The Bishop, on seeing Fafner was beside himself with excitement. He was certain he had within his grasp, one of the guardians of a messenger.

418

His desire to embellish himself to Lucifer was so strong he sent a message prematurely.

"We've been waiting, we've always known a messenger would one day visit London," said the bishop as he approached Fafner, "good was our decision to take this vile house."

"In sixteen hundred years I've seen many gatherings of serpents," said Fafner with contempt, "I know your weaknesses and have no fear. I'm a War God and trained by the greatest. You don't frighten me."

"Even you War Gods cannot defeat The Darkness," said the bishop, "you are weak in its presence and will fail."

"Out of the darkness came the Light," said Fafner, "it has shone brightly since the beginning of time and it will never succumb. If it's surrounded, as I am, it will always find a way, as I will. You know not with whom you're dealing."

Fafner touched a nerve and the Bishop's anger grew, "Do you think we're fools? Look around, we have planned for this day, Dragon Lord."

The bishop raised his hand then clicked his fingers. Hundreds of Dark Angels exited from the surrounding houses holding many prisoners. The terror and fear in the Londoners eyes touched Fafner; he recognised many of them to be carriers of Jacob's message. He also recognised some to be descendants of those who had, in the past, met with Panya, Oba, or Mulan. It was obvious Lucifer had changed his strategy and was now targeting the carriers.

The Bishop opened a portal and showed Fafner the cages of hell, he said, "Look what awaits you, see them fill up with descendants of the carriers, watch their souls being tortured and torn from their bodies."

The Bishop then dismissed the portal before beckoning some of the angels to kill their captives. Fafner raised his sword until he looked across at Faer who slightly moved his head as a sign not to react.

The Bishop noticed, "Fool! We can't be deceived. We see the other one on the roof yonder?" Fafner felt compromised and wondered how to deal with this new power Hell had acquired. Faer remembered how the mountain nymphs gave him flight, closed his eyes and called on them yet again. Immediately he took to the sky to land alongside Fafner.

"Ah two guardians, this day gets better," said the bishop, "all we are missing is the messenger, where is she?"

Faer responded, "You will not lay your hands on her, she is of the Light and the most protected."

The Bishop laughed, "Either she is the bearer of the goddesses, or she is the consort of the boy king. I see no Asgard army above so she must be the consort. Can you imagine his pain when we catch her? We know she is somewhere in London."

The Bishop demanded to know the location of Eala but all he got in response was two smirking guardians. He pounded his staff off the steps before transforming into a most hideous dark demon. Faer recognised him as one of the generals who attended the council of Hell when Lucifer was discussing his plans for the attack on earth. He knew they were now dealing with a most powerful force of evil.

Faer was troubled and tried to mentally reach Fafner but Fafner was already in a moment of trance, he was calling for assistance using an inaudible low frequency murmur that was so low, only he and the dragons were aware of it.

The Bishop snarled while turning to Fafner, "Your call for aid will not be answered. We've sealed the entrances to your realm, Dragon Lord."

Fafner smiled, "You say you sealed the entrance to my realm? Now I ask as to who is the fool? I've been trained by the best. Three entrances are known, others not. Be afraid demon, the Light is soon to unleash its power, and you will be sent back to the depths of Hell. Go do your worst."

Fafner could hear the flapping of wings but they were too far away so he decided to try some delaying tactics. He turned to Faer, "We're in real trouble here. Did you sharpen your sword as I asked?"

Faer understood the question and responded, "Are you trying to rile me? Don't start on that again; I'm fed up with you ordering me about."

Fafner punched him, "Idiot, you've put us in danger." Faer responded with an equally forceful punch causing Fafner to stumble. Some of the Dark Angels began to enjoy the simmering tension and moved forward to watch the growing anger. Even the demon Bishop began to smile.

The delaying tactics were working and both Faer and Fafner continued with their pretend posturing until the sound of flapping wings became audible to all. In the meantime Eala had arrived and was using her invisibility to help rescue the carriers. She moved among the Dark Angels and placed her hand on each of their shoulders, immediately incapacitating them, allowing the captured carriers to escape.

It wasn't long before the demon Bishop realised the captives had been freed and was furious when he saw his angels all in a frozen state causing him to unshackle his power and send bolts of lightning in all directions. The lightening compromised Eala, "Ah, there she is!" yelled the bishop, "it seems the messenger has graced us with her presence."

He raised his hands and released more bolts, this time targeting Fafner but Fafner's training kicked in and he leapt to somersault out of danger. As he leapt he drew his sword and targeted the priest demons destroying a number of them in one swoop. The demon Bishop stepped back and directed his angels to attack.

From the windows of the houses nearby those people who escaped capture watched as a battle between the forces of Hell and the warriors of the Light was fought out with an unheard of ferociousness. In the meantime Eala made her way to the entrance of a nearby alleyway and placed the rescued carriers behind her.

As the minutes passed many more serpents arrived and were moving towards her, putting her in serious danger, that was until she felt a presence, it was Jacob, "Eala, my love, don't be afraid, you are now a most powerful Goddess of the Light, use your powers and be safe."

Eala raised her hands and the Light came, it was at its strongest and rose up to form a barrier across the entrance to the alleyway. As the serpents attacked and touched the shield they were incinerated and sent back to where they came from.

The battle on the steps was very one sided with Faer and Fafner being overwhelmed, they were having difficulty dealing with the serpents and Dark Angels who were coming at them from all directions. Whenever they got the upper hand the demon Bishop would step in and send the fires of Hell towards them. As the battle progressed Hells fires began to take its toll. They were struggling and any relief would be welcome.

That relief soon arrived when three dragons appeared above London. They were visible and looked to be very powerful. They flew alongside each other before crossing the entrance to the cathedral. They unleashed their fire and incinerated most of the Dark Angels on the lower steps. They then re-formed and swooped again this time they succeeded in taking out most of the remaining demons in the square.

What nobody had planned for was a second group of demons who were hiding in the shadows, they emerged and began attacking. They succeeded in bringing down one of the dragons who, when he hit the ground, was subjected to a fearsome onslaught that was only momentarily relieved when Fafner came to his aid.

The serpent attack was so relentless and vicious it seemed that the young dragon had no hope. He transformed into his human form and called out, "Father, help me."

Fafner turned and saw it was his second son, Evan. He began to breathe erratically and then rapidly, his throat was reddening and the straps on his armour weakened before falling from him and then he changed. When transformed he was bigger and broader than when last he was a dragon. His rage was building and he let out an almighty roar before releasing his fire. He targeted every last serpent and held his ruthlessness for his attack on the Dark Angels. His vengeance was fuelled by the thoughts of Heulwyn lying dead in his arms all those years ago. He was desolate; the attack in Spain never left his memory but the thoughts of an attack in London taking his son was just too much.

Faer in the meantime had followed the demon Bishop into the cathedral where he had difficulty finding him. After searching, the Bishop finally revealed himself while standing below an inverted black cross. Faer shouted, "I warned you that you will not lay your hands on her, she is the most protected."

The Bishop sneered, "Have you not grasped at how close we came, we are getting stronger and one day we will prevail, each time we meet we learn more, we will defeat the Light and The Darkness will be supreme." He transformed back into a demon, disappeared and returned to Hell.

Faer ran out to join Fafner who was on his knees holding Evan in his arms. He could see his eyes had welled up and were ready to release their tears. Fafner just kept shaking his head and rubbing his sons face. His two other sons stood close by and were in total shock. Afan went to his knees and rested his head across Evan's chest, he and his brother were the closest any brothers could be and were never apart. Derwyn then went to his knees and tried to comfort his father. It was a tragic scene to see such grief.

Eala joined them, "Fafner, listen, he's not gone; there's a faint heartbeat. I can hear it." Faer reached forward and took Fafner and his sons away to allow Eala to work her magic. She raised her arms, closed her eyes and called on the Light and it came, it illuminated the whole square and many of the people who were infected by the plaque were no longer in pain. The hidden carriers came out of hiding and stood at the base of the steps and were joined by the people who were cured.

Eala slowly lowered her arms and her light travelled into Evan. It seemed to take a long time which bothered her. She shook her head, "What magic is this, they've sent the evil deep into his soul. I need help. I'm not strong enough."

She called on Danu, Merlin, anybody, to answer and didn't have to wait too long, for high above a bright light appeared and when it arrived on the steps, it was Faer who was first to react. His heart beat faster, so much so that Fafner who was still being held by him noticed. "Is that her?" Faer was speechless and just nodded.

Eala smiled and took Danu's hand and they together called on the Light. Again it came and with its full force they expelled the poison allowing Evan to recover. Eala and Danu then sent the Light out over the city. It penetrated every street, alley, house, hovel and drain. It drove all infected rats and fleas out to be incinerated in its burning beams. London was now free

424

of plague and its people were healed, many rejoiced. "To rejoice is folly," said Eala, "London's fate is sealed, nothing can be done. His revenge will be swift and brutal. The screams of terror and pain are already ringing in my ears. A further calamity will make itself known and it'll be within the next year."

Fafner held his son who was now in a deep sleep. He gently rocked him saying, "I can't do this. Jacob will have to understand, my family must come first. I'm returning to the dragon realm." He lifted his son and began to transform only to be stopped when Evan woke, "Father, you have a task to complete, we're safe under Derwyn's protection. If you leave now, what happened here will happen in our realm and all will be lost. The Darkness will see this as a weakness and find a way in; you must stay and protect Eala."

Fafner was taken aback and asked, "When did you become so wise?"

Danu joined Faer, touching his cheek. He said, "Please tell me you can stay a little longer."

She shook her head, knowing her presence had the capacity to attract Lucifer and would complicate the task Eala had to complete. She placed her fingers over his lips, "I must go, he still seeks me and I feel him probing everywhere. We'll meet again. Remember, seek the Fair Land and there you'll find me." She disappeared.

Eala walked among the carriers and said, "Gather your families and move to the south coast and wait for the call. Today you witnessed the power of Hell and it now knows you are here. His vengeance will be merciless. Go now." Eala rejoined Faer and Fafner and watched the carriers gather their families and their belongings to begin their exodus south.

Fafner's sons retook their dragon form to prepare for their journey home. Derwyn turned to his father, "Climb up father, it's time I carried you."

Fafner never moved so fast, he felt any differences there was between them were long gone but most of all he just wanted someone to carry him for a change. The shock of nearly losing one of his sons had taken a terrible toll and wasn't far from his mind.

Eala, before mounting Evan looked out over the square and realised that too many people had seen the battle. "I hope they heed my warning," she said, "I worry for them, Lucifer always attacks the towns and cities visited by messengers and he knows we were here."

Faer, as they travelled high above England, took every opportunity to send out the Light, highlighting serpents biting their way through many places.

They continued their flight and eventually reached the Welsh mountains where Derwyn opened a secret portal allowing them to enter the realm of the dragons where they remained for almost fifty years. On arrival they were greeted, and then a great celebration was organised. The older dragons were still in awe of Fafner, they remembered the way he brought back their pride and gave them all the tools they needed to prepare for the End Times battle. He was still revered as their emperor but he never allowed this to take away from the rule of Derwyn who had grown into a just and wise king.

Eala continued to worry about London and her fears were well founded. One year after reaching the dragon realm, word reached her of how, in a small baker's shop, on a street called Pudding Lane, a fire was started that spread through the old city, wiping out everyone and everything. That night, in her dreams, she saw his chiselled good looking face rise up before her; she recognised him and saw his smile as St Paul's burned. She then knew his revenge on London was complete.

Chapter 15

Fafner normally loved being in his homeland, it was there where he was at his most contented, but not this time. Everywhere he walked reminded him of his beloved Heulwyn. Walking by the lakes, through the forests and across the meadows released scents and sounds that flooded his mind with missed memories. What kept him going was not only the companionship of Eala and Faer, it was the love he had for his sons and daughters.

Time was up to its usual tricks, it allowed fifty years to pass without anyone realising it. As the years passed Fafner became more agitated. His sleep was being interrupted continuously by ever increasing nightmares. They were getting more vivid alerting him to a hidden danger beneath his feet. They showed him tunnels being dug but not the diggers and this bothered him. It was when the drilling became incessant and louder he realised he had to take action. He left the palace after another series of particularly gruelling nightmares. He didn't make it too far when he was approached by his younger sons, "Father, Evan and I are aware of your nightmares, we're sharing them. They show us following you through tunnels, and we sense your fears, it's time you told Derwyn to prepare."

Fafner was taken aback, "Nightmares in my head shouldn't be shared. They're not real but if you're sharing them something is wrong. I'm on my way to investigate and must insist you say nothing to anybody until I'm ready." He said while gripping Afan's arm, "In Olympus we learned how the volcanoes were being used by Lucifer for his attacks. We also learned how the hot springs have their source in the depths of the earth where the volcanoes begin their journey. There are thermal springs beneath our realm and that's where I'm going. You and Evan must remain here; keep your eyes open and ears to the ground. Don't alert Derwyn, he has enough to do." It was then he felt a movement beneath his feet, Afan also felt it.

Fafner continued his journey out into the vastness of the dragon realm. He was totally focused on what was ahead but was also keenly aware he was not alone. On glancing back he caught glimpses of his sons, jumping behind any rock or tree that was near them. It pleased him that they cared enough to disregard his instructions but he was very annoyed they didn't do what he asked and resolved to deal with them later.

He became distracted when thinking of the happy times he and Heulwyn shared. He thought of his three sons constantly teasing him about his great age. He then thought of his parents and smiled to himself when he thought of Jacob speaking about how much they loved him. He realised he never grieved and sought solace in the knowledge they were taken to the Elysian Fields where they were placed among the heroes of old. He hoped they were there to greet his beloved Heulwyn. He resolved to visit and place flowers at their tomb.

After several hours he reached a small concave style indentation in the centre of the grass lands and had no memory of it being there in the past. He smelt sulphur and this bothered him. When he crouched he knew he was getting close. His sons broke cover and joined him saying they too smelt sulphur. Fafner gestured for them to be quiet by placing his finger over his lips. He slightly turning his head, at times to the right and then to the left, he was straining to hear something. His instincts told him that a sinister evil was at work below their feet.

"Return to the city and fetch Faer," said Fafner to Afan, "it's time to explain my suspicions to Derwyn. Tell him to place the city on alert." When Afan left, Fafner extracted his staff and sent out the Light. Evan's eyes widened, "Wow dad, I've never seen you call on the Light before. Its power is awesome; see how it penetrates the ground." Fafner didn't reply; he was horrified.

After a while he said, "The Light has revealed a gaping breach in our underground defences. It has shown me a gathering of serpents and they seem ready to attack. I don't understand. Our realm is like that of the elves, totally protected from evil."

Fafner placed his fingers to his forehead and called on the power of Merlin who immediately answered. His arrival was announced by continuous flashes of lightning. Soon twenty elderly dragons arrived followed by Derwyn, Faer and Afan.

"All is not what it seems," said Merlin as he bowed to Derwyn, "I sense the serpents have breached your defences but they've no idea where they are and we must keep it that way."

Merlin summoned Apollonius who quickly arrived. Together they re-tested the breach and again were satisfied the serpents had no idea where they were.

"My lord," said Apollonius to Derwyn, "you and your army must leave the grasslands. We believe your realm is safe but as a precaution Merlin and I will place a spell around the city. Allow your realm to be under the protection of the wizards."

Fafner turned to Afan and Evan, "Return with your brother and help with the protection of the city."

Evan reacted with incredulity, "Are you for real? You're an old dragon and need us young ones to keep an eye on you."

Faer couldn't help himself, he was in his element, "I love it, I've got allies, the great Fafner will rue this day."

Derwyn said trying to suppress a laugh, "That was brave, little brother. I can't believe your wings are still intact after that comment," he turned to Fafner, "father, I agree with Evan. They stay. They will have your back."

"I'm not happy with this decision," said Fafner.

Merlin and Apollonius followed the dragons back to the city and when all was secured they raised their staffs and called on the Light. The Light arrived and quickly surrounded the city. It formed a dome and then everything under its protection faded into invisibility.

When Merlin and Apollonius rejoined Fafner and Faer they continued with their plan to assist. Merlin conjured up images of ancient structures that once existed on Salisbury plain, including Stonehenge. His intention was to deceive the serpents by leading them to believe they were in the south of England and not in the realm of the dragons.

Apollonius searched for any entrance that would take Fafner and Faer deep underground but found none until he observed a quivering near a low rocky outcrop some distance away. He approached it and using his magic he was able to unlock its secrets, the quivering was a shield concealing a long forgotten entrance into the Underworld.

Fafner was shocked; he feared Hell could have used this exit to reach his realm. He was reassured when Faer said, "Relax friend, my power as the God of Travel tells me that no serpents or Dark Angels have ever passed through this entrance."

Fafner relaxed until Merlin said, "Its best we leave now. The light of a wizard is strong, the light of two even stronger. We are a danger to the dragon realm. Follow the tunnel and sort out what lies beneath."

When they disappeared Fafner and Faer walked into the tunnel. They hadn't walked far when Fafner hesitated and said while staring at his sons, "I suppose there's no way I can persuade you to return to the city?" Afan said after rushing passed, "No."

Fafner responded, "I admire your fearlessness, don't allow it bring you to the point of being reckless."

They continued walking along the tunnel, following a faint orange light that took them deeper into the Underworld. Although armed, Fafner was uneasy. His sons were not trained by the War Gods and this unsettled him. Faer sensed his uneasiness and said, "I'm the only one who has walked deep into Hell, I should take the lead."

Evan scoffed and Afan said after casting his eyes towards the heavens, "Shit, we've two old men on our backs now."

This time it was Fafner who sniggered but he also knew things could go seriously wrong. He raised his foot, sending Evan flying forward with an unmerciful kick as his companion. His sons got the message allowing Faer to take the lead.

Faer touched the walls and noted how alike they were to the walls in the caverns of Hell near Rome. He sensed that Lucifer's plans to enter the realm of man would be through similar tunnels that were drilled all over the world, tunnels strategically placed to be camouflaged by hot springs or volcanoes.

As they travelled deeper they soon reached a portal that led into Hell. At the entrance was hundreds of serpents, many of which had transformed into Dark Angels and they seem to be preparing for war.

Faer removed his armour and weapons from his satchel and then extracted his spare set and gave it to Evan. Fafner also took two sets from his satchel. All four then prepared.

Evan and Afan last saw their dad dressed as a warrior at the battle outside St Pauls in London and saw how he looked as powerful now as he did then. When they were all ready Faer said, "You three are clones of each other, you're dressed identical, are all the same height and equally as broad," he continued as he walked marginally ahead, "this is the plan, Fafner and I will go into invisibility and you two will be the bait." He waited for a reaction and when none came, Fafner said,

"I know you two will be visible and vulnerable to any attack. You wanted a fight, now you've got one. Begin walking towards the serpents and let us see your skills."

Afan looked shocked, he didn't anticipate this plan. He knew he was not as skilful as his brothers, or his father, but was reassured when he heard his father say, "I'll be by your side and won't let them near you. Remember you're only the bait, they will respond and we'll destroy them."

When Afan and Evan came into the view they got a reaction. A sense of excitement travelled through the ranks of the serpents causing many more of them to transform into Dark Angels. They were amazed that two warriors would have the nerve to challenge them and called for their general. When he arrived, Faer recognised him as another of the demons who was with Lucifer before the rescue of Danu.

"This is more serious than I thought," whispered Faer, "there are hundreds, far more then when last I fought."

Fafner asked, "How many more than when you last fought?"

Faer said after looking about, "About double."

"Well there are two of us now, so tell me what to do," replied Fafner.

Afan piped up "What about me and Evan? Do we count for nothing?"

Faer said, "This will be a battle like no other, you must back off when they attack and let us deal with them."

Evan wasn't impressed, "You're typical of old men, never trust the young. I take exception to that. We are dragon warriors and our fire can bring down these walls and sort this problem once and for all."

Fafner rebuked him, "Son, shut it. Faer and I have a plan; we can read each other's minds and always work together. Let us do our jobs and only when they are sent back to Hell, bring theses tunnels down using our breath of fire." He then turned to Faer, "Help me allow Athena in." He needed no help; Athena was already in his head.

Faer closed his eyes and soon felt he had the power of Athena. He looked across at Fafner and saw that he too had her power. They were now not only powerful Olympus warriors, they were also under the control of the most powerful and ruthless goddess of them all.

The general stepped forward and after looking at the emblems on the armour of Evan and Afan said, "Ah, guardians of a messenger. Which one do you protect? The consort of the boy king or is it the mother of the goddesses? Tell me, where is she?" Fafner whispered, "Sons, say nothing."

The general stepped forward sniffing the air, "I smell your fear, Dragon Lord. Say goodbye to your realm, we know it's nearby, the stench of dragon is everywhere."

Fafner saw Evan was about to react until the demon spoke again, "You try to deceive me? You're not the guardians. You're both dragons," he became confused, "how can this be?"

It was then when Faer and Fafner materialised. "I'm the Emperor of the Dragons," yelled Fafner, "prepare to be sent back into the bowels of Hell. You have wreaked havoc for the last time."

The demon's excitement grew, "Four Olympus warriors stand before us, an Emperor, two dragons reeking of fear, and one whom I met before. The goddess of the Light you rescued, she'll be ours again. Her light dims as her people allow all memory of her to fade. You'll all be ours before this day is out."

Faer tried not to react but his fears for the safety of Danu unsettled him. He said, "That day in the depths of Hell, I knew nothing of the goddess. Now she's all I think about. Trust me when I say - I will protect her with my life."

He felt a presence; it was Danu and she said, "I'm with you. Unleash your power and assist in protecting the realm of the dragons, unleash it now while Athena is present."

At the same time the general again detected fear in Fafner's sons and instructed his serpents to target them. What wasn't expected was the new ability the serpents had garnered. They had gained the ability to grip and slither along the smooth and shiny walls and travel across the ceilings. They succeeded in placing themselves above Evan and Afan, and just like a cascading waterfall they dropped to the ground to begin their attack. Faer and Fafner never took their eyes from the Dark Angels or the demon general, they depended on the boys to be the warriors they claimed to be, and deal with the serpents alone.

Fafner couldn't help himself; he occasionally glanced back to ensure his sons were coping with the onslaught. They were, and he felt a sense of pride. His training of the old dragons over a thousand years earlier had been passed on to his sons.

Evan and Afan found the strength needed to successfully destroy all the serpents without showing any fear or favour. The general was seen to twitch as his anger grew.

Faer suggested backing away towards the entrance so as to draw the remaining demons and Dark Angels out into the open. Fafner agreed. The demons followed and when they exited there were so many they formed a dense circle around Faer, Fafner and his sons.

The demon general, being the tallest, could see above all their heads and out into the distance, "Three thousand years it's been, since last I walked through Stonehenge. Strange how not much has changed. I watched the stones fall and the druids succumb to my will. That was a good time. These lands will be ours again and will be made ready for The Darkness."

He continued to look around and looked a bit unsure causing Fafner to get rattled, he feared the shield wasn't holding but he needn't have worried, it was the invisible presence of Danu the demon sensed.

Danu had arrived and after materialising said, "I remember you, Demon. You were one who got great pleasure in torturing me and my people. What you did to me and to my followers will be avenged. Beware my wrath."

The demon and his angels didn't care; they seemed immune to her threats. Some released their arrows which were quickly dealt with by the speed of both Faer and Fafner. Then, just like in the bowels of Hell, Faer retaliated. He unleashed the power of Athena and was immediately joined by Fafner. They travelled through the ranks of Hell like a violent tornado, systematically taking out angel after Dark Angel leaving very few for Danu, Evan or Afan to deal with. The speed at which they travelled through the ranks of evil was astounding and when the battle was over only the demon general was left standing.

Faer and Fafner approached him then placed their swords to his neck but he showed no fear. He sneered then said, "Kill me now and 'He' will just bring me back. He has plans and they include me. I am a Hell Lord and can't be destroyed." The general had two swords resting against his neck and when they were flipped he was decapitated. The general spoke the truth, his body fell to the ground but his spirit remained standing. It was still sneering and then, at the speed of light, it raced into the tunnel and made his way back into the bowels of Hell.

Fafner, Evan and Afan followed and raced to where the hot springs got their power. They transformed into dragons and using all their strength they destroyed the source of the springs. As they backed away they released their fire to bring down the ceilings and collapse the walls. They didn't stop until certain the dragon realm was safe.

In the meantime while waiting for the dragons to return, Danu said, "What is it about you that breaks through my sleep and wakes me? The first sign of danger and I come to your aid only to find you are always in control. Is this love?"

Faer embraced her, "If that's the case I promise to put myself in more danger ......and look forward to you rescuing me."

She laughed then got serious, "Our meetings must be fleeting. Remember, Lucifer always knows when I'm about. He senses my power. My Light is like a beacon and he uses it to destroy all I hold dear. I fear a weakness and its targeting my realm."

"It breaks my heart to say this," said Faer, "you best go. Your light is blinding, definitely bright enough to attract Hell." He moved his head forward and received his first real kiss. "Just a few more moments," he whispered, "your kiss is doing things to me and I like it." She then disappeared, leaving him alone, slightly bent forward with puckered lips.

After Fafner, Evan and Afan emerged from the tunnel they destroyed the entrance then called on the plains nymphs to use their magic to cover the fire scars with lush greenery.

Fafner was confident his realm was safe again but chose to wait a little longer before making his way to the city. When the false monuments and other structures placed as a deception by the wizards faded, he totally relaxed. He used the journey back to the city to berate his sons for ignoring his instructions. He repeated himself several times, each time saying the same thing using different words. Afan and Evan had difficulty keeping composed; they were trying to prevent themselves from laughing. Fafner knew his sons weren't taking him serious and started yelling, Faer intervened, "Hey, enough! Be proud of your sons, they did well. Thank the gods they were there. The realm of the dragons is safe in their hands and that's because of you."

"Of course I'm proud of them; they just need a kicking now and then," responded Fafner.

By the time they reached the city limits the shield had totally dissolved revealing the magnificent home of the dragons. At the main gate an anxious Derwyn was waiting. He embraced his brothers and after bowing to his father said, "I was so worried. Father, I have new powers, it's as though the Ancient One is helping, look," He pointed to the sky and parted the blue showing them the night, "see into the depths of space and see how vast swathes are now in darkness. Watch the pulsating star to the right, keep watching. It's gone. The distant stars are dying at a faster rate than what was foretold. The Darkness is closer and preparing to enter the realm of man."

The next morning Eala joined Derwyn for breakfast, "I heard about what you showed Fafner. The darkness is close but it's still not close enough. Three hundred years have to pass before it reaches our nearest suns."

"I'm going to revisit our plans," said a worried Derwyn, "I'm going to test them; check them. Increase the training of our army. I'm uneasy. There's also something bothering me about Isidra and I can't put my finger on it."

Eala tried to reassure him, "Dangerous times are coming and no realm will escape unscathed. Loved ones will die but there will be enough to rebuild. I see your son as Emperor of the Dragons when the next age begins. I see your sisters, Aneira and Glain. They are special and will be elevated to be Goddesses of the Light. All is not bad."

"You see a son," said Derwyn. "Yes. Not just one."

Eala excused herself and joined Fafner who was out in the meadows carrying Isidra, "She's beautiful," said Eala, "I see her with a war god, one whose face is hidden from me. There is love."

"She constantly reminds me of Heulwyn," said Fafner reaching down for a kiss. "Is it time for us to leave?"

"Yes, I'm afraid it is."

Chapter 16

It was now the year 1720CE and the journey towards the Fair Lands began. Fafner, at times was torn between his feelings for the dragon realm and his loyalty to the task but his loyalty to Jacob made his decision to leave easy.

On the day of their departure Derwyn escorted them to the northern portal. It was emotional for him; he feared it would be his last time to see his father for many years. "Father," he said on reaching the portal, "have you ever forgiven me? Mother would still be alive if I hadn't run away. It breaks my heart to think I'm responsible for her death, and your loneliness."

"Derwyn, son!" said a surprised Fafner, "I've spent a thousand years with your mother and will always cherish those memories. When I look on you I see her, when I look on your brothers and sisters I also see her. When I carry your daughter I look into her eyes and see your mother. I feel I am holding your mother one more time. She lives through all of you, never forget that. I'm so proud. You've become the king I could never be. Look after our people and make sure they are all prepared for the call."

Derwyn bowed, "No need to bow to me, son, stand tall for you are King of the Dragons and will one day be their emperor," Fafner walked a short distance, and then stopped. He had more he wanted to say, "Son, the day your mother died my heart also died. I've never loved another. Those restless nights, lying awake I sometimes call on the Ancient One to take my immortality. At those times, all I want is to lie in the Elysian Fields and share eternity alongside your mother."

Derwyn said while welling up, "But what about us, don't you think we need you?"

"That's exactly what keeps me from doing something stupid," Fafner said while leaning in to whisper in Derwyn's ear, "always remember, I've never stopped loving you."

Walking through the portal took them close to Hadrian's Wall, a place that brought back some bad memories for Fafner. He shuddered remembering his treatment at the hands of Morgana. It also reminded him that Hadrian's Wall was the place where he met Heulwyn for the first time.

Faer never shirked in his duty, he sent out the Light throughout their journey and was always happy to report there were no serpents about. They continued north and continued to pass the message to those who were worthy. They reached the highlands and then made their way towards the Mull of Kintyre on the west coast. From there they looked across into the Fair Lands.

The northern Irish Sea was, as normal, very rough making their plans to cross difficult to put in place. Eala was about to ask Fafner to carry them across but changed her mind when she saw how depressed he was. He was missing his family. She placed her hands into the water wondering if Poseidon would help. He did, he sent hundreds of dolphins and they formed into the shape of a carriage, and when ready, they called Eala and boys to climb aboard. They then rode the waves and crossed to the land of Danu.

On arrival they walked north towards the Giants Causeway where they set up camp for several weeks. They then made their way west into the wilds of Donegal before travelling to Croagh Patrick. From there they walked further south towards the cliffs of Moher, all the time spreading the message among the Celtic peoples. After some time in the south west they crossed to the holy islands and stayed there among the seabirds.

Knowing their journey's end was getting closer, they returned to the mainland and made their way to the cathedral rock where they chose to stay for several weeks. Faer sensed the presence of Danu and couldn't understand why she never appeared. As the days passed he became more alarmed, her presence was fading. Eala suggested travelling to the north midlands to a place she felt his search would end.

Fafner took over sending out the Light and was always ready with a smart response when reporting no signs of serpents. His favourite was, "Patrick did a great job."

After several days they reached the hill of Slane and from there they saw across to Tara where a dim light was glowing. "It has to be her," said Faer, "I recognise the Light but it seems in trouble." Without thinking he raced the twenty kilometres to be with her only to be shocked by what he found.

Danu was leaning against the Stone of Destiny and her Light had faded so much it was near extinction. He couldn't believe the gods would allow this to happen especially after all he had done to get Eala safely into the Fair Lands.

When he composed himself he took Danu into his arms believing she was so weak there seemed to be no way back. When Eala arrived, she too tried to help but the Light didn't answer.

It was then when an elderly man approached carrying a pail of water. He knelt before Danu and bathed her face and neck. "My queen," he said holding a cup to her lips, "I've found none. They've forgotten and laugh at the old ways." He sat beside her and moved her head to rest on his shoulder while she moaned in pain "How has it come to this?" he asked, "How is it you've lasted this long?"

"I've lasted this long waiting on him to find the Fair Lands," she said gasping for breath, "I want to touch his face one last time. The Fields, they call me."

"Please, my lady, don't answer the call of the Fields," the old man mumbled, "I cannot bear to lose you too. I'm the last of the druids and need you to be the goddess you always were."

Faer materialised, "I sought the Fair Lands not expecting to find what is before me now. How did this happen?" The old man reacted, demanding to know who was there; he waved his arms about, it was obvious he was blind.

Eala materialised and her aura was so bright it made itself known to the old man, healing his damaged eyes. When he looked at Danu he was shocked to see her so gaunt, he remembered her as a beautiful goddess, but nothing prepared him for when he saw Eala, he was awe struck. When he refocused he pleaded, "My lady, this darkness you spoke of, please fight its power. Give me more time. I will go out again and look for believers." Before he left he said glancing at Faer, "I am Mug Ruith, last of the druids. I've remained loyal to my queen. She is the lady Danu, Goddess of the Light and protector of these lands." He pleaded with Faer not to allow the white mist rise and backed away. Faer never left Danu's side and held her, hoping his Light would sustain her for a while longer.

Mug Ruith went to the nearest village where he shocked the people with his new appearance. He challenged the local ministers and sought out the hidden priests. He spoke of the old ways and how they were not so different to what was being taught now. He spoke of how all should be at one with nature, and revere the ones who were present at the creation, for they are the ones who are the favourites of the Ancient One.

When he found no one, he left and quickly made his way to the next village, and then the following village. He told the people of the Ancient One and then pleaded with them to search their consciousness and try to remember. Some did, and began walking towards the Hill of Tara. The more villages and towns he visited the more the elderly began to remember and then the young began to hear the spirits of their ancestors speak of their past. They too began to make their way to the seat of the High Kings.

Almost immediately things began to change, the sound of people walking slowly but purposely got louder. It was as though an ancient magic was at work and calling the people home. Within days there were thousands standing all around the Hill and they weren't tired, hungry or thirsty. They stood in silence and after three days they went into a trance-like state where they received visions showing them the power of their ancestors in the distant past. The visions walked them through history showing them that they were of the druids, and descendants of the guides and healers. They discovered that they too were carriers of the Light.

When the visions ended a calm and warm silence descended all around the hill. It was so quiet the least movement was heard. It was then when a young girl uttered one word, 'Danu' and then repeated it. Those beside her joined in, within seconds the crowds were sending out a continuous and repetitive call, Danu...Danu...Danu, and the call went on for days.

The power generated by the continuous chanting eventually reached into Danu's soul and her strength began to return. She moved from total helplessness to placing her arm behind Faer's back and resting her head on his chest. The constant call of her people eventually gave back to her the strength of a goddess, and from that strength came a shaft of a very translucent light. It travelled from deep out in the universe and came to surround both her and Faer, causing them to stand upright. Danu immediately materialised and moved to walk among her people, giving them hope.

At the time the Fair Land was under the control of the British army who were instructed to suppress all gatherings for fear of rebellion. A contingent of troops, based in a nearby barracks, had become aware of the gathering and was sent to disperse the crowds using any force necessary. They were commanded by a general from Dublin who had a reputation for being ruthless.

What the army didn't realise was that this gathering was brought about by the coming together of a Goddess of the Light and a God of Olympus, and was no threat to the British Empire but they didn't care. The general ordered his soldiers to move on the crowds.

Fafner was alert to the danger and being invisible he was able to get close to the soldiers and send out his Light. What his Light showed was the first sign of serpents in the Fair Lands. It also showed the mark of the serpent on several of the sergeants as well as the general but the general was different, he carried the mark but was clearly a disguised Dark Angel.

The soldiers had moved to surround the people, taking up positions covering all exits. They were just waiting to be unleashed and were also under instruction to execute anyone who resisted.

From the hill, Faer watched the trap being set and used his magic to set up a shield around the people. He then materialised alongside Danu showing to the army what they were up against. He stood as a fully armed War God and made sure he looked every part of one, the people also saw he was a guardian of their goddess. His golden armour, imperial helmet and his long flowing cape showed he was of high status and great power. When he extracted his sword he was sending a clear message that he was prepared to fight.

In the meantime Eala maintained her invisibility and made her way to join Fafner as he moved among the soldiers. She reached him and together they chose those whom they felt should receive the message. Every soldier chosen weakened the ranks of the army.

The first order was given ordering the arrest of the ring leaders but there were no ring leaders. The commanders couldn't understand why there was no panic or why the people were just calmly staring back at them, what they couldn't see was the impregnable magic shield that was protecting them. A further order was then given to fire on Faer but the bullets were skilfully sent to the ground by his stunning swordsmanship.

Danu instructed her followers to leave and bathed them with her Light ensuring their journey home would be safe. Many of the soldiers also left, they too received her Light and made it safely home leaving the general and a few bitten soldiers to be dealt with.

The general and the remaining soldiers climbed the hill with the intention of capturing Faer and Danu; they didn't seem interested in Mug Ruith. The general said as he got closer, "We meet again, guardian. It's been a long time since you walked into the bowels of Hell. Tell me, where's the messenger?" He didn't wait for an answer, he turned and opened a portal to Hell and ordered one of the soldiers to rush through and report to Lucifer the presence of a messenger in the land of Danu. Fafner materialised with the intention of preventing the soldier getting through but was too late and Danu's face said it all, she knew Hells armies would now attack her realm.

The general's face lit up when he saw Fafner; he surmised that the messenger had to be close by. Eala knew the game was up and decided to materialise and when the general saw her he was beside himself with glee. Eala joined Danu and they backed away to protect Mug Ruith, who was the most endangered. He had no magic protection to help him so Eala and Danu placed him between them and waited.

The portal unexpectedly widened and this time it looked like Lucifer himself had arrived. All observed how he seemed to fear stepping out and surmised he still feared wakening the gods but they did see he was moving closer to the exit. He said as he looked passed Faer and Fafner towards Eala and Danu, "The Light is brighter in you both, but still it won't defeat The Darkness." He then turned back to Faer and Fafner, "How does it feel to have failed? You didn't make it to your resting place. The messenger is soon to be mine and your souls will be fed to the hounds of Hell."

A smile of delight crossed his face when he looked directly at Fafner, "I was there. I released the black crystals that penetrated your golden armour. It was I who threw the spear that killed your beloved and it was I who watched with glee as the pain took you. My revenge on you is almost complete, you will fall before me and the destruction of your realm will begin, Dragon Lord."

Eala reached into Fafner's mind and said as she brought him the calmness, "He's one of the seven Princes of Hell but which one I cannot see. He may or may not have been there. Remember, Lucifer is one of the princes and the greatest deceiver. He may have sent someone who looks like him to play with your mind."

Lucifer then said, "Morgana sits by my side and waits for the day you are brought down. Before that happens we will make you watch as she devours your beloved daughters." Eala was still in his head, "Fafner, remain calm, we now know who he is. He's Asmodeus, lover of Morgana. He's trying to rile you."

Asmodeus then said while staring at Danu, "Sister, we stood alongside each other at the creation, come back to us, we can rule together."

Danu had had enough; she stepped forward and used all her strength to send a powerful light-beam towards him. It was so powerful it sent him reeling back into the depths of Hell. Faer and Fafner then moved on the general and his soldiers but unfortunately, they successfully scurried through the portal before it was destroyed by the strongest light ever produced by either Eala or Danu.

There was no relief when the portal was destroyed. Danu was distraught and walked to the highest point on the hill to look out across her green and fair land. She saw the bon-fire being prepared on the hill of Slane and saw the preparations on the hills of Screen, Tailte, Uisneach and Slieve Gullion. She looked with sadness across to the Hill of the Witch and out as far as the Mountains of Mourne. She said turning to Faer, "I lived for the time when you would seek the Fair Land; look all around for it shows before you. Never did I think that 'He' would come and bring the fear. I saw him look and stare at the villages; all he sees are the souls. He will wreak his vengeance upon the innocents and show no mercy. I fear his vengeance will come when least expected, It'll be ruthless and unrelenting. It will bring pain and a great hunger. I already sense the pestilence. His actions will kill many and cause the dispersal of my people."

"I too see what you see," said Eala reaching across to comfort her, "I look around at this beautiful land and despair at what's coming. The dispersal of your people will enrich foreign lands but it will be at a terrible cost. I see Poseidon escorting the coffin ships, he will take their bodies and place them among the Celtic heroes; he will give back to them their dignity."

Danu was still despondent and fought hard to find the strength and when she did she said to Mug Ruith, "I'll leave you as my emissary among the peoples of the Fair Lands. Rebuild the council of the druids and wait for my return." She then turned to Faer, "Your journey is just about over. Allow me share your long sleep and when we awaken, together we will wield the Light and assist Olympus during the Battle of the End Times."

Fafner was very quiet; he was troubled, "How did he know I am the Dragon Lord?" he asked, "how did he put in my head visions of my realm being destroyed? Should I go back?"

Eala joined him, "He still plays with your mind and is doing the same to me, the visions are showing my babies being attacked but I know they are safe under the protection of the Elves."

Both Fafner and Faer sent out the Light and were happy no serpents or forces of Hell were present at that time.

Chapter 17

Fafner sent out the Light and was happy Ireland was safe for the moment. He remained on high alert during the journey that took them to Dublin, where, for the next one hundred and twenty years, they walked through the city passing on the message to those they felt worthy. They were so engrossed in their work they didn't realise it was now the year 1820CE and their journey was over.

They moved south of Dublin and climbed towards Montpelier hill from where they looked back over the city and most of the towns that spread out towards the mountains of the north. Faer instinctively send out the Light for the last time and satisfied himself all was safe. They then walked into the dense forests and across the peat laden mountain top marshes to eventually reach the Glenmacnass waterfall where they set up camp and rested for several days. At the base of the waterfall there was a small pool where, each day, Faer and Danu would bathe, that was until, on the final day, the water turned from a torrent into a trickle before stopping completely. They dressed and decided to investigate.

Faer stood at the base of the falls and rubbed his hand along a smooth stone slab that to him looked to be a very large door. He went on alert and prepared for an attack but was stopped, "What will I do with you," said Danu, "ever the guardian, this time have no fear. I know of such places, wait."

The door began to creak open and when fully opened, a soft and soothing voice was heard, "Welcome my friends to the domain of the Mountain Elves." It was Kalen and he stood before them as supreme Lord of all Elves.

They entered and were taken aback at what was before them, a cavern so vast it seemed to have no end; they saw cities and farmlands, lakes and rivers, all surrounded by majestic mountains and bathed in the heat and light of its own sun. To their left, on a wide plateau, stood thousands of warriors set in stone.

Kalen saw the expression of awe on Faer's face and said, "Don't be so shocked, Warrior of Olympus, we've been waiting for the call. We are ready to assist Olympus in defending the realm of man. The battle is close, see how the dust falls from our warriors, they are beginning to stir."

He turned to Danu, "My sister, it's been too long. I'm happy love has brought you and Faer together. How things have changed since you and I stood watching the creation." She acknowledged his comments, bowed and said while holding Faer, "Twice he has come to my rescue."

Kalen turned back to Faer, "Your work is done; it's time for you to find your grotto and sleep."

Faer was still speechless and had difficulty finding the words and when he did, he asked, "This army? Are there more?"

Kalen was pleased he asked, "There are many! On every continent we are prepared. We expect heavy losses for elf kind but there is no other way. We believe the Light must, at all costs, prevail. Mankind will see the flow of the great waterfalls slow, then cease, and only then will they know of the Elves and the Astrals. We will remove their armies and only allow those of myth and legend fight."

Kalen turned to admire his army, he was proud of what he had achieved but he still worried, "We know Jacob must alone fight Cronus and we know this will be an epic fight. Jacob's son, Obelius, was heard to whisper a prophecy which describes how the battle begins. He spoke of Jacob sending out the Light and we know this is the invitation for Hell to unleash its fury. Then there is The Darkness."

Faer agreed, "I was there after he gave his prophecy, I worried then and I'm worried now." He was about to say more when Kalen turned towards the entrance, "Ah, more visitors; welcome my Lady Ealasaid and Lord Fafner." When Eala reached him he said, "We sensed your pain and your concerns. Be assured your children are safe and well protected. Lucifer creates doubts in everybody's minds, trust us."

Fafner moved towards the edge of the ridge allowing him look out over the vastness of the elf realm and was shocked, "My dragons are ready to fly," he said, "will they be needed with such power I see before me?"

"The Darkness will take everything before it," replied Kalen, "all armies will be needed for the defence of their own realms. They will also be needed to assist with those who are in trouble."

"I see the need to sleep has becoming overwhelming, your journey ends in but a few hours," he said, giving them directions, "follow the road to the next village, turn right and walk into the valley of the two lakes. Seek out the hermit monk, Kevin is his name. He's been waiting for over thirteen hundred years and will be there to open the doors to your resting place. Go now with the blessings of the elves." They bowed to Kalen and turned to leave.

When they exited they saw they were being watched and as they walked, those watching were moving along the summits. When they reached the village they turned towards the valley as instructed. Again, high on the summits, they saw their escorts, and never once did they feel threatened because their escorts were the ancient spirits of the Great Elks who once ruled over these mountains.

A short time later they reached a monastery and circled its iconic round tower then continued their walk towards a cliff face where they were met by a golden stag who was the spirit of the last emperor of the now extinct Elks. He bowed and then led them to a place, known locally as 'St Kevin's bed'.

There standing was the hermit monk who turned and faced the bed. He said nothing, just raised his arms and called on the Light. When it arrived it opened a portal leading to a cavern hidden deep within the cliff. In the cavern stood four thrones, their resting place for the next two hundred years.

Fafner walked in and was first to take his seat, followed by Faer and Danu. Faer reached across and took Danu's hand, kissed it and then the stone came and took all three. Eala stood back and just stared, she remarked to herself as to how handsome her guardians were and how beautiful Danu was. She walked over and placed her arms around the stag, whispering in his ear, "My lord and spirit of the mountains; protect us well."

She bowed to Kevin and took her seat then slowly turned to stone but not before she thought of Jacob and their children. It was then, from a Goddess, a single tear flowed.

𝔖o began their long sleep

It was to be a restless sleep because Danu's prophecy came to pass and Lucifer sought his revenge. He poisoned the potato's causing the worst hunger in history, millions were to die and millions more dispersed. To ensure his success he unleashed the Wraiths of Hell who possessed the landlords and their agents, they also possessed those of influence in government. Those not possessed were bitten; especially the one in London who controlled the corn, clouding his judgement so no action was taken to help those in need. When the time came his soul was taken and sent to the darkest recesses of Hell.

The End

Jacob - Walk of the Messengers

Epilogue

For around two hundred years, in four locations across the world, the messengers and their guardians slept, all around them the forces of Hell probed and searched for their whereabouts, but they had no chance because the power of the Light ensured they'd never be found.

All across the world there was no real peace because anarchy, famine, genocide, pestilence and war became part of life. Tyrants and despots rose and fell taking millions of souls with them.

Those who had received the Message continued to pass it down through the generations by keeping a low profile. During this turbulent time they were the peacemakers, the healers and the guardians, providing subtle assistance to many villages, towns and cities. They watched and waited for the arrival of the Light

In Olympus, the gods remained in their deep sleep, and as time marched on centuries of accumulated layers of dust began to fall from the statues. For Jacob the process of wakening started when he sensed the rise of Hell.

All over the world rumblings were detected bringing a degree of fear. When the tremors reached Olympus the stewards knew to prepare for the impending arrival of the gods, especially Jacob. They knew the battle of the 'End Times' was about to begin.

Jacob
Journey of A God
Eamon Blake

'Jacob - Journey of a God' is the first in a gripping series of five books. It chronicles the journey of a troubled youth who, since his twelfth birthday, has been haunted by disturbing visions showing horrific events set in the past. As the visions escalate he learns of a future filled with turbulent and violent times.

Its 2016, and although living the normal life of a Dublin teenager - school, studies, rugby, and girls, he soon discovers his true identity. His mother tells him the story of his birth and her efforts to protect him from forces beyond his comprehension. He begins to understand his extraordinary abilities especially when he realises those abilities are actually the powers of a God.

Amidst the unfolding drama of his life, Jacob's visions show him to be leading a battle against two malevolent forces - one is 'The Darkness' and the other, the nefarious 'Prince of Hell'. Both have made him a target of their venom, they know he has been chosen to be the defender of the Light and they fear his power.

Why does The Darkness loathe the Light?

What fuels the Prince of Hell's hatred of Jacob?

In the face of these existential questions, will Jacob embrace his divine destiny and become the God he was born to be?

Jacob
War of the End Times
Eamon Blake

For centuries, there've been epic battles fought across vast battlegrounds. There've been empires that rose and then fell to the sound of powerful armies using weapons designed for mass killing. None of that compares to what is put together for the battle between the forces of the Light and the servants of Hell.

Jacob - War of the End Times - is the third book in a riveting series of five and tells the story of a monumental battle that threatens the very fabric of all existence. Apart from open battlefields, it also takes the reader into villages, towns and cities to witness the destruction of all infrastructures that makes those cities function.

Defence of the Light is led by Jacob, and using the power of the Gods, he brings together those of myth and legend. He also calls upon the overwhelming might of the Carriers, the millions of Carriers assembled over the centuries by his messengers.

Opposing Jacob is a massive army of pure evil led by Lucifer, the Prince of Hell, and Cain, the first murderer. Both of whom are being manipulated by the stifling shadow of The Darkness.

Does Jacob possess the strength to successfully command the armies of the Light?

Will humanity survive the relentless onslaught from the forces of evil?

Will the well-planned tactics of the Olympus and Asgard War Gods be enough to defeat Hell?

460

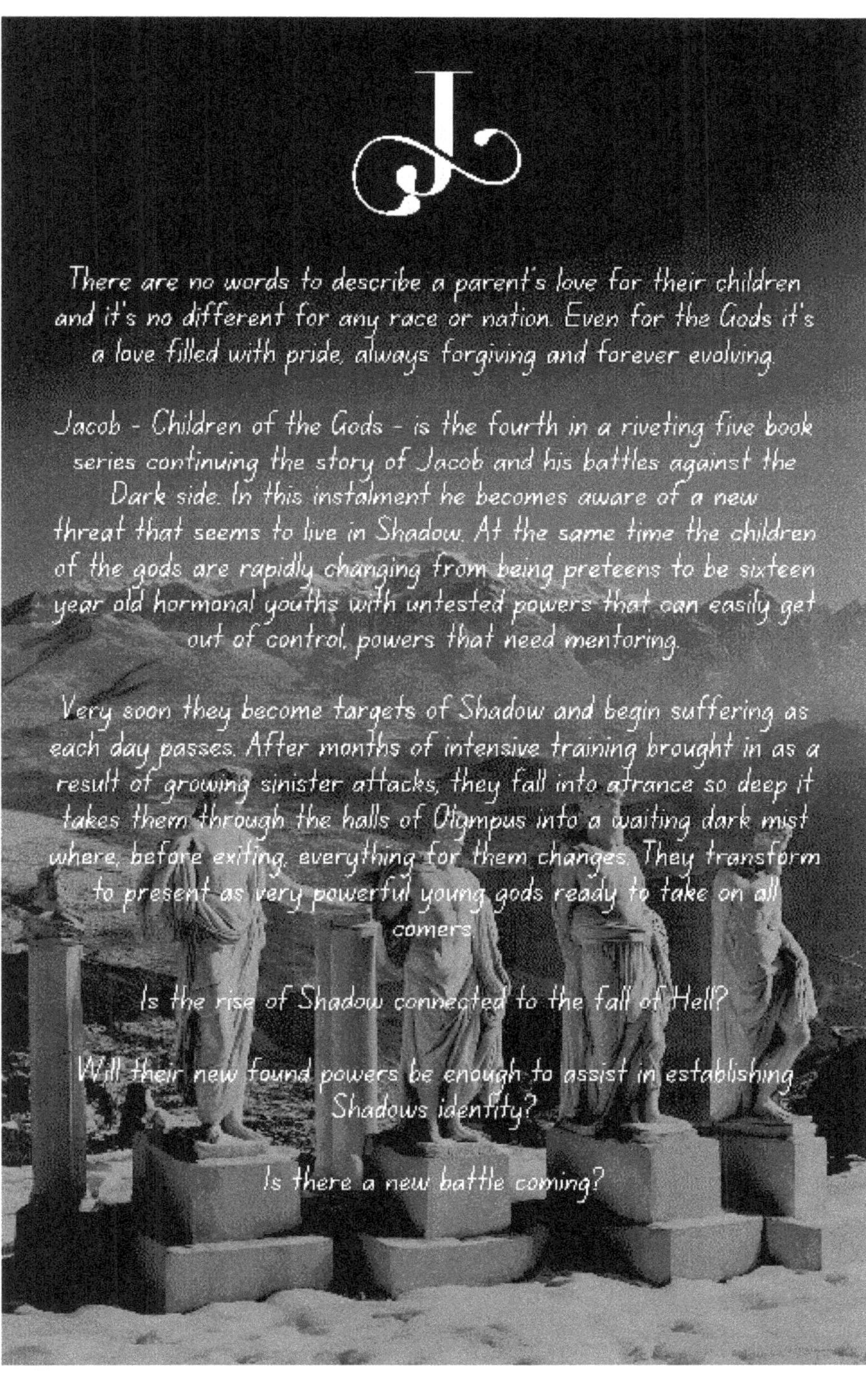

There are no words to describe a parent's love for their children and it's no different for any race or nation. Even for the Gods it's a love filled with pride, always forgiving and forever evolving.

Jacob - Children of the Gods - is the fourth in a riveting five book series continuing the story of Jacob and his battles against the Dark side. In this instalment he becomes aware of a new threat that seems to live in Shadow. At the same time the children of the gods are rapidly changing from being preteens to be sixteen year old hormonal youths with untested powers that can easily get out of control, powers that need mentoring.

Very soon they become targets of Shadow and begin suffering as each day passes. After months of intensive training brought in as a result of growing sinister attacks, they fall into a trance so deep it takes them through the halls of Olympus into a waiting dark mist where, before exiting, everything for them changes. They transform to present as very powerful young gods ready to take on all comers

Is the rise of Shadow connected to the fall of Hell?

Will their new found powers be enough to assist in establishing Shadows identity?

Is there a new battle coming?

Jacob
Battle for Olympus
Eamon Blake

A mysterious and frightening shadow has been skulking its way through all the realms of myth and legend. Its sinister presence is always followed by an attack of such evil violence that few survive.

Jacob - Battle for Olympus - is the last in a riveting five book series. It concludes the story of his battles against the Dark side. In this instalment he finally establishes who Shadow is and quickly learns it can only be defeated with the assistance of the Ancient One.

Jacob's heart breaks on learning of attacks by Shadow on the Dragon, Elf and Yeti nations and is devastated when he discovers many of his friends and allies have been killed.

When Asgard is destroyed he concludes that Shadow's plan, just like that of The Darkness, is to destroy all that has been created by the Ancient One. This emboldens him to awaken the defenders of Olympus who have, since long before the time of Zeus, been sleeping deep in the caverns below the temple.

Can Jacob rescue the remnants of those of myth and legend?

Will the Ancient One come to Jacob's assistance?

Is the Battle for Olympus to be the battle to end all wars?